P9-DNO-466

CC17

TO HOLD
the BRIDGE

ALSO BY GARTH NIX

THE OLD KINGDOM SERIES
Clariel

Sabriel

Lirael

Abhorsen

Across the Wall: A Tale of the Abhorsen and Other Stories

The Ragwitch

*One Beastly Beast: Two Aliens, Three Inventors,
Four Fantastic Tales*

Shade's Children

A Confusion of Princes

TO HOLD THE BRIDGE

HARPER

An Imprint of HarperCollinsPublishers

"To Hold the Bridge: An Old Kingdom Story" copyright © 2010 by Garth Nix,
first published in *Legends of Australian Fantasy*, edited by Jack Dann and Jonathan Strahan, 2010.
"Vampire Weather" copyright © 2011 by Garth Nix, first published in *Teeth*,
edited by Ellen Datlow and Terri Windling, 2011.
"Strange Fishing in the Western Highlands" copyright © 2008 by Dark Horse Comics Inc., first published in
Hellboy: Oddest Jobs, edited by Christopher Golden, 2008. Reprinted here with the kind permission of Mike
Mignola. Hellboy™, BPRD™, Abe Sapien™ and all related characters are trademarks of Mike Mignola.
"Old Friends" copyright © 2008 by Garth Nix, first published in *Dreaming Again*, edited by Jack Dann, 2008.
"The Quiet Knight" copyright © 2009 by Garth Nix, first published in *Geektastic*,
edited by Holly Black and Cecil Castellucci, 2009.
"The Highest Justice" copyright © 2010 by Garth Nix, first published in *Zombies vs. Unicorns*,
edited by Holly Black and Justine Larbalestier, 2010.
"A Handful of Ashes" copyright © 2012 by Garth Nix, first published in *Under My Hat*,
edited by Jonathan Strahan, 2012.
"The Big Question" copyright © 2012 by Garth Nix,
first published in *Elsewhere*, Edinburgh Festival Special, 2012.
"Stop!" copyright © 2009 by Garth Nix, first published in *The Dragon Book*,
edited by Jack Dann and Gardner Dozois, 2009.
"Infestation" copyright © 2008 by Garth Nix, first published in *The Starry Rift*,
edited by Jonathan Strahan, 2008.
"The Heart of the City" copyright © 2009 by Garth Nix, first published in *Subterranean* magazine, 2009.
"Ambrose and the Ancient Spirits of East and West" copyright © 2011 by Garth Nix,
first published in *The Thackery T. Lambshead Cabinet of Curiosities*, edited by Ann and Jeff VanderMeer.
"Holly and Iron" copyright © 2007 by Garth Nix, first published in *Wizards*,
edited by Jack Dann and Gardner Dozois, 2007.
"The Curious Case of the Moondawn Daffodils Murder: As Experienced by Sir Magnus Holmes
and Almost-Doctor Susan Shrike" copyright © 2011 by Garth Nix, first published in *Ghosts by Gaslight*,
edited by Jack Dann and Nick Gevers, 2011.
"An Unwelcome Guest" copyright © 2009 by Garth Nix, first published in *Troll's-Eye View*,
edited by Ellen Datlow and Terri Windling, 2009.
"A Sidekick of Mars" copyright © 2012 by Garth Nix, first published in *Under the Moons of Mars*,
edited by John Joseph Adams, 2012.
"You Won't Feel a Thing" copyright © 2012 by Garth Nix, first published in *After*,
edited by Ellen Datlow and Terri Windling, 2012.
"Peace in Our Time" copyright © 2011 by Garth Nix, first published in *Steampunk!*,
edited by Kelly Link and Gavin J. Grant, 2011.
"Master Haddad's Holiday" copyright © 2012 by Garth Nix,
first published as a bonus story in the Australian edition of *A Confusion of Princes*, 2012.

To Hold the Bridge
Copyright © 2015 by Garth Nix
All rights reserved. Printed in the United States of America. No part of this book
may be used or reproduced in any manner whatsoever without written permission
except in the case of brief quotations embodied in critical articles and reviews. For
information address HarperCollins Children's Books, a division of HarperCollins
Publishers, 195 Broadway, New York, NY 10007.
www.epicreads.com

Library of Congress Control Number: 2014952735
ISBN 978-0-06-229252-0

Typography by Henrietta Stern
15 16 17 18 19   PC/RRDH   10 9 8 7 6 5 4 3 2 1
❖
First Edition

To Anna, Edward, and Thomas, and all my family and friends, and also to all the editors and anthologists who commissioned these stories in the first place, with my thanks for the impetus!

TO HOLD
the BRIDGE

CONTENTS

TO HOLD THE BRIDGE

An Old Kingdom Story

Morghan stood under the arch of the aqueduct and watched the main gate of the Bridge Company's legation, across the way. The tall, twin leaves of the gate were open, so he could see into the courtyard, and the front of the grand house beyond. There was great bustle and activity going on, with nine long wagons being loaded and a tenth having a new iron-bound wheel shipped. People were dashing about in all directions, panting as they wheeled laden wheelbarrows, singing as they rolled barrels, and arguing over the order in which to load all manner of boxes, bales, sacks, chests, hides, tents, and even a very large and over-stuffed chair of mahogany and scarlet cloth that was being carefully strapped atop one of the wagons and covered with a purpose-made canvas hood.

The name of the company was carved into the stone above the gate: THE WORSHIPFUL COMPANY OF THE GREENWASH & FIELD MAR-KET BRIDGE. That same name was written on the outside of the old and many-times folded paper that Morghan held in his hand. The paper, like the company, was much older than the young man. He had seen only twenty years, but the paper was a share certificate in an enterprise that had been founded in his great-grandfather's time, some eighty-seven years ago.

The Bridge Company, as it was universally called, there being no other of equal significance, had been formed to do exactly as its full name suggested: to build a bridge, specifically one that would cross the Greenwash, that wide and treacherous river that marked the Old Kingdom's northern border. The bridge would eventually facilitate travel to the Field Market, a trading fair that by long-held custom took place at the turn of each season on a designated square mile of steppe some sixty leagues north of the river. There, merchants from the Old Kingdom would meet with traders from the nomadic tribes of both the closer steppe and the wild lands beyond the Rift, which lay farther to the north and west.

Despite the eighty-seven years, the bridge was still incomplete. During that time the company had constructed a heavy, cable-drawn ferry; a small castle on the northern bank; a fortified bastion in the middle of the river; and the piers, cutwaters, and other foundation work of the actual bridge. Only the previous summer a narrow planked way had been laid down for the company's workers and staff to cross on foot, but the full paved decking for the heavy wagons of the merchants was still at least a year or two away. Consequently, the only way to safely carry loads of trade goods across the river was by the ferry. The ferry, of course, was also a monopoly of the company, as per the license it had obtained from the Queen at its founding.

The ferry, and the control it gave over the northern trade, was the foundation of the company's wealth, nearly all of which was reinvested in the bridge, which would one day enormously expand the northern trade and repay the investment a hundredfold. It was this future that made the old, dirty, and many-times folded share certificate Morghan held in his hand so valuable.

At least, he had often been told it was very valuable, and he hoped that this was true, since it was the sole item of worth that his recently dead, feckless, and generally disastrous parents had left him. The only doubt about its value was that they *had* left the share certificate to him, rather than selling it themselves, as they had sold all other items of worth that had been handed down from his grandmother's estate.

There was only one way to find out. The grim and cheerless notary who had wound up his parents' estate had told him the share could not be freely sold or transferred without first being offered back to the company, in person, at Bridge House in Navis. Of more interest to Morghan, the notary had also informed him that the share made him eligible to join the company as a cadet, who one day might even rise to the exalted position of Bridgemaster. Then, true to his miserable nature, the clerk had added that very few cadets were taken on, and those only after most rigorous testing, which none but the best-educated youngster might hope to pass. The implication was clear that he did not think Morghan would have much of a chance.

But it *was* a chance, no matter how slim. So here Morghan was in Navis, after a rough and literally sickening three-day sea voyage from Belisaere, a passage that had cost him the single gold noble he possessed. It had been the gift of one of his mother's lovers when he was fourteen, not freely given but offered to buy his silence. The weight of the unfamiliar gold coin in his hand had so shocked him that the man was gone before he could give it back, or tell him that he had no need to bribe him. He had learned young not to speak of anything his parents did, whether singly or together.

One of the gate guards was looking at him, Morghan noted, and not in a friendly way. He tried to smile inoffensively, but he knew it just made him look even more suspicious. The guard rested his hand on the hilt of his sword and swaggered across the road. After a moment's hesitation, Morghan stepped out from the shadow under the aqueduct and went to meet him. He kept his own hand well clear of the sword at his side. It was only a practice weapon anyway, blunt and dull, not much more than a metal club. That was why Emaun had let him take it from the Academy armory, it had already been written off for replacement in the new term.

"What are you up to?" demanded the guard. His eyes flickered up and down Morghan, taking in the cheap sword but also the Charter Mark, clear on his forehead. The guard had the mark too, though this didn't necessarily mean he was schooled in Charter Magic, as Morghan was—at least to some degree. Not that he could do any magic, even if the guard decided he was some sort of threat and attacked him. There were probably a dozen or more proper Charter Mages within earshot, and many more around the town. They would note any sudden display of magic and come to investigate. A penniless trespasser would not be accorded much consideration, he was sure, and misuse of magic—Charter or Free—was a serious offense everywhere in the Old Kingdom.

"I . . . I want to see the Bridgemaster," said Morghan. He held out his share certificate, so the guard could see the seal, the crazed wax roundel bearing the symbol of the half-made bridge arching over the wild river.

"Bridgemistress, you mean, till tomorrow," said the guard, but his hand left his sword-hilt. "What's your name?"

"Morghan."

"In from the ship this morning? From Belisaere?"

Morghan shrugged. "Most recently."

"And what's your business with the Bridgemistress?"

"I'm a shareholder," said Morghan. He lifted the certificate again.

The guard glanced at the paper, and then at Morghan. He didn't have to say anything. Morghan knew the man was looking at his frayed doublet, which showed no blazon of house or service. Morghan's shirt also had too few laces, and his sleeves were of very different colors, and not in a fashionable way. Even his boots, once of very high quality, did not quite match, the left boot being noticeably longer and more pointed in the toe. Both had been his father's, but not at the same time.

"You'd better see her, then," said the guard amiably, which was not the reaction Morghan had been expecting.

"Th-thank you," he stammered. "I . . ."

He waved his hand, unable to say that he'd been expecting to be kicked to the roadside.

"Don't thank me yet," said the guard. "If you have real business here, that's one thing. If you don't, you'll get worse from the Bridgemistress than you'd ever get from me. Go on in, across the court, up the stairs."

Morghan nodded and walked on, past the other three guards at the gate, into the courtyard. He wove his way through all the activity, ducking aside or stepping back as required, trying to keep out of the way. It was difficult, for there were at least a hundred people hard at work. As he weaved his way through and caught snatches of conversation, Morghan picked up that the entire caravan was leaving soon, and he had arrived just in time to catch the seasonal changing of the work crew on the bridge. This was the winter expedition, near to setting off, and when it arrived the autumn crew would return to Navis and refit for the spring.

There was as much bustle inside the house as out. Morghan walked gingerly through the open front door into a high-vaulted atrium dominated by a broad stair. The room, though very large, was entirely full of clerks, papers, maps, and plans. A long table stretched some forty feet from the rear wall and was heaped with stacks of ledgers, books, map cases, and rolled parchments tied in many different-colored ribbons.

There were several people sitting on the steps, with their papers, books, inkwells, and quills piled around them so widely that Morghan had to tread most carefully.

At the top landing, another guard waited patiently for Morghan to step over an abacus that was precariously perched next to a clerk stretched out asleep on the second-to-last stair.

Though she was at least six inches shorter than him, wore only a linen shirt and breeches rather than a mail hauberk like the gate guards, and had a long dagger at her side instead of a sword, Morghan knew that he would not last a second if he was foolish enough to try to fight this woman. The dark skin of her hands and wiry forearms was covered in small white scars, testament to a score or more years of fighting, but more telling than that was the look in her bright blue eyes. They were fierce, the gaze of a well-fed hawk that has a pigeon carelessly held, and though it can't be bothered right now, could disembowel that prey in an instant. She also bore a Charter Mark on her forehead, and Morghan instinctively knew that she would be a Charter Mage. A real, trained mage, not someone like him who had only a smattering of knowledge and power.

"Pause there, young master," she said, and held up one hand.

Morghan stopped below the topmost step, so that their eyes were almost level. The woman pointed two fingers toward the Charter Mark on his forehead, and waited.

Morghan nodded and raised his hand to touch the woman's own mark at the same time she laid her fingers on his brow. He felt the familiar, warm flash pass through his hand, and the swarm of Charter symbols came close behind, a great endless sea of marks rising up to him as he fell into it and was connected with the entirety of the world . . . and then they were gone, as he let his hand fall and the woman stepped back to allow him up the final step, both their connections to the Charter having proven true, neither one corrupted or faked.

"It pays to be cautious," she said. "Though it is some forty years since Bridgemaster Jark was assassinated by a Free Magic construct."

"Really?" asked Morghan. He wanted to ask why anyone would want to assassinate a Bridgemaster, but it didn't seem like the moment.

"Really," said the woman drily. "What is your name and your business here?"

"I am Morghan, and . . . uh . . . I wish to see the Bridgemistress."

"So you are," said the woman impatiently. "I am Amiel, Winter Bridgemistress of the Greenwash Bridge Company."

"Oh," said Morghan. He looked down at the share certificate, unfolded it, and proffered it to Amiel. "I . . . I . . . uh . . . inherited a share in the company from my parents. . . ."

Amiel took the paper, flicked it fully open, and glanced across the elegantly printed lines, the handwritten number, and the gold-flecked seal. Then she leaned forward and prodded the sleeping clerk on the steps below. "Famagus! Wake up!"

The clerk, an elderly man, grunted and slowly sat up.

"I told you everything has been done, to the last annotation," he complained. "A nap is the least I deserve!"

"I need you to look up a share," said Amiel. "Number Four Hundred and Twenty-One, in the name of Sabela of Nerrym Cross."

"My grandmother—" said Morghan.

"Yes, yes," Famagus interrupted. He groaned again as he stood up, and tottered down several steps to pick up a very large and thick ledger that was bound in mottled hide and reinforced with bronze studs and corner-guards. He opened this expertly at almost the right place, turned two pages, and ran his index finger along the lines recorded there.

"Share Four Hundred and Twenty-One, dividends anticipated for the next seven years, the maximum permitted, paid to one Hirghan, son of Sabela—"

"My father—"

"Care of the Three Coins, an inn in Belisaere," concluded Famagus. He shut the ledger with a snap, put it down, and yawned widely.

"This share is essentially worthless," said Amiel. "Your father borrowed from the company against it, and it cannot be redeemed or sold until that sum is repaid."

Morghan's hand shook as he took the paper back. He sucked in an urgent breath, and just managed to stutter out what he had come to say.

"I—I don't want money . . . I want to join the company."

Amiel looked him up and down. Though her gaze was neutral, neither scornful nor encouraging, Morghan blinked uneasily, knowing that what she saw was not promising. He was tall and thin and did not look strong, though in fact he had the same wiry strength and constitution that had allowed his father to take far longer to drink himself to death than should otherwise have been the case. His dark eyes came from his mother, though not her beauty, and he had nothing of the selfishness and cruel disregard for others that had been the strongest characteristic of both his parents.

"You want to enroll as a cadet in the company?" asked Amiel. "The indenture is five years, and there's no pay in that time. Board, lodging, and equipment, that's all."

"Yes," said Morghan. It was precisely the certainty of food and a roof over his head that he sought. "I know."

The Bridgemistress looked at him with those fierce blue eyes. Morghan met her gaze, though he found it very difficult. Somehow he knew that if he looked away, whatever slim chance he had would be gone.

"Very well," said Amiel slowly. "We'd best see if you are suitable. It is no small thing to be a cadet of the company. Come."

She led the way across the landing into a roomy chamber that had tall windows overlooking the front courtyard. There was a desk against one wall, with several neatly organized stacks of paper arranged on its surface, lined up behind an ink-stained green blotter that had a half-written letter secured upon it by a bronze paperweight in the shape of a nine-arched bridge. A bookshelf occupied the opposite wall, the top shelf taken by a case of swords and the lower shelves occupied by at least a hundred volumes of various sizes and bindings.

"Do you have any knowledge of the art mathematica?" asked Amiel. She ushered Morghan into the room and went to the bookshelf to take down a small volume.

"Yes, milady," answered Morghan. "I have studied at the Academy of Magister Emaun in Belisaere for the past six years."

"You have a letter attesting to your studies with the Magister?" asked Amiel.

Morghan wet his lips.

"N-no, milady. I was not a paying pupil. I—I worked in the kitchens and yard for the Magister, from dawn to noon, and attended lessons thereafter."

He did not mention that the Magister's lessons had been erratic and depended much on his whim. Morghan had learned more by himself than he had ever been taught, but at least working for the Academy had gained him access to the Magister's library. He had worked more regularly and longer hours at the Three Coins, where his parents were sometimes guests and always debtors. He knew stables and cellar better than any schoolroom. He had also learned more at the inn than from the academy. Hrymkir the innkeeper was an educated and well-traveled man, and, as a former guardsman, both an experienced fighter and a minor Charter Mage. He had passed much of his knowledge on to Morghan, in return for his work as stable hand, potboy, and occasional cook. The lessons were all the pay Morghan ever saw, though his labor supposedly helped to reduce his parents' debt.

"Then we shall see what you have learned," said Amiel. She flicked through the pages of the book and placed it open on the desk, next to a writing case and a sheaf of paper offcuts, intended for informal notes or jottings. "Prepare your paper, cut a new pen, and answer the mathematical problems set out on these two pages. You may have until the noon bell to finish."

Morghan glanced out the casement window at the sun, which was already rather high. Noon could not be far off. He took off his sword-belt and leaned the weapon against the desk, hilt ready to hand, before he sat down on the polished, high-backed chair and leaned over the desk to focus on the open book. His hand shook as he drew the volume closer. But the shaking eased as Morghan read, and he found that he readily understood the problems. They were not particularly difficult, but there were eleven questions, addressing various matters of practical geometry, calculation, and mathematical logic, though all in practical settings, concerned with the wages of artisans and laborers, the cost and quantity of goods, the time required for works, and so on. All the questions required a lengthy series of workings to arrive at the correct solution or solutions.

Morghan was halfway through question six when the great bell in the tower above the town's citadel boomed out, its deep voice sounding to him like the roar of one of the disgruntled customers at the Three Coins upon discovering their ale had been watered beyond even their low expectations.

The young man set his pen down and dropped a pinch of sand on his current paper. Four other sheets lay to the side, covered in his careful script. Morghan was fairly confident he had answered the questions correctly, but he hadn't finished, and his stomach knotted as he waited for Amiel to come in and dismiss his pathetic effort.

The Bridgemistress strode in before the echo of the bell had faded and, without speaking, picked up the papers and looked through them. As she finished each sheet, she let it fall back onto the desk. Morghan sat uncomfortably, watching her.

Amiel dropped the last page and looked down at Morghan.

"I—I didn't finish . . ." stammered Morghan.

"You've done well," said Amiel. "If you had done more, or shown less of your working, I would have suspected you of reading the explicatory chapters at the back. Now, your mark is true. I presume you also studied Charter Magic with Magister Emaun?"

"A little, milady," said Morghan. "It . . . it is not the fashion in Belisaere these last few years—"

"Fashion?" snorted Amiel. "By the Charter! If some of those

guild popinjays ever left the peninsula they'd . . . well, you say you did some study?"

"Yes, milady, but not much at the Academy. The innkeeper at the Coins, where we lived, he was a retired guardsman. He taught me a lot of things, and my father . . . my father did give me a book once, a primer of a thousand useful marks."

"Do you still have it?" asked Amiel.

Morghan shook his head. "He took it back, to sell it."

"How many Charter marks do you remember?"

Morghan blinked in surprise.

"All of them. I had the book for almost a year."

"Then you had best show me," said Amiel. "Not here. We will go into the inner court, and I will also have Sergeant Ishring test your skill with weapons."

Morghan nodded and made a curious movement with his left arm, raising and lowering it with a rotation outward. Amiel noticed it, but did not comment. Instead she turned away to lead the young man through the house, out onto a squat tower at the back where two sentries watched. Their crossbows lay ready in the embrasures and each had a dozen quarrels neatly stood up against the wall, ready to hand.

"All's well, Bridgemistress," reported the closer guard as Amiel and Morghan stepped out.

"Good," said Amiel. She looked over the crenellated wall, and Morghan did likewise. The inner court was a large grassed area, the grass worn to dirt in patches, behind the house proper but within the perimeter wall. There were sentries on the outer wall as well, walking the ramparts, and more atop a taller square tower in the northeast corner.

Morghan wondered why the sentries were necessary. After all, the Bridge House was well within the town's own walls, which were in good repair and patrolled; and it was also well protected against the Dead or Free Magic creatures, being inside both the main aqueduct ring and a smaller one that encircled the Bridge House and several of its neighbors, which were also the headquarters of other major commercial operations.

"We are a rich company," said Amiel, answering his unspoken question as they descended the steps to the courtyard, pausing at the bottom for the iron-studded door to be unlocked. "Wealth attracts trouble, of every stripe, and lack of the same can make even the most steadfast stray. We must always be on guard."

Morghan nodded. The courtyard was empty save for one very broad-shouldered man with a short neck. Unlike the other guards, who wore tan surcoats over mail, he had on a knee-length coat of gethre plates that rippled as he moved. He was chopping at a pell—a target post—with a poleaxe, sending chips flying from the tough wood on both sides as he switched his angle of attack. He made it look effortless.

"That's Ishring, my Sergeant-at-Arms," said Amiel. "Come on."

Morghan followed, nervously touching the hilt of his practice sword. He was reasonably competent with swords and short blades, but he'd never wielded a poleaxe. He rotated his left arm again, trying to loosen the elbow as much as he could. A poleaxe needed the full strength and flexibility of two good arms.

As they stepped out into the courtyard, Ishring stabbed the pell at eye-height with the spear point of the poleaxe, then stepped back to the guard position and swiveled on his left foot to face Amiel and Morghan, though as far as Morghan could tell no one had warned him of their approach and he doubted their footsteps could have been heard over the sound of the chopping and striking at the pell.

"Bridgemistress!" bellowed Ishring, slapping the shaft of his pole-arm in salute.

"Sergeant," acknowledged Amiel. "This is Morghan, a potential cadet to be put to the test. Arms first, I think, and then I shall assay his knowledge of the Charter."

"You know how to use that sword, Morghan?" asked Ishring.

"Ah . . . yes—" began Morghan. Out of the corner of his eye he saw Amiel step smartly away from him, and a more complete answer faltered and remained unspoken.

"Use it, then!" bellowed Ishring, and suddenly swung the pole-axe toward Morghan's head, though not directly at it. Morghan jumped back and drew his sword, ducked under another swing and scrabbled sideways.

Ishring backed away, poleaxe at guard once more. Morghan eyed him warily, keeping his sword high.

"How do you deal with an opponent who has a longer weapon or greater reach?" asked Ishring.

Morghan gulped, and kept watching the sergeant's eyes.

"Get in close," he said.

"What are you waiting for, then?" taunted Ishring. He began to circle around the young man. Morghan circled the other way, so as not to be maneuvered into facing the sun, and when Ishring circled back, he feinted a lunge at the sergeant's knee, which he hoped would provoke a counter and provide an opening for a proper attack. But Ishring merely stepped back just far enough to avoid this strategy and kept his poleaxe ready.

"Nasty thing, a poleaxe," said Ishring conversationally, as they circled around each other. "We need them to crack open the nomad spirit-walkers, but they'll do fearful damage to unarmored flesh and bone, shockin—"

He swung in midword, without any telltale tensing of muscle or flicker of eye. Morghan jumped back and stepped back again as the axe blade came whistling in from the other side, then before it could come again, he leaped forward with his sword shortened to stab, and then he was lying dazed on the ground, uncertain what had actually happened other than the blunt haft of the poleaxe beating his blade aside and tapping him behind the knee.

Instinct made him roll away, a good response, as the spear-point of Ishring's poleaxe stabbed the ground where he'd been, though it was more punctuation than an actual attack. Morghan knew it would already have been in his throat in a real combat.

"Good enough," boomed Ishring. He stepped well back. "Sheathe your blade."

Morghan returned his sword to its scabbard with a shaking hand. He could feel blood trickling down his chin. He wiped it away, the slight stain of bright red confirming that it was only a graze from his fall.

"You move quite well," said Ishring. "But you hold your left arm strangely. You have injured your elbow?"

Morghan looked down. He had hoped they would not notice, at least not immediately, but he should have known that an armsmaster like Ishring would spot it straight away.

"My elbow was broken," he said. "A long time ago, and not set properly."

"Hold out your arm," commanded Ishring. "Grip my hand. Hard as you can."

Morghan did as he was told. He could not completely straighten his left arm, but he had worked very hard to make sure that his left hand was as strong or stronger than his right.

Ishring probed around his elbow joint, pushing with his fingers. It hurt, but no more than it would have hurt his other elbow.

"Old break, grown wrong," confirmed Ishring to Amiel. She came over and prodded as well, while Morghan stood there, scarlet-faced.

"Why was it not mended?" asked Amiel. "A simple spell, at the time, and it would have reknit."

"It was an accident," mumbled Morghan. "My mother was . . . was ill, and didn't mean to hit me. My father wasn't home. No one tended to it for days, and then . . . there was no money . . ."

"How old were you?" asked Amiel.

"Nine or ten," said Morghan. He remembered every detail of what had happened, but not exactly when it was. His mother had been taking some concoction that addled her wits and had lashed out at him with a curtain rod, thinking he was someone—or something—else, and had then lapsed into a drugged coma for three days. She had been lucky to survive, and he had been fortunate not to lose his arm completely by the time his father returned and belatedly sought help. They had been living in a grace and favor house of his grandmother's then, on the sea cliffs near Orchyre, a beautiful but lonely spot with no near neighbors.

"It could perhaps be made new, but it is far beyond my skill," said Amiel. "It really should have been dealt with at the time. The Infirmarian at the Glacier might be able to do something . . ."

Morghan nodded glumly. He knew that only a most powerful and experienced Charter Mage, one who was also a surgeon, might be able to mend his elbow. The Infirmarian of the Clayr, off in their remote glacier home, would be one such possibility. But the Clayr demanded payment for all their services, be it foretelling, research in their famed library, or anything else.

He had once thought to petition the King in Belisaere to be healed. There was a tradition that the ruler of the Old Kingdom would consider such petitions on certain feast days, but Morghan had found that in modern times, putting the petition into the hands of the right people who would convey it to the King cost far more money than he had ever had. Besides, the King, though a powerful Charter Mage, was not a surgeon.

With his weak elbow known, he supposed that Amiel would now decide he was unfit to join the Bridge Company, and he would have to come up with some other plan. The only problem was that he couldn't think of anything else. Joining the company had seemed the one possibility that might lead to decent work and regular meals. If he failed here then he supposed he could try to gain employment in an inn or tavern. He knew the work, after all. But such relatively unskilled jobs always had many takers, and he had seen enough beggars in the walk from the docks to know that there were few prospects in Navis, and he had no money for the return journey to Belisaere. It would be a long and hungry walk back to the capital, if he had to make it—though with winter coming, he would probably die of cold before he had the chance to starve.

Morghan stood and tried to be stoic, preparing himself for the bad news. Perhaps he could begin his begging here, and ask for a loaf and cheese, to see him on his way. They were certainly loading provisions enough in the front courtyard.

"Try the poleaxe," said Ishring unexpectedly. Amiel said nothing.

"Uh, on the pell?" asked Morghan. He took the poleaxe, forehead knitting as he felt its weight. It was much heavier at the head than the axe he had used to split wood at the Three Coins, but the shaft was also longer and had a counterweighted spike, so its balance was far superior.

"On the pell," confirmed Ishring. "Three strokes to the left, three strokes to the right, and finish by jamming the spear into the middle, hard as you can."

"Hard enough to stay there?" asked Morghan doubtfully. He had done little spear work, but the old guard who had taught him had been insistent that you thrust a spear in only as far as you could pull it out, to avoid disarming yourself in the middle of a battle.

"Aye, for this test," said Ishring. "But it is good you asked the question."

Morghan took a deep breath, stepped forward, and swung, rapidly delivering three hefty chops to the left side of the pell. As he had expected, they were not quite as powerful as they would have been if he could straighten his left arm, but a satisfying number of wood chips flew from the timber.

Reversing the momentum of the poleaxe was also tricky, but Morghan managed it, rolling his wrists and pivoting on his foot to address the right side of the pell. But his first swing was weak, and at a bad angle, so that the axe-blade was almost pinched, caught in the tightly grained wood. Desperately, he wrenched it free, though it put him off-balance. He nearly panicked and swung back immediately, but all the lessons in the inn courtyard had their effect. He almost heard Hrymkir bellowing at him to calm down, that balance was more important than sheer speed.

Morghan regained his focus, delivered two more forceful strikes, then rammed the spear-point of the poleaxe as hard as he could at the very middle of the pell. The impact jarred his hands and he felt a savage jab of pain in his bad elbow, but he held on long enough to make sure the weapon was firmly embedded before he let it go, the shaft quivering as it slowly leaned toward the ground. But the spear-point did not come out.

"Good," said Ishring. "Now, draw your sword with your left hand. Take guard."

Morghan grimaced with the pain, but he drew his sword. His elbow felt like it was burning up inside, but it hadn't locked up. He could fight left-handed, after a fashion, but Ishring only needed a few passes to disarm him.

"The elbow *is* a weak point," pronounced the sergeant-at-arms while Morghan bent to pick up his blade. "If we used longbows I would say we could not take him. But we don't, and a crossbow should present no difficulty. He can wield a sword well enough and can manage a poleaxe. He can be trained to be considerably better with both. Is he a useful Charter Mage?"

"That we shall presently see," said Amiel. "Come, Morghan."

"Yes, milady," Morghan replied hurriedly. He nodded thankfully at Ishring, who inclined his head a fraction in return. The sergeant had a hard, scarred face, but his eyes showed considered thought, rather than anything else, and Morghan felt none of the fear that other such faces had provoked in him, back at the Three Coins. Eyes showed true intent, and he had learned young to make himself scarce when he saw the glint of need, anger, or just plain madness in a gaze, usually intensified by too much drink or one of the more vicious substances you could buy in the alleys behind the inn.

Amiel took him to the very center of the courtyard, as far from the wall and the house as possible. There was a large flat paving stone under the dust there. It was some ten feet square and had a bronze grille set in the middle, above a sump or drain to the town sewer.

"Stand next to the grille," instructed Amiel. She walked away from him, off the paving stone. "Now, I am going to ask you to cast some basic Charter spells. If you do not know the spell, do not attempt it! Simply tell me that you do not know. Similarly, if you begin a spell and lose your way or the marks begin to overwhelm you, stop at once. I do not wish you to kill yourself, or me, for that matter, by attempting magic beyond your knowledge or skill."

"I understand," said Morghan. This was also a basic principle that had been drummed into him by Hrymkir, and he had a dim memory of the consequences of overreaching with Charter Magic. His grand-mother had tried to bespell his father, to make him stop drinking and become responsible, but it had completely failed. She had been struck blind and dumb as a result and had died soon after. Morghan had been six, but he still remembered her withered hand clutching at him as she tried to tell him something, her words no more meaning-ful than the cawing of a crow.

Morghan was very careful with Charter Magic.

"Make a small flame, as if to light a candle," called out Amiel. She had retreated another dozen feet. Morghan briefly wondered just how catastrophically other potential candidates had fared with such a simple spell, but forced himself not to dwell on that. Instead he took a deep breath and reached out for the Charter, immersing himself in the endless flow of marks, visualizing the two he needed, reaching for them as they swam out of the rush of symbols. He caught them and let them run through him, coursing with his bloodstream to the end of his index finger. He held that finger up, and the marks joined and became what they described, a small yellow flame that did not burn his skin, though if he touched it to wick or paper it would set them ablaze.

"Good," said Amiel. "Dismiss it."

Morghan stopped concentrating on the two marks. They retreated back into the great body of the Charter, and the spell instantly faded. A wave of tiredness passed through Morghan as the marks fled, a kind of weary farewell. It must have shown in his face or perhaps he shivered, for Amiel immediately asked if he was able to continue.

"Yes," answered Morghan, as strongly as he could. He felt that his voice hardly reached Amiel, but she nodded.

"Call forth water from the air, to cup in your hands," she instructed.

Morghan knew this one well. It was a simple spell, but could save a traveler's life. It could be difficult in a very dry place, but the air was moist in Navis.

Once again he reached into the Charter, summoning the marks he needed. This time, when he connected with them, he sketched them in the air with his fingers, completing the tracing by cupping his hands under the glowing signs that hung in the air before him. They turned to sweet water, which trickled through his fingers. Morghan found himself thirsty, and drank.

As before, the conjuration made him tired, but the drink helped a little. He wiped his face with wet fingers, took a breath and looked to Amiel, signaling his acceptance for the next challenge.

"Call a bird to your hand, from the sky," said Amiel.

Morghan hesitated. He knew some of the sequences of marks that identified particular birds, and he knew some marks that could be used together to call to someone, to let them know that the caster wanted to see them. But he did not know any specific spells for calling birds.

"Uh, I don't . . . I don't know how to do that, milady," he said. Better to confess it, he thought, than to accidentally summon a thousand birds, or perhaps something far more dangerous. There were Free Magic creatures that could fly, and were not deterred by running water. Sometimes such creatures slept beneath cities, or had been imprisoned in bottles or jars, and a slipshod Charter spell could help them escape their confinement.

"You are wise," said Amiel. "Do you know the spell of the silver blades?"

"Yes," answered Morghan. This was a very old, much-used spell for combat. He could feel the three marks already, rising up from the swirl of the Charter, pressing to come into his mind and mouth.

"Cast against the pell," said Amiel.

Morghan raised his hand and pointed at the wooden post. It was already almost hacked in half by the attentions of Ishring and Morghan's own efforts. The sergeant had left it now, and the space was clear around it.

"Anet! Calew! Ferhan!" roared Morghan, the use-names of the marks flying from his mouth, leaving the burn of power against his lips. The marks became silver blades as they flashed across the gap between him and the pell, and then the timber exploded as they struck, the top of the post bouncing across the yard in a cloud of dust and wood chips.

"That will do," said Amiel.

Morghan blinked, wiped his sweating forehead, and tried to suck in air without making it too obvious that he was absolutely shattered. His legs felt weak, barely able to support his weight, and he wished there was something he could unobtrusively lean against.

"You have done well," said Amiel. She surprised Morghan by taking his arm and helping him walk back toward the house. He tried to not lean on her, but found he was too exhausted. In any case, she seemed to have no difficulty holding him up.

"I have tested many a cadet who has fainted after their first spell-casting," said Amiel as they slowly ascended the stairs in the rear tower. "Few manage three spells in so short a time with no allowance for rest, and I think on only two occasions has a cadet candidate managed four."

"Will you . . . will I . . . may I join the company?" croaked Morghan as they came back out on the main landing, above the grand stair. It was much as they had left it. Famagus had not returned to sleep on the step, but instead was sitting up and writing in a different but equally large, ledger.

"Yes," said Amiel. She sat him down on the top step, next to Famagus. "You are accepted as a cadet of the Worshipful Company of the Greenwash & Field Market Bridge."

"Sign here," said Famagus, balancing the open ledger on Morghan's knees.

Everything was already written out, in neat lines of script, indenturing Morghan, son of Hirghan and Jorella, to the Company for the next five years in the position of cadet, one share of the company to be put in trust as a surety for his conduct and application, a further share to be issued should he on the completion of four years be commissioned as a Bridgemaster's Second.

Morghan took the pen, signed with a shaking hand, and passed out.

Though he had been allowed to sleep on the step for an hour or so after he signed his indentures, his awakening marked the beginning of Morghan's training. Even before he rubbed his eyes, a passing

Bridgemaster's Second whose name he missed thrust a book called
Company Orders into his hand, with the instruction that he was to
read it before he next saw the Bridgemistress, as among many other
things, it detailed the comprehensive duties of a cadet. He had barely
opened this small but thick volume, printed very clearly and precisely
on onionskin paper, before a different Bridgemaster's Second took
his elbow and led him away to another part of the main house, where
he met someone he initially thought was called Sutler before he realized that was her title, as she was in charge of a veritable treasure
trove of clothing and equipment.

Before he could protest, Morghan was stripped to his under-
clothes by the Sutler's assistants, one of whom was a woman not
much older than he was, and when the Sutler saw the state of disre-
pair of the undergarments, though they were clean, those came off
too.

Morghan almost lashed out at his helpers as they stripped him,
but just in time he realized that they were not trying to humiliate
him, just trying to get on with their jobs as quickly as possible and
that the Sutler herself was piling up new undergarments and other
clothes on the table, ready for Morghan to put on immediately.

Newly attired in the livery of the Company, Morghan was loaded
up with more new stuff than he had ever had before, the assistants
piling things onto his outstretched arms as the Sutler wrote them
in her ledger. When the pile of five undergarments, three leather
tunics, six sleeveless shirts, six sleeves with laces, one pair breeches
short, two pairs breeches long, one heavy greasy wool cloak with
enamel Company badge, one light cloak lined with silk, two leather
jerkins, four belts, one pair doeskin boots, one pair metaled leather
boots, one pair woolen slippers, one broad felt hat, one cap, six pairs
assorted neckerchiefs, and one sewing wallet reached Morghan's
chin, he was tapped on the elbow by the first Bridgemaster's Second,
back again, and led out of the Sutler's store to yet another part of the

house, this time a long, high-ceilinged room that had to be a wing all on its own. It was lined with trestle beds, forty along one wall and thirty on the other, each of them with two chests at the foot of the bed, a large one and a smaller one with leather straps.

Morghan was told this was the barracks, which was usually about half full as the greater majority of the company's people lived in private accommodations in the town, and the senior officers had their own chambers above. But when on guard duty, this was home for a week at a time, and for their first year at least, the cadets were required to live in the barracks.

"Not that you'll be here long," said the Second, whose name Morghan still didn't know and didn't want to ask. "You're joining the Winter Shift, under Bridgemistress Amiel, and you move out tomorrow at dawn."

"How many Shifts are there?" asked Morghan. Under the Second's direction, he chose a bed, even if it was only for one night.

"Four, of course. I'm in Summer, under Bridgemaster Korbin. But I was loaned to Winter, under Amiel, last year. She's a tough one."

Morghan must have looked worried, because the Second added, "She's just, mind you. Or, not exactly just . . . I mean she's . . . ah . . . just do what you're told willingly and you'll be all right. Now, get your things stowed. Your small chest will go with you, so make sure you have everything you'll need in it. I'll be back to take you to the armory for your weapons and hauberk, the refectory for supper, and then the Bridgemistress wants to see you before her evening rounds."

Morghan muttered his thanks and immediately packed away all the things he had been given, carefully sorting and inspecting them. Everything went into the smaller chest. He had nothing personal to put in the larger one, and he belatedly realized that the Sutler had not returned his former clothes, his ill-fitting mail shirt or his blunt training sword. He supposed they might be sold, and that would be part of the business of the company, or perhaps the Sutler's personal perquisite. In either case, he didn't care. They were a reminder of a life that he hoped he had left behind forever.

After a final, satisfied look at his well-packed traveling chest, and mindful of the Second's parting comment about the Bridgemistress wanting to see him, Morghan tried to read as much as he could of *Company Orders* before he was led away again.

He managed thirty-six pages before he was hustled out of the barracks to become reacquainted with Sergeant Ishring in the armory: a large, split-level room that opened out into a smaller courtyard of yet another wing of the main house. It held more weapons and armor than Morghan had ever seen in one place before, including the large swordsmith's that had been near the Three Coins and was supposed to be one of the best in Belisaere.

Ishring explained that while he was Sergeant of the Winter Shift, and so would be training Morghan on the road and at the bridge, command of the house had been formally handed over to the Spring Shift just that past hour, and thus it was Sergeant-at-Arms Corena who now ran the armory. So it was she who carefully measured him for a hauberk of ringed mail that would be adjusted and ready for him to pick up after he saw the Bridgemistress that evening, a promise made concrete by the sound of the smiths working at the forge in the courtyard outside the armory.

Morghan was also issued a poleaxe; a sword, a proper long hangar with a rounded point; two daggers, thin and merciless; a knife of more general purpose and rougher make; and the number of a crossbow that would be his to use and care for, but when not in active use would be stored in the armory wagon or, when they reached the bridge, in the fort on the northern bank or the midriver bastion, depending on his assigned station.

"You can ride, I suppose?" asked Ishring as he helped Morghan back to the barracks with his gear.

"Yes," said Morghan. "I . . . I worked a lot with horses."

He did not say that this consisted mostly of mucking out the stables, cleaning tack, and wiping down and brushing the mounts of guests at the inn. But he had been taught to ride properly when he was very young and his grandmother was still alive, and though he had not ridden far since, he had had plenty of practice taking horses in and out of the city, the Three Coins being located near the Western Wall, and so was a convenient place to exchange horseback for a litter or to go afoot, horses being prohibited in most parts of Belisaere.

"We walk, mostly," said Ishring. "With the wagons. But there's always a mounted patrol as well, and cadets and guards alike take their turn."

"How long does it take to reach the bridge?" asked Morghan.

"You mean, 'How long does it take to reach the bridge, *Sergeant*,'" said Ishring. "You're a cadet now, not a visitor. Don't forget."

The sergeant's tone was formal, but not aggressive.

"Beg pardon, Sergeant," said Morghan. He felt his back straighten by reflex as he asked again, "How long to reach the bridge, please, Sergeant?"

"Sixteen days, weather permitting," said Ishring. "Twenty or more if there's snow. Now, in barracks, your poleaxe goes across behind the bedhead, you see the brackets? You wear sword and knife at all times, and daggers as well when mustered to the guard. When you get your hauberk and gambeson, you will wear them at all times, except when you're asleep, when they go on the stand here, half-unlaced and ready to put on. When I think you're used to the weight, you can wear leather and cap when not on duty, but not until I say so. You'll learn more about your duties and service on the march, from tomorrow. Understand?"

"Yes, Sergeant," said Morghan. He spoke softly, as he usually did, a habit born of not wanting to draw attention to himself at the inn.

"I can't hear you!" roared Ishring. "Do you understand me?"

"Yes!" Morghan roared back, surprising himself.

"Good," said Ishring, in conversational tones. "Ah, here comes Second Nerrith to show you to supper. Welcome to the company, Cadet Morghan. Good evening, Second Nerrith."

"Good evening, Master Ishring," said Nerrith, who was the first Bridgemaster's Second who had rushed him hither and yon. She didn't look much older than him, but had far more self-assurance. "Cadet Morghan."

Ishring departed. As he strode away, Morghan relaxed a little, but not too much. He remembered Hrymkir's stories of life in the Royal Guard, and though he didn't fully understand the hierarchy of the company, he'd read enough in his new book to understand that the Bridgemaster's Seconds were junior officers and could not only give any cadet orders, but also subject them to a long list of punishments for any perceived infraction of courtesy or duties. He had not read about the status of the sergeants-at-arms, but it was clear they were to be obeyed. As for the Bridgemistress herself, she had already attained a status for Morghan as a figure of vast authority, who was not only to be obeyed, but worshipped.

"Have you read the *Orders*?" asked Nerrith.

"Ah, some of it," said Morghan. Belatedly he added, "Bridgemaster's Second."

"Just call me Second," said Nerrith. "The Bridgemistress is 'milady' or 'Bridgemistress.' Cadets call the sergeants 'Sergeant.' The guards you address by name, or 'guard,' if you absolutely have to. You'll need to learn everyone's name as quickly as you can. I'll get you a copy of the full roster, but you'll need to try and fix the names in your head as you meet people. Do you have any questions right now? We have a few minutes before the first sitting for supper."

"Are there many cadets?" asked Morghan. He was a little anxious about how he might get on, particularly after his experiences at the Academy. Working in the stables was not conducive to good relations with the richer and more important students and their highly inflated views of their own standing and how it might be affected by deigning to even notice, let alone befriend, a stableboy, even if his family had once been important at court.

"You're it in the Winter Shift," said Nerrith. "Didn't you know? Each Bridgemaster only takes on one new cadet each season, and only then if they're short of Seconds. You were lucky the Bridgemistress only has two Seconds right now and she didn't care for the cadet candidates we've had these past months. I thought she might have to borrow a Second from one of the other Shifts, which is what happened to me last year, but I suppose she always knew you'd turn up."

"How?" asked Morghan.

Nerrith gave him a look that he supposed was one of kindly scorn.

"She's a Clayr, of course. You don't see those blue eyes and that dark skin on anyone else, do you? And her hair was all gold before, so they say."

"But the Clayr live in the Glacier," said Morghan. "They See the future there, in the ice. What's she doing here, with the company?"

"Maybe she'll tell you one day," said Nerrith, with the air of someone who already knew this secret, though Morghan doubted that she did. But he did believe Amiel was a Clayr, though he had never heard of one who had permanently left the Glacier. He had seen Clayr from time to time in Belisaere. But they were only visiting, and always traveled in groups, on the business of their strange community.

"Where are the Bridgemistress's Seconds?" he asked next.

"Gone on ahead, to check the road and the way stations," said Nerrith. "They're all right. Terril, the senior, will probably be a Bridgemistress herself in a few years, and Limmie, I mean Limath, he was a cadet till only last summer, so he'll remember what it was like and not be too hard on you."

They're often the worst, thought Morghan pessimistically. *Keen to pass on whatever horrible things happened to them.*

His thoughts were interrupted as Nerrith announced it was time for supper. On the way to the refectory, she told Morghan that there were usually two sittings and that it was important to be on good terms with the chief cook and the stewards or else one might be served more gristle than meat, and that at some time, he would spend three months working in the kitchens and the refectory, as part of his training.

Morghan did not mention that he already knew this kind of work well, though he quickly discovered that the food in the refectory was better than that of the Three Coins. He had to force himself to eat slowly. If he'd been alone, he would have bolted down everything in sight, and tucked half a dozen of the small brown-crust pies under his shirt for later. But the refectory was crowded, and Nerrith sat next to him and talked and talked, so he ate slowly but steadily, and listened.

Nerrith told him he would have an unprecedented three meals a day, including breakfast, luncheon, and supper. She detailed the traveling rations they would draw, and what the food was like at the bridge, and where he should sit, or more importantly not sit, some tables being reserved by custom if not actual regulation for particular officers of the company. For example, Famagus, the chief clerk, who after the four Bridgemasters was the most important officer, had a favorite table and a particular chair. On no account must a cadet ever sit on his chair, for as the keeper of all records he was a very important figure in the lives of both cadets and Seconds. Though he did not leave the headquarters in Navis, Nerrith said it felt like he was always around, because his letters fell upon them like arrows. There were dozens each day, always wanting some count of equipment, a tally of goods, or an explanation of work, and replying was always the work of the junior officers.

"I hope you have a good writing hand," she added. "And you can spell. If a report is untidy or misspelled, Famagus sometimes makes us write it out again, three times."

"You mean when you were a cadet," suggested Morghan.

"You're in for some disillusionment if you ever make it to Second," replied Nerrith. "We get paid and all, but no one thinks we're worth much more than the cadets."

"Sometimes with good reason," said a voice behind them. Nerrith choked on a mouthful as she hastily stood up, and Morghan almost fell backward over his chair as he followed suit.

"I said I wanted to see Cadet Morghan before my evening rounds, not at the commencement of them," said Bridgemistress Amiel. "I am not pleased, Second Nerrith. Please let Bridgemaster Korbin know that you have let me down."

"Yes, milady," said Nerrith. She turned on her heel and left.

"I expect my cadets and Seconds to be punctual, within reason," said Amiel. "It is now a quarter after the hour. Did you not hear the town clock strike, Cadet Morghan?"

"No, milady."

"Here we take our time from the town clock. At the bridge, horns are blown in the North Fort, the Midriver Bastion, and the Work Camp, on the hour, every hour. Doubtless you will be responsible for such timekeeping at some point. You have been provided with a book of Company Orders?"

"Yes, milady."

"You will find a section on timekeeping between pages eighty-seven and ninety-one. Do you possess one of these timekeeping eggs the artificers are making in Belisaere?"

"No, milady," said Morghan. He was about to add that they called them "watches" now, but decided against it.

"You can tell the hour from the sun? Or the moon?"

"Yes, milady," said Morghan. He hesitated again, but this time he did speak. "And . . . and from the Charter, milady."

Amiel looked surprised.

"Good. That is an old spell, not often known these days, save among folk who need careful count of time."

"My grandmother taught me," said Morghan. "It is the only spell that I had from her that I can remember. I was six and . . . and wondering when I would get my dinner."

It had been one of the last of the regular dinners. His grandmother had attempted to "fix" his father not long after she taught him how to find and recognize the marks that spun in time with the passage of the sun and waxed and waned in keeping with the hours of light and darkness. She had said it could sometimes be very important to know how long it would be before the sun would rise.

"It is the first small part of weather lore," said Amiel. "Do you know anything more?"

"No, milady," answered Morghan.

"I have some small knowledge of weather magic," said Amiel. "If time permits from your regular instruction, we may look into it. Speaking of such, as doubtless you already know from your reading of *Company Orders*, part of the regular duty of cadets and Seconds is to accompany the Bridgemistress on her rounds, whether at house, bridge, or camp. As my two Seconds have gone ahead to scout the road, this privilege is solely yours this evening. Follow me."

Morghan learned a lot about the company and the Bridgemistress in the next hour and a half, as he followed Amiel all over the "house," as she called the whole sprawling array of buildings. Though preparations had been under way for more than two months for the Winter Shift to move to the bridge, and everything had supposedly been done, Amiel checked into everything. On nearly every inquiry she was satisfied with the result. The one occasion when she was not satisfied, and the nature of her dissatisfaction, made Morghan very thoughtful. He had been beaten, shouted at, spat on, and worse on numerous occasions by his supposed superiors and customers at the inn, by older students at the Academy, and by his own parents when they were drunk or drugged. He had nursed his wounds alone and had sworn that one day he would be richer, and more powerful, and more important than his tormenters. Their dominance over him was only temporary, a fleeting moment that would be forgotten.

Amiel did not swear or use force. On discovering that one of the wagon drivers had not replaced a broken axle with a new one, but had had repairs done instead and presumably pocketed,the difference, she merely looked at the axle, then at the driver, and had said, "This is the second infraction, Werrie. There is the gate."

Werrie had fallen to his knees and begged and pleaded for another chance. He'd sobbed out a story, made incoherent by his tears, something about debts and family. But Amiel had merely pointed at the gate again, and when Werrie groveled at her ankles, she gestured to summon two of the gate guards, who picked him up and dragged him out. Morgan made particular note that they tore the company emblem from the sleeve of Werrie's coat, and unpinned the enameled badge from his hat.

"Cadet Morghan," said Amiel conversationally, as she continued to the next wagon, "you have seen a very rare occurrence. This company looks after its people well, but we expect much in return. While you may err out of stupidity, or weariness, or simply make less than ideal choices, if you intentionally put the company's goods, persons, or premises at risk, you will be warned once only. The second time, you will be expelled, your share or shares forfeit, and your name published across the Kingdom as an offender against the company. In some very few cases, we take even sterner action, as we may under our original patent from Queen Hellael the Second."

Morghan thought about that later, as he lay in his narrow bed and tried to sleep. There were many people in the barracks, a lot of them still preparing gear, or talking, but it was not this busy noise that kept him awake.

It was pure amazement that forestalled sleep. He could not believe how much his life had changed for the better, a wonderment that was accompanied by a deep-seated fear that something would happen to take it all away again.

Finally, Morghan did sleep, but he felt like he had only just closed his eyes when he was roused again, by a rough shake on his shoulder.

"Come on, lad! The day won't wait for you."

The next few weeks were a golden time for Morghan. He wasn't necessarily happy, as such, for he did not really know that such a state existed, or how he might reach it. But he was content and busy, a combined state that he was equally unfamiliar with, the result of finally finding a respectable place among a well-ordered community, rather than the confusion of never knowing what the next day would hold, apart from the petty miseries that were his lot at the Three Coins, or the arbitrary actions of his parents.

The company's wagons traveled the Royal Road north, and had right of way over almost everyone, so they rarely had to leave the paved and well-drained highway for the muddy shoulder. They were lucky with the weather, too. To begin with the days were cold but fine, and the morning frosts light, not much more than a tonic to wake up a tired cadet.

He *was* tired, for his every waking hour was occupied, mostly following the Bridgemistress everywhere or dashing off at her orders, usually to discover something she already knew but Morghan did not. She also set him passages of *Company Orders* to memorize, and showed him Charter marks that he had to summon for her the next day, with the promise that in time he would also learn how these marks could be combined with others to become useful spells.

Amiel did not sleep very much herself, which made things even more difficult. By the fourth day he was very tired indeed, so tired that he could not even summon the energy to be nervous about the imminent arrival of the Bridgemistress's two Seconds, who were due to arrive that evening, having already been to the Bridge to check the road and discover anything unusual, before doubling back.

The two Seconds rode into camp at dusk, the hails of the sentries alerting Morghan before he saw them. He was holding a washing basin and a ewer of warm water for Amiel in her tent, for her to wash the dust from her face and hands. She heard the calls too, and gestured for him to set basin and ewer on their stands.

"Go and meet my Seconds," she instructed. "Tell them to report when they have taken some repast."

"Yes, milady."

"For your instruction, if they have anything urgent to report, they will refuse and come straight to me," added Amiel. "As you will do, if returning from a similar task."

"Yes, milady," repeated Morghan. He bowed and went outside into the orderly camp and walked between the rows of tents to the horse lines. The guards there nodded to him.

"Good even, Romashrikil and . . . Kwor . . . Kworquorakan."

The guards smiled and nodded again. Morghan walked past them, still unsure if they were playing tricks on him. They had told him their names themselves, but they were like nothing he had ever heard before, and they did not look as if they were from so distant a country as to have such names. He had yet to hear anyone else address them, which in itself suggested it was all some kind of elaborate joke to play on the new cadet.

The Seconds were taking off their saddles. Terril was a slim, serious-looking woman easily eight or nine years Morghan's senior. Limath looked to be much the same age as himself, Morghan reckoned, though he was considerably broader in the shoulders and sported a rather splendid beard as jet-black as his hair. He was also much more mud-splattered than Terril, some of it above his belt, though Morghan noticed neither of the horses was particularly dirty, and not at all above the knees.

Limath saw him first as he turned around with his saddle and gear over his shoulder.

"Terril!" he cried. "By all that is marvelous! A cadet!"

"A cadet indeed," said Terril. She inclined her head.

Morghan bowed, not quite as deeply as he did to Amiel.

"My name is Morghan," he said carefully. "The Bridgemistress desired me to inform you that you need not report to her until you have taken some repast."

"I am Second Terril," said Terril. "This rag-bag is Second Limath."

"Rag-bag is rather extreme," said Limath. He clapped Morghan on the shoulder. It was a companionable touch, though the younger man had braced for a testing blow. "I fell off, if you must know. There was a storm, and bandits, and . . ."

"Perfect calm and an empty road, in truth," said Terril. "Limath just isn't a very good rider."

"True, true," sighed Limath. "But perhaps the luck that has given us a new cadet will also allow me to walk to the Bridge, and I need not ride till . . . oh, damn . . ."

Morghan turned his head to see what had stopped the flow of Limath's speech and instinctively braced as he saw Sergeant Ishring.

"Need not ride until tomorrow morning, Second Limath, I think you were saying?" asked Ishring. "To the seventh milepost and back, perhaps you were about to say?"

"Indeed, Master Ishring," said Limath. Morghan was surprised to see him smile, as if perfectly happy at being caught out. "I daresay I could use the practice."

"I daresay," said Ishring. "I beg your pardon for my intrusion, Second Terril."

He turned his attention to Morghan. "Cadet Morghan, the Bridgemistress has decided that now the Seconds have returned, she can spare you from tomorrow for additional arms drill. You will have the first hour after dawn and the first hour from the halt with me, for poleaxe and other work."

"Yes, sergeant!" bellowed Morghan.

Ishring nodded and stalked off past the torch-poles, out into the darkness toward the nearest of the outer guard posts. Morghan had already been taken around the outer ring of sentries, learning where they all were so that he could at least in theory find them in the dark. In this careful preparation, as in so many other things the company did, the young cadet saw the very real expectation of trouble.

"Show us our tent and the refectory wagon, then," said Limath. "I could eat a horse."

"You'd probably do that better than you ride them," said Terril.

"Ah, I shall miss your wit when you are made Bridgemistress," said Limath. "Now, Morghan, is it? Was the watch list for the Bridge made up before you joined?"

"I don't know, Second," said Morghan.

"Ah, you would know, because you would have been writing out a dozen copies if it had," said Limath with great satisfaction. "Fortune smiles upon us, Terril."

"I suspect that rather you should say the Bridgemistress knows her business," said Terril drily.

Morghan was unable to stop a flicker of puzzlement wrinkling his brow, though he did suppress a question. Terril saw it pass across his face, like a swift cloud across the sun.

"Tell Cadet Morghan why you are so pleased to see him . . . or rather, any cadet . . . and the associated matter of the watch list."

"Ah, it is simple!" roared Limath, clapping Morghan on the back. "You know that the Bridgemistress must always be accompanied about by a Second or a cadet? We must buzz about her like bees around the queen of the hive, ready for anything, to sting or fly at her order. You follow?"

"Yes . . ." said Morghan cautiously.

"But unlike bees, who only work under the sun, the Bridgemistress moves by night as well as day. You see now?"

"I'm not sure . . ."

"It is simple! You comprehend that the day and night is divided into four watches?"

Morghan nodded.

"With only two Seconds, we must divide all four watches between us, to follow the Bridgemistress about and do her bidding. But there is also weapon work, and writing work for Famagus, and all manner of other works that must be done, and if we must serve the Bridgemistress watch-by-watch, it leads to a terrible lack of that wonderful thing that we know as sleep."

"Ah, I do see now," said Morghan. He paused for a moment, wondering if he should admit a weakness that might be used against him. "I admit that I am a little bit—"

"Tired?" interrupted Terril. "That is the lot of cadets, and even for such exalted beings as Seconds. But you will be more tired still by the time we reach the Bridge. It is in many ways a test, Morghan."

"A test! But I have been tested . . ."

Morghan's voice faltered, and stopped for a moment, before he resumed.

"I see. I shall not fail."

"That's the way, young cadet!" boomed Limath. "Let's get this gear cleaned up, Terril, and then . . . food!"

"You'd best go back to the Bridgemistress," said Terril. "If I were you, I'd run. The Bridgemistress does not make much allowance for the chattering we have just done. We will not be far behind."

"Yes, Second!" replied Morghan. He turned and raced back past the tents, jumping over guy ropes rather than taking the time to go around them.

"Keen," remarked Limath.

"Yes," said Limath. "I hope he makes it to the bridge. I confess that I do not fancy watch-and-watch for the whole winter."

Morghan did make it to the bridge, though he was battered and scratched from his daily practices with Sergeant Ishring and other guards, and weary beyond reckoning, for he had never walked so far for so long and had so little sleep.

None of that mattered as he stood on the hilltop and looked along the road that wound down to the river valley. The Greenwash ran there, in slow curves, at its narrowest more than two thousand paces wide. But the river, for all its majesty, did not hold Morghan's eye. He looked at the bridge, the greatest bridge he had ever seen. Nine vast arches sat on piers the size of houses, their flanks extended by cutwaters that divided the river's flow into nine swift channels. Though the stone deck was not yet laid, it was clear that when finished the bridge would be wide enough for four carts to pass abreast.

The Midriver Bastion, built on an all but submerged islet that underpinned the middle of the bridge, was complete, barring all passage along the temporary boardwalk or the side parapets. It was a square tower, eighty feet higher than the bridge deck, which was itself forty-five feet above the water. The bastion's gates were shut, and guards walked along the battlements, the company's banner flying high above them.

As Morghan watched, a horn sounded on this tower. It was answered a few moments later from the castle on the northern bank. Morghan switched his attention to that, noting that while it was a relatively small fortification of only four towers around a single bailey or courtyard, it was built on a rocky spur that rose from the river, and a small stream wound about it before rejoining the Greenwash. The castle was thus protected by swift water and sat on the highest point for at least a league, till you reached either the southern hill where Morghan was, or the slowly sloping land to the north, which led to the high steppe, somewhere beyond the far horizon.

Ahead of Morghan, the Bridgemistress raised her hand in the air, and a single bright Charter mark flew into the sky. It whistled as it sped, a single pure note that was louder and clearer than the horn-blasts of the two fortifications, loud enough to be heard for leagues. Morghan wondered what mark it was, for he did not know it, and wished he did.

"Onward!" ordered Amiel. "Let the Winter Shift take possession of our Bridge!"

Three months later, Morghan felt it was indeed his bridge, as much as anyone else's in the company. He had walked and climbed every accessible inch of it, slipped on its icy stones, been bruised by it, and almost drowned shooting the rapids under its arches in a too-flimsy craft. He knew every nook and cranny of the North Fort, the Midriver Bastion, and the work camp on the southern shore. He had learned and even understood *Company Orders* and could recite any part of it. He had grown a fingersbreadth in height and a fraction broader in the shoulders and arms, though he was still thin. He had come to know several hundred new Charter marks, and forty-six particular spells. Though his elbow held him back from reaching the standard Sergeant Ishring expected with a poleaxe, he had been graded as very good with a crossbow, and the Sergeant had once hinted that another year or two of constant practice might . . . just might make Morghan a worthwhile addition to the company's fighting strength.

It was more difficult to tell what the Bridgemistress thought about his value. She was not generous with praise, but did not criticize unduly either, not unless it was deserved. Morghan had made his small mistakes and had taken his punishments without complaint, which were usually designed to ensure that he learned whatever he had gotten wrong the first time.

But he still worried that he might not be considered good enough, a fear that slowly grew as the winter waned and the first signs of spring began to show in sky and field. Eventually, he broke his habit of caution and on one of their last evenings spoke to Terril about it. They were on watch in the Midriver Bastion, Terril commanding the small garrison, while Limath was off with the Bridgemistress, inspecting the southern ferry station, which was a league to the west, far enough away to avoid the rapids created by the bridge. With the Field Market only a week away, the ferry was very busy, and there was a line of waiting wagons, trains of mules, and even footsore peddlers that stretched from the ferry station to the bridge and then halfway up the southern side of the valley.

"Second Terril, may I ask a question?" Morghan said as he stood at her side on the top of the tower.

"You may, Cadet Morghan," said Terril. She was always formal and deliberate, unlike Limath, who treated Morghan as something of a cross between a pet dog and a little brother, with great enthusiasm and friendliness, but not a lot of thought.

"I have been wondering," Morghan said carefully. "I have been wondering if cadets are often dismissed."

Terril turned her complete attention to him.

"Very rarely," she said. "Only in circumstances of incompetence, or gross turpitude. Selling our secrets, for example. Or weapons or something like that."

"What exactly might comprise incompetence?" asked Morghan. He swallowed and thought of his elbow and Sergeant Ishring's frowns at his poleaxe work.

Terril put her head on side and looked Morghan in the eye.

"You have nothing to worry about, Cadet Morghan," she said firmly. "You have worked well, and I am sure that you will get a very good report."

"I will?" asked Morghan.

"Yes," said Terril firmly. "And if you keep on as you have, I expect that one day you will make an excellent Second, and in time, will be a redoubtable Bridgemaster yourself."

Morghan nodded gratefully, unable to speak. He had not been able to think past their return to Navis. But to one day be a Bridgemistress's Second, and then . . . to reach the impossible peak of becoming a Bridgemaster!

"Now go and get some sleep," instructed Terril. "I expect we'll swap watches a little early, when the Bridgemistress comes back tonight, and you go with her, and Limath takes over here."

"But the dusk rounds, shouldn't I go with you?"

"Not tonight," said Terril. "I'll go in a moment, and Farremon will keep watch here. I'll wake you in good time for the Bridgemistress, have no fear of that. We won't see her much this side of midnight."

"Thank you, Second," said Morghan gratefully. He bowed, and climbed down the stairs to the guardroom on the second floor, where everyone off-duty slept. The bastion was garrisoned by a dozen guards and an officer, and six of the beds were occupied by variously silent or snoring guards. Morghan found his own, wearily shrugged off his hauberk and hung it and his weapons on their stands, and sat on the bed. He thought about taking off his gambeson and boots, but before he could decide one way or another, he fell sideways and was instantly asleep.

Morghan awoke from the grip of a terrible, frightening dream to find himself in total darkness, and immediately felt waking panic too. There should have been a lantern lit, as per standing orders, and the Bridgemistress might be there at any moment. He leaped up and felt for his armor and weapons, dressing and equipping himself with practiced speed, despite the absence of light.

It was only when he fastened his belt that he fully woke up and realized something was wrong, much more wrong than one unlit lantern.

He couldn't hear any snoring, or even the soft breath of his companions, and there had never been, nor could there be, a guardroom so quiet.

They've been called to arms, was Morghan's immediate thought, and panic choked him. *I've slept through an alarm! I'll be dismissed after all!*

He caught a sob in his throat, choked on it, and coughed, the sound harsh and loud in the silence. With the intake of breath after the cough came a sour, nasty taste, as if the air itself was tainted with something like the hot, metallic air of a forge. . . .

"Free Magic," whispered Morghan, and a different fear rose in him and washed away all other fears. Instinctively he reached for the Charter, and found that it was already there, that he must have reached for it in his sleep. A faint, almost extinguished mark glowed feebly just below his heart, and it was joined to other marks that ran in a chain around his chest. Morghan touched them one by one and remembered a spell he had forgotten he knew, a spell his grandmother had taught him when he was too young to know what she guarded him against. But somewhere deep inside, the child within had remembered, in the time of need.

Morghan called the marks again and rebound them to himself, winding them around like the armor they were. Armor against spells of ill-wishing, that, if strong enough, might still a beating heart, or close mouth and nose against the life-giving air.

With the new marks came light, but not enough. Morghan reached into the Charter again and found the mark he sought. He drew it in the air, and it hung above his head, a companion brighter than the best of candles. In its light, Morghan surveyed the room.

Wisps of fog, thick and unnatural, oozed in through the shuttered arrow-slits and clustered around the beds. One quick glance across the silent, still figures and the winding fog was enough for Morghan to know that all his sleeping companions were dead, even the three who also had the Charter Mark.

Morghan picked up his poleaxe and ran down the steps.

Morghan did not immediately recognize that the five guards below were no longer alive, for though their chests were still, they were moving. Four of them were clumsily unbarring one of the northern gates, while the fifth kept walking into the wall, bouncing off it, and walking into it again. The reek of hot metal was stronger than ever, and the fog flowing in under the gates was as thick as wool.

"Stop! Stand!" he shouted. But they did not stop, or stand still, or even turn. They had one end of the bar lifted out of its bracket, and he realized they would have it off entirely in a minute.

Morghan shouted again, then dashed forward and struck the closest man across the back of the legs with the shaft of his poleaxe. Bone cracked, but the man did not turn. Still he lifted the beam, and Morghan belatedly saw what he was dealing with.

The poleaxe swung, and a head rolled on the floor. The decapitated body kept at its work for a few seconds, then lost coordination and began to flail angrily at the gate.

Sobbing, Morghan swiftly beheaded the other guards and beat the headless bodies back from the gate. The Dead tried to keep opening the door, but without heads they could not see, so they crashed into each other and fell over, and felt about blindly and worked at cross-purposes.

For an instant Morghan thought he was done with them and could take a moment to think. But then he heard something from outside, something that at first gave him heart, for it was the pure, sweet sound of a bell, before the sound was overlaid with something else, something he felt rather than heard, that made his stomach cramp, and bile come flooding into his mouth.

The dead guards, headless as they were, answered the bell as if a guiding intelligence had occupied them all. They came at him together, hands grasping, trying to bring him down, and he swung and bashed and cut and kicked at them with everything he'd learned from Sergeant Ishring and in the alleys behind the inn, but it was not enough, and at last he had to jump back to the stairs.

He was only just able to slam shut the heavy door as the Dead charged against it. One dead guard's hand was caught in the doorway and severed. It scuttled at him as he swung down the bar, and he had to stomp it to pieces before it lay still.

Morghan stood for a moment, trying to regain his breath. He could hear the Dead going back down to unbar the gate. There had to be a necromancer there, maybe more than one, or several Free Magic sorcerers. There might be an army of the Dead. . . .

Morghan stopped that thought. There would not be an army of the Dead. They could not cross fast running water. In fact, it was only because the bastion was built on a rocky island that the Dead below could survive. The necromancer outside could only use those people in the bastion who had already been slain with Free Magic to raise the Dead—

Like the sleeping guards upstairs.

The thought had barely formed in Morghan's mind before he was running again, jumping up the steps four at a time in a desperate race to get above the guardroom and bar the next door. If he could make it past, then there would only be the sentry above . . . and Terril.

Maybe Terril's alive, thought Morghan. *Please, please, let Terril be alive!*

Kworquorakan stepped into his path, eyes still half shut as if he merely slept, but his skin was pallid and blue around the mouth and eyes. He held a sword in a weak and clumsy grip, for the Dead spirit within him was not his own, and was too new to the body.

Morghan swept the sword to the floor and hammered the Dead guard to one side, rushing past before it could get up. He caught a glimpse through the open guardroom door, of the other Dead shambling from their beds, arming themselves slowly and stupidly.

Morghan shut the next door and barred it twice. This door was almost as heavy as the lower gate, but he had no illusions about how long wood and iron alone could hold against the Dead and Free Magic. Despite his lack of breath and the wave of shock and weariness that threatened to overwhelm him, he calmed himself and found the Charter. For a moment he almost lost himself in the welcoming sea of marks, before training and desperation asserted control. He found the symbols he needed, cupped them in his hands, and pressed them against the door while he whispered their use-names.

Warm, soft light spilled out between his fingers and ran through the tight grain of the wood, swirling round and round as it sank deeper, strengthening and binding. Rivulets of gold ran from wood to stone, like tree roots seeking water deep underground. The iron hinges spewed rusty flakes as they took on a deep, yellow glow that was sunlight and gold and a comforting, well-banked fire.

Morghan turned away from the door and fell over, momentarily too weak to support himself. He jarred his bad elbow on the stone, but the pain helped, the old familiar sensation cutting through his exhaustion. He got up and picked up his poleaxe, only to see that the axe was notched and there was a crack in the shaft. His fight against the Dead below had been desperate indeed.

Morghan left the poleaxe where it lay and stumbled to the rack of crossbows on the wall. He took down his own, and the cranequin and quarrel, and quickly wound back the string and loaded a shaft. Then he thrust four more quarrels through his belt and slowly began to climb the stairs.

He tried to be as quiet as he could, but within five steps this became unnecessary, as the Dead below attacked the door he had spelled shut. He heard the deep boom of heavy timber against timber and realized that they had made a battering ram from one or more of the beds. *Beds which should be made less sturdy so as not to be used against us,* Morghan thought. Something to be noted for the Bridgemistress, and if she approved, a memorandum sent to Famagus for the other shifts.

Morghan slowed near the top. The battlements were reached by a ladder through a hatch, and this was open, when it should not be. Tendrils of fog came spiraling down through the hatch, as if some hideous, tentacled sea creature of mist and dark vapor was squatting on the tower.

His crossbow held ready, Morghan moved underneath and looked up. But he couldn't see anything but the fog, and he couldn't hear anything, either, apart from the repeated crack and boom of the ram below.

Morghan started to climb the ladder with the crossbow at the ready, and found that he could not. He could not pull himself up or balance with his left arm. It would not support him, the elbow locking up or giving way, all flexibility lost. Morghan cursed under his breath and put the crossbow down to take up one of his thin daggers in his left hand. He could barely manage even that slight weight, but at least he could climb with his right hand.

But I won't be much use in a fight, Morghan thought. *When I stick my head up through that hatch, there'll be . . . there'll likely be two Dead on me right away . . . I can't win . . . I can't do any good . . . but I have to try . . . whoever is attacking us, they mustn't cross the bridge . . . they will not cross the bridge . . . my bridge . . .*

Morghan took a breath and began to climb. Slowly at first, then as he neared the top, it became a sudden, scrabbling rush and he burst out onto the battlements like a startled pheasant from the heath, sending the fog swirling in all directions.

Two bodies lay near the hatch. The guard Farremon was dead, pale and blue. But Terril's chest rose and fell slowly. Morghan put his dagger down, ready to hand, and quickly pushed Farremon's body through the open hatch, slamming it shut afterward and locking the bar. Then he turned to Terril. Her eyes were half open, but she looked drugged and insensible. Her hand was on her breast, and there were three faint Charter marks drawn there, pulsing in time with a very slow heartbeat.

"Terril!" said Morghan. "Terril!"

There was no answer. The death magic that had come with the fog had not claimed Terril, but it had left her fighting for her life. Perhaps the spell was weaker higher up, Morghan thought. Not that it mattered.

He reclaimed his dagger, drew his sword, and went to the northern battlements to look over the side. All he could see was thick, white fog, completely cloaking the bastion, hiding it from the North Fort and the southern shore. He couldn't even see directly below, though he could hear the clank and jangle of armor and weapons on the boardwalk, in between the booms of the ram on the lower door. There were a lot of enemy out there, scores of them, if not more.

But the continued booming was oddly reassuring. It meant that the door, or more likely at this point, the spell alone, still held. When he didn't hear it, but heard instead the clatter of feet on the stair, that would be . . . well . . . the end.

I'm not thinking straight. I need to warn the fort, and the ferry . . . and all the waiting merchants . . .

Morghan's head hurt, almost as much as his elbow, and he now knew that it was possible to feel even more exhausted than was the usual lot of a cadet on the bridge. It took a supreme effort to prise himself from the embrasure and walk over to the great horn that hung between two iron posts.

He leaned forward to set his lips to the horn, ready to blow the alert, when he saw that it was split at the mouth, riven in two. At the same time, he tasted hot metal that blistered his tongue. The horn had been split by magic, and that was no mean feat, unseen from below.

Or was it done unseen? Morghan thought. *Is there someone else up here, in the fog?*

Morghan stepped back and almost fell over before he managed to spread his feet and steady himself. Despite his pain and weariness he was thinking faster now, aware that he might have very little time.

One of the several hundred new Charter marks he had learned over the winter was the one that was the scream of the saffron-tailed kite, only the Bridgemistress wound into it another mark, one of magnification, that made the scream louder, more than a hundred times louder.

But they were difficult marks, not old familiar ones that he knew well. He might well meet the death of his grandmother, seeking to find and wield such marks when he was already so weary.

So be it, thought Morghan. *Better to die here than in an alley in Belisaere. I have had my winter, and it is enough.*

He kneeled down and rested his hands on the hilt of his sword, setting the point deep in a crack between the flagstones. Then he went into the Charter once more, knowing it was one time too many, that his weary body could not bear to harness the power he sought. Not and live to speak of it.

The first mark, the cry of the bird, he found easily, and he let it slide from his hands into the sword. The second was more difficult, and his vision swam and his breath grew ever more ragged before at last he pushed through a swarm of too-bright marks and caught the one he sought, and sent it into the blade too.

With the spell ready, and his strength fading fast, Morghan left the flow of the Charter and brought himself back to the foggy battlements. Slowly, ever so slowly, he rose to his feet and prepared to lift his sword, to send his signal flying to the night sky above the fog.

But the blade was stuck. Morghan pulled at it, and almost had it free when he saw that he was no longer alone. Someone . . . or something . . . was slipping over the battlements. It stopped to fix its gaze upon him, and then came stalking toward him.

Morghan knew what it was at once, for it was part of his lessons. It was why the company's guards carried poleaxes, to fight such a thing of stone, impervious to lighter weapons. Carved from solid rock to match the fetish of one of the tribes of the far steppe and infused with a Free Magic spirit to make it live and move, this was a Spirit-Walker.

It moved toward him, not lumbering as one might expect a statue to do, but more like a stalking insect, all sharp starts and flurries. It was manlike in the sense that it had two legs and two arms, but the legs were long, and the arms jointed backward and ended in wedges of sharpened stone.

One cruel wedge shot forward. Morghan twisted aside, too slowly, and his hauberk was sliced open as if it were no more than thin cloth, and he felt the sudden pain of a deep wound. At the same time, he wrenched his sword free and thrust it forward in riposte, though he knew no mere blade could harm a Spirit-Walker.

The riposte missed, but drawing back, the tip of the sword touched the Spirit-Walker on its backward-jointed elbow.

Morghan felt the connection to his very bones. He felt the ancient, malevolent spirit inside, striving to do as it was bid and slay him, and he felt the stone that it inhabited, and at once knew every fissure, every faint crack and weakness.

"Go," whispered Morghan to his spell, and he fell backward, all strength gone.

The marks left the blade, and not hundreds but thousands of saffron-tailed kites screamed their hunting scream inside the

Spirit-Walker's stony flesh, the sound resonating and echoing along every crack, growing and expanding, fighting to get out.

The Spirit-Walker took one further step, then exploded into powder as the distress call of the bastion echoed through the river valley, to the North Fort, and the ferry stations, and up the road and beyond the hills, to Navis and even to the very walls of Belisaere.

The great scream blew away the fog, and under sudden moon and starlight, a necromancer cursed and hurried back along the boardwalk. His Dead bashed once more at the door, then fell, the spirits too weak to sustain themselves in Life without their master. Hundreds of nomad tribesmen, spread out along the bridge, heard what they thought was the death-cry of their Spirit-Walker. They saw their necromancer flee and turned to run with him. The great raid upon the southern lands, so long in the making, had failed before it had really begun.

At the ferry station, Amiel cast a spell that sent a night-bird of dull Charter marks flying faster than any bird to the Glacier of the Clayr, and then another, like as a twin, winged south to Navis. But even as the magical birds left her hand, she was running for her horse and shouting orders, with Limath at her heels, spitting out the over-large mouthful of cake he had just wedged in his mouth.

Atop the bastion, Morghan looked at the stars, now so clear in the sky. They looked welcoming to him, something he had not thought about before. If he had the strength, he would have raised a hand to them, but he could not. Besides, he could feel the river calling to him, could hear the roar of the Greenwash—or perhaps it was some other river, for it did not sound entirely the same. . . .

"You are *not* allowed to die, cadet," said a voice near at hand.

Morghan slowly moved one eye to see who was speaking to him.

It was Terril, who was crawling over to him. Her hand moved across his face and climbed to his forehead, and two fingers touched the Charter Mark there. He felt some small spark of power flow from her, a faint thread that nevertheless was strong enough to arrest the pull of the unseen river and lessen the attraction of the distant stars.

"I said you are not allowed to die, Cadet Morghan! Do you understand?"

"Yes, Second," whispered Morghan. He did understand, and in that moment, he knew that he would not die. Terril held him back, and Terril was the company, and the company was the bridge, and he was part of it, and always would be, and one day he would be a Second and a Bridgemaster, too, for he had not failed the test.

He had held the bridge.

CREATURES OF DARKNESS AND LIGHT

VAMPIRE WEATHER

You be home by five, Amos," said his mother. "I saw Theodore on my way back, and he says it's going to be vampire weather."

Amos nodded and fingered the chain of crosses he wore around his neck. Eleven small silver-washed iron crosses, spread two fingers-breadths apart on a leather thong, so they went all the way around. His great-uncle told him once that they used to only wear crosses at the front, till a vampire took to biting the back of people's necks, like a dog worrying at a rat.

He took his hat from the stand near the door. It was made of heavy black felt, and the rim was wound with silver thread. He looked at his coat and thought about not wearing it, because the day was still warm, even if Theodore said there was going to be a fog later, and Theodore always knew.

"And wear your bracers and coat!" shouted his mother from the kitchen, even though she couldn't see him.

Amos sighed and slipped on the heavy leather wrist bracers, pulling the straps tight with his teeth. Then he put on his coat. It was even heavier than it looked, because there were silver dollars sewn into the cuffs and shoulders. It was all right in winter, but any other time all that weight of wool and silver was just too hot.

Amos had never even seen a vampire. But he knew they were out there. His own father had narrowly escaped one, before Amos was born. His great-uncle, Old Franz, had a terrible tangle of white scars across his hand, the mark of the burning pitch that he had desperately flung at a vampire in a vain attempt to save his first wife and oldest daughter.

The minister often spoke of the dangers of vampires, as well as the more insidious spiritual threat of things like the internet, television, and any books that weren't on the approved list. Apart from the vampires, Amos was quite interested in seeing the dangers the minister talked about, but he didn't suppose he ever would. Even when he finished school next year, his life wouldn't change much. He'd just spend more time helping out at the sawmill, though there would also be the prospect of building his own house and taking a wife. He hoped his wife would come from some other community of the faith. He didn't like the idea of marrying one of the half-dozen girls he'd grown up with. But, as with everything, his parents would choose for him, in consultation with the minister and the elders of the chapel.

Amos felt the heat as he stepped off the porch and into the sun. But looking up the mountainside, a great white, wet cloud was already beginning to descend. Theodore was right as usual. Within an hour the village would be blanketed in fog.

But an hour left Amos plenty of time to complete his task. He set off down the road, tipping his hat to Young Franz, who was fixing the shingles on his father's roof.

"Off to the mailbox?" called out Young Franz, pausing in his hammer strokes, speaking with the ease of long practice past the three nails he held in the corner of his mouth.

"Yes, brother," answered Amos. Of course he was, it was one of his duties and he did it every day at almost the same time.

"Get back before the fog closes in," warned Young Franz. "Theodore says it's—"

"Vampire weather," interrupted Amos. He regretted doing so immediately, even before Young Franz paused and deliberately took the nails out of his mouth and set down his hammer.

"I'm sorry, brother," blurted out Amos. "Please forgive my inci-
vility."

Young Franz, who was not only twice as old as Amos but close to
twice as heavy, and all of it muscle, looked down at the young man
and nodded slowly.

"You be careful, Amos. You sass me again and I'll birch your
backside from here to the hall, with everyone looking on."

"Yes, brother, I apologize," said Amos. He kept his head down
and eyes downcast. What had he been thinking to interrupt the
toughest and most short-tempered brother in the village?

"Get on with you, then," instructed Young Franz. He kept his
eye on Amos, but picked up the nails and put them back in his mouth.
Every second nail had a silver washer, to stop a vampire breaking in
through the roof, just as every chimney was meshed with silver-
washed steel.

Amos nodded with relief and started back down the road, faster
now. The fog was closer, one arm of it already extending down the
ridge, stretching out to curl back around toward the village like it
usually did, to eventually join up with the slower body of mist that
was coming straight down the slope.

He liked going to the mailbox. It was the closest thing the community had to an interface with the wider world, even if it was only
an old diesel drum on a post set back twenty feet from a minor
mountain road. Sometimes Amos saw a car go past, impossibly swift
compared to the horse buggy he rode in once a month, when they
visited with the cousins over in New Hareseth. Once a coach had
stopped and a whole bunch of people had gotten out and tried to take
his photograph, and he had almost dropped the mail as he tried to
run back and keep his face covered at the same time.

The flag was up on the box, Amos saw as he got closer. That was
good, since otherwise he would have to wait for the mail truck to
get back out on the main road. Sometimes the postal workers were

women, and he wasn't allowed to see or talk to strange women.

He hurried to the box and carefully unlocked the padlock with the key that he proudly wore on his watch-chain as a visible symbol that while not quite yet a man, he was no longer considered just a boy.

There were only three items inside: a crop catalog from an old firm that guaranteed no devil-work with their seeds; and two thick, buff-colored envelopes that Amos knew would be from one of the other communities, somewhere around the world. They all used and reused the same envelopes. The two here might have been a dozen places, and come home again.

Amos put the mail in his voluminous outer pocket, shut the lid, and clicked the padlock shut. But with the click, he heard another sound. Right behind him, the crunch of gravel underfoot.

He spun around, looking not ahead but up at the sky. When he saw that the sun was still shining, unobscured by the lowering cloud, he dropped his gaze and saw . . . a girl.

"Hi," said the girl. She was about his age, and really pretty, but Amos backed up to the mailbox.

She wore no crosses, and her light sundress showed a bare neck and arms, and even a glimpse of her breasts. Amos gulped as she moved and caught the sun, making the dress transparent, so he could see right through it.

"Hi," the girl said again, and stepped closer.

Amos raised his bracer-bound wrists to make a cross.

"Get back!" he cried. "I don't know how you walk in the sun, vampire, but you can't take me! My faith is strong!"

The girl wrinkled her nose, but she stopped.

"I'm not a vampire," she said. "I've been vaccinated like everyone else. Look."

She rotated her arm to show the inside of her elbow. There was a tattoo there, some kind of bird thing inside a rectangle, with numbers and letters spelling out a code.

"Vacks . . . vexination . . ." stumbled Amos. "That's devil's work. If you're human, you wear crosses, else the vampires get you."

"Not since maybe the last twenty years," said the girl. "But like you said, if I am a vampire, how come I'm out in the sun?"

Amos shook his head. He didn't know what to do. The girl stood in his path. She was right about the sun, but even though she wasn't a vampire, she was a girl, an outsider. He shouldn't be looking at her, or talking to her. But he couldn't stop looking.

"I don't have a problem with crosses, either," said the girl. She took the three steps to Amos and reached over to touch the crosses around his neck, picking them up one by one, almost fondling them with her long, elegant fingers. Amos stopped breathing and tried to think of prayers he couldn't remember, prayers to quench lust and . . . sinful stirrings and . . .

He broke away and ran a few yards toward the village. He would have kept going, but the girl laughed. He stopped and looked back.

"Why're you laughing?"

She stopped and smiled again.

"Just . . . men don't usually run away from me."

Amos stood a little straighter. She thought he was a man, which was more than the village girls did.

"What's your name?" asked the girl. "I'm Tangerine."

"Amos," said Amos slowly. "My name is Amos."

Behind the girl, the fog kept coming down, thick and white and damp.

"It's good to meet you, Amos. Are you from the village, up the mountain?"

Amos nodded his head.

"We just moved in along the road," said Tangerine. "My dad is working at the observatory."

Amos nodded again. He knew about the observatory. You could

see one of its domes from the northern end of the village, though it was actually on the crest of the other mountain, across the valley.

"You'd better get home before the fog blanks the sun," he said. "It's vampire weather."

Tangerine smiled again. She smiled more than anyone Amos had ever known.

"I told you, I'm vaccinated," she said. "No vampire will bite me. Hey, could I come visit with you?"

Amos shook his head urgently. He couldn't imagine the punishment he would earn if he came back with an almost naked outsider woman, one who didn't even wear a cross.

"It's lonely back home," said Tangerine. "I mean, no one lives here, and Dad works, there's just me and my grandmother most of the time."

The fog was shrouding the tops of the tallest trees across the road. Amos watched it and even as he spoke he wondered why he wasn't already running back up the road to home.

"What about your mother?"

"She's dead," said Tangerine. "She died a long while back."

Amos could smell the fog now, could almost taste the wetness on his tongue. There could be vampires right there, hidden in that vanguard of cloud, close enough to spring out and be on him in seconds. But he still found it difficult to tear himself away.

"I'll be back tomorrow," he said, and bolted, calling over his shoulder, "Same time."

"See you then!" said Tangerine. She waved, and that image stayed in Amos's head, her standing like that, her raised arm lifting her breasts, that smile on her face, and her bright hair shining, with the cold white fog behind, like a painted background, to make sure she stood out even more.

Amos wasn't home by five, or even half past, and he just barely beat the main body of the fog, which came straight down. The home door was shut and barred by the time he got there, so he had to knock on the lesser door, and he got a cracking slap from his mother when she let him in, and when his father finished his bath he ordered an hour-long penance, which left Amos with his knees sore from kneeling, and made the words he'd been repeating over and over so meaningless that he felt like they were some other language that he'd once known but had somehow forgotten.

Through it all, he kept thinking of Tangerine, seeing Tangerine, imagining what might happen when he next saw her . . . and then he'd try to pray harder, to concentrate on those meaningless words, but whatever he did, he couldn't direct his mind away from those bare arms and legs, the way her unbound hair fell . . .

Amos slept very badly, and earned more punishments before breakfast than he'd had in the past month. Even his father, who favored prayer and penance over any other form of correction, was moved to take off his leather belt, though he only held it as an unspoken threat while he delivered a homily on attention and obedience.

Finally, it was time to get the mail. Amos took no chances that this plum job might be taken from him. If anyone else saw Tangerine he'd never be allowed to go to the mailbox again. So he put on his bracers, coat, and hat without being asked and went to tell his mother he was going.

She looked at him over her loom, but didn't stop her work, the shuttle clacking backward and forward as she trod the board.

"You be back by five," she warned. "Theodore says the fog today will be even thicker. It is a shocking month for vampire weather."

"Yes, Mother," said Amos. He planned to run to the mailbox as soon as he was out of sight of the village. That would give him a little extra time with Tangerine. If she came. He was already starting to wonder if he might have imagined her.

He also made sure to wave and nod to Young Franz, who was working on the roof of his father's house again. But as soon as he was around the bend, Amos broke into a run, pounding along the road as if there was a vampire after him.

Tangerine was at the mailbox, but so was the post truck and a postal worker, a man. He was chatting to Tangerine while he put the letters in the slot, and they were both smiling. Amos scowled and slowed down, but he kept going. Since he'd already talked to a girl, talking to a postman wasn't going to be any bigger transgression.

They both turned around as he approached. Amos had seen that postman before, in the distance, but up close he saw details he'd never noticed before. Like the fact that the postman didn't wear crosses either, and there were no wrist bracers under his uniform coat. It also looked too light to be sewn with silver wire or set with coins.

"Hi," said Tangerine. She had a different dress on, but it was just as revealing as the one the day before. Amos couldn't take his eyes off her, and he didn't notice the postman wink at him.

"Howdy, son," called the postman. "Good to see you."

"Brother," replied Amos stiffly. "We don't call each other 'son.'"

"Fair enough, brother," said the postman. "I guess I'm old enough to be your dad, is why I said son. But I'd better be on my way. Plenty of mail to deliver."

"And the fog is coming down," said Amos. He was trying to be friendly, because he didn't want to look bad in front of Tangerine. But it was difficult.

"Oh, the fog's no problem," said the postman. "I'll drive down out of it soon enough, and the road is good."

"I meant it is vampire weather," said Amos.

"Vampire weather?" asked the postman. "I haven't heard that said since . . . well, since I was no older than you are now. I doubt there's a wild vampire left in these parts. With nothing to drink, they just wither away."

"My uncle's wife and daughter were killed by vampires, not eight years ago," said Amos hotly.

"But that's . . ." The postman's voice trailed off, and he looked at Amos more intently, tilting his head as he took in the necklace of crosses and the bracers. "I knew you folk were old-fashioned, but you can't tell me you're not vaccinated? That's against the law!"

"There is no law but the word of the Lord," said Amos automatically.

"I gotta get going," said the postman. He wasn't smiling now. "Miss Tangerine, you want a lift down to your dad's?"

"No, thanks, Fred," said Tangerine. "My grandma's coming past a bit later, I'll go back with her."

"Well, say hello to your dad for me," said the postman. "Goodbye . . . brother."

Amos nodded, just a slight incline, which if he'd done it to an older man back home would have gotten him into serious trouble.

"I've been waiting for a while," said Tangerine. She leaned back against the mailbox and tilted her head, so that her hair fell across one of her eyes. "I thought maybe you'd come early."

"Everything's got its time," said Amos gruffly. He took out his key and held it nervously, his mouth weirdly dry. "Uh, I have to . . . to get the mail. . . ."

"Oh, sure," laughed Tangerine. She moved aside, just enough that Amos could lean forward and open the lid. She was so close he almost touched her arm with the back of his hand. He reached past and quickly took out the mail. Just two buff-colored envelopes today.

Tangerine moved behind him as he locked the mailbox, so that just like the day before she was blocking his way.

"I have to get back," said Amos. He jerked his thumb at the fog, which was once again eddying down the hillside.

"Can't we just . . . talk awhile?" asked Tangerine. "I mean, I'm curious about you. I've never met anyone like you before."

"What do you mean like me?" asked Amos.

"Nothing bad!" exclaimed Tangerine. She came closer to him

and gave a little tug at the lapel of his coat. Amos took a half step back and almost didn't hear what she said next, the blood was rushing so in his ears. "I mean, you're a really good-looking guy, but it was kind of hard to tell at first, with the big hat and the coat and everything. And I never saw so many crosses—"

"I told you, it's for . . . to protect us . . . against the vampires," said Amos.

"But you don't need them," said Tangerine. "Like Fred said, there's no wild vampires left. When most everyone got vaccinated, they just died out."

"I don't know about that," said Amos. "People see them, in the fog, through the windows."

"Have you seen them?" asked Tangerine.

Amos shook his head. He'd looked, but all he ever saw were drifts of fog, occasionally spurred into some strange eddy.

"There you go then," she said. "Besides, if you did think they were still around, you could get vaccinated too."

Amos shook his head.

"But it's just like getting a shot for polio, or measles," said Tangerine.

Amos shook his head again. His little sister had died of measles, but everyone said that it was the Lord's will. Amos had taken the measles too, at the same time, and he hadn't died.

"If the Lord wants to take you, then that's it," he said. "No amount of vaxinating can stand against that."

Tangerine sighed.

"I guess you hold to some pretty strong beliefs," she said. "Do you even get to watch television?"

"Nope," said Amos. "That's just a door for the Devil, straight into your head."

"My dad would kind of agree with you on that," said Tangerine. "Not enough to stop me watching, thank heavens."

"*You* watch television?" asked Amos.

"Sure. You could come down and watch it too, sometime. My place is only half a mile along the road."

She pointed and Amos suddenly realized that the fog was upon them. Tendrils of cold, wet whiteness were undulating past, weaving together to make a thicker, darker mass.

He looked up the mountain and could no longer see the sun. The two arms of the fog had already joined, and he would be in darkness all the way back to the village.

He must have made a noise, a frightened noise, because Tangerine took his hand.

"It's only fog," she said.

"Vampire weather," whispered Amos. He tried to look everywhere at once, peering past Tangerine, turning his head, then spinning around so that somehow he ended up with Tangerine's arms around him.

"I can't get back," Amos said, but even in the midst of his panic, he was thinking how wonderful it was to have Tangerine's arms around him, and then out of nowhere her mouth arrived on his and he supposed it was a kiss but it felt more like he'd had the air sucked out of his lungs, but in a good way; it wasn't something horrible, and he wanted it to happen again but Tangerine tilted her head back and then settled her face into his neck, all warm and comfortable.

He patted her back for a little while, something he'd seen his father do once to his mother, before they'd seen that the children had noticed their embrace. Tangerine said something muffled he couldn't hear, then she stepped back and disentangled herself, but she was still holding his hands.

"Don't go back, Amos. Come down to my house. You can stay with me."

"Stay with you?" mumbled Amos. A great part of him wanted more than anything to always be with this wonderful, amazing girl, but a possibly greater part was simply terrified and wanted him to sprint back up the road and get home as quickly as possible. "I . . . I can't . . . I have to get somewhere safe . . ."

A noise interrupted him. Amos flinched, looking wildly around, arms already coming up to make a cross. But Tangerine dragged his arms back down and hugged him again.

"It's just Grandma's car, silly," she said.

Amos nodded, not trusting himself to speak. He could see the car now, turning in off the main road. A small, white car, which sent the fog scurrying away as it pulled up next to the mailbox.

The car's headlights turned off, and the light inside came on. Amos saw a white-haired old woman in the driver's seat. She waved and smiled, a tight smile that bore no relation to Tangerine's open happiness.

Tangerine held Amos's hands as they watched the little old lady get out of the car. There was something strange about the way the woman moved that Amos couldn't quite process, how she kind of unbent herself as she rested her hands on the roof and got taller and taller, maybe seven feet tall, with her arms and legs out of normal human proportion, and then she didn't look like a little old lady at all.

"Oh, God, Grandma, I can't do this," said Tangerine, and all of a sudden Amos's hands were free and the girl was pushing at his chest, pushing him away. "Run!"

Amos glanced back over his shoulder, only half running, till he saw that the old woman's mouth was open, and Amos wished it wasn't, wished he'd never seen that mouth, never met Tangerine, never got caught in vampire weather, and he was running like he'd never run before, and screaming at the same time.

The vampire stalked past her granddaughter, who held a necklace of crosses in her hand and wept, a girl crying for her grandmother the vampire, and for a boy she hardly knew.

Amos felt the cold, wet air against his bare neck, missed the jangle of the crosses and knew that Tangerine had taken his protection when she kissed him. He wept too, tears full as much of the hurt of betrayal as fear, and then something fastened on his coat, and he was borne down to the ground, sliding and screaming, trying to turn onto his back so he could cross his arms, but the vampire was so much stronger, her hands like clamps, gripping him to the bone, keeping him still, and he wet himself as he felt the first touch of those teeth he'd seen on his neck and then—

Then there was a heavy, horrible thumping, cracking sound, like a big tree come down on a house to smash it to bits. Amos felt suddenly lighter, and with a last surge of desperate energy he rolled over and brought up his bracers to form a cross—and there above him was Young Franz, in full silver-embroidered coat and hat, a bloodstained six-foot silver-tipped stake in his hand. Behind him was Old Franz, and Amos's father, and all the older Brothers, and his mother and the aunts in their silver-thread shawls, argent knives in hand.

Amos sat up and a bucketful of tainted dust fell down his chest and across his legs. It smelled like sulfur and rotten meat, and the reek of it made Amos turn his head and vomit.

As he did so, his mother came close and raised a lantern near his head. When Amos turned to her, she pushed his head back, so that the light fell clear upon his neck.

"He's bit," she said heavily. She looked at Amos's father, who stared blankly, then held out his hand. Young Franz gave him the bloodied stake.

"Father . . ." whispered Amos. He reached up to touch his neck. He could, quite horribly, feel the raised lips of two puncture wounds, but when he looked at his fingers, he could see only a tiny speck of blood.

"It is the Will of the Lord," said his father, words echoed by the somber crowd.

He raised the stake above his head.

Amos let himself fall back on the ground and shut his eyes.

But the stake did not enter his heart. He heard someone scream-ing, "Stop! Stop!" and he opened his eyes again and tilted his head forward.

Tangerine was running through the crowd of villagers, who parted quickly ahead of her, but closed up behind. She had his neck-lace of crosses in her left hand and a small golden object in her right.

"Another one," said Amos's mother. She raised her knife. "A young one. Ready your stake, Jan."

"No!" shouted Amos. He twisted himself up and grabbed his father's leg. "She's human. Look, she's holding crosses! She's a per-son!"

Tangerine stopped at Amos's feet and glared at his parents, not even looking at the stake. She was shouting too, and holding up the gold object.

"I've already called the police! And my dad! You can't kill Amos!"

Amos's father looked her up and down, the stake held ready in his hand. Then, without taking his eyes off her, he spoke to his wife.

"She's holding crosses, sure enough."

The older woman sniffed.

"This isn't any of your business, outsider. A vampire's bit my son, and we must do what must be done."

"But he can be vaccinated!" sobbed Tangerine. "Within twenty-four hours of a bite, it still works."

"We don't hold with vaccination," answered Amos's mother. She looked at her husband. "Do it."

"No!" shrieked Tangerine. She threw herself over Amos as Jan raised the stake. Amos put an arm around her and shut his eyes again.

"I said do it, Jan!"

Amos opened his eyes. His father was looking down at him, with an expression that he had only ever seen once before, when Jan had broken his favorite chisel, broken it beyond repair.

"My phone is still connected to the nine-one-one operator," said Tangerine. "Listen for yourself, *Jan*."

She held up the tiny gold object. There was a distant voice speaking from it.

Jan took it from her. For a moment Amos thought he would throw it away, or crush it beneath his heel, but instead he lifted it to his ear and spoke slowly and heavily.

"This is Jan Korgrim, from New Rufbah. We need an ambulance for a vampire-bit boy. He'll be by the mailbox. No, the vampire's dealt with. I reckon it was an old family one, let loose."

Jan handed the phone back to Tangerine. His wife looked at him with eyes sharper than her silver knife, and turned away. The other villagers followed watchfully, lanterns held high to illuminate the fog, stakes and knives still kept ready.

"Father, I—"

Jan held up his hand.

"There's nothing to be said between us, Amos. You're an outsider now."

"But Father, I don't want—"

Jan turned away and strode quickly up the hill, toward the fuzzy, fog-shrouded lantern light that marked the way home.

Tangerine rolled off Amos and stood up. He looked dully up at her and saw that she was crying.

"My name's not Tangerine," she said. "It's Jane."

Amos shrugged. He didn't want to know this, he didn't want to know anything.

"And I've got a steady boyfriend."

Amos just wanted to lie on the ground and die.

"Grandmother wanted me to find someone she could drink. Someone unvaccinated. She was tired of reheated plasma. She promised she wouldn't kill you, but then when I saw her . . . I saw her go full vampire . . . I'm sorry, Amos. I'm sorry!"

"Doesn't matter," said Amos. "You'd better go, though."

"Go? I'll help you down to the road, to meet the ambulance."

"No," said Amos. He got up on his knees and then slowly stood up, pushing Tangerine . . . Jane . . . aside when she tried to help. "I'm not going down to the road."

"What?"

"There's a cold lake in a kind of hollow up near the peak," said Amos. He staggered forward a few steps, almost colliding with a tree. "The fog sits there, day and night. I'm going to take a rest up there. Just for a few days, and then—"

"But you'll turn," exclaimed Jane. She tugged at his arm, trying to drag him downhill. "You'll be a vampire!"

"I'll be a vampire," agreed Amos. He smiled at the thought. "And then I reckon I'll go home and . . . despite crosses and silver and everything, I'll—"

He stumbled and would have fallen, but Jane held him up. He kept mumbling about drinking the blood of girls with names Jane had never heard of, like Hepzibah and Penninah, and killing someone called Young Franz, and was so intent on this litany that he barely noticed when they reached the mailbox and Jane sat him down against it.

The ambulance came with two police cars. The police spoke to her briefly, before driving on up the road to the village. The paramedics gave Amos a sedative and then the antivampire shot, and chatted cheerfully with Jane as they loaded Amos into the ambulance.

As Jane climbed in the back, one of the paramedics, the older one, looked around the shrouded landscape and took a deep breath.

"Ah, I like a lungful of mountain fog," he said. "Sometimes you just can't beat a touch of vampire weather."

STRANGE FISHING IN THE WESTERN HIGHLANDS

I t is forty years and more since I first went fishing with Hellboy. I was a young man then, with a fresh-minted medical degree from St. Andrews and what I thought was a wholly rational view of the world. Bachelor of Medicine and Bachelor of Surgery I was, with "Mb ChB" after my name, and a head stuffed full of scientific knowledge and a bare modicum of practical surgery from the hospital in Dundee.

The last few years of my medical studies had been extraordinarily busy, and in that time I'd seen very little of my father, my sole living relative. He hadn't made it any easier, choosing when he retired to live not in our comfortable former family home in Edinburgh, instead moving to the house he had inherited from his uncle, a remote place on the shore of Loch Torridon in the Western Highlands. It was four miles from where the road terminated, had no telephone and only occasional electricity from a diesel generator, and for the most part, could only be easily reached by boat from Lower Diabaig or Shieldaig, across the loch.

So, having unexpectedly been given four days off duty from the hospital due to what I supposed was a rostering error but may have in fact been a direction from on high that I was working too hard, I decided to visit my father. I sent a telegram to advise him, but as it was February, and the winter storms busy on the west coast, I thought it unlikely it would reach him before I did. Though I had no doubts about his filial affection, we did not enjoy the closest of father-son relationships. So I took the precaution of purchasing a ham, a dozen bottles of his favorite burgundy, and a few other odds and ends to offer as gifts, all of which went into a hamper that I could only just jam into the very slim boot of my senior colleague Dr. Teague's Austin-Healey 3000, which he had reluctantly lent me for my journey.

The road trip was uneventful, save that I drove toward bad weather rather than away from it, and regretted borrowing a convertible rather than something more sensible from one of my other friends, as while the car looked very fine and was quite fast, it also leaked and the heater was either too hot or completely ineffective.

I arrived at Lower Diabaig around four o'clock and parked near the pier, which marked the terminus of the road. It was already quite dark, and the latest in a steady series of heavy showers was coming down, with the promise of more to follow. There were two fishing boats tied up at the pier, so I walked up to see if anyone was aboard who might take me to my father's. If not, I would have to knock on some doors to see who might be at home in the village, as there was no pub or hotel where I might otherwise find a fisherman.

I thought I was in luck as I saw someone aboard the first vessel, as I even knew the man slightly. His name was Toller, though I didn't know if this was his Christian or surname. He had taken me to my father's on several previous occasions, so I was rather surprised when he answered my cheerful greeting with a grunt and immediately returned his attention to coiling a rope that he had in fact just perfectly coiled, only to unroll it at my approach.

"I'm sorry to interrupt, Mr. Toller," I called. "I was hoping you might be able to take me over to Owtwauch House."

Toller turned away from me, ignoring me completely, as I stood stupidly in the rain looking at his broad, oilskin-clad back. I was surprised, for Toller had never shown me any animosity before. True, he was a Highland Scot, and I a Lowlander born and bred, and an Anglified one at that, but I'd never felt that this was a problem before, though I'd heard of such prejudices.

I was momentarily tempted to step aboard his boat and give him a piece of my mind, but fortunately was prevented from doing so by a hail from the other fishing boat. A fisherman I hadn't met before waved at me, so I left Toller and walked along the pier.

"Old Toller's having a Presbyterian sulk today," said the man, who was not much older than myself, though considerably more weathered. His accent was unusual. He spoke excellent English, and sounded Scottish most of the time, but he placed a different emphasis on the syllables of some words. "Did ye' say you wanted to go over to the Owtwauch?"

"Aye," I answered. "It's my father's house, Colonel MacAndrew. I'm his son, Malcolm."

"Pleased to meet you, then," said the fisherman. "I'm Erik Haakon. I'll take you over."

"That's very kind," I said, leaning down to shake hands as he reached up from the deck. "I'll just nip back and get my things. You don't think the weather's too tough to cross, then?"

Erik looked startled, following this by a glance at the sky.

"Ach, no! There's plenty of rain, but the wind's dying already. Full moon tonight, and all."

I'd forgotten it was a full moon. If it cleared, it would be a beautiful night. The view from my father's house was particularly spectacular on a moonlit night, with its panoramic vista of the loch and the western sea toward Skye. I supposed that was why it had been called Owtwauch House, "Owtwauch" being Gaelic for something like a sentry post. My father was very keen on the Gaelic and spoke it fluently, and it had been drummed into me as a small boy, but like any rarely used language it had faded from my mind. Mostly to be replaced by medical Latin, which I had been required to memorize far more than was really sensible in the modern age.

Erik and I chatted a little as we chugged away across the loch. He was Norwegian, but had married a local girl, and was older than I thought, in his midthirties at least. We discussed the parlous state of the fisheries and the recent purchase by the National Trust of most of the land around Loch Torridon from one of the old estates. In fact my father's property was one of the few remaining pockets of freehold not to go to the National Trust. It had been held by our family for a very long time, apparently all the way back to Somerled, King of the Isles, and perhaps before.

We were bumping up against the rough wooden jetty that served as a landing stage for Owtwauch House before I noticed, through the curtain of rain, that there was a helicopter sitting on the front lawn, a broad expanse that ran down almost to the stony beach, ending in a retaining wall that was as green with tidal weed as the grass of the lawn. There were also many more lights than usual burning in the house, far more than the one generator could support.

"Remember me to your father," said Erik, and he made a curious gesture, a fist hammering the air, as I gaped at the helicopter. "I'd best make for home."

Absently, my mind awhirl, I tried to pay him for the short voyage, but he would have none of it, instead helping me get my hamper onto the jetty and helping me out as well, as I continued to try to press a five-pound note into his hand.

I had hardly taken four steps when I saw two men emerge out of the rain-hazed lights and block the end of the jetty. They were dressed in the typical style of country gentlemen, as I was myself, in Harris tweed, corduroy, and Wellingtons, and it would not have been too out of place if they had shotguns under their arms. But it was definitely out of place for them to be carrying Sten submachine guns, relics of the past war, instantly recognizable to me both from hundreds of comic books of commando adventures, but also from many visits to the various bases where my father had served the latter part of his thirty-five years under the colors.

Fortunately, I half recognized one of the two men, and perhaps even more fortunately, he knew me.

"Malcolm MacAndrew! What are you doing here?"

"I've come to see my father," I stammered. "What's going on?"

"You'd better come inside," replied the man. He was a major, or had been when I had last met him, though I'd forgotten his name. He was one of my father's former subordinates from his last posting before retirement, when he commanded the King's Own Scottish Borderers.

Cradling the Sten in the crook of his left elbow, he shook hands with me. I almost dropped the hamper in the process, and felt a clumsy fool in the presence of these soldiers.

"Colonel Strahan," said the man, reminding me. "Call me Neil. This is Bob Mumfort."

The other man nodded, but it couldn't be described as an overly friendly gesture. Reluctant acceptance at best.

Strahan led us across the lawn, past the helicopter. It wasn't a type I recognized, and the only marking on its dark grey hull was a small acronym in darker grey on the door.

"BPRD? What's that?"

"Your father will explain," said Strahan. We continued past the helicopter, farther into the light. There were portable floodlights like those used in filmmaking rigged up around the house, encircling it with harsh white illumination, and I could hear the deep thrum of several diesel generators out the back.

The front door was open, but guarded by two more men, this time with Lee-Enfield rifles, who looked familiar and were almost certainly some of my father's former military colleagues.

There were a lot more men inside the house, dozens of them in the reception rooms, all armed to the teeth, with rifles, submachine guns, and even a couple of Bren light machine guns. They stopped talking as I was led through to the kitchen.

My father was there, tall and authoritarian-looking as ever, though I had never before seen him as he was now, with his face painted in strange whorls of a blue so dark it was almost black and a wreath of holly in his silver hair. He was also wearing a long white robe with the hood pushed back.

He was waving a green stick, a branch recently torn from a tree, over a pile of .303 ball ammunition boxes on the kitchen table, tapping the boxes as he chanted something in what was not exactly Gaelic. There was also a pile of what looked like gilded pruning hooks under the table, thirty or forty of them, and every third tap he bent down to wave the stick over them as well.

I started to go in, but Strahan held me back and emphasized his grip on my arm with an urgent whisper.

"Wait! Not until he puts the rod down."

I opened my mouth, but shut it again before anyone needed to tell me. I suppose I was in mild shock, the kind of dissonance you experience when you see your extremely proper military father wearing a white robe while he performed something that could only be described as a rite or spell of some kind.

Then I really did go into shock, as I took in the figure at the far end of the room. A man, or a manlike humanoid, whose skin was as red as a boiled lobster, and his head a strange confabulation of angular lines, with two circular growths sprouting from his forehead like opaque goggles of that same red flesh. He wore a khaki trench coat, and I was further staggered when I saw a tail twist out behind the coat, a tail that could only be described as demonic.

I must have gasped, for Strahan pulled me back, and the strange red creature looked at me. He put down his pewter mug and waved, shocking me still further, as his right hand was a massive, oversize fist that, apart from being the same color as his flesh, would have been more in keeping on a mighty statue of some medieval hero.

My father finished his chant and laid the wand upon the

ammunition boxes. The branch withered as he did so, and crumbled into a light ash, which he bent down to blow off with three carefully controlled breaths. Then he turned to see who had almost inter-rupted him, controlled anger on his painted face, which eased as he saw me staring, the hamper clutched to my chest almost like a shield.

"Malcolm! What are you doing here?"

"I . . . I got some days off," I stammered. "Spur of the moment—"

I was looking past him at the creature. I couldn't think of him as a man, for he looked to be so far beyond the physical norm. In fact I didn't know what to think, and a good part of my previously extremely secure worldview was crumbling.

My father saw me looking and clearly understood.

"Let me introduce you to a colleague," he said. "Hellboy, may I present my son, Dr. Malcolm MacAndrew. A medical doctor, not one of those philosophers."

"Hi," growled the apparition. He sounded human enough, with the hint of an American accent. "How ya doing, Doc?"

"Fine, thank you," I said automatically. Then I dropped the hamper. I heard the wine bottles break, but it didn't really register.

"But I don't understand what is going on," I added, and suddenly felt ten years old again, and not at all a well-qualified professional with a grasp of every situation, which was how I liked to perceive myself. "Why is your face painted? And why are you wearing a . . . a robe?"

"It's not the right time to tell you," said my father slowly.

"Got to tell the kid sometime, Mac," said the red apparition, this Hellboy. "Must be a shock to see your father wearing a dress."

"It's not a dress, it's a druidical robe," said my father. "As you very well know, Hellboy. But I wasn't initiated into the mysteries until I was thirty-three, that is the proper age—"

"What mysteries?" I interjected. "Just tell me what is going on, please!"

"We might need a doctor to come along," said Hellboy.

"We have a doctor," replied my father.

"Doc Hendricks is a bit old to be wandering across the bottom of the loch," said Hellboy. He looked at me and winked. "What say you come along, Doc?"

"The bottom of the loch?"

"Oh, very well, I suppose I don't have much choice," grumbled my father. "You BPRD types just don't respect tradition sometimes. Strahan, issue the blessed ammunition and the sickles to the men. You come upstairs with me, Malcolm, and I'll fill you in. Hellboy . . . I don't suppose there's any point giving you any orders, is there?"

"Nope," said Hellboy. He finished whatever he was drinking from the pewter mug, took a cigar from an inside pocket of his trench coat, and lit it up. "I might take a walk along the water's edge, see if anything pops up."

"Nothing will happen till the moon is high," said my father.

"The Russians might not know that," replied Hellboy. He bit down on his cigar and talked through a clenched jaw, while he busied himself checking the most oversize handgun I'd ever seen, at least outside the picture of a medieval hand-cannon that had adorned the cover of one of my childhood books.

"The Russians?"

I felt like I'd inadvertently taken some delirium-inducing drug. My father was apparently a druid in charge of some paramilitary organization in league with an American semihuman. . . . I felt a strong urge to get out my medical bag and take my own temperature, except that I knew it would not indicate a fever. I had stumbled into a hidden world, but I knew it was a real one, as real as the discovery of my father's secret relationship with my cousin Susan, after my mother died. That had been a shock too, but to some degree it had prepared me for this, the realization that my father had a number of layers to his life, many of them hidden from me.

I followed him upstairs to his study, which was as orderly as ever, his books of military and natural history arrayed in alphabetical order by author behind the glass doors of the bookshelves, his desk devoid of paper, several pens lined up on the green baize top in order of size.

We sat in his studded leather armchairs, and he looked at me with an expression I knew well, that of a gentleman of a certain age uncertain how to impart to his son the facts of life. He took a breath to start, stopped, let it out, took another breath, and started off all while not really looking me in the eye.

"We come from a long line of what many people call druids, Malcolm. Uncle Andrew, your great-uncle, was in fact the Arch-Druid of Britain until his death and in due course I will probably succeed him. At present I hold the post of Sentinel of the West and the Isles, and it is in that capacity that I have gathered the lesser druids and deodars here and sought the help of the BPRD—"

"Deodars? BPRD?"

"Deodars are sworn laymen in our service. The Bureau for Paranormal Research and Defense is an organization that has a lot of experience in dealing with the kind of situation we're facing. Particularly Hellboy, who is their chief operative—"

"What situation? And what is Hellboy, anyway?"

"Hellboy is a fine young man," replied my father stiffly. "Just think of him as having a different background. Like a Gurkha or a chap from Africa. I met him in Malaya during the Emergency, got a lot of respect for the fellow."

"He's not a Gurkha," I protested weakly. "He's got a tail, and he's red—"

"Hellboy is an absolutely essential ally in the fight we face tonight," interrupted my father grimly. "I expect you to show him the respect you would accord one of my brother officers."

"I don't understand, but of course I will behave properly toward him," I said. "What exactly is the situation? What fight?"

My father walked to the window and drew back the curtain. Beyond the floodlights, the surface of the loch glimmered silver, catching the light of the full moon, which had begun to climb up, half its disc now visible.

"This house has been here a very long time," he said. "It is not called the Owtwauch for nothing, for it is indeed a sentry post, from where we druids have watched over the sacred circle of Maponos since time immemorial."

He gestured out toward the water.

"When the moon is full, there is a silver road to the stone circle that now lies at the bottom of the loch. A silver road that we guard against those who would attempt to use the circle for evil ends. Hellboy has brought us word that just such evildoers will seek to enter the circle tonight, and we must prevent them."

"Russian evildoers?"

"Their nationality is not their primary identification. They serve a Russian master, and have bent the power of the Soviets to their own ends. Now, there is little time, and I must prepare you. We cannot do the full initiation of course, but Maponos will need to know you as one of his own."

"I've heard that name before," I said. "I vaguely remember . . . when I was a child . . ."

"Aye, I'd forgotten you'd met a presence of the god," said my father, as matter-of-fact as if he were talking about the village grocer. "That will help. You were eight or nine at the time, it would have been 1946, when we were last all here."

"I thought he was a fisherman," I said. I had forgotten the name, but I remembered the occasion very well. There was a stream not far away that ran into the loch, and I had been paddling in it. A man had come out of the water and given me a very large and splendid sea trout, which I'd taken back to my mother, who had not been as thrilled as I was to receive it.

"Well, he might remember you anyway, but we shall paint your face to make sure, and you can wear one of my spare robes."

I acquiesced to this without protest. It didn't even feel particularly strange to have my father smear the curiously sweet-smelling dye upon my cheeks. He'd painted my face before, when I was a child. Perhaps those occasions had been more significant than I thought.

The robe was slightly more troublesome, since it was extremely reminiscent of a large, loose dress. But if my battle-veteran father could wear one, I supposed I could too, and when we went downstairs I was not that surprised to see several others also wearing the white robes, though most of the younger men were not. I supposed they were the deodars.

Hellboy was back inside too. A man wearing a similar trench coat was talking to him, reading from a clipboard. Hellboy nodded as the man spoke. When he'd finished, he stood up and raised that strange clublike fist. Everyone fell silent and looked at him.

"Okay, guys, the sonar buoy says there's a sub in the loch. Gotta be the Russians. Mac, what's the deal with the silver road?"

My father looked out the window.

"The road is forming. They will be able to enter it, from the mouth of the loch, as will you. We had best deploy."

"Yeah, we'd best," said Hellboy. "Remember, you hold 'em off from the circle, while I come at them from behind."

"They will not reach the keystone," said my father grimly. "Not alive, at any rate."

"That's what I'm worried about," growled Hellboy. "I don't want any of them reaching the keystone dead, either."

"None of the unworthy will gain a boon from Maponos," added my father. "Dead or alive."

"They'd better not or we'll all be into some serious regretting time. Those old gods ought to be more choosy who they dish the goods out to. I'll see you later. Good luck, guys."

Pausing only to throw his cigar butt into the fireplace, Hellboy left. He moved very swiftly, I noted, weaving through the men with deft, precise movements that belied his bulky chest and that massive fist. I thought then that he would be a very interesting subject to examine more closely, before I even knew about his immense strength and durability.

We all left the house soon after Hellboy. I carried my doctor's bag and one of the gilded pruning hooks. I had declined the offer of a Browning Hi Power pistol, having a somewhat romantic notion of being true to my Hippocratic oath. I wished I had taken it soon enough.

The moon was not quite completely risen, but its light was bright enough to cast shadows. By virtue of the surrounding mountains or some meteorological phenomenon it did shine most brightly on the surface of the loch, lighting a silver trail that extended from the sheltered waters far out to sea.

"The silver road is present," pronounced my father, and he added something in Gaelic that I didn't catch, but was repeated by the men around me.

We marched down to the water's edge. I had no idea what was to happen next, but given the earlier events of the night, I was not overly surprised when we just kept going into what should have been water, but was not. My father gestured, and the men spread out into a skirmish line and I followed them into the strange, silver-lit atmosphere that was neither air nor water.

After a few yards I noted that though I could see a membrane above my head that was where the water level should be, and the ground beneath my feet was by turns both weeded and stony, there were no fish sharing this temporary environment we had entered. The water had not been made breathable to us, it had been transformed entirely, and that transformation had also removed the usual inhabitants of the loch's waters.

We continued down the slope of the loch floor for several minutes, in watchful silence. I found it both frightening and wonderful,
that I should be walking deeper and deeper into the heart of the sea.
But even this strange experience could not hide the underlying fear
I felt, that soon I would be under fire, that I would be taking part
in a battle and my father would see that I had not chosen a medical
career because of some deep calling to the profession, but because
it represented a respectable way for me not to become a soldier like
him. It had even allowed me to avoid National Service, and I had
fully expected that my occupation would keep me safe even in the
event of another world war.

It was not being wounded that I feared. I had treated all kinds
of wounds, and could easily imagine myself being shot, or peppered
with shell fragments, or burned. I was afraid of being put in a position where I might show my fear, where my natural instinct to run
would take over.

I knew that my father would soon know I was a coward. But I
had no choice. I was under his eye and, deeply programmed from my
earliest years, I knew no other course but to obey.

Half a mile from the shore, at the deepest part of the loch, I saw
the ring of standing stones. We were easily six hundred feet below the
notional surface, but the same soft moonlight continued to illuminate everything. My father gestured again, and his troops quickened
their pace as he circled his hand and indicated that we should form a
defensive ring, mimicking the posture of the stones themselves.

"The enemy have to take the longer way, coming from the western end of the silver road," said my father quietly as the two of us
continued on and entered the ring of stones. "We may take a quicker
path, as befits the children of Maponos."

"Where is Hellboy?" I asked. I could see no sign of our fire-
skinned friend.

"He, too, must take a longer path. He is not a child of Maponos.

Now, we must pay our respects, before the hurly-burly starts."

There was a single stone in the middle of the circle. It was no higher than the others, and in fact all the stones of the ring were quite modest sarsens, little taller than myself, and of a not particularly inspiring grey-green color.

Even so, I knew that central stone was different. If I looked at it from the corner of my eye, it was not a stone I saw, but a hunched figure, with the hint of a grin too wide for a human face, and clasped hands that were not hands, but taloned claws.

I fell back as we drew closer. My father stopped and looked at me.

"There's nothing to be afraid of. Maponos knows his own. Those others who come, they will seek to bend him to their will. He would never turn against us of his own accord."

I felt six years old again, listening to my father explaining why I should not be afraid of a cow in a field, because it was not a bull. Only when we did cross the field, there was a bull there that we hadn't seen and it had frightened me so much I dreamed of it for years afterward. He'd thought it was funny at the time and, of course, was not the parent who responded to a small boy's nightmares.

"We need merely grant him a small taste of our blood," continued my father. He lifted his pruning hook and sliced the end of his finger, and wiped the blood upon the stone.

Out of the corner of my eye, I saw a tongue curl and lick it off, and then there was no blood.

"Hold your finger up."

I shook my head.

"I *am* a surgeon," I answered. "I can cut my own finger when necessary."

I did it too, clumsily enough that if I'd been doing a prac I would never have passed my finals. Without looking, I wiped my finger on the front of the stone and suppressed a shudder as I felt a warm, soft touch upon my flesh.

My father recited something in Gaelic and stepped back. I stepped back too, very readily.

The stone was the same, but there was no blood, and I saw that grin again.

"Right, that's done. I wonder where these Reds are?"

He sounded confident, as perhaps he had every right to be, with some forty heavily armed men in position, their ammunition blessed by ancient ceremony, and the god Maponos along for the ride.

Then we saw the first of the approaching enemy. I don't know what my father expected, but I had a hazy idea that some sort of Soviet marine force would be attacking, that apart from our strange location, it would be a relatively conventional battle.

But the figures who came toward us did not walk across the loch floor as we had, but descended from above, floating down as if they still moved through sea, not the silver atmosphere we experienced.

They were not Soviet marines either, but the rotten, skeletal remnants of long-dead men, clad in waterlogged rags that had once been the working uniforms of Hitler's Kriegsmarine.

They were dead U-boat crews from the last war, and they were coming for us.

"Aerial targets! Open fire!" shouted my father, and before even the word "open" was out of his mouth, the sharp crack of rifles and the chatter of the Stens and the deeper beat of the Brens exploded all around us. I kneeled down and opened my bag, but continued to look up at the enemy. They looked like target dummies, or puppets on long, loose strings being lowered to a stage, jumping and dancing as they were struck by bullets, bits of uniform and bone and faint fragments of decayed flesh spraying out above them.

"They have some protection," muttered my father, who was watching them intently. "The bullets are charged with the power of

Maponos. They should be falling apart."

But the dead sailors kept coming, inexorably drifting toward us. The first of them touched down some twenty yards distant, and for a moment I thought it would just settle in place, a sodden, long-drowned relict, its flesh long stripped away. But it jerked upright, as if those puppet strings were suddenly under command, and advanced upon the nearest of our defenders. He emptied the magazine from his Sten into its head, but even though its skull was blown to pieces, the headless thing kept coming, skeletal hands grasping as he chopped at it with his gilded pruning hook. He took one arm off, but it got a grip on the blade and pulled it from his grasp and before he could retreat, another revenant fell upon his head and thrust its long fingers through his eyes and into his brain.

"We must call the god himself," said my father quickly. He looked down at me. "We will need a sacrifice."

I gaped up at him as he loomed over me, his sickle in hand. Long-dead German submariners sank like falling flowers behind and above him, far too many for us to fight off, even if they had been susceptible to our weapons.

"Dad—"

"Not you, Malcolm!" exclaimed my father testily. He pulled me to my feet and forced the sickle into my hand. "Do you really know me no better than that? Now cut my throat and let the blood fall upon the stone!"

Those taloned hands were cupped now, ready to catch my father's blood and drink it up.

"Hurry!"

I raised the sickle. My father quickly gripped it and tried to bring it down across his throat. But I was faster, and held it back. I had seen something, beyond the outer stones. A red shape, moving fast, accompanied by a sound like a miniature sonic boom, or a mallet struck against a giant kettledrum—or the sound of an arcane fist smashing undead skulls.

Hellboy came charging through the undead sailors, smiting them as he advanced. Where his fist hit, the enemy simply blew apart, the fragments being carried away on unseen tides.

I dragged the sickle back, and the grin on the stone became a scowl, and the clawed hands twisted together in annoyance.

"Hellboy!" I exclaimed.

"What?" asked my father. He craned his head around to look, and stopped trying to drag the sickle down. I let my own grip ease, and the sickle suddenly moved of its own accord, falling across my father's throat.

At almost the same moment, two of the undead sailors threw a net of steel mesh and heavy lead weights over Hellboy's head, and down he went.

I threw the sickle away and held my father as he slowly fell. The cut to his neck was deep, but I saw in a moment that it had missed the major blood vessels. I pressed my hand against the wound and lowered him down as I groped about for my bag.

I so badly wanted to run, but while my father no longer held me back, I was holding him. His right hand scrabbled at his neck, painting his fingers with blood, and then he splayed that same hand against the stone.

I felt a voice speak to me, a voice that felt as if it was coming from deep inside my own heart, the words rushing to my head with the pulse of my blood.

"There," said Maponos angrily. "Our foe! Strike him down!"

I looked and saw that amid the melee of our few remaining men and the undead sailors, there was one who I knew was different. He looked like a ragged skeleton, but he hung back from the fray, and when he walked, he did not bounce and glide as if he moved through some other more buoyant medium.

Hellboy had torn the steel net apart and was using it to snag enemies and drag them into smashing range, but there were just too many of them. From the look of things he'd definitely beat them, but it would be too late for me, and far too late for my father. I needed to investigate and suture the wound, and there was no time to lose.

"Hellboy!" I shouted, pointing with my free hand. "Maponos says shoot that one at the back!"

"You got it!" replied Hellboy. His hand-cannon boomed out, and this time I saw the bloom of real red blood. The man fell, and so did the U-boat crews, all at once, before the echo of Hellboy's shot even came back from the sides of the loch.

"Mine," said the voice inside me.

"Drag that one Hellboy shot over here!" I shouted, not looking to see who heard. I was busy, plying my trade, my hands bloody in a different way.

I had just finished stitching up my father's wound when Hellboy himself dumped the still-bleeding corpse at the foot of the keystone. I saw the talons reach, but also saw nothing, the stone completely still. But the body was gone, and I heard a self-satisfied chuckle that slowly faded.

"Thanks," I said to Hellboy as I stood up and looked around for other wounded. My father raised a finger at me from where he lay, by way of a salute.

"No trouble, kid," said Hellboy. But it was a distracted answer and I saw that he was looking at the sole small remnant of the man Maponos had consumed. A metal badge, which the man had worn on his tunic, a swastika variation that incorporated some kind of serpent.

Hellboy suddenly stomped on the badge, mashing it beyond recognition. One of our men called to me, and I picked up my bag. At the same time, my father croaked, his voice barely understandable.

"Moonset . . . early . . . feel it. Get . . . moving!"

We moved. I stabilized the few wounded who had managed to

survive, but we had to leave our dead. There were only ten of us left, eleven counting Hellboy. He carried my father, and Maponos made no trouble about all of us taking the short way back.

We went fishing the next day, just Hellboy and I. Hellboy had a purpose-made strap to lash a rod to his fist, so he could wind the reel with his left hand. A friend of his called Abe had made it for him, or so he said. He caught a dozen salmon to my three sea trout, the fish teeming on his side of the boat, which was certainly unnatural, but by that point I did not find it particularly strange. We didn't talk, but I believe he enjoyed the shared solitude.

He must have done, for we have been fishing a dozen times or more since then, not always when there is also business to be done for the BPRD, though always at the loch.

Hellboy is quite a regular visitor here, and has become known to some of the locals as a lucky fisherman, which stands him in even better stead than being known as the friend of the only doctor for miles, or even for those who know that I am more than a country doctor, but also the Sentinel of the West and the Isles, and favored son of the sunken god Maponos.

Who, I think, should work *much* harder to help me catch more fish than Hellboy.

OLD FRIENDS

I'd been living in the city for quite a while, lying low, recovering from an unfortunate jaunt that had turned, in the immortal words of my sometime comrade Hrasvelg, "irredeemably shit-shape."

Though I had almost completely recovered my sight, I still wore a bandage around my eyes. It was made from a rare stuff that I could see through, but it looked like dense black linen. Similarly, I had regrown my left foot, but I kept up the limp. It gave me an additional excuse to use the stick, which was, of course, much more than a length of bog oak carved with picaresque scenes of a pedlar's journey.

I had a short-lease apartment near the beach, an expensive but necessary accommodation, as I needed both the sunshine that fell into its small living room and the cool, wet wind from the sea that blew through every open window.

Unfortunately, after the first month, that wind became laden with the smell of rotting weed and as the weeks passed, the stench grew stronger, and the masses of weed that floated just past the breakers began to shift and knit together, despite the efforts of the lifesavers to break up the unsightly, stinking rafts of green.

I knew what was happening, of course. The weed was a manifestation of an old opponent of mine, a slow, cold foe who had finally caught up with me. "Caught" being the operative word, as the weed was just the visible portion of my enemy's activities. A quick examination of almanac and lodestone revealed that all known pathways from this world were denied to me, shut tight by powerful bindings that I could not broach quickly, if at all.

I considered moving to the mountains or far inland, but that would merely delay matters. Only the true desert would be safe from my foe, but I could not go there.

So I watched the progress of the weed every morning as I drank my first coffee, usually leaning back in one white plastic chair as I elevated my supposedly injured leg on another. The two chairs were the only furniture in the apartment. I slept in the bath, which I had lined with sleeping moss, which was comfortable, sweet-smelling, and also massaged out the cares of the day with its tiny rhizoids.

The day before I adjudged the weed would reach its catalytic potential and spawn servitors, I bought not just my usual black coffee from the café downstairs, but also a triple macchiato that came in a heavy, heat-resistant glass. Because I lived upstairs they always gave me proper cups. The barista who served me, a Japanese guy who worked the espresso machine mornings and surfed all afternoon, put the coffees in a cardboard holder meant for takeaways and said, "Got a visitor today?"

"Not yet," I said. "But I will have shortly. By the way, I wouldn't go surfing here this afternoon . . . or tomorrow."

"Why not?"

"That weed," I replied. "It's toxic. Try another beach."

"How do you know?" he asked as he slid the tray into my waiting fingers. "I mean, you can't . . ."

"I can't see it," I said as I backed away, turned, and started tapping toward the door. "But I can smell it. It's toxic all right. Stay clear."

"Okay, thanks. Uh, enjoy the coffee."

I slowly made my way upstairs and set the coffees down on the floor. My own cup in front of one white chair, and the macchiato at the foot of the other. I wouldn't be resting my limb on the spare chair today.

I had to wait a little while for the breeze to come up, but as it streamed through the room and teased at the hair I should have had cut several weeks before, I spoke.

"Hey, Anax. I bought you a coffee."

The wind swirled around my head, changing direction 270 degrees, blowing out the window it had come in by and in by the window it had been going out. I felt the floor tremble under my feet and experienced a brief dizziness.

Anax, proper name Anaxarte, was one of my oldest friends. We'd grown up together and had served together in two cosmically fucked-up wars, one of which was still slowly bleeding its way to exhaustion in fits and starts, though the original two sides were long out of it.

I hadn't seen Anax for more than thirty years, but we scribbled notes to each other occasionally, and had spoken twice in that time. We talked a lot about meeting up, maybe organizing a fishing expedition with some of the old lads, but it had never come together.

I knew that if he were able to, he would always answer my call. So as the coffee cooled and the white plastic chair lay vacant, my heart chilled and I began to grieve. Not for the loss of Anax's help against the enemy, but because another friend had fallen.

I sat in the sunshine for an hour, the warmth a slight comfort against the melancholy that had crept up on me. At the hour's end, the wind shifted again, roiling around me counterclockwise till it ebbed to a total calm.

Even without the breeze, I could smell the weed. It had a malignant, invasive odor, the kind that creeps through sealed plastic bags and airtight lids, the smell of decay and corruption.

My options were becoming limited. I took up my stick and went downstairs once more to the café. The afternoon barista did not know me, though I had seen her often enough through my expansive windows. She did not comment on my order, though I doubt she was often asked for a soy latte with half poured out after it was made, to be topped up again with cold regular milk.

Upstairs, I repeated the summoning, this time with the chill already present, a cold presence of somber expectation lodged somewhere between my heart and ribs.

"Balan," I called softly. "Balan, your lukewarm excuse for a drink is ready."

The wind came up and carried my words away, but as before, there was no reply, no presence in the empty chair. I waited the full hour to be sure, then poured the congealed soy drink down the sink.

I could see the weed clearly in the breakers now. It was almost entirely one huge, long clump that spanned the length of the beach. The lifesavers had given up trying to break it apart with their Jet Skis and Zodiac inflatables, and there were two "Beach Closed" signs stuck in the sand, twenty meters apart. Not that anyone was swimming. The beach was almost empty. The reek of the weed had driven away everyone but a sole lifesaver serving out her shift and a fisherman who was dolefully walking along in search of a weed-free patch of sea.

"Two of my old friends taken," I whispered to the sun, my lips dry, my words heavy. We had never thought much about our futures, not when we were fighting in the war, or later when we had first escaped our service. The present was our all, our time the now. None of us knew what lay ahead.

For the third time, I trod my careful way downstairs. There were a dozen people outside the café, a small crowd that parted to allow me passage, with muffled whispers about blindness and letting the sightless man past.

The crowd was watching the weed, while trying not to smell it.

"There, that bit came right out of the water!"

"It kind of looks alive!"

"Must be creating a gas somehow, the decomposition . . ."

". . . check out those huge nodules lifting up . . ."

". . . a gas, methane, maybe. Or hydrogen sulfide . . . nah . . . I'm just guessing. Someone will know . . ."

As I heard the excited comments I knew that I had mistimed my calls for assistance. The weed was very close to catalysis and would soon spawn its servitors, who would come ashore in search of their target.

I had meant to ask the owner of the café, a short, bearded man who was always called "Mr. Jeff" by the staff, if he could give me a glass of brandy, or at a pinch, whiskey. A fine Armagnac would be best, but I doubted they'd have any of that. The café had no liquor license but I knew there was some spirituous alcohol present, purely for Jeff's personal use, since I'd smelled it on his breath often enough.

But as I said, it was too late for that. Palameides might have answered to a double brandy, but I secretly knew that he too must have succumbed. It had been too long since his last missive, and I accounted it one of my failings that I had not been in touch to see where he was and if all was well with him.

"Someone should do something about that weed," complained a thickset young man who habitually double-parked his low-slung sports car outside the café around this time of day. "It really stinks."

"It will be gone by morning," I said. I hadn't meant to use the voice of prophecy, but my words rang out, harsh and bronze, stopping all other conversation.

Everyone looked at me, from inside and outside the café. Even the dog that had been asleep next to one of the outside tables craned his neck to look askance. All was silent, the silence of an embarrassed audience who wished they were elsewhere without knowing why, and were fearful about what was going to come next.

"I am a . . . biologist," I said in my normal tones. "The weed is a known phenomenon. It will disperse overnight."

The silence continued for a few seconds, then normal service resumed, at a lower volume. Even the double-parking guy was more subdued.

I spoke the truth. One way or another, the weed would be gone, and likely enough, I would be gone with it.

As the afternoon progressed, the stench grew much worse. The café was shut, staff and customers retreating to better-smelling climes. Around five o'clock, nearby residents began to leave as well, at the same time the fire department, the Water Board, the police, and several television crews arrived.

An hour after that, only the firefighters remained, and they were wearing breathing apparatus as they went from door to door, checking that everyone had left. Farther afield, way down the northern end of the beach, I could see the television crews interviewing someone who was undoubtedly an expert trying to explain why the noxious odors were so localized and dissipated so quickly when you got more than three hundred meters from the center of the beach.

The "DO NOT CROSS" tapes with the biohazard trefoils got rolled out just before dusk, across the street about eighty meters up from my apartment. The firefighters had knocked at my door and called out, gruff voices muffled by masks, but I had not answered. They could probably have seen me from the beach, but no one was heading closer to the smell, however well protected they might be. The sea was bubbling and frothing with noxious vapors, and weedy nodules the size of restaurant refrigerators were bobbing up and down upon the waves. After a while the nodules began to detach from the main mass of weed and the waves carried them in like lost surfboards, tendrils of weed trailing behind them, reminiscent of broken leg-ropes.

I watched the nodules as the sun set behind the city, mentally mapping where they were drifting ashore. When the sun was completely gone, the streetlights and the high lamps that usually lit the beach didn't come on, but that didn't matter much to me. Darkness wasn't so much my friend as a close relative.

The lack of artificial light caused a commotion among the

HAZMAT teams, though, particularly when they couldn't get their portable generators and floodlights to work, and the one engine they sent down the street choked and stalled before it had even pulled away from the curb.

I had counted thirteen nodules, but more could be out in the weed mass, or so low in the water I'd missed them. My enemy was not underestimating me, or had presumed I would be able to call upon assistance.

I had presumed I would be able to call upon assistance, a foolish presumption built upon old camaraderie, of long-ago dangers shared, of the maintenance of a continuum. I had not thought that my friends, having survived our two wars, could have had a full stop put to their existence in more mundane environments, or at least not so soon. Which meant that they had met the same fate that now threatened to be mine.

"Anax, Balan, Palameides," I whispered. By now there would be three new death-trees laid out in a nice row in the arboreal necropolis, with those nameplates at their feet. There was probably a Nethinim carving my name onto a plaque right now, and readying a sapling. They always knew beforehand, the carriers of water and hewers of wood.

I dismissed this gloomy thought. If my time had come, it had come, but I would not wait in a dark apartment, to acquiesce to my fate like a senescent king grown too tired and toothless to act against his assassins.

I took off the blindfold and tied it around my neck, returning it to its original use as a scarf. It became my only item of apparel, as I shucked white cotton trousers, white T-shirt, and underwear.

The stick I gently broke across my knee, sliding the two lengths of wood apart to reveal the sword within. I took the weapon up and made the traditional salute toward my enemies on the beach.

Courtesies complete, I shaded my skin, hair, and eyes dark, a green almost heavy enough to match the blackness of the night, and with a moment's concentration, grew a defensive layer of young bark, being careful not to overdo it, while overlaying the sheaths in such a way that it would not limit my movement. Novices often made the mistake of armoring up too much, and found themselves extraordinarily tough but essentially sessile. I had not made that mistake since my distant youth.

The wind lifted a little, and the stink of the weed changed, becoming more fragrant. I heard thirteen soft popping noises come from the beach and knew that the nodules were opening.

There was little point in dragging things out, so I simply walked down the street to the beach, pausing to bid a silent farewell to the café. Their coffee had been quite good.

I paused at the promenade railing, near the block of stone surmounted by the bronze mermaid, and looked across the beach. There was a little starlight, though no moon, and I thought both sea and sand had never looked prettier. The humans should turn the lights off more often, though even then they would not see the way I saw.

The thirteen had emerged from their nodules, or perhaps I should call them pods. Now that I saw them clearly, I knew I had even less chance than I'd thought. I had expected the blocky, bad imitations of human women that looked like Bulgarian weightlifters, armed with slow, two-handed axes that, though devastating when they hit, were fairly unlikely to do so provided I didn't make a mistake.

But my enemy had sent a much superior force, testament I suppose to the number of times I had defeated or evaded previous attempts to curtail my activities. This time they were indeed what long-gone inhabitants of this world had called Valkyries: female human in form, tall, long-limbed, and very fast, and the sensing tendrils that splayed back from their heads could easily be mistaken for a winged helmet, as their rust-colored exoskeleton extrusions could look like armor.

They lifted their hatchets—twenty-six of them, as they held one in each hand—when they saw me, and offered the salute. I returned the greeting and waited for the eldest of them (by a matter of seconds, most like) to offer up the obligatory statement, which also served as a disclaimer, thrust all liability for collateral damage upon me, and usually offered a chance to surrender.

"Skrymir, renegade, oathbreaker, and outcast!"

I inclined my head.

"Called to return eight times; sent for, six times."

Had it been so many? I'd lost count. Too many years, across too many worlds.

"Surrender your sword!"

I shook my head, and the Valkyries attacked before I could even straighten my neck, running full-tilt at the seawall that bordered the promenade. Six stopped short before the wall and six leaped upon their backs to vault the railing, while the last, the senior, stood behind in a position of command.

I lopped two heads as I fell back, the Valkyries concerned momentarily confused as their major sensory apparatus went bouncing back down to the sand. As per their imprinting, they stopped still, and if it had not been for the others I could have felled them then. But the others were there, attacking me from all sides as I danced and spun back to the road, my sword meeting the helves of their hatchets, nicking at their fibrous flesh, but their weapons in turn carved long splinters from my body.

If they could surround me, I would be done for, so I fought as I had not fought since the wars. I twisted and leaped and slid under parked cars and over them, around rubbish bins and flagpoles, changing my sword from left hand to right hand, kicking, butting, deploying every trick and secret that I knew.

It was not enough. A skilled and vicious blow caught my knee as I took off another head, and in the second I was down, a dozen other blows put paid to my legs. I rolled and writhed away, but it was to no avail. The Valkyries pinned me down and began to chop away.

The last memory I have from that expression of myself was of the starry sky, the sound of the surf a deeper counterpoint to the thud of axework, and the blessed smell of fresh salt air, the stench of that particular rotten weed gone forever.

I cannot smell anything where I am now, nor see. I can sense light and shade, the movement of air, the welcome sensation of moisture on my extremities, whether above or below the earth.

Neither can I speak, save in a very limited fashion, the conveyance of some slight meaning without words.

But I am not alone.

Palameides is here, and Balan, and Anax too. They have grown tall and overshadow me, but this will not last. I will grow mighty once more, and one day, *They* will have need of us again . . . and then, as we whisper, tapping with our roots, signaling with the rustle of our leaves, then our hearts will bud new travelers, and we shall go forth to do the bidding of our masters, and perhaps, for as long as we can, we four friends shall once again be free.

STANDING UP
COMING-OF-AGE STORIES

THE QUIET KNIGHT

No going out till you've split that wood, Tony. All two tons, you hear?"

Tony looked up from lacing his outdoor boots and made a gesture to indicate he'd already done the job. His father understood the sign, but he still went outside to check, returning a few minutes later as Tony was finishing winding the lace around the top of his left boot.

"When did you do it?"

Tony held up five fingers and curled back his forefinger, to make it four and a half.

"Four thirty? This morning before school?" his father exclaimed. "You're crazy, son. But good on you for getting it done. You must have chopped like crazy."

Tony nodded. He had chopped like crazy. He'd enjoyed it, though, crossing the lawn to the shed, the frost cracking under his boots. It had been cold to start with, and quite dark, under the single lightbulb high above his head. But as he'd swung the blockbuster, split the wood, and stacked it, he'd gotten hot very quickly, and the sun had come up bright and strong.

"What is it tonight? Basketball practice?"

Tony nodded again and shrugged on his backpack. It was a full-on hiker's backpack, not a school satchel or day bag. He carried it everywhere outside school, notionally for all his sporting equipment, and his father had gotten used to it long ago and didn't inquire what was actually inside.

"Considering how much practice you do it's a wonder you guys never win a game," said his father. He'd been an all-round athlete in his youth, and he couldn't help but needle Tony a little about his lack of sporting success. He didn't come to the games, either, not for the last few years. He didn't like being with the other dads when Tony's team didn't win. He was also too busy. Though they lived on a farm on the outskirts of the city, it was a hobby farm, a tax deduction and sideline interest for his dad, who was a senior executive in some shadowy government intelligence outfit. Tony's mother and younger sister lived on the other side of the city, almost an hour's drive away. He spent some time with them, but not much. He preferred the farm, even though it took him forty minutes to get to school on the bus.

Tony settled his pack, then mimed turning a car key to his dad.

"You want to borrow the monster again?"

Tony nodded.

"You know, it wouldn't hurt you to talk to me."

"Sorry," mumbled Tony. His voice was low and scratchy. It sounded like a rough scrubbing brush being drawn across broken stones. He'd accidentally drunk some bathroom cleaner when he was little, and it had burned his throat and larynx. His mother had blamed his father for it, and his father still blamed himself. "Can I borrow the car?"

"Of course. Be careful. No drinking after practice. None at all, you hear?"

Tony nodded. He looked old enough that he could easily pass for legal drinking age. He stood six foot four in bare feet, and took after his father in both his heavy build and an early onset of dark stubble on his face. But he planned no drinking and he wasn't going to basketball practice anyway.

He took the keys to the farm truck. His father moved as if to hug him, but didn't follow through. Tony waited stolidly, ready to hug if that was what was required to get the keys.

"Okay. I'll see you later. I'll be in my study, working till late.

Check in when you get home."

Tony nodded and walked out into the cool, near-freezing air of the night.

The backpack held his armor, belt, helmet, and mask. His foam-wrapped PVC pipe "boffer" sword was in a sack in the tray of the truck. Tony checked it was still there, unlacing the top. His dad hardly ever used the truck, and practically never looked in the back, but a good knight always checks his weapons before venturing to battle.

That night's game was being held in the usual place, the old woolshed and farm buildings on Dave Nash's family property. Dave was a big mover and shaker in LARP circles; he'd been involved in live-action role-playing for more than twenty years. He was in his forties, heavier and slower than in the old pictures and videos Tony had seen. He was still a tough fighter, though he mostly ran the games rather than participating in them.

Tony parked the truck off the road a half mile from the Nash property, edging it well behind a fringe of trees. It was a rural road, and not much traveled, but there would be other LARP gamers heading along it later and he didn't want them to spot him or the vehicle.

It took him ten minutes to get his armor on. First there was the athletic supporter and the padded undergarment, which were easy enough. It was the thigh-length hauberk made of thousands of steel rings that was the hassle. It was a lot easier if you had help to lace the back up, but he'd worked out a method using a long leather strap and a lot of wriggling about.

He didn't change his boots, but tied on a pair of gaiters that disguised them so they looked more medieval. The hauberk was long enough to protect his thighs, but he strapped on converted ice-hockey armor to his knees and shins. It was painted black and looked okay, or at least it would in the partially lit game that would occur tonight.

Tony's helmet was fairly basic. Unlike the hauberk, which he'd bought with the unwitting assistance of his mother, he'd made it himself in Dave's workshop, with a lot of help. It was modeled on a classic Norman nasal-bar helmet and went on over a padded lining and a mail coif, which also protected his neck.

With almost everything on, Tony added the final, unique touch: a half mask of beaten gold (actually gold paint over tough plastic) that covered his face from his chin to just below his eyes. It locked on to the nasal bar and the sides of the helmet and was perforated so he could breathe. And talk, if he wanted to do that.

All armored up, Tony tested his movement, jumping, springing, lunging, and stepping back. Everything was on right and tight, so he strapped on his belt and put on his leather gauntlets. Last of all he took up his sword, practiced a few test swings and cuts, then laid it at rest on his shoulder.

There was a beaten track made by the sheep along the inside of the barbed wire fence that paralleled the road some ten yards in. Tony had made a rough stile when he first started going to the LARP sessions a few years before, just a log up against a corner post that he could run up and jump down on the other side. He checked that too, before he went over. It would be very embarrassing to break a leg out here alone, in full armor. . . .

As he always did, Tony stopped at the edge of the roadside trees to observe who was waiting outside the woolshed before he went on. The woolshed itself was huge, a vast barnlike relic of bygone days when two hundred shearers had worked inside, shearing several thousand sheep a day. Dave Nash had partitioned it up inside with moveable walls and scenery like a theater, so he could arrange all kinds of different scenarios. The LARP group used the paddocks outside as well, and the smaller buildings. For evening games, like this one, they always chose a night when the moon was full. It wasn't up yet, so all the exterior lights were on, including the big floodlights

at the front of the woolshed. They lit up the bare dirt field in front
that was used as a car park.

There were half a dozen cars there now, parked as far from
the woolshed as possible, in the half dark so they wouldn't detract
from the atmosphere. Tony recognized all but one of them. Seeing
a strange car made him cautious, so he carefully scanned the group
around the front steps of the woolshed.

Dave Nash was standing there, wearing his wizard's robes, which
meant he would be the gamesmaster and not an active participant.
Next to him were the twins, Jubal and Jirah, equipped and dressed
as elven scouts in green and tan leather, with their boffer long swords
at their sides. They didn't have their bows. Dave didn't allow even
boffered bows, since he'd nearly lost an eye a few years before. Other
groups did use them, and Jubal and Jirah were fine archers, even with
the very light draw bows used in LARP.

Besides Jubal and Jirah, there were five regulars Tony knew, all
of them already geared up in armor from Dave's Orc armory, with
an array of foamcore axes, halberds, and other pole-arms. Their latex
masks and helmets were stacked on the steps. No one put them on
until they had to. It got hot and sweaty very quickly fighting in a
latex mask. But it looked good.

That meant the strange car belonged to the two people Tony
didn't know. A girl he guessed was around his age, who wasn't wearing armor, but a serviceable dress of red and gold, square-cut around
the neck. She had a lute on her back and a reed pipe through the gold
cloth belt she wore, so was clearly a bard.

The boy at her side was younger and had the same dark but
slightly strange good looks as the girl, so Tony guessed they were
brother and sister. He wore leather trousers, a leather brigandine
coat, and a leather cap that was a bit like a WWI aviator's helmet.
Two long daggers were thrust through broad loops on his belt. Boffer
weapons didn't scabbard very easily. The foam cladding made them

bulky, but was of course essential to not getting hurt.

Dave walked up to the top step, tapping his way with his six-foot oaken staff that was tipped with a cyalume chemical light. He turned at the top and spread his arms wide.

"Are all who would essay tonight's adventure present?"

"Aye!" called the people around the steps.

Tony hesitated, then strode forward toward the light, stamping his feet as he walked so he made more noise.

"Ah, the Quiet Knight approaches!" declaimed Dave, a smile flitting across his face. He was the only one who knew who Tony actually was, and he respected the confidence. "You are welcome, as always, Sir Silent."

Tony saluted with his sword and went to stand off to one side, near but not close to Jubal and Jirah.

"We have two newcomers, recently moved to our fair realm," said Dave. "Sorayah the Bard, and Horace the Halfling Rogue. Welcome, Sorayah and Horace."

Sorayah was cute, Tony thought, and she and Horace were definitely sister and brother. They had the same nose and eyes, and probably the same ears, though it was hard to tell as Horace had stuck artificial hairy ears over his own.

"Tonight we seek to find a passage through the ancient tunnels of Harukn-Dzhur," said Dave. He nodded at the Orcs, who picked up their masks and helmets and walked off to one of the entrances around the side of the woolshed. "If we can but find a way, we may escape those who have pursued us from the wilds . . ."

Tony listened carefully as Dave set up the scene. "Tunnels" meant that Dave would have spent the last week rearranging the walls and lowering the temporary ceilings inside the woolshed, and there would be lots of close combat, with only enough light for safety. Dave liked strobe lights too, and color effects for magic, and he had a lot to work with, since he'd bought all the old lighting gear, sets, and props when the city had condemned the Alder Street Theatre.

"We begin with the long crawl through the zigzag way," intoned Dave. "Horace, will you scout a little way ahead? Not too far, mind. Ten feet, no more."

"Aye," said Horace. He drew his daggers and moved to the door.

"Sir Silent, if you would follow, and Sorayah behind you," said Dave. "I task you with protecting the Bard, for she wears no armor, and we will need her magic and her song in times to come. I will follow, and Jubal and Jirah will guard our rear."

Sorayah came over to Tony and curtseyed, inadvertently giving him a good look down the front of her dress.

Tony bowed back. He was glad she couldn't see him blush.

"I thank you for your protection, gallant knight," she said. He liked her voice. It sounded cool and pure, and she had the trace of some foreign accent that sounded real, not like it was put on for the game.

He bowed again and led the way up the steps. Horace was lying on his stomach, listening at the gap in the bottom of the door. As Tony approached, he stood up and slowly opened it. There was darkness within, but slowly a weak red light blossomed, revealing a narrow passage no more than three feet high.

"The long crawl!" hissed Dave. "Let the adventure begin!"

Tony didn't get home till just before midnight, his curfew time. It had been a great game, one of the best, and the others had stayed behind to have a drink and chat around the fire, wrapped in the cloaks from a long-ago Alder Street production of *Henry V.*

Tony had wanted to stay too, to talk to Sorayah, and it wasn't the curfew that stopped him. It was his inability to talk. He knew that as soon as he opened his mouth and she heard his hoarse crow-voice her face would show scorn, or even worse, pity. He didn't want that. She respected him as the Quiet Knight, they had enjoyed playing their parts, it was best to keep whatever they had in the game.

Tony laughed at himself for thinking such stupid thoughts. Whatever they had! They didn't have anything. He'd protected her in the game, sure enough, and had taken bruises enough to show for it, including the one across the back of his left hand that was coming up purple and brown. But that didn't mean anything in real life. He didn't even know her real name, or where she lived, or anything.

Tony was sore and his arms and legs were very stiff the next morning. Splitting two tons of wood for the potbelly stove and later fighting for four hours was way too much, too much even for a blindingly hot shower to totally remedy. His bruises had come up as well, on his hand and forearms, and the back of one leg. He applied anti-inflammatory cream to the worst of them, but didn't take a painkiller.

The bus trip to school was normal. Tony sat two-thirds of the way to the back, alone as always, with the hood of his sweatshirt pulled up over his head. He was big and mean-looking enough that the bullies and the petty annoyers left him alone, but since he didn't talk, no one else interacted with him either. In fact, most of them, including the bullies, were afraid of his dark, hooded presence, though he didn't know that.

He spent the time looking out the window, wondering what the hell he was doing with his life. There was one more year of school to get through, which he could do. His grades were good, better than anyone ever expected from a silent ox. But he had no friends. Not real friends. Dave was the closest to a real friend that he had, but Dave had a family and a job and was just being kind to a kid.

Tony supposed he could be friends with Jubal and Jirah. They went to the same school, though they were a year behind. They had lots of friends too, gamers and fantasy freaks and alternative drama types. That was the trouble. Tony already felt he was an outcast. A disguised outcast, to be sure. He looked normal enough. No one in the street would ever know that he had a weird voice and liked to dress up and play pretend fighting.

If he revealed himself to Jubal and Jirah as the Quiet Knight, they probably would welcome him as a friend, and he could hang out with their friends. But everyone would know he was a real weirdo. Besides, if he had friends they'd expect him to talk. . . .

What would the Quiet Knight do? Tony asked himself. *Not talk, that's for sure. He'd just get on with things, in his own quiet way. . . .*

The bus stopped outside the school. Tony waited for everyone to get out, then slowly followed, steeling himself for another day of trying to minimally answer questions. The teachers usually didn't push him too much now, not after a long trial with one particular English teacher a few years before, which had ended with Tony still stubbornly refusing to deliver a speech, his father raging in the headmaster's office, and the teacher requesting a transfer to another class.

The usual stream of student foot traffic filled the front drive, most of them heading for the main doors, with knots of people here and there delaying the inevitable. Tony strode through them, his mind on last night's game. Younger students scattered out of his way without him noticing. He didn't know that he was a legend to the lower years, his reluctance to talk transformed into a story of backwoods tongue mutilation and bloody revenge. Even if the backwoods in question were only ten miles past the outer suburbs.

There was a small commotion just before the doors, to the left of the front steps in the blind spot that was hidden from the security cameras out the front and the gaze of the teacher on door duty. There often was something going on there; it was a favorite spot for some casual bullying or lunch-money shakedowns. Tony never paid much attention to this kind of thing. It never happened to him.

This time, he stopped. Two students were being terrorized by five of the spoiled brat girls, the ones who liked to think they were rough and tough and had some kind of gang readily identifiable by infected eyebrow piercings without the studs (since the school wouldn't allow it) and expensive leather jackets bought by their daddies and driven over to rough up.

The two students being terrorized were Sorayah and Horace. Sorayah was wearing another medieval-style dress, this time in dark yellow. She looked good, but totally out of place at school. Horace, though in jeans and a T-shirt, still had on the stupid hairy ears. Two of the self-proclaimed bad girls were holding Sorayah back with difficulty, two more were holding Horace, and the five-eyebrow-piercing leader, whose name was Ellen, was trying to tear the ears off Horace.

"They're stuck on, he can't get them off!" Sorayah shouted. She shook off one of the girls and swung at Ellen, but there were too many of them and she was dragged back.

"Help! Someone!"

A baseball cap was shoved in Sorayah's mouth, muffling her shouts. She kept struggling, kicking back at her captor's knees. Horace was trying to bite his enemies, tears of pain welling up as his real ears were twisted every which way.

Tony saw Sorayah's frantic gaze as she looked for help. But her gaze swept across him and then she was bundled farther back into the shadow of the stairs.

He'd been invisible to her. Just another student who wasn't going to help, who didn't want to get involved or cross Ellen and her gang. It wasn't just her and the girls. There were their boyfriends as well, most of whom were bad-tempered second-string jocks who weren't good enough to focus all their energy on sports.

Tony stopped for what felt like ages, but could not have been longer than a second. Then he continued on up the steps, crashing through several slower students.

I can't intervene, he thought. *She's in a medieval dress. He's got hobbit ears on. They won't really hurt her. . . .*

He stopped before the doors as another thought struck him like a blow to the heart.

What would the Quiet Knight do?

Tony turned around and pulled back his hood, before taking a very deep breath. The students coming up the stairs parted like the Red Sea as he stood there, taking another breath, sucking in the air as if he were taking in strength.

I must do it, he thought. *And I will talk to her, even if she does laugh.*

He ran down the stairs. Students sprang aside and dragged their friends out of his path and turned to watch as Tony rounded the wall at the base of the stair, picked up Ellen by elbow and knee, and pitched her aside onto the pavement.

"Let them go," he ordered. His voice was as peculiar and scratchy and variably pitched as ever, but coming immediately after throwing their leader six feet through the air, incredibly effective. The bad girls released Sorayah and Horace and backed away.

"They are under my protection," rasped Tony. "You will never even talk to them again, understand?"

The bad girls nodded.

"Go to class," added Tony. He pointed to Ellen, who was sullenly picking herself up, blood beading through her faux-punk stockings where she'd grazed her knees. "Drop her off at the infirmary, and keep your mouths shut."

He turned back to Sorayah, and the words that had so gloriously issued from his mouth failed him. She smiled and curtseyed. He looked up and blushed and averted his gaze to Horace, who shrugged and rubbed his ears.

"Superglue, all right?" said Horace. "So it was a bad idea. It goes with being called Horace in the first place. Stupid parents. They can't organize laundry either or my sister—"

"Thank you again, Sir Silent," interrupted Sorayah, with a quelling glance at her brother. She stepped closer to Tony and looked up at him. He thought that it would be very easy to rest his chin upon her silky head and draw her close.

Tony tried to ask her how she knew who he was. No sound came out, but his puzzled frown was clear enough.

"Your eyes are very distinctive," said Sorayah. "And the bruise on your hand."

Tony nodded slowly and gulped again. He was making a fool of himself, he knew, and he felt an incredibly strong compulsion to back away, to pull his hood up and just disappear.

But he wanted to stay, he wanted to talk, and so he fought against the urge to run.

"My name really is Sorayah, by the way."

Tony cleared his throat. Sorayah waited patiently, smiling, looking straight into his eyes. The world faded away around them as Tony gulped at the air again and searched for the words that he knew he had to say.

"Tony," said the Quiet Knight at last. "My name is Tony."

THE HIGHEST JUSTICE

The girl did not ride the unicorn, because no one ever did. She rode a nervous oat-colored palfrey that had no name, and led the second horse, a blind and almost deaf ancient who long ago had been called Rinaldo and was now simply Rin. The unicorn sometimes paced next to the palfrey, and sometimes not.

Rin bore the dead Queen on his back, barely noticing her twitches and mumbles and the cloying stench of decaying flesh that seeped out through the honey-and-spice-soaked bandages. She was tied to the saddle, but could have snapped those bonds if she had thought to do so. She had become monstrous strong since her death three days before and the intervention by her daughter that had returned her to a semblance of life.

Not that Princess Jess was a witch or necromancer. She knew no more magic than any young woman. But she was fifteen years old, a virgin, and she believed the old tale of the kingdom's founding: that the unicorn who had aided the legendary Queen Jessibelle the First was both still alive and would honor the compact made so long ago, to come in the time of the kingdom's need.

The unicorn's secret name was Elibet. Jess had called this name to the waxing moon at midnight from the tallest tower of the castle, and had seen something ripple in answer across the surface of the earth's companion in the sky.

An hour later, Elibet was in the tower. She was somewhat like a horse with a horn, if you looked at her full on, albeit one made of white cloud and moonshine. Looked at sideways, she was a fiercer thing, of less familiar shape, made of stormclouds and darkness, the horn more prominent and bloody at the tip, like the setting sun. Jess preferred to see a white horse with a silvery horn, and so that is what she saw.

Jess had called the unicorn as her mother gasped out her final breath. The unicorn had come too late to save the Queen, but by then Jess had another plan. The unicorn listened and then by the power of her horn, brought back some part of the Queen to inhabit a body from which life had all too quickly sped.

They had then set forth, to seek the Queen's poisoner and mete out justice.

Jess halted her palfrey as they came to a choice of ways. The royal forest was thick and dark in these parts, and the path was no more than a beaten track some dozen paces wide. It forked ahead, into two lesser, narrower paths.

"Which way?" asked Jess, speaking to the unicorn who had once again mysteriously appeared at her side.

The unicorn pointed her horn at the left-hand path.

"Are you sure—" Jess asked. "No, it's just that—"

"The other way looks more traveled—"

"No, I'm not losing heart—"

"I know you know—"

"Talking to yourself?" interjected a rough, male voice, the only other sound in the forest; for if the unicorn had spoken, no one but Jess had heard her.

The palfrey shied as Jess swung around and reached for her sword. But she was too late, as a dirty bearded ruffian held a rusty pike to her side. He grinned and raised his eyebrows.

"Here's a tasty morsel then," he leered. "Step down lightly, and no tricks."

"Elibet!" said Jess indignantly.

The unicorn slid out of the forest behind the outlaw and lightly pricked him in the back of his torn leather jerkin with her horn. The man's eyebrows went up still farther and his eyes darted to the left and right.

"Ground your pike," said Jess. "My friend can strike faster than any man."

The outlaw grunted and lowered his pike, resting its butt in the leaf litter at his feet.

"I give up," he wheezed, leaning forward as if he might escape the sharp horn. "Ease off on that spear, and take me to the sheriff. I swear—"

"Hunger," interrupted the Queen. Her voice had changed with her death. It had become gruff and leathery and significantly less human.

The bandit glanced at the veiled figure under the broad-brimmed palmer's hat.

"What?" he asked hesitantly.

"Hunger," groaned the Queen. "Hunger."

She raised her right arm and the leather cord that bound her to the saddle's high cantle snapped with a sharp crack. A bandage came loose at her wrist and dropped to the ground in a series of spinning turns, revealing the mottled, blue-bruised skin beneath.

"Shoot 'em!" shouted the bandit as he dove under Jess's horse and scuttled across the path toward the safety of the trees. As he ran, an arrow flew over his head and struck the Queen in the shoulder. Another, coming behind it, went past Jess's head as she jerked herself forward and down. The third was struck out of the air by a blur of vaguely unicorn-shaped motion. There were no more arrows, but a second later there was a scream from halfway up a broad oak that loomed over the path ahead, followed by the heavy thud of a body hitting the ground.

Jess drew her sword and kicked her palfrey into a lurching charge. She caught the surviving bandit just before he managed to slip between two thorny bushes, and landed a solid blow on his head with the back of the blade. She hadn't meant to be merciful, but the sword had turned in her sweaty grasp. He fell under the horse's feet and got trampled a little before Jess managed to turn about.

She glanced down to make sure he was at least dazed, but sure of this, spared him no more time. Her mother had broken the bonds on her left arm as well, and was ripping off the veil that hid her face.

"Hunger!" boomed the Queen, loud enough even for poor old deaf Rin to hear. He stopped eating the grass and lifted his head, time-worn nostrils almost smelling something he didn't like.

"Elibet! Please . . ." beseeched Jess. "A little longer—we must almost be there."

The unicorn stepped out from behind a tree and looked at her. It was the look of a stern teacher about to allow a pupil some small favor.

"One more touch, please, Elibet."

The unicorn bent her head, paced over to the dead Queen, and touched the woman lightly with her horn, briefly imbuing her with a subtle nimbus of summer sunshine, bright in the shadowed forest. Propelled by that strange light, the arrow in the Queen's shoulder popped out, the blue-black bruises on her arms faded, and her skin shone, pink and new. She stopped fumbling with the veil, slumped down in her saddle, and let out a relatively delicate and human-sounding snore.

"Thank you," said Jess.

She dismounted and went to look at the bandit. He had sat up and was trying to wipe away the blood that slowly dripped across his left eye.

"So you give up, do you?" Jess asked, and snorted.

The bandit didn't answer.

Jess pricked him with her sword so he was forced to look at her.

"I should finish you off here and now," said Jess fiercely. "Like your friend."

"My brother," muttered the man. "But you won't finish me, will you? You're the rightful type, I can tell. Take me to the sheriff. Let him do what needs to be done."

"You're probably in league with the sheriff," said Jess.

"Makes no odds to you, anyways. Only the sheriff has the right to justice in this wood. King's wood, it is."

"I have the right to the Middle and the Low Justice, under the King," said Jess, but even as she said it, she knew it was the wrong thing to say. Robbery and attempted murder in the King's wood was a matter for the High Justice.

"Slip of a girl like you? Don't be daft," the bandit said, laughing. "Besides, it's the High Justice for me. I'll go willingly along to the sheriff."

"I don't have time to take you to the sheriff," said Jess. She could not but help glance back at her mother. Already there were tiny spots of darkness visible on her arm, like the first signs of mold on bread.

"Better leave me, then," said the bandit. He smiled, an expression that was part cunning and part relief beginning to appear upon his weather-beaten face.

"Leave you!" exploded Jess. "I'm not going to— What?"

She tilted her head to look at a patch of shadow in the nearer trees.

"You have the High Justice? Really?"

"Who are you talking to?" asked the bandit nervously. The cunning look remained, but the relief was rapidly disappearing.

"Very well. I beseech you, in the King's name, to judge this man fairly. As you saw, he sought to rob me, and perhaps worse, and told his companion to shoot."

"Who are you talking to?" screamed the bandit. He staggered to his feet as Jess backed off, keeping her sword out and steady, aimed now at his guts.

"Your judge," said Jess. "Who I believe is about to announce—"

Jess stopped talking as the unicorn appeared behind the bandit, her horn already through the man's chest. The bandit walked another step, unknowing, then his mouth fell open and he looked down at the sharp, whorled spike that had seemingly grown out of his heart. He lifted his hand to grasp it, but halfway there nerves and muscles failed, and his life was ended.

The unicorn tossed her head, and the bandit's corpse slid off, into the forest mulch.

Jess choked a little and coughed. She hadn't realized she had stopped breathing. She had seen men killed before, but not by a unicorn. Elibet snorted and wiped her horn against the trunk of a tree, like a bird sharpening its beak.

"Yes. Yes, you're right," said Jess. "I know we must hurry."

Jess quickly fastened her mother's bandages and bonds and rearranged the veil, before mounting her palfrey. It shivered under her as she took up the reins and looked back with one wild eye.

"Hup!" said Jess, and dug in her heels. She took the left-hand path, ducking under a branch.

They came to the King's hunting lodge at nightfall. It had been a simple fort once, a rectangle of earth ramparts, but the King had built a large wooden hall at its center, complete with an upper solar that had glass windows, the whole of it topped with a sharply sloped roof of dark red tiles.

Lodge and fort lay in the middle of a broad forest clearing, which was currently lit by several score of lanterns, hung from hop poles. Jess grimaced as she saw the lanterns, though it was much as she expected. The lodge was, after all, her father's favorite trysting place. The lanterns would be a "romantic" gesture from the King to his latest and most significant mistress.

The guards saw her coming, and possibly recognized the palfrey. Two came out cautiously to the forest's edge, swords drawn, while several others watched from the ramparts, their bows held ready. The King was not well loved by his subjects, with good cause. But his guards were well paid and, so long as they had not spent their last pay, loyal.

"Princess Jess?" asked the closer guard. "What brings you here?"

He was a new guard, who had not yet experienced enough of the King's court to be hardened by it, or so sickened that he sought leave to return to his family's estate. His name was Piers and he was only a year or two older than Jess. She knew him as well as a princess might know a servant, for her mother had long ago advised her to remember the names of all the guards and make friends of them as soon as she could.

"Oh, I'm glad to see you, Piers," sighed Jess. She gestured to the cloaked and veiled figure behind. It was dark enough that the guards would not immediately see the Queen's bonds. "It is my mother. She wishes to see the King."

"Your Highness!" exclaimed Piers, and he bent his head, as did his companion, a man the other guards called Old Briars, though his name was Brian and he was not that old. "But where are your attendants? Your guards?"

"They follow," said Jess. She let her horse amble forward, so the guards had to scramble to keep alongside. "We came on ahead. My mother must see the King immediately. It is an urgent matter. She is not well."

"His Majesty the King ordered that he not be disturbed—" rumbled Old Briars.

"My mother must see His Majesty," said Jess. "Perhaps, Piers, you could run ahead and warn . . . let the King know we will soon be with him?"

"Better not, boy, you know what—" Old Briars started to say.

He was interrupted by the Queen, who suddenly sat straighter and rasped out a single world.

"Edmund . . ."

Either the King's name, spoken so strangely by the Queen, or the desperate look on Jess's small, thin face made Old Briars stop talking and stand aside.

"I'll go at once," said Piers, with sudden decision. "Brian, show Their Highnesses into the *hall.*"

He laid a particular stress on the last word, which Jess knew meant "Keep them out of the solar," the upper chamber that the King had undoubtedly already retired to with his latest mistress, the Lady Lieka—who, unlike Jess, actually was a witch.

They left the horses at the tumbledown stable near the gate. The King had not bothered to rebuild that. As Jess untied the Queen and helped her down, she saw Brian working hard to keep his expression stolid, to maintain the professional unseeing look all the guardsmen had long perfected. The King being what he was, the outer guards usually did not want to see anything. If they did want to watch, or even participate, they joined his inner retinue.

The Queen was mumbling and twitching again. Jess had to breathe through her mouth to avoid the stench that was overcoming spices and scent.

"Ed-mund . . ." rasped the Queen as Jess led her to the hall. "Ed-mund . . ."

"Yes, Mother," soothed Jess. "You will see him in a moment."

She caught a glimpse of Elibet as Brian stood aside to let them pass through the great oaken door of the hall. Piers was waiting inside, and he bowed deeply as they went in. He didn't notice the unicorn streaming in ahead, the smoke from the fire and candles eddying as she passed.

The King was seated at the high table as if he had been there all the time, though Jess could tell he had just thrown a richly furred robe of red and gold over his nightshirt. Lady Lieka, clad in a similar robe, sat on a low stool at his side and poured a stream of dark wine into the King's jeweled goblet, as if she were some ordinary hand-maiden.

None of the King's usual henchmen were with him, which suggested a very rapid descent from the solar. Jess could still hear laughter and talking above. The absence of courtiers and the inner guards could be a bad sign. The King liked an audience for his more ordinary deeds of foulness, but preferred privacy when it came to mistreating his own family.

"Milady Queen and my . . . thoughtful . . . daughter," boomed out the King. "What brings you to this poor seat?"

He was very angry, Jess could tell, though his voice did not betray that anger. It was in the tightness in his eyes and the way he sat, lean-ing forward, ready to roar and hurl abuse.

"Ed-mund . . ." said the Queen, the word half a growl and half a sigh. She staggered forward. Jess ran after her and took off her hat, the veil coming away with it.

"What is this!" exclaimed the King, rising to his feet.

"Edmund . . ." rasped the Queen. Her face was grey and blotched, and flies clustered in the corners of her desiccated eyes, all the signs of a death three days gone, returning as the unicorn's blessing faded.

"Lieka!" screamed the King.

The Queen shambled forward, her arms outstretched, the ban-dages unwinding behind her. Flesh peeled off her fingers as she flexed them, white bone reflecting the fire- and candlelight.

"She was poisoned!" shouted Jess angrily. She pointed accusingly at Lieka. "Poisoned by your leman! Yet even dead she loves you still!"

"No!" shrieked the King. He stood on his chair and looked wildly about. "Get her away. Lieka!"

"One kiss," mumbled the Queen. She pursed her lips, and

grey-green spittle fell from her wizened mouth. "Love . . . love . . ."

"Be calm, my dove," said Lieka. She rested one almond-white hand on the King's shoulder. Under her touch, he sank back down into his high-backed chair. "You—strike off her head."

She spoke to Piers. He had unsheathed his sword, but remained near the door.

"Don't, Piers!" said Jess. "Kiss her, Father, and she will be gone. That's all she wants."

"Kill it!" shrieked the King.

Piers strode across the hall, but Jess held out one beseeching hand. He stopped by her side, and went no farther. The Queen slowly shambled on, rasping and muttering as she progressed toward the raised dais, the King, and Lady Lieka.

"Traitors," whined the King. "I am surrounded by traitors."

"One kiss!" shouted Jess. "You owe her that."

"Not all are traitors, Majesty," purred Lieka. She spoke in the King's ear, careless of the Queen's pathetic, faltering step up onto the dais. "Shall I rid you of this relict?"

"Yes!" answered the King. "Yes!"

He turned to look the other way, shielding his face with his hands. Lieka took up a six-branched silver candelabra and whispered to it, the candle flames blazing high in answer to her call.

"Father!" screamed Jess. "One kiss! That's all she wants!"

Lieka thrust out the candelabra as the Queen finally made it onto the dais and staggered forward. The flames licked at dress and bandages, but slowly, until Lieka made a claw with her hand and dragged it up through the air, the flames leaping in response as if she hauled upon their secret strings.

The Queen screeched and ran forward with surprising speed. Lieka jumped away, but the King tripped and fell as he tried to leave his chair. Before he could get up, the Queen kneeled at his side and, now completely ablaze, embraced him. The King screamed and writhed but could not break free, as she bent her flame-wreathed, blackened head down for a final kiss.

"Aaaahhhh!" The Queen's grateful sigh filled the hall, drowning out the final muffled, choking scream of the King. She slumped over him, pushed him down into the smoldering rushes on the floor, and both were still.

Lieka gestured. The burning bodies, the smoking rushes, and the great fire in the corner pit went out. The candles and the tapers flickered, then resumed their steady light.

"A remarkable display of foolishness," the witch said to Jess, who stood staring, her face whiter than even Lieka's lead-painted visage. "What did you think to achieve?"

"Mother loved him, despite everything," whispered Jess. "And I hoped to bring the murder home to you."

"But instead you have made me Queen," said Lieka. She sat down in the King's chair. "Edmund and I were married yesterday. A full day after your mother's death."

"Then he knew . . ." said Jess stoically. It was not a surprise, not after all this time and the King's other actions, but she had retained some small hope, now extinguished. "He knew you had poisoned her."

"He ordered it!" Lieka laughed. "But I must confess I did not dare hope that it would lead to his death in turn. I must thank you for that, girl. I am also curious how you brought the old slattern back. Or rather, who you got to do it for you. I had not thought there was another practitioner of the art who would dare to cross me."

"An old friend of the kingdom helped me," said Jess. "Someone I hope will help me again, to bring you to justice."

"Justice!" spat Lieka. "Edmund ordered me to poison your mother. I merely did as the King commanded. His own death was at the Queen's hands, or perhaps more charitably by misadventure. Besides, who can judge me now that I am the highest in the land?"

Jess looked to the darkest corner of the hall, behind the dais.

"Please," she said quietly. "Surely this is a matter for the Highest Justice of all?"

"Who are you talking to?" said Lieka. She turned in her seat and looked around, her beautiful eyes narrowed in concentration. Seeing nothing, she smiled and turned back. "You are more a fool than your mother. Guard, take her away."

Piers did not answer. He was staring at the dais. Jess watched too, as the unicorn stepped lightly to Lieka's side and gently dipped her horn into the King's goblet.

"Take her away!" ordered Lieka again. "Lock her up somewhere dark. And summon the others from the solar. There is much to celebrate."

She raised the goblet and took a drink. The wine stained her lips dark, and she licked them before she took another draft.

"The royal wine is swee—"

The word never quite quit Lieka's mouth. The skin on her forehead wrinkled in puzzlement, her perfectly painted face crazing over with tiny cracks. She began to turn her head toward the unicorn and pitched forward onto the table, knocking the goblet over. The spilled wine pooled to the edge and began to slowly drip upon the blackened feet of the Queen who lay beneath, conjoined with her King.

"Thank you," said Jess. She slumped to the floor, raising her knees so she could make herself small and rest her head. She had never felt so tired, so totally spent, as if everything had poured out of her, all energy, emotion, and thought.

Then she felt the Unicorn's horn, the side of it, not the point. Jess raised her head, and was forced to stand up as Elibet continued to chide her, almost levering her up.

"What?" asked Jess miserably. "I said thank you. It's done, now, isn't it? Justice has been served, foul murderers served their due portion. My mother even . . . even . . . got her kiss . . ."

The unicorn looked at her. Jess wiped the tears out of her eyes and listened.

"But there's my brother. He'll be old enough in a few years, well, six years—"

"I know father was a bad king, that doesn't mean—"

"It's not fair! It's too hard! I was going to go to Aunt Maria's convent school—"

Elibet stamped her foot down, through the rushes, hard enough to make the stone flagstones beneath ring like a beaten gong. Jess swallowed her latest protest and bent her head.

"Is that a unicorn?" whispered Piers.

"You can see her?" exclaimed Jess.

Piers blushed. Jess stared at him. Evidently her father's outer guards did not take their lead from the King in all respects, or Piers was simply too new to have been forced to take part in the King's frequent bacchanalia.

"I . . . I . . . There is someone in particular . . ." muttered Piers. He met her gaze as he spoke, not looking down as a good servant should. She noticed his eyes were a very warm brown, and there was something about his face that made her want to look at him more closely. . . .

Then she was distracted by the unicorn, who stepped back up onto the dais and delicately plucked the simple traveling crown from the King's head with her horn. Balancing it there, she headed back to Jess.

"What's she doing?" whispered Piers.

"Dispensing justice," said Elibet. She dropped the crown on Jess's head and tapped it in place with her horn. "I trust you will be a better judge than your father. In all respects."

"I will try," said Jess. She reached up and touched the thin gold circlet. It didn't feel real, but then nothing did. Perhaps it might in daylight, after a very long sleep.

"Do so," said Elibet. She paced around them and walked toward the door.

"Wait!" cried Jess. "Will I see you again?"

The unicorn looked back at the princess and the young guardsman at her side.

"Perhaps," said Elibet, and was gone.

A HANDFUL OF ASHES

There's the bell again," groaned Francesca. She reluctantly lifted her eyes from the copy of *An Introduction to Lammas Night Curses and Counter-Curses* that she'd been studying and looked across at the indicator board that dominated one entire wall of the servants' dining room. "Miss Englesham this time. Whose turn is it to go?"

"Mine," answered Mari, with a sigh. She had three books open on the table in front of her, and was in the middle of making some very precise and careful notes that required great concentration. She balanced her pen back on its stand next to the inkwell, slid off the cuffs that kept the sleeves of her blouse ink-free, and stood up.

"I'll go for you, Mari," said a cheerful young woman who was toasting her feet by the huge kitchen range, without a book in sight.

"Oh no you won't, Tess," instructed a much older and larger woman who was making pie cases on a neighboring bench. "You're finished for the day, and them sizars knows they only study as work allows. Which it don't, right now."

"Yes, Cook," said Tess, subsiding back into her chair.

"Thank you anyway, Tess," said Mari. "Cook is, of course, quite right."

Francesca made a face behind Cook's back and handed Mari an apron. Cook was mistress of the kitchen and a powerful curse-cooker, so they could not afford to cross her. Particularly as the two of them were sizars, poor students who were allowed to study at Ermine College in return for menial service. Ermine was one of the seven colleges at the University of Hallowsbridge, the only one for

witches, the other six colleges being exclusively for wizards. Only
Ermine and the wizard college Rolyneaux still continued the tradition of sizars.

Mari tied the apron behind her back as she ran up the kitchen
stairs and out across the North Quadrangle, being careful to stay on
the path. Walking on the grass was prohibited except for senior members of the college or university, visiting dignitaries like Inspectors of
Magery, and the Head Gardener. The lawn was not to be touched by
the feet of undergraduates, and certainly not by the ugly worn-out
boots of a sizar.

Across the quad, she slowed to take a shortcut along the narrow lane between the ancient, mossy stones of the western wall of
Agstood Hall and the smooth brick of the eastern wall of the Oozery.
It was the quickest way, though not without its perils, the foremost
being that it was off-limits to servants and sizars. But, as it was
already dusk, Mari thought it worth the risk in order to save time.
The young ladies, as the sizars were supposed to refer to the proper,
fee-paying undergraduates, were generally not very patient. Most of
them came from homes with a large and attentive domestic staff, and
they did not adapt well to the far less available services of the sizars
and the limited number of college servants.

The Miriam Oakenwood Quadrangle on the other side was a
much smaller version of the North Quadrangle. It was lined on two
sides by an L-shaped four-story building officially called Oakenwood
Hall, but known to everyone as Mo'Wood. It housed most of the first-
year students. Mari went to the western arm and rapidly ascended to
the top floor, where the best rooms were located, and knocked on
the door that had a plain white card with "Englesham, Miss C."
inserted in its bronze nameplate.

"Enter!"

Mari pushed the door open. Four carefully made-up faces on
four elegantly attired young women turned to look at her. The four

were sitting on two leather chaise longues that were lined up opposite each other, with a low table in between that currently hosted a
very expensive and definitely noncollegiate collection of tea things,
including a large enameled bronze samovar that Mari was fairly certain she'd seen in *The Mercury* as being the property of the recently
deceased Prince-Wizard Athenanan, sold for a record price at the
auction disposing of his worldly goods.

"You rang, Miss Englesham," Mari stated calmly, though inside
her heart was racing, and she stood on her toes, ready for flight, all
prompted by the sight of her reception committee.

Caita Englesham herself was a typically harmless first year, if
thoughtless. But the other three were third-year students, and a con-
sistent problem for Mari and the other sizars. Aphra Lannisa was a
bully of the worst stripe; Susyn Clairmore was a liar and a cheat; and
their leader, Helena Diadem, was the worst of the lot, since in Mari's
opinion she was well on the way to becoming a bane-witch, though
Diadem was too clever to let anyone in authority see that.

"Yes," said Englesham nervously, with a sideways glance at the
others. "I had some questions."

Mari stood, waiting for the questions. None were forthcoming
for several seconds.

"Ah, I believe . . ." Englesham wet her lips and hesitated again.
"I believe that you grew up in the servant's quarters of the College,
Mari?"

"Yes, miss," replied Mari woodenly. Lannisa and Clairmore were
giggling, but Mari still couldn't see where this was going. Everyone
knew that she had been found on the steps of the porter's lodge as a
baby and had been taken in by Mrs. Garridge, the porter's wife. She
and her husband had died of the Great Ague three years previously
when Mari was sixteen, but not before Old Garridge, as everyone
knew him, had managed to call in the many favors owed to him to
have Mari made a sizar of the College, so that she might take her

degree and thus ensure her future.

"You're smart, my girl," he'd said on his deathbed. "Smarter than three-quarters of them here. You might even be Mistress of the College one day. You get your degree and you'll be set for life."

Or so he had thought. But the Great Ague had come again the next year, and the next, and twelve months ago had taken the former Mistress of Ermine College. The new one, Lady Aristhenia, did not approve of the tradition of sizars. She liked her servants to be servants, she'd said, and her scholars to be gentlewomen.

Since Lady Aristhenia's installation as Mistress, Mari had been doing a lot more serving and a lot less studying, and with her final exams only a month away, she feared that she would not pass, would not gain her degree, and then would either have to stay on simply as a servant, or leave the College that she loved, to find her way in an economically depressed outside world that would not welcome an unqualified witch.

"And you . . . um . . . weaseled . . . your way into becoming a sizar student in the Beltane term three years ago," continued Englesham, her eyes darting to the other girls and back again.

I know who's really speaking here, thought Mari. *Helena Diadem.*

"Yes, miss," she replied, trying to stay calm. "Is there anything I can do for you? More coal for your fire, perhaps?"

"No," said Englesham quickly, eager to be done with what she had been told to say. "It's just that . . . we . . . that is I . . . I have found a scrap of the Original By-Laws of the College . . ."

Mari's eyes narrowed. The Original By-Laws were potent magical artifacts, written in Brythonic and inscribed on stone tablets in the Ogham script to bind everyone in the College to obey their draconian strictures. But fortunately for all concerned, some three hundred years previously the then Mistress of the College, the fabled Alicia Wasp, aided by the Witch-Queen Jesmay I, had nullified the Original By-Laws and buried the stone tablets under the moondial in the Library Garden. Then Mistress Wasp had promulgated the New By-Laws, which were considerably more liberal, and being merely in Latin, were also much easier to read.

As far as Mari knew, the stone tablets were still under the moon-dial, and even if they weren't, it was very unlikely that Englesham could understand Brythonic, or read even a sentence written in Ogham script.

It was clearly going to develop into some sort of attack upon her, but Mari couldn't work out what the nature of it was going to be, or where the forgotten and nullified Original By-Laws were going to come into it.

"I found a parchment," continued Englesham. She looked over at the wall. "When I moved in, the wallpaper had to be changed, really it was too awful . . ."

Helena Diadem looked at her. Englesham gulped and continued.

"There was a parchment under the plaster, and the workmen pointed it out to me. It was a rubbing of part of one of the old tablets. I was going to take it to my tutor, but Diadem said—"

"That's enough," said Diadem. "Suffice to say, Mari, that we have found a paragraph of the Original By-Laws, which, curiously enough, concerns sizars in the College. We thought you should be the first to know, before it is invoked."

"That's old magic," said Mari. She tried to look unconcerned, but inside she was scared. "Deep magic. You shouldn't mess with it."

"It's only a sentence or two of the Original By-Laws," sneered Aphra Lannisa. "Most sensible by-laws, I think."

Mari took a step back, toward the door. But Diadem pulled a wand out from between the cushions of the chaise longue. It wasn't a weak student wand, a mere stick of wych elm, carved with some simple runes granting minor magics. This wand was very old and very, very dangerous. Carved from a human shinbone, it was cov-ered in minute inscriptions that called upon serious powers: powers of the past, powers of the present, and powers that were yet to be.

"You shouldn't have that," whispered Mari. She felt like someone had just pressed an icicle lengthways against her spine, and her heart faltered in its steady rhythm.

Wands like that weren't just forbidden. They were outlawed. Owning one was a very serious offense. Actually using one put the wielder beyond the law: every witch and wizard who witnessed such activity was then empowered to do whatever was necessary to disarm or even kill the user and keep the wand in place till it could be made safe by the authorities. The only problem being that any sensible witch or wizard would run a mile before tackling the wielder of such a wand.

"Why?" asked Diadem. "It's a family heirloom, and besides, I *don't* have it, as all my friends here will attest if you claim otherwise."

She looked at Englesham.

"Give the fragment to Mari, Caita."

Englesham, anxious to obey, took a small folded piece of parchment out from inside the sleeve of her gown and proffered it to Mari, who locked her hands into fists at her sides.

"That won't do," said Diadem. She made a slight gesture with the bone wand and spoke three words that curdled the milk in the silver jug on the table and frosted the cake with a hideous fuzzy green mold.

Mari found her hands opening, and her right arm lifting up, her joints moving like an old puppet brought out of the attic and forced to answer once more to the strings.

"Read it," said Diadem. "Aloud."

Mari's hands unfolded the parchment, even though she didn't want to. Nor did she want to raise the parchment to eye level, but her arms lifted, answering the gentle string-pulling movements of Diadem's wand.

"I . . . I can't decipher Ogham," muttered Mari, through clenched teeth. "Or pronounce Brythonic."

"Liar!" exclaimed Lannisa. "Oh, let me have a turn with the wand, Helena!"

Diadem ignored her friend.

"Really?" she answered Mari. "What was that essay of yours last year? 'The Augmentation of Incantation: Brythonic, Ogham, and a Choir of Seven,' I believe it was called. You certainly convinced our *old* Mistress of your familiarity with both language and cipher. She gave you a prize, as I recall."

"Swot," said Clairmore venomously, almost spitting at Mari.

"Read it," commanded Diadem.

Mari tried not to, but she had no choice. Diadem had her in the grip of a geas, which was bane-witch territory for certain, not that any of the others would ever testify against her, and Mari's word alone would not count for anything. She regretted that she had not thought to equip herself with a defensive charm, as she usually did when called to Diadem's rooms. But she had not considered that the inoffensive Miss Englesham would be recruited to Diadem's flock of harpies.

She started to read, roughly translating the Brythonic in her head as she spoke aloud. Most of the words were harmless enough in themselves, but they were joined by words of power in such a way that the totality of the phrase became a very powerful spell.

Scholar-servants of low estate
brought into learning, of this date
Shall with ashes adorn their face
And must not be adorned with lace
Their coats shall be—

The fragment was torn there, and ended.

"What does that mean?" asked Englesham anxiously. Lannisa

and Clairmore did not ask, but looked to Diadem, who was certainly the only other person in the room who had understood the Brythonic original of this small evocation of the Original By-laws.

"You'll see in a moment," said Diadem. She pointed the wand at Mari.

"You will find you cannot speak of this wand. But you are otherwise released."

She slid her wand up her sleeve, and Mari felt the geas lift. Her arms fell, boneless for a second, till she got control.

But even though she was no longer under Diadem's spell, Mari still felt a strong compulsion. It was different, more inside her head than physically controlling, but she could not resist it any more than she had the geas. She ran to the fireplace, knelt down and in lieu of immediately available wood-ash, ran her finger along the grate and smeared the resulting sticky black coal residue across her face, two messy tiger-stripes down each cheek.

A slight smile curled up one corner of Diadem's mouth. Lannisa and Clairmore shrieked with laughter. Englesham bit her lip and looked away.

Mari stood up and returned to the door.

"Will that be all, miss?" she asked calmly. Inwardly she was suppressing a fierce rage. If she'd had a bone wand like Diadem's, four . . . or perhaps three . . . lady undergraduates would be smoking corpses, and Mari would be a murderer and a bane-witch, to be hunted across the Protectorate and all the civilized lands beyond.

So it was probably just as well she hadn't had an evil wand, thought Mari as she ran furiously along the Agstood-Oozery Lane. She would have to find another way to be revenged upon Diadem that did not involve banecraft and outlawry. And more pressingly, she needed to find out how to nullify or overcome the Original Law that even now was sharp inside her mind, insisting that the black coal stripes on her face must be replaced with fine gray wood ash, in the approved pattern that hadn't even been mentioned in the fragment but that she somehow now knew.

Back in the kitchen, Francesca, her face daubed with coal soot like Mari's, was lighting a fire of hazel sticks in the corner of the vast old range that was only used now once a year to roast the Beltane ox. The other two current sizars in the College, Rellise and Jena, were helping her by breaking sticks. Rellise's face was streaked with what looked like mascara, and Jena's with something gray that defied immediate identification but was possibly a mixture of cigarette ash and toothpaste.

Cook, still working on her pies, was watching the fire-building out of the corner of her eye. When Mari came back in, the huge outside door clanking shut behind her, Cook gestured with a floury thumb at the firemakers.

"I don't suppose you can explain this, Mari?"

"It's in the Original By-Laws," said Mari. "Someone found a rubbing—one paragraph—from the stone, and invoked it. It says we sizars have to daub our faces with wood ash, in a pattern."

"Someone?" asked Francesca. The fire was burning merrily now. There would be a nice pile of ash soon. A handful of ash mixed with olive oil would do nicely to make the lines and swirls that all the sizars now knew, without knowing why they did.

"Diadem and her lot," replied Mari. "As usual."

Cook nodded grimly. Taking up a chopper, she began to split pig's trotters. While she did not particularly care for the sizars, who she considered neither fish nor fowl, Cook was a stern guardian of the other servants who had often been the target of Diadem's mistreatment.

"I don't suppose it'll do any good going to Lady Aristhenia then," said Francesca.

The sizars all nodded in mournful agreement. The Mistress of the College was some sort of relative of Diadem's, and in any event, would never take the side of the sizars against the "proper students."

"What about the University proctors?" asked Rellise.

Cook stopped splitting trotters and looked over at the four sizars thoughtfully. They didn't notice. Mari was shaking her head.

"They wouldn't believe us, either. Besides, Diadem hasn't done anything illegal with this, or even gone against the University rules. They've just brought to life an old College regulation. I wish we could get her investigated, since she's definitely a bane-witch. She used a geas on me."

"But surely she's not strong enough!" protested Francesca.

Mari opened her mouth, but couldn't speak of the wand.

"Well, she is," said Mari. "Not that I can prove it, worse luck. How's that ash coming along?"

Francesca stirred the fire with the poker.

"It needs longer. I suppose we should be grateful there isn't a By-Law to make us wear sackcloth as well."

"It did say we can't wear lace," said Mari. "Not that I've got any."

Rellise and Jena exchanged a look.

"What?" asked Mari.

"I had to change my . . . my unmentionables," said Jena, blushing. "I was wearing some with lace trim . . . it was lucky I was in our room."

"We have to do something," said Mari. She hesitated, not wishing to alarm the others, but then carried on. It was better to have everything out. "It's not just the ash and the lace, well it *is* the ash . . . it occurred to me that it might stop us sitting examinations."

Three pairs of frightened eyes fixed on her.

"What!?"

"You know to sit the exams we have to present ourselves in 'hat and gown, with wand and athame.'"

The others nodded.

"There's also a bit about being sober and *clean*," said Mari. "I don't know how we'll go with ash-streaked faces."

"But it'll be because of a College By-Law!" protested Jena.

"The University's examination rules came in with the Protectorate," said Mari. "*After* our By-Laws were buried, so they were never taken into account. Even in the best case, it will go to the Chancellor's Court, and we'll still miss the examinations this year. And if I . . . if Francesca and I miss them this year, we'll never get another chance!"

"She planned it," said Francesca furiously. Like Mari, she was in her final year, while Jena and Rellise still had a year to go. "Diadem the Arch-Bitch. She's always hated us. Now this, to make us *fail*—"

"No one's going to make us fail," said Mari, summoning up all her reserves of determination. "We will sit the exams and we *will* graduate!"

"How—" Francesca started to say, but the fire fell in on itself, crumbling into ash, and all four sizars were gripped by the By-Law demanding they clean their faces of their temporary indicators, prepare the ash, and then paint stripes ending in swirly marks on their cheeks.

That took several minutes, some splashing about with cool water and olive oil, and concluded with a depressed silence as the young women looked at one another.

"How?" repeated Francesca.

Mari frowned. She'd been thinking about the problem ever since the Brythonic words had left her mouth.

"I'm not sure," she said slowly. "This is Deep Magic; there might be all kinds of complications. I shall have to look up the spell the Queen and the Mistress used, and we'll have to get the parchment as well."

"Who has it now?" asked Francesca.

"Englesham," said Mari. "I don't think Diadem or her cronies would touch it. It's sure to be spelled against bane-witches."

"If it was burned . . . destroyed . . . would that release us from—"
Mari shook her head.

"It can't be destroyed, not now it's been invoked," she said.
"It's not just a parchment. I mean, even Alicia Wasp and Queen
Jesmay couldn't destroy the Original By-Laws, only nullify them.
But maybe we can do the same, if we can get the parchment. And
since Englesham is too frightened of Diadem to hand it over freely,
I suppose . . ."

Mari stopped talking and looked at Cook, who was listening
intently. The older woman reddened, sniffed, and paced down to
the other end of the kitchen to noisily rattle through the pots on the
shelves there.

"We'll have to steal it from her rooms," whispered Mari.

The other three women drew back. Being caught stealing would
mean instant dismissal from the College and probably charges from
the civilian authorities as well.

"But we . . . we can't do that," whispered Jena. Rellise nodded
vigorously by her side, like a puppet at a village fair.

"*You* won't have to," said Mari. "In fact, it would be best if you
and Rellise stay out this completely. Francesca and I are the ones who
won't get a second chance at Finals. You still have next year."

"Oh, good," said Jena, with relief.

"Yes," said Mari. She smiled, though it took some effort. She'd
always had a low opinion of Jena and Rellise, who were never to
be seen when there was any threat to the sizars, leaving it to Mari
and Francesca to sort everything out. But for the sake of civility and
kindness she tried not to show her contempt. "If you two stay here
and take over our shift, Francesca and I will go and work out what
we need to do."

She hesitated, then added, "Whatever we decide, it won't happen
for a few days, anyway. So just sit tight, and do your work as normal."

"We will," chorused Jena and Rellise together.

"Come on," Mari said to Francesca. They got up together and started packing up their books, prompting a sudden inquiry from Cook.

"Hey, where are you girls off to? There's three hours yet—"

"Jena and Rellise are taking over tonight," replied Mari. "If you don't object, Cook."

"Don't suppose it would make any difference if I did," sniffed Cook. She fixed Mari with one of her famously fierce looks, and added, "Don't you two do anything foolish. Or if you do, you might want to consider that the Mistress is dining out tonight, and will be flying home."

Mari nodded gratefully, and she and Francesca hurried out into the kitchen garden, where they paused to note that the sun had almost set behind the spire of the College tower, and then they continued past the radishes and the rosemary, out through the garden gate into the Old House and along the back corridor there to the room they shared with Jena and Rellise. Unlike the lady undergraduates, who all had their own rooms, the sizars were housed with the servants, but in even more cramped conditions, since there were four of them in a room meant for three, and they also had to keep all of the para- phernalia of student witches: brooms, wands, staves, daggers, books, scrying globes, basic alchemical apparatus, and, most of all, books. Even with daily sorties to and from the library, the room was always overflowing with books.

"So we go and steal the parchment tonight," said Francesca. She kept pacing backward and forward as Mari carefully made her way between two piles of books to the window seat.

Mari laughed. "Was I so transparent? Jena won't be as worried if she thinks nothing will happen for a few days, and Rellise only ever echoes Jena. So they'll be happy, and they won't give us away."

"What's the plan?" asked Francesca. "Fly over as soon as it's dark, nip in Englesham's window, and nab the parchment?"

Mari looked out the window. Though they were on the ground floor, it had a good view over the North Quadrangle toward the Oozery. One of the gardeners was doing something to the turf, working in the light of a flaming branch that hung suspended in the air without actually being attached to a tree. A fairly typical illusion for light, but not one she'd ever seen employed by the gardeners, who usually just conjured a simple marsh light or dead man's lantern. Apart from him, there was no one around. In another hour it would be full dark, the tower bell would sound, and the College gates would be locked for the night.

"It's not going to be easy," she said slowly, as she looked up at the night sky framed by the College buildings, with the dark bulk of the tower looming above in the distance, a few stars beginning to make their appearance around it. "Diadem's no fool. She'll be expecting us to try to steal the parchment. And as Cook was just kind enough to tell us, the Mistress will be flying in at some point. She'd be bound to notice anyone else flying about the place."

"She won't be back till late, not if she's out to dinner," replied Francesca.

"We can't count on that. What if she has a stomachache, or the dinner's awful, or even more boring than usual?"

"So what do we do?" asked Francesca impatiently. She was always impatient, her temper matching her red hair. Valiant but foolhardy, in Mari's loving opinion, which she had often expressed to her friend. Francesca for her part thought the dark-haired Mari was too controlled, too thoughtful. Together, they made a formidable pair. Both, though they did not know it, were almost beautiful, and would be in time, if they were not worn down in servitude. That was one of the reasons Diadem and her friends were jealous of them, for their incipient beauty and their fierce intelligence, and thus their potential to transform from downtrodden ducklings into academic swans.

Mari kept staring out the window, arranging and rearranging all the salient facts in her head. Every now and then she glanced at the gardener. There was something about him that was prompting a thought, but it wasn't quite rising to the surface.

"What did Cook's nephew end up doing after he took his degree last year?" she asked finally, interrupting Francesca's pacing.

"You mean Bill? What's that got to do with anything?"

"I'm not sure," replied Mari. "Do you know, though?"

"Yes," said Francesca, coloring slightly. "He went away to join the Metropolitan Police. I believe he is already a detective."

"But he hasn't been back?" asked Mari.

"No," said Francesca. She paced over to Mari and looked down, her cheeks red and eyes bright. "Don't be a beast, Mari, you know—"

"Sssh," said Mari, taking her by the wrist. "Come here and have a look at this gardener. Remind you of anyone?"

Francesca looked through the window. Suddenly her whole body stiffened and her head lurched forward, like a hunting dog on point.

"Bill!" she exclaimed. "But . . . what's he doing here?"

"Police work, I suppose," said Mari. "I bet it's to do with . . . that . . . well, anyway . . . I'm beginning to get an idea of how we might sort all this out. I'm off to the library to look up how Alicia Wasp and the Queen got rid of the Old By-Laws in the first place. You go and say hello to Bill and tell him—"

"I can't talk to him looking like this!" protested Francesca, pointing at her ash-smeared face.

"You'll have to pretend he's just a gardener you don't know, anyway," said Mari. "It's important. Stop and make it look like idle chat, but tell him to be on the lookout for bane-witches flying around outside Mo'Wood later tonight. I hope he's got some help . . ."

"I don't . . . I don't want to get him into danger," said Francesca.

"He's a police officer!" exclaimed Mari. "He's probably been in all sorts of danger already, only you don't know about it."

"It's easier if I don't know," said Francesca. "Not that it's any of my business."

"You could make it your business," suggested Mari. "Starting now. I mean, if this all comes off according to plan, he'll be here for a while. You'll see him again. Without the ash on your face."

"It's not just the ash," said Francesca. She gestured at her rough cotton blouse, sensible but ugly woolen skirt, holed stockings, and clumpy boots.

"He was a sizar too," said Mari. "He knows to look past the wrapping paper."

"Does he?"

"He's Cook's nephew!" exclaimed Mari. "And he was at Rolyneaux. They spend half their time staring into the dark there. You know what they say, 'What you don't want known, a Rolyneaux knows.' Probably why he joined the police."

"I'm not sure that's any better," said Francesca. "Do you think he can read my thoughts?"

"No," said Mari, carefully not mentioning that mind reading would not be necessary, Francesca's main thought regarding Bill being clearly visible in her face and eyes. "Look, we haven't got much time. After you tell Bill, pick a coven of radishes and start carving faces. Do it here, but don't let Jena and Rellise see if they come in before you're finished."

"Radish-girls?" asked Francesca. "Should I gather some yew twigs as well?"

"No, I'll get them on the way back from the library. Oh, we'd both better put on charms. Not that they'll be all that much use against—"

"Against what?" asked Francesca.

Mari groaned through clenched teeth.

"Something you can't talk about," guessed Francesca. "Something Diadem's got—"

Mari clapped her hand over Francesca's mouth and shook her head violently. The questions were making the geas adopt sterner measures, beginning with her tongue swelling to block her throat.

Francesca raised her eyebrows, acknowledging that she'd worked out that a geas was in effect. Mari took her hand away.

"Lovely night," commented Francesca, careful to make sure it didn't sound like a question. "Full moon later. Lovely. I'd better be off."

"Yes," croaked Mari. "Don't forget your charms."

Both of them put on silver necklaces, the thin, spindly ones that were lent by the College to the sizars, courtesy of some ancient bequest. Francesca added a moonstone ring that was the only thing her debt-ridden father had left her, and Mari put on the turquoise and silver bracelet that had been her foster mother's. Mrs. Garridge had never worn it, because she said it was too old and precious, and had been in the Garridge family for centuries. Mari had only worn it once or twice, when she had felt particularly at risk from malevolent magic—which essentially meant the two occasions when she had been unable to avoid responding to a call to Helena Diadem's rooms without a witness.

"I think Diadem and company will be waiting for us to try Englesham's rooms," said Mari as they went out. "But if you do run into them—retreat to the kitchen."

"You do the same," said Francesca. "Or stay in the Library. Be careful."

Mari nodded. They turned away from each other and went their separate ways: Francesca out to the North Quadrangle and Mari through the Old Building, out along the path that ran the length of the Scholar's Garden, around the base of the Tower, across the Foreshortened Court and into the hexagonal, six-turreted Library.

The College Library was open all hours, though it was not much used at night, since most undergraduates borrowed books and took them away to read in the comfort of their rooms. But there was always at least one librarian in attendance, sometimes more, though they were usually engrossed in their own tasks and paid little attention to the students, other than to get requested books from the stacks. They did not record what went in and out. All the College's books were ensorcelled. They could not leave the grounds, and would return of their own accord in due course if kept too long out of the Library.

Mari was rather surprised to find the Librarian herself strolling between the desks of the reading room, idly flicking a feather duster at every second or third green-shaded lamp. Professor Aiken was not only the Ermine College Librarian, she also held the University Chair of Bookmaking, lecturing in magical type, paper, and binding. Mari had attended several of her lectures, but did not know her, unlike most of the senior members who she had waited on as a sizar or known since she was a child in the porter's lodge. Aiken did not live in at the College, and was a very infrequent diner there.

Professor Aiken looked across as Mari came in and then surprised the young woman still more by coming over to join her at the index files, the feather duster still flicking as she zigzagged between the desks.

"Miss Garridge, I believe?"

"Yes, Professor," replied Mari. Aiken was looking at her face, evidently curious about the ash.

"Keeping up old traditions, I see," remarked the Professor. "Tribute to Mistress Wasp, I suppose?"

"I beg your pardon?"

"The sizar ash," said Aiken, pointing with her feather duster, which now Mari saw it closely, was not a feather duster at all, but a wand with a feather duster end. "You know, you *do* look rather like that first portrait. A fine copy of the bracelet, too. Well done."

"*Mistress Wasp* was a sizar?" asked Mari.

"Didn't you know?" asked Professor Aiken. She wrinkled her

nose, then reached into the pocket of her rather horsey tweed coat and pulled out a snuffbox, flicked it open expertly with one hand, and scooped out some snuff on the back of her thumbnail. Inhaling it carefully, she closed the box and stowed it away, as Mari stood there gaping at her.

"I suppose they do leave it out of that nasty little college brochure these days," she continued, occasionally taking small, nasal breaths as if she was about to sneeze, but never actually doing so. "But she was a sizar. In her memoirs she wrote it was the greatest advantage she had."

"Advantage? Being a sizar?" spat Mari. "Uh, I beg your pardon, ma'am. About Mistress Wasp's memoirs, in fact I was hoping to look at them tonight—"

"The memoirs are forbidden to undergraduates," said the Librarian. "You can read them next year. But, yes, Mistress Wasp wrote that being a sizar gave her a great advantage. She said, 'I have been forged in a hot furnace, my metal is of the strongest proof. Had I been born higher, I would have not striven to rise so high.'"

"Oh," said Mari. "I didn't know."

"There is a portrait of her as a sizar. Not the big painting in the Hall with her in lace ruff and cuffs. There was an earlier one, that used to hang in the Mistress's Lodge, but was lost a century or so ago. Spring-cleaning gone awry. But there is a fine plate of it in *Landsby's Colleges of Hallowsbridge*. I'll fetch it down for you."

"Thank you," said Mari, who was rather stunned by this information. She had never imagined that Alicia Wasp, the most famous Mistress of the College ever, had been a sizar.

"What else were you wanting?" asked Professor Aiken. "I could get it on the way."

"Ah," said Mari. "Well, I'm . . . I'm looking into the . . . that is . . . how Mistress Wasp and the Queen nullified the Original By-Laws. I was hoping to find a reference. . . ."

Her voice trailed off as Professor Aiken leaned in close and looked at her face again.

"Hmmm," said the Librarian. Her pale grey eyes were very sharp behind her half-moon spectacles. "More to this than meets the eye, I see. The Wasp Memoirs would be the best resource, as it happens. Though there is some relevant material in some of the court correspondence of Queen Jesmay, which we don't have here, though there is an *almost* complete collection over at Jukes."

"I see," said Mari despondently. "And the Memoirs are forbidden to undergraduates?"

Professor Aiken leaned back and took another thumbnail of snuff. Mari looked at her with a hopeful expression, trusting that it was not too spaniel-like to be effective.

"You sit your Finals in three weeks, I believe?" asked Professor Aiken.

Mari nodded.

"I thought so. I read your essay on a choir of seven. You know, your foster father was always very helpful to me, when I first came here as a Junior Fellow. . . ."

"Was he?" asked Mari.

"Very helpful. I'll bring you the relevant volume of the Memoirs. Sit down."

Mari slid behind a desk and turned on the green-shaded lamp. When the professor had gone, zooming up the circular stair in the corner to the stacks above, she looked at her bracelet. It was very old, and her foster father's mother had given it to his wife, and the Garridges had been porters at the College for generations . . . but surely it couldn't have once belonged to the fabled Alicia Wasp?

Professor Aiken was back in under ten minutes, which was interesting. The stacks occupied four floors above the reading room, and three beneath it, and a book request, even in the daytime when there might be a half dozen librarians available, often took an hour or more to be delivered.

"There we are. The portrait is the frontispiece of this one, and here is Volume Six of the Wasp Memoirs. The part you need starts on page one hundred and ten, but I would start at one hundred and six for a little more context."

"Thank you, Professor," said Mari. "Thank you, very much."

"I wondered why I needed to come here tonight," mused the Librarian. "Sizar ash-face, and Alicia Wasp's bracelet . . . yes, I'm a little slow but I now realize it's not a copy. Tell me—is that ash the result of the Original By-Laws being invoked?"

"Yes. A fragment, anyway."

"Oh, dear," replied Aiken. "I wonder if whoever did it fully comprehends what it means?"

"I don't know," said Mari. "Um, what does it mean?"

"I'm not entirely sure myself," replied Aiken. "But I believe there is a good chance that if even part of the Original By-Laws are released, the New By-Laws might be at risk, and the safety of the college . . . what time is it?"

"Half past eight," said Mari. The library clock was behind Professor Aiken.

"We have until midnight then," said Aiken briskly. "Do you have the fragment?"

"No," said Mari. "I'm . . . I'm going to try and get it."

"Good. Read the Memoirs," said Aiken. "I must go and find the Chancellor, pity he won't talk on the phone, ridiculous superstition, entirely unfound—"

"The Chancellor!" exclaimed Mari. Raised in the college, she regarded the involvement of any of the university authorities as a very last resort, and the Chancellor . . . well, the less he had to do with the College, the better.

"Shouldn't you tell the Mistress? I mean, I think she's out, but surely—"

"No, I don't think so," replied Professor Aiken firmly. "I really *don't* think so. I'll be off now. Do whatever you can, Miss Garridge. And good luck."

Before Mari could get another word in, the Librarian was striding off toward the revolving doors that led outside.

"But, Professor!" she called. "Couldn't you . . ."

The doors whisked around. The Librarian was gone.

"Couldn't you just take over?" muttered Mari. Somehow everything had got even more complicated, but she wasn't sure what it all meant. What had seemed to be just a petty act of bastardry against her by Diadem was assuming a new dimension. Where had the bone wand come from? Why were the police secretly watching inside the College? Why did the Librarian not want the Mistress to know what was going on?

"One thing at a time, Mari," she whispered to herself, echoing her foster father's advice. "Get the fragment, and get it done with."

She opened *Landsby's Colleges of Hallowsbridge* and looked at the tipped-in, hand-colored plate. It showed a young Alicia Wasp standing against what looked like the south wall of the kitchen garden. She was wearing a simple muslin dress and had the ash design on her cheeks and the bracelet on her wrist. The inscription on the painting simply read, "A Sizar of Ermine College."

Mari stared at the painting for a long time. Alicia Wasp did not look at all like her. She had straw-colored hair and freckles. But there was something in her eyes, something Mari recognized in herself. Not the color. Alicia's eyes were green, and Mari's so brown they were almost black. It was something else. Determination. An indomitable will.

At least Mari hoped that was what she saw in both sets of eyes.

She closed the Landsby volume, picked up the Memoirs, and turned to page 106.

An hour and a half later, she hurried back to the sizars' room, pausing along the way to break off and collect a bundle of hazel twigs from the branches that overhung the path alongside the Scholar's Garden. Outside the room, she knocked and called out who it was, then entered. Francesca was sitting at the one desk that they all shared, cutting a face in the last of thirteen radishes. Twelve others sat upright around the rim of a silver bowl.

"Almost done," she called out. "Did you bring the twigs?"

"Here," replied Mari, dumping them on the desk. "Did you tell Bill?"

"Yes. I told him. But he didn't want to talk, and he practically ordered me back inside."

"You don't seem to mind," said Mari.

"He cares about me," said Francesca proudly. "He was worried."

"We should all be worried," replied Mari. "There's something bad going on here. I mean, really, really bad, not just Diadem making life miserable for a bunch of sizars."

"What do you mean?"

"I'm not entirely certain," replied Mari. "But I think that because part of the Original By-Laws have been invoked, the New By-Laws will cease to work. At midnight tonight."

"Does that matter?" asked Francesca. "I mean, they're mostly about what time the gates are locked, the lights go on, what time breakfast stops, and so forth."

"The By-Laws aren't just about the mundane stuff," said Mari. "They also describe the bounds and wards. Without the full By-Laws, Original or New, the College is vulnerable to banecraft and . . . summoning."

Francesca's happy look faded. Summoning wasn't *always* bane-craft, but it tended to be, because the things that could be summoned were enormously powerful and dangerous. Summoning was not taught to undergraduates, and was only used under strict supervision at Cross-Hatch House, the university's most secure laboratory, where summoned creatures could be properly restrained and, if necessary, banished.

"You think *Diadem*'s going to summon something?"

"I don't know!" exclaimed Mari. "All I know is that we have to get that fragment back, and we have to get it in the ground under the shadow of the moondial. At midnight, between the chimes of the tower bell."

"And what exactly is the plan?"

Mari knelt down by the desk, selected a hazel twig and broke it into small pieces. She plucked one of Francesca's red hairs and, tak-ing a longer stick, used the hair to tie the smaller pieces on the end, making a serviceable miniature broom.

"We make the radish-girls and brooms lively at quarter to twelve," she said. "We send them to Mo'Wood to fly around out-side Englesham's window, drawing out Diadem and her cronies. At the same time, we go into Mo'Wood on foot, get into Englesham's room, and get the fragment. Then we dash to the moondial, do the incantation—"

"What incantation?"

"Sorry, the spell to nullify the fragment. I got it from Alicia Wasp's memoirs, I've written it out, here—it's only seven words. She was a sizar—"

"What!?"

"Yes . . . look, I'll explain later. It must already be half past ten. We do the incantation, bury the fragment between the bell chimes at midnight, and all will be well."

"All will be well!" exclaimed Francesca with a disbelieving snort.

She finished carving the face of the last radish and picked up some twigs to work on another broom. "I suppose we use your keys to get into Mo'Wood? Even though you swore you wouldn't ever again, after that time we were nearly caught in the Dean's office?"

"Yes, we'll use the keys," said Mari. "It's too important not to this time—even if we do get caught."

The keys were a set that properly belonged to the Porter of the College, and were imbued with magic that was recognized by college locks, as mere mechanical copies of the keys would not be. Mari's foster father had given the set to her, with a heavy wink.

"Not in anyone's inventory, these keys," he'd wheezed out. "Don't use them idly, Mari. Keys can turn into trouble, easily enough."

"Jena and Rellise will be back at half past eleven," said Francesca. She plucked one of Mari's hairs and tied off her first broom. "We'd better clear off before then."

"We can wait in the Library Garden," replied Mari. "I want to look at the moondial anyway. We'll launch the radish-girls from there, then run through the New House into Mo'Wood."

"Why couldn't my stupid father have just saved his money and stopped gambling?" asked Francesca rhetorically. "Other fathers manage it. Then I wouldn't be a damned sizar."

"Like I said, this isn't just a sizar thing now," said Mari. "But would you really want to be just another rich and self-satisfied undergraduate?"

"Yes," said Francesca. "It would be so much easier."

"Alicia Wasp said being a sizar was the greatest advantage she had."

"I bet she never said that when she actually was one," replied Francesca. She tied off another bundle of twigs. "There, that's my six done."

"And my seven," replied Mari. She picked up a radish girl and speared it through the middle with the stick, to make the little vegetable figure look like it was sitting on the broom. Francesca followed suit, and within a few minutes they had the whole lot done and sitting back in the silver bowl, the brush-ends in and the radish-faces pointing out.

"You take them," said Mari. "I'll get our wands and the keys."

They only had student wands, green wych elm that would not take on much power. But Mari and Francesca had worked hard to make them as puissant as possible, gradually adding rune after rune in the last three years, and impressing them with cantrips and lesser spells. Mari took out her foster father's keys as well. There were only three of them, huge old iron keys on a bronze ring, but one or another of them would open every door, gate, hatch, or cupboard in the college.

"We should put on our academic gowns," Francesca said. "It might be the last time we get to wear them. And our hats."

Mari paused to think about this, then slowly nodded.

"Yes. You're right. We will be on college business. I hope."

They put down their various objects and slipped on their black academic gowns over their clothes, topping them with the shorter, student version of a graduate witch's two-foot-high pointy hat. The sizars' hats were mostly cardboard and blacking, unlike the sleek velvet of the lady undergraduates' headgear. But, from a distance, no one could tell.

It was quiet outside as they carefully made their way around the tower. The air was still and cool, and the moon was rising, big and bright and full. Mari and Francesca tried to stay in the shadows, moving swiftly through the occasional pools of bright light from the gas lanterns that hung over the Old House door, the tower gate, the corners of the Foreshortened Court, and outside the Library.

It was darker around the back of the Library, the light from the windows falling over their heads as they sneaked along the southern wall. The garden itself was darker still, lit only by the dappled moonlight filtering through the leaves of the guardian rowans, their branches thick with late spring leaves and bunches of berries.

The moondial was in a small clearing in the center of the garden. It was a modest thing, merely a rectangular silver plate hung verti-cally on a thin stone plinth, so that the moonlight fell on its face and the stubby gnomon cast a moonshadow down to the correct hour, indicated by deeply etched numbers that were gilded with fine lines of gold. In addition to the hours, the plate was also etched with a table for calculating the correct time at phases of the moon other than full, and the college's motto ran around the edges. It was in Brythonic, but written in Anglic letters, not Ogham, and was usually translated as "I make women of girls and witches of women."

"Stay here," said Mari to Francesca as they huddled in the shadow by the trunk of one of the larger rowans. "I need to look at the moondial."

Francesca nodded. She was looking up at the clear night sky, watching for signs of flying witches, and also keeping an eye on the tower clock. It was already twenty-five minutes to twelve.

Mari crept forward, bending low. At the moondial, she lay down on her side and pulled her legs up, spreading her gown across her body so that she might blend in with the ground as much as pos-sible. Then she reached out and thrust her fingers into the turf close to the base of the moondial, pulling back the grass and then the dirt beneath, grubbing away until she'd made a hole some ten inches deep and as wide as her hand.

That done, she crawled back to Francesca, who was staring up at the sky.

"What's up?"

Francesca pointed at the moon. A thin film of red was begin-ning to spread across its surface, flowing like spilled blood across a smooth-tiled floor.

"Potent banecraft," whispered Mari. "Someone's started a summoning already!"

"Shouldn't we make the radish-girls lively now?" asked Francesca anxiously.

"Five minutes," said Mari, looking at the tower clock. It was already becoming indistinct, as a strange fog began to fall across the College, rather than rising from the ground—another indication of most serious banecraft at work. Chill air rolled in front of the fog, making the two young women shiver. "Too early and they'll get picked off, and then they'll be after us."

It was a long five minutes. The fog grew so thick that they couldn't see the tower clock, and the air grew so cold that frost began to form on the grass and on the trunks of the rowans.

A single chime, muffled by the fog, sounded high above them. It was the quarter-hour before midnight.

"Now!" whispered Mari. She held Francesca's hand, and they both bent down to breathe over the radish-girls before quickly stepping back. Brandishing their wands, they recited the spell that would make the vegetables and their brooms lively.

The fog stirred as a breeze wafted through the garden. There was a sound like an ancient gate creaking open, and then instead of thirteen carved radishes speared by hazel-twig brooms, there were thirteen witches standing astride proper broomsticks. Seven of them looked rather like Mari, and six rather like Francesca, though all of them had redder skin and greenish hair.

"Fly to the Miriam Oakenwood Quadrangle, and there play hide-and-seek," instructed Mari and Francesca together.

The witches nodded, pointed their broomsticks, and rose into the air. Mari and Francesca didn't wait to see them take off. They ran through the garden toward the New House, Mari fumbling with her keys for the one that would open the door. New House had no accommodation, it was all tutorial rooms, so she hoped no one would be inside.

She and Francesca were barely inside the door when they heard the first scream, immediately followed by a police whistle, both coming from the direction of the Miriam Oakenwood Quadrangle. It was answered almost immediately by more whistles, coming from other parts of the College, and the air above.

"Bill!" exclaimed Francesca. She half turned to go back out the door, but Mari grabbed her sleeve.

"No! The best way to help is to get that fragment!"

Together, they ran through the New House to the eastern door that led straight into Mo'Wood. Mari fumbled the keys there, uncertain which one was needed. As she tried each key, more screams could be heard, and more whistles, and then a horrible sound that was more a sensation, as if the air around them had been sucked into a void.

"Implosion," said Francesca. "Hurry up, Mari!"

Mari's hands shook as she tried the third key. It turned easily. With a cry of relief, she swung the door open. Francesca ran ahead of her and raced straight for the stairs, her wand held ready. Mari wrestled the key out and followed as quickly as she could.

First-year students were peering out nervously through partially opened doors on the top floor as Mari and Francesca ran past.

"Evacuate!" shouted Mari. "Go to your assembly points! This one, Francesca!"

Francesca had run past Englesham's door. She skidded to a stop and turned back. Mari didn't knock. She thrust in a key, turned it, and pushed the door open.

Englesham must have been close up on the other side of the door, because now she was on her knees, awkwardly crouched on her very nice and expensive carpet, her hand going up toward a bleeding nose. Mari gripped her hard on the shoulders and looked around, ready for an attack.

"Where's the fragment?" she shouted.

Englesham started to cry, tears streaming from her eyes to mingle with the blood from her nose.

"Where is it?" Mari shouted again.

Englesham pointed at the sleeve of her nightgown.

Mari felt inside the elasticized wrist. Her fingers tingled as she felt the familiar magic of the fragment. She gripped it tightly and pulled it out.

There was the sound of glass breaking and timber splintering in Englesham's bedroom. Through the half-open door, Mari saw a shadow on the wall, the shadow of a witch throwing a shattered broomstick on the floor.

Francesca saw it too and dashed across to slam the door shut. She began to trace the frame with her wand to seal it closed, but even as she did so, the door itself began to froth and bubble like whisked milk, and a terrible stench of decayed flesh filled the room. One of the bubbles popped, making a hole three inches in diameter. Through it, Mari saw a pallid hand holding the bone wand.

"Leave it!" screamed Mari. She let go of Englesham. "Everyone run!"

The three of them were barely out of the room when the door exploded in a sickening gout of rancid matter, bits of it splattering into the hall beyond.

Mari didn't need to repeat her instruction. Englesham ran one way, and Francesca and Mari the other, back the way they'd come. Terrified undergraduates ran with them, and the two sizars had to fight their way through the crush to reach the connecting door to the New House, rather than out to the quadrangle.

They ran through the New House without any thought for silence, heavy boots clattering on the polished wooden floors. There was still a great deal of screaming going on outside, though fewer whistles.

"Almost there!" called Mari as they burst out the other side, down the steps and into the Library Garden. "Get ready!"

"Get ready for what?" asked a cold voice that came from a tall, impeccably dressed witch who was just stepping off her hovering broom a dozen paces in front of the moondial.

It was the Mistress of the College. Lady Aristhenia.

"Something that must be done, ma'am," answered Mari carefully, as she slid to a halt, Francesca cannoning into her back.

"Indeed?" asked Lady Aristhenia. "I will be the judge of that. Ah, Helena. You have been hasty, I see."

Mari looked behind her. Helena Diadem was coming down the steps of the New House, the bone wand in her hand.

"Let me finish them, Aunt," said Diadem. "Please!"

Lady Aristhenia looked at her niece. It was not the look of a fond aunt, but rather that of someone who has found something displeasing in their morning porridge.

"Where are the others?"

Diadem gestured toward Mo'Wood. "Distracting the constabulary and the proctors," she said.

"Who should not be here," replied Aristhenia. "And would not be, save for your foolishness. I told you not to use the wand before I needed it."

"I am the heiress, Aunt," replied Diadem stiffly. "The wand is mine to use."

"But you need me to tell you how to use it *properly*," snapped Aristhenia.

Mari slid one foot forward as the two bickered, hoping they were sufficiently distracted to not notice. Francesca slithered a little to the side, her own wand slipping out of her sleeve into her hand.

"I know how to use it," said Diadem. "It's in my blood. You

only married into the family—"

"Don't talk nonsense!" barked Aristhenia. "We haven't got time. The summoning must be made complete. Give me the wand."

"When I've done these two," said Diadem. She turned toward Francesca and raised the bone wand.

In the fog above, the tower clock chimed the first of the twelve strokes of midnight.

Mari screamed a word of power and threw the heavy bunch of keys at Diadem, at the same time diving toward the moondial. Francesca flung herself behind a rowan.

Diadem's curse struck the tree. Its leaves all fell at once, like a truckload of mulch being dumped, and the bark on its trunk curled and withered. Any lesser tree would have crumbled into dust, but the rowans of the Library Garden were ancient, and very strong.

Even as the leaves fell, the bunch of keys hit Diadem on the face. One of them stuck there, the ensorcelled metal suddenly red-hot. The bane-witch screamed, dropped the wand, and tried to pull the burning key from her flesh.

"Idiot!" said Aristhenia. In two quick strides she was at Diadem's side. She snatched up the wand from the ground and gestured with it. The key flew off the younger witch's face, leaving a ghastly, burned brand on her cheek. Diadem fell to the ground, whimpering, little wisps of smoke still rising from her ruined face.

Mari reached the hole she'd made. She stuffed the parchment in it and was about to open her mouth to speak the incantation when she was caught in the grip of a geas even more powerful than the one Diadem had used on her before.

"Judicious application of power is to be preferred," said Aristhenia. She jerked the wand, and Mari found herself standing up as the tower clock struck for the third time. "The wand may prefer the traditional banecraft, with all its gore and foulness. I do not."

Mari couldn't move anything except her eyes. She looked down at her wrist. Surely, Alicia Wasp's bracelet would do something now to protect her from this dread magic?

Aristhenia saw her looking and smiled.

"It's only a silver bracelet. Even if it was once owned by the fabled—"

Whatever she was going to say was lost in the loud report of close gunshots, as Bill suddenly dropped down from the sky behind her, a flying cloak whipping around his shoulders, a service revolver in his hand. He fired three times, the first bullet silver, the second petrified wood, and the third lead reclaimed from the gutter of a house where wizards had lived for more than a hundred years.

None of them had any effect. They went into and through Aristhenia, sure enough, and gaping wounds opened—but no blood came out. Instead a pale fire flickered behind the holes in her clothes.

It was a very unwelcome sign that whatever was being summoned had already mostly arrived and taken up residence—inside the Mistress of the College.

But the bullets did have one small, positive side effect. As the clock struck its ninth, or possibly tenth, chime, Mari turned her head to listen and found she could move again.

Aristhenia turned around toward Bill and raised the dreadful wand.

"Run!" screamed Francesca to Bill. She ran out from behind her tree and dived to the moondial, taking Mari's outstretched hand. Bill's cloak flapped as he leaped up into the air, even as Aristhenia's curse flew like an arrow, passing a fingersbreadth beneath the silver hobnails on the soles of his size 11 police boots.

Together, Mari and Francesca said the words. They were in Brythonic. In translation they said something like: "Rest you here, under the moon, if you wake it will be too soon."

The parchment sank into the earth and was gone. A fierce wind blew in across the College, wrapping up the fog and rolling it away.

The bloody haze across the face of the moon vanished, wiped away by an unseen, cosmic hand.

"Interfering brats!" shrieked Aristhenia. She swiveled back toward Mari and Francesca, who were crouched by the moondial. In that second, all three of them were caught in the moment of the clock's twelfth and final chime.

The bone wand shivered in the Mistress's hand. She spat out a sound, but the word faltered in her mouth and was never completed. Her fingers came unstrung, and the wand fell to the grass as the last echo of the chime faded into the night.

The Original By-Laws were once again made naught, and the New By-Laws sprang back into force with renewed vigor.

Lady Aristhenia looked down at herself and saw the blood gushing from the wounds in her chest and stomach. She took a step toward the moondial, crumpled forward, and fell facedown in front of the two trembling sizars.

There was a flurry in the air above, and half a dozen proctors in flying cloaks plummeted down, silvered swords in hand. They were followed by a large, bearlike man in a red-and-gold dressing gown over blue striped pajamas that had the University coat of arms on the pocket, who was sitting in a well-upholstered armchair that landed with a heavy thump on the lawn. He was followed a moment later by Professor Aiken coming to a sliding stop on a broom.

The Chancellor had a saucer and a cup of tea in one hand, with most of the tea slopped in the saucer, and he looked extremely irritated, until he saw the body of Lady Aristhenia and the bone wand lying near her lifeless body.

"Hmmm. That old stick up to its tricks again," he muttered. He got out of his chair, handed his teacup to the air, where it stayed, and took a handkerchief out of his dressing gown pocket. He laid this over the bone wand, drew his own silver-inlaid ebony wand out of his sleeve, and tapped the handkerchief twice. When he picked up the handkerchief and stuffed it back in his pocket, the wand had vanished.

"That'll hold it till morning," he said. He touched the body of Lady Aristhenia with the toe of his dun-colored, fleece-lined slipper and sniffed. "Who did she invite in then?"

"One of the dwellers of the most far regions," replied Professor Aiken, peering at the corpse through her half-moon glasses. "I suspect her niece will know which one. Fortunately it couldn't manifest entirely, thanks to Miss Garridge and her friend restoring the New By-Laws."

"Mmm. Yes, well done, you two," said the Chancellor, smiling and nodding at Mari and Francesca. "Grand tradition of Mistress Wasp and all that. Expect nothing less from an Ermine sizar."

"You'd better take over here as temporary Mistress, Joan," he said to Professor Aiken. He indicated Diadem, who was curled up in a ball, pallid with shock, and added to the nearest proctor, "Take her to the Infirmary, but keep her under guard. I expect the police will want to talk to her in the morning."

"Yes, sir, we will," said Bill, from the top of one of the rowans. He was untangling himself from his flying cloak. Its trailing edge had been caught by the curse and the whole garment was being eaten away by a rapidly spreading and highly unpleasant mold.

"Bill!" exclaimed Francesca, letting go of Mari's hand to run to him. He fell from the tree as she reached the trunk, and they embraced tightly before Bill remembered he was on duty and gently pushed her away.

Mari smiled at them and gingerly pulled herself upright, using the moondial's pillar as a support. Everyone seemed to have forgotten her. The Chancellor was talking to Professor Aiken; the proctors were picking up Diadem and clustering around in a "guarding the scene of the crime long after it was necessary" kind of way; Bill was taking out his notebook to write something while Francesca clung to his arm; several other policemen were dragging in Lannisa and Clairmore, both of them handcuffed; and large numbers of scared-looking undergraduates in a bewildering assortment of sleeping garments were filtering in from the New House and the Mo'Wood quadrangle.

Because we swapped duty with Jena and Rellise, I'll be doing breakfast in five hours, thought Mari. She sighed and was about to go and pick up her keys, hopefully before anyone in authority wondered exactly whose they were, when she felt someone lightly touch her wrist, just next to her bracelet.

She turned and saw Alicia Wasp, the young woman of the sizar portrait, not the older Mistress of the College from the portrait in the Great Hall.

"It is quite true that had I been born higher, I would not have striven to rise so high," said Alicia Wasp. "However, I forgot to say that you have to *make* being a sizar an advantage. Never just accept your lot, Mari. And thank you, for my College."

Mari nodded, and then blinked, because Alicia Wasp wasn't there anymore and, as no one else had noticed her, possibly hadn't been there in the first place.

"Never accept your lot," whispered Mari to herself as she briskly walked over and picked up her keys. Then she positioned herself in front of the Chancellor and Professor Aiken and waited for a break in their conversation, which came quite soon as they both turned politely toward her.

"I beg your pardon, Mistress Aiken," said the Sizar Mari Garridge. "But I wondered if, on account of all that's been done tonight, Francesca and I might have a holiday tomorrow . . . that is, today? I believe that Jena and Rellise will most *happily* fulfill our duties."

THE BIG QUESTION

A long time ago, as people measure time, but not so long that the stars have changed in the heavens or the rocks have turned to dust, a young man left his home to go hunting on the mountain that loomed above his village. He took two spears and a knife with him. One spear was short, for throwing, and that was his hunting spear. The other was long, and that was his fighting spear, should he meet any enemies.

He took the fighting spear even though no one from his village had ever met or seen any enemies. Indeed the young man had never seen any strangers at all, and had heard only dim legends of outsiders who long ago had somehow managed to climb up to his home, a secret and very high valley, which lay nestled between three mountains.

Two of the mountains were very high indeed and permanently covered in snow and ice. The third mountain was smaller, and a forest grew from the valley floor almost to the icy pinnacle that stood in the shadow of its much higher companions. The forest was full of animals to hunt and be taken home to fill the pot.

The young man, who was called Avel by his family, was lucky that day. He speared two rabbits and one of the small deer that made such tasty venison. But as he skinned the deer, his hands moving almost without conscious direction, performing the task he had done so often, Avel found himself looking out from the mountainside, to the permanent carpet of clouds that shrouded the world beyond and below, and he wondered what lay beyond those clouds. Were there other animals he might hunt, and were there other people? Did they hunt deer, and eat venison, and raise corn?

That night, he asked his mother, who was the wisest person he knew, what the world was like outside their valley.

"I do not know, Avel," she replied. She thought for a while longer, and then added, "When I was a girl, there was a wise woman . . . or perhaps a wise man with a womanish voice . . . who lived in a cave near the big waterfall. My mother told me that this wise woman knew about the world beyond. I have not thought of her in years, or heard if she still lives. Perhaps if you go there, you will learn the answer to your question."

Avel nodded. The big waterfall was four days' walk away, at the foot of the valley. He had only been there once before, with his father, when he still lived and Avel was a child. It was a long way to go to get the answer to an idle thought.

"It is not an important question," he said, and hugged her, before getting up to make sure his two younger brothers and three younger sisters did not eat all the cornbread, and that they had properly cleaned his spears, without injuring one another in the process.

But Avel could not forget his question. Every time he went hunting and looked out from the upper slopes to the cloud-shrouded lands below, he wondered what was out there. Finally, he decided that he would go and talk to the wise woman who lived by the big waterfall and ask her his question.

He left just after dawn the next day, bidding farewell to his mother, his brothers, and his sisters, as they prepared for the day's work: weeding in the cornfield, fishing in the river, and, for his next-oldest brother, taking over Avel's hunting grounds for a while.

Other villagers waved or called out to him as he strode down the terraced hill below his house. Avel was well liked, for he was an amiable man, and a good hunter who readily shared his kills when he had more meat than he needed for his family's needs.

He met other villagers farther down the hill, who waved as they waded around their fish traps in the river that was meandering on its way to his own destination, the big waterfall.

Avel reached the waterfall three days later, after an easy journey, walking downhill all the way, with occasional stops to hunt or gather food. He had dined well on rabbits, berries, and various roots, and had even enjoyed his solitary nights, without the press of the family and all their noise around him.

The waterfall marked the boundary of Avel's world. The river spread wide as it approached the mighty cliff face of the mountain, before plunging over it, down into the clouded lands beneath.

The cave his mother had told him about was under the cliff face, on the very edge of the waterfall. Avel saw where it was easily enough, looking along the line of the cliff. But the path down to the cave followed a very narrow, very steep, and very slippery ledge. It would be easy to fall, and if he did, there was nothing but cloud beneath.

Nevertheless, Avel followed the path down, though he was careful to keep a handhold on the cliff face at all times, in case he put a foot wrong. But he managed to get all the way to the cave without incident, arriving just as the sun began to shine directly against the cliff.

Avel cautiously went inside the cave and leaned his two spears against the wall, as was polite. It was dry inside, and the floor was covered in rushes that were no more than a week old. Avel smelled smoke, and as he went farther in, he saw a fire burning on a raised platform, most of the smoke going up through a hole in the ceiling.

Next to the fire, lying on a bed of rabbit skins, was a very, very old woman. Her long white hair trailed down from the bed, and her gnarled, crooked hands were folded on her breast. Her eyes were shut, and Avel could not tell if she was dead or alive.

"Hello!" called Avel, but the woman did not reply. Avel took a few steps forward, very slowly. He was remembering stories of ghosts and spirits, and there was not enough sun or firelight to banish the shadows in the cave. Not all the shadows looked as if they belonged there, and they did not move as they should when the fire flickered or the sunshine paled for a moment.

One of the woman's hands suddenly moved. Avel jumped, his heart pounding. Still she did not speak, but she indicated for him to come forward. Avel obeyed, though he did not want to go any closer. He wanted to turn around and run.

When he stood next to her, she turned her head, just a little, and her eyes opened. They were a very light blue, a color unknown to Avel's people, and clear. She smiled, which unnerved him, and in a voice so quiet that Avel had to bend close to hear it over the roar of the waterfall outside, she spoke.

"I knew you would come. Take my place, with my blessing."

She raised her hand again, there was a rattle in her breath, and then those light blue eyes dulled, and one eyelid drooped half-shut.

The wise woman of the waterfall was dead, before Avel could even ask his question.

Avel looked at the shadows. They seemed to him to be clustering closer, and he didn't know what to do. The old woman had said, "Take my place," but he was not wise—he knew nothing beyond the everyday things that everyone knew. She must have thought he was someone else, Avel considered. The very old often saw things no one else saw.

The best thing to do would be to leave her here, he thought, and tell everyone what had happened. In time, someone wise would come to live in the cave, and Avel could ask his question then.

The question didn't seem that important anymore, now that he was here alone with the dead woman and the shadows of the cave. He felt an overpowering desire to hurry out of there, to get back to his village and return to his normal life.

Avel hurried from the cave. But he was in too much of a hurry, was too frightened by the shadows he felt were following at his heels. As he stepped out on the wet ledge, his sandal slipped. The hide strap around his ankle snapped. Avel spun halfway around, trying to rebalance himself, his fingers grasping at air instead of the cliff face.

With a despairing cry, he fell into the waterfall. For what felt like an interminable, never-ending time but in fact could only have been a minute or so he struggled to get a breath out of the all-encompassing water, and his legs and arms flailed, hoping against hope that he might grab something to stop his fall. Through it all he felt a more intense fear than any fear he had felt before, a fear that mercifully was soon replaced by unconsciousness as he failed to get his breath and failed to grab hold of anything.

He went into that darkness knowing that it must be his death. So when he found himself waking, and his breath coming into his mouth, he was bewildered. Surely ghosts did not breathe?

Avel was even more bewildered when he opened his eyes. Soft light fell upon his face, and he wasn't in the waterfall, or even in a river. He was wrapped in furs, and there were people nearby, sitting with their backs to him. Slowly, every muscle aching, he sat up. One of the people—a man about his own age—turned around and said something to him, but it was gibberish, the words all sounding the same.

"I am Avel," said Avel, before he passed out again.

The next time he awoke, Avel found himself on the back of a cart drawn by oxen. This was strange, for his people had neither carts nor oxen, but it was not the strangest thing. When he tried to sit up, he found heavy manacles of a reddish metal around his ankles, joined together by a chain of the same material. Later, Avel would come to learn that this metal was bronze, and that he was a slave. His rescuers had not dragged him from the water out of kindness, but because they thought that he might be a saleable commodity.

It was from the back of that cart that Avel had his last glimpse of the waterfall. It stretched up into the clouds, looking impossibly high. Later, when he had learned enough of the language of his captors to tell his tale, they would not believe he had fallen all the way down the waterfall. As far as they were concerned, the gods lived above the clouds. Avel was a liar and had simply fallen in the river, probably trying to escape from one of the lowland villages where he was already a slave.

Slaving was not the primary trade of the group that had taken Avel; they dealt in many different things, traveling between the villages of the lush lowlands all the way down to the great city where the river emptied into the sea. It was in this city that they sold Avel, and he became the slave of a merchant whose name was Sernam, though of course to Avel he was always simply "Master."

For more than ten years Avel traveled as part of Sernam's household. They went across seas, and through deserts, and over mountains, traveling from city to city. Avel learned five languages, three alphabets, and two systems of counting and arithmetic. He fell in love with a fellow slave, Hebela, and was heartbroken when she was sold to a trader, to be taken away to be sold again, a thousand miles away, beyond a desert uncrossable save with the secret knowledge of its oases and waterholes.

In the eleventh year of his slavery, Sernam's ship was wrecked upon an unfamiliar shore. Only Avel survived, for he was the only one who knew how to swim, and even then, it was pure luck that the wind and tide conspired together to bring him ashore.

Taken in by more hospitable people than on his first near-drowning, Avel once more became a hunter in a mountain forest, a provider of meat to a village both like and unlike the one of his birth. The people had different colored eyes and skin, and spoke a different language, and lived in houses made of bricks rather than timber, but beyond that, they were much the same. Avel fell in love again, with a woman named Kikali, and together they built a new house of bricks, and in time Kikali bore three children, who Avel named after his long-lost brothers and sisters of the village in the high valley.

The children grew, the village prospered, and all was well—until one hot summer day when a caravan slowly shambled in, the mules, as always, going straight to drink at the great stone trough where a spring splashed out cold, fresh water from under the earth. But there was no one leading the mules. The caravan master was unconscious astride one mule, and apart from him, there was only a boy, who was tied across the very last mule and was already dead.

The villagers who helped the caravan master down from the mule died soon after he did, coughing until they could cough no more. After three days, everyone in the village was dead, all save Avel. He had coughed, and sweated, and shouted against invisible enemies, but he had lived.

As was the custom in that village, though it was not his own, Avel carried the bodies to the hill and left them for the carrion-eating birds. It took a long time to take everyone, for he was weak from the sickness, and there were so many.

When he was done, he laid himself down with Kikali and his children and tried to be completely still, so the birds would come and eat him as well. But even though he did not move a muscle, the birds kept circling above and would not come down.

Eventually, Avel got up. The villagers had believed it was necessary for bodies to be eaten, otherwise they would become unhappy ghosts. Avel did not believe that, but he wasn't sure.

He said a farewell in all the languages he knew, and walked away.

A year later, he was a slave again. He had walked to the coast and taken over an abandoned hut and a hide boat and become a solitary fisherman, until the day he and his catch were taken by a galley of triple-tiered oarsmen that had a ram of green-shrouded bronze.

Avel rowed in the galley for four months. It was hard and thirsty work, for there was never enough fresh water for all the rowers. But it was this need for fresh water that helped Avel escape, when the watering party he was with was surprised by enemies, who came riding out of the dunes as the slaves filled dozens of water casks at a beachside stream.

All the galley's crew and guards were slain, and the slaves were taken to serve new masters. But Avel spoke the language of the raiders, as he had learned it from his first love, Hebela. So he was thought to be one of their own, and was given weapons and clothing, and joined their band.

Avel did not enjoy his time with the raiders. They roamed the coast, robbing and looting wherever they could, and they also took many slaves, selling them every full moon at a vast slave market on a beach, with the buyers' ships riding offshore, beyond the breakers.

It was a dark of the moon, a year or more later, when Avel managed to leave the band, sneaking into the night on the back of a not very good horse.

A thousand miles away, the horse was exchanged for a sack of sugar-cured fruits and passage on a ship, and after a month at sea, Avel came to the city at the end of the river that was born of the great waterfall.

The sack of sugar-cured fruits was valuable in that city, enough for two horses and some odds and ends that might prove useful. Avel rode the horses in turn, never slackening his pace, following the river back to its source.

He came to the foot of the waterfall late in summer. The river was low, mud extending for many yards from its banks to the central channel. The waterfall, too, seemed less impressive, its mists thinner, and the clouds not quite so high above. But perhaps, thought Avel, it was simply that he had seen so many other waterfalls now.

He had also seen many mountains, and climbed them, in company and alone. He had learned how to find a way among and through rocks, and how to cut hand- and footholds in ice with a bronze pick.

Even so, the way was hard. There was not one cliff to climb, as he had thought, but many, and here he learned how he had survived his fall so long ago. The waterfall did not plunge straight down from the clouds. There were many waterfalls, and many pools, coming down the mountainside in giant steps.

Finally, Avel came to the top of the waterfall. He pulled himself up over the last lip of stone and looked out on the valley of his youth. It was exactly as he remembered it; nothing had changed. Only four days' walk away he would find his mother, if she still lived, and his brothers and sisters, and all the folk he had once known so well.

He was keen to go on, but the sun was setting, and the air was already cool. Avel had forgotten how cold it could be, up in the valley, and he was very tired from the climb. He looked again, at the way he would go, and then turned about to walk along the edge of the waterfall.

It did not take long to find the path down to the wise woman's cave. It was wider than he remembered, and there were marks on the stone that suggested someone had worked to make the way easier.

Avel hesitated at the cave entrance. There were two spears against the wall, marking the presence of a visitor. Then he remembered leaving his own spears there, and when he looked, he saw the obsidian points and recognized the patterns he had chipped himself. They were his spears, still in place after twenty years or more.

He took up his hunting spear, but the shaft was rotten and broke in his hands. The fighting spear fared no better. Avel let the broken pieces fall, keeping only the obsidian heads.

There were no fresh rushes on the floor, and the bed of rabbit skins was long gone, and with it the body of the wise woman. But there was a load of dry firewood laid ready on the raised stone, with an obsidian flint and tinder by it, though Avel used his own bronze firewheel for the spark. Then he unrolled his cloak and lay down. For a little while he looked at the obsidian spearpoints, turning them every which way against the light, and within moments was asleep.

He awoke soon after dawn, the cave still dark. It was cautious, quiet footsteps that had brought him from slumber. Avel had learned to sleep lightly among the raiders.

"Careful, grandmother," whispered a voice by the cavemouth. A young man's voice, speaking in the tongue of Avel's people, the words sounding strange and familiar at the same time.

Avel sat up. He could see two silhouettes in the cave mouth. One, young and straight, the other bent and old, leaning on the first.

"Who comes?" he asked. He was used to speaking in different ways now, his tongue felt wrong, the shape of his mouth odd and uncomfortable. It made his voice much more higher-pitched than usual.

"We saw the smoke," said the young man. "And thought to see if a new wise woman had come to the cave at last."

"I am not a woman," answered Avel grumpily, his voice more his own. He stood up slowly and stretched, his muscles and joints aching from the waterfall climb. "Where did you come from? The village is days away."

"It was," said the bent silhouette. Her voice was weak and shaky, and she took a few steps forward, old eyes peering eagerly into the dark. "We moved down in the terrible winter, when the river froze."

Avel stopped his stretching. His heart felt like it might rise up through his chest and come out his mouth, and he could not speak. He knew that voice.

"I have a question," continued the old, bent woman. "Twenty-two summers ago, my son Avel came to ask the wise woman a question, and he was never seen again. What happened to him?"

Avel opened his mouth, shut it, and opened it again. He thought back across the years, of the joy and the misery, the happiness and the suffering, of Hebela and Kikali and his children, and of all the people he had loved, and liked, and hated, and feared, and everything in between.

"He found the answer to his question," said Avel, as he walked forward, unable to even breathe, and held out his hands. As he reached the visitors, the rising sun peered in just enough to light up his face, and he embraced his mother.

"And then he came home."

CHECK YOUR FAINT
HEART AT THE DOOR
COMBAT AND STRUGGLE

STOP!

They spotted him an hour after dawn, as the two jeeps drove along the ridge road. It was Anderson in the lead jeep who saw him, which was kind of ironic since he was the only one who wore glasses, sand-blasted GI-issue things with black frames a finger thick. He called out to stop, and Cullen stomped the brake so hard the jeep fishtailed off into the loose gravel and almost went over, and Breckenridge, driving the jeep behind, almost ran into them because he did the same thing.

When they finally stopped with the dust blowing back over the top of the vehicles, they debused as per the S.O.P. and shook out into something approaching a line along the road, with Master Sergeant Karadjian shouting at them not to f—ing do anything unless he told them to, most particularly not to let their stupid fat f—ing fingers go anywhere near any f—ing triggers unless he f—ing well ordered them to shoot.

When the dust cleared, the guy Anderson had seen was still walking toward them. Just walking through the desert like it was some kind of park, or maybe a neighborhood he was visiting since he was done up in one of those brown robes, the ones with the hood like the old Mexican monks wore, who ran the orphan school over near the border, but that was eighty miles away, so if it was one of those monks he'd walked a hell of a long way.

"Okay, priest or whatever you are, stop right there!" called out Karadjian. "Can't you read?"

He meant the signs that peppered the Proving Ground, the ones that said the Army would shoot you if you came in. The man had to have seen the signs, not to mention climbed over at least three fences, the last one still just in sight, a steel blur shimmering in the heat haze, looking like a mirage only it was real, and twelve feet high with concertina wire hung all along the top, so who knew how the guy had got over it, or under it, which was more likely the way as the ground was a bit unsteady due to previous tests.

"I said stop!" shouted Karadjian again and he racked the slide on his .45 and raised the pistol, aiming over the guy's head. But either the guy couldn't hear or he was nuts from the heat, because he kept on coming and he still kept on coming even after Karadjian fired one then two shots over his head.

Karadjian swore and quickly looked at the men then back at the approaching cretin and wished that he'd never signed back on again after Korea, but then you could never expect what was going to happen in the f—ing Army from one day to the next, and before you knew it you had to shoot a damned priest or a monk or whatever and he'd been brought up Orthodox and his mother would never forgive him—

"Stop or I will shoot to kill!" he shouted. The idiot was only twenty feet away now, just walking with his head down, Karadjian couldn't even see his face, though maybe that was better, and then he was taking aim and tap-tap two rounds straight into the chest and the guy didn't fall down!

"Crap! Anderson! Four rounds rapid!" barked Karadjian as he fired another two shots, this time at the man's head. Anderson fired too, his M1 a higher, sharper report, bang-bang-bang-bang. The fourth round was a tracer and they all saw it go straight through the guy, chest-high, no doubt about it.

Panic rose in Karadjian. He was back at Koto-ri, with the Chinese pouring over the forward positions, a tide of men in the moonlight that the machine guns hadn't stopped and the artillery hadn't stopped, and he knew that his rifle and bayonet weren't going to make no difference but the training took over and he mechanically loaded and fired and then when the platoon sergeant pulled them back by squads he did as he was ordered and somehow they survived. . . .

Training took over again.

Treat the f—ing bulletproof walker as a tank, he thought, and *get out of its way.*

He pointed urgently at the jeeps.

"Patrol! Fall back on the front jeep! Steady!"

When he was satisfied they were moving right, keeping the line, and weren't going to stumble together, he shouted again.

"Opportunity fire! Nice and slow, take your shots, watch your flanks!"

The walker kept going as they shot at him, five M1s and a .45 shooting as steady and true as any sergeant could wish, and they kept shooting till he got too close to the rear jeep and Karadjian shouted to cease fire.

In the immediate quiet, they heard another noise, one that had been drowned by the gunfire. A noise they didn't want to hear, shrieking out of the rear jeep, the high squeal of a recently issued, almost-brand-new Detectron Geiger Counter, even more terrible to hear because it'd been turned right down, the background squeaking a pain to listen to on the long patrols.

"Stay back," croaked Karadjian. "Don't nobody move."

The guy didn't stop. He just went on walking, straight toward the inner cordon, and the next fence, two miles to the east. The bullets had shredded his robe or habit or whatever it was, and it looked like he was naked underneath, only he was caked in dust or mud or something. Karadjian holstered his pistol, fumbled for his binoculars, and got them up and twiddled the focusing knob, his hands shaking so much he couldn't get a good look till he clamped his elbows in and then he saw the flash of a thin, scrawny leg slide out of the shredded robe. It was red, all right, but it didn't look to him like it was from mud or dust.

Karadjian lowered his binoculars. The men were looking at him, the Detectron was easing off its scream but was still loud, too loud to be anything but bad news.

"Back up twenty yards that way," ordered Karadjian. He pointed along the road. Away from the jeeps. Away from the path of whatever was inside that robe. "Keep a look out, see if there's any more of those guys."

"More!?" muttered someone. Probably Breckenridge.

"Shut up and move!"

Karadjian lit a cigarette and coughed. His throat was dry. It was always dry in the desert but it was even drier now.

"What we going to do, Sarge?"

"Pass the shitty buck," said Karadjian. He threw the cigarette down and ran to the lead jeep. The Geiger counter in the backseat of that was screaming too, only not as loud as the one in the other jeep. The sergeant snagged out the field radio and ran back and, thinking about it, moved everyone back another hundred yards, so the shriek of the radiation detectors wasn't scaring him so much he felt like taking a dump right there in front of everyone and he had to suck air and try and think of other stuff to stop himself.

Karadjian had been on the Proving Ground security force for three years. He talked to the scientists, particularly the troubled ones, who roamed around at night and wanted to talk, and wanted to hear him tell them about Korea, and how they needed the Bomb and more and bigger and better bombs because when it came down to it there were billions of Chinks and Russkies out there and there wasn't anything else that was going to stop them. But the scientists talked about other stuff too, and so did the guards, and all of them had seen what it meant to die of radiation poisoning, and anyone who'd been slack early on was dead now, or wished they were.

The radio worked, which Karadjian hadn't been sure about. He'd bet the one in the other jeep was fried, but that's why they had two, that was the Army way, only you could never be sure if the gear was any good in the first place, so often you had two pieces of crap that didn't work instead of just one.

He called in a contact report, not that it was like any normal contact report. He could tell they thought he was drunk or heatstruck or something, so he put Anderson on, the College boy, and then they thought he was drunk too and there was a stupid little dance with every guy taking turns on the radio to tell the looey, then the captain, then the colonel, all telling the same story over and over again while the f—ing superman guy was walking in toward the test site without anybody doing anything about it.

The radio died while the Colonel was still asking dumb questions. Karadjian put it down and they backed up from the jeeps again, till they were three hundred yards away, and he wondered if that was enough. He put the men into all-round defense, a little circle of green on the rocky desert ground, and they propped there and smoked and watched. He didn't let them talk. It wouldn't help and would only crystallize the fear they were all keeping a lid on.

Half an hour later, a helicopter went over pretty low, a CH-21 Shawnee heading toward the test site. A couple of minutes later they heard its machine guns firing. Karadjian stood up with his binoculars and watched the bird do a figure eight and come back into a slight backward hover, the guns still firing.

Then its engine cut out. It was too low to autorotate and just smacked into the ground and blew up. The gunners kept firing pretty much till it hit; it happened so quickly they probably hardly knew what was going on.

An hour after the helicopter crash, when the oily column of smoke from the crash was hardly more than a crematory wisp, Karadjian saw a convoy coming up the road, five jeeps, two with

.50-cal mounts, and four deuce-and-a-half trucks loaded with what looked to be everyone who could carry a rifle from the base, including the cooks and the laboratory techs.

Half a mile in front of the military vehicles, Karadjian was more pleased to see the blue '57 Chevy Bel Air convertible of Professor Aaron Weiss, the chief scientist. It would be quicker explaining everything to him than to the White Streak of Shit, which was what everyone called Colonel White behind his back, or very occasionally just "Streak" when he could overhear. He thought it meant like lightning and indicated speed and power and the healthy respect of the men.

Karadjian waved Weiss down well before the jeeps. The professor must have heard the radio traffic because when he got out he had his gloves and overshoes on and was carrying one of the Geiger counters with the long probe. He stretched it out and ran it over Karadjian at four inches away, watching the dial.

"You're somewhat hot, Sergeant," said Weiss. "Not too hot. Portable decontamination's coming up, you might as well do stage one here. Strip and pile everything over there, and I mean everything, from dog tags out, it'll all have to be buried. You say this man in the robe walked over there—past your jeep? You fired at him to no effect?"

"Yes, sir, the jeep behind. He just walked in a straight line, in from the desert and on toward the test site. I put six shots into him myself, and the boys at least fifty, maybe sixty rounds. We saw the tracer going through, but he just went on walking. He just went on!"

Karadjian could feel the hysteria rising, and fought to hold it back. Only now could he recognize that he had survived something that might have killed him, or maybe not survived it, because "not too hot" might be a kindness, not a real accurate appraisal.

"Stay away from everyone but the decontamination team," said

Weiss. "I'll make sure the Colonel understands. When did this all happen?"

"Seven oh eight," said Karadjian.

"And he was walking at a normal speed?"

"I guess so. Steady. He never slowed down or speeded up."

"He'll almost be at the site by now," said Weiss. "Presuming he continued on."

There was a moment of silence between them. They both knew the test was scheduled for noon. Everything was set for it to fire; normally the only delay would be if the wind changed direction and blew hard toward civilization.

"Bullets couldn't hurt him," said Karadjian. "They went straight through. His skin was dark red like dried blood, oh, mother of Christ, it was—"

"That's enough, Sergeant!" snapped Weiss. He looked over his shoulder. The convoy was close now, and the White Streak would soon be exerting his military authority all over the place, without pausing to think first.

"Get your men ready for decon," he ordered, and walked toward the second jeep, holding out the Geiger counter's probe and watching the dial. The needle edged up as he approached and then jumped as far across as it would go when he got near the rear wheels. A year ago, he would have scurried back like a cockroach caught in the light, but since he was on borrowed time following the accident in Lindstrom's lab he didn't bother.

He crossed backward and forward a few times, confirming that it was indeed the track of the man that was still intensely radioactive some hours after he passed. The actual footprints were hotter still, impossibly so—it was as if a chunk of pure uranium was buried in every faint indentation in the ground.

Weiss got back in the Chevy convertible as Colonel White's

jeep pulled in behind. The White Streak jumped out before the jeep stopped rolling and ran up to the window as Weiss gently moved his foot over the accelerator, but he didn't press it down.

"Professor!" shouted the Colonel. "Where are you going?"

"The test site." Weiss smiled. "Keep everyone back. There's a trail of very high radiation. Run a phone line to the nearest junction and I'll call in from the site."

"What? You can't go in alone! We've lost a helicopter, we don't know what that thing is. Those morons at Groom Lake won't say if it's something of theirs but I tell you whatever it is we'll finish it off with that goddamned A-bomb if we have—"

"Good-bye, Colonel," said Weiss. He let his foot pivot forward from the heel, and the Chevy accelerated away, TurboGlide smooth through the gears. Weiss jinked the car around the jeeps and then off the road, plumes of dust spurting up as the rear wheels spun for a moment in the loose roadside gravel before getting traction on the stony desert floor.

Weiss sang as he drove, Puccini's "*E lucevan le stelle.*" In his head he could hear the clarinet solo, repeating over and over again, no matter what part he sang. He did not want to die, but it could not be helped. It was only a matter of time. Perhaps in the next few hours, but if not, then in the next few weeks, a horrible and painful death.

There was no obvious gap in the inner fence, no way for the walker to have gotten through. Weiss swung the car around and reversed through, wincing as the barbed wire scratched the beautiful blue paintwork and shredded the folded-back roof of the Chevy. He ducked down and avoided being scratched himself, only to wince again as a thick strand of triple-barb scraped across the hood.

Closer to the test site, he let himself wonder what he was following. Before the first test, way back in '45, he had been an atheist. Since then, he was not sure what he believed, but it certainly included things that could not be immediately measured or similarly known. He knew of no scientific reason why a man could be immune to bullets, or would leave a radioactive trail, but that did not mean that no scientific reason existed. He was quite curious to find out . . . anything, really.

Colonel White obviously thought it was an alien, for there were inexplicable and possibly alien artifacts under study over at Groom Lake, but they were sad remnants for the most part and did not include anything alive. Unless the Air Force had been hiding them from the atomic scientists who had assisted in some of the early investigations, which was possible.

Weiss saw the robed man shortly thereafter. He was climbing the tower that held the Pascal-F device. A ten kiloton bomb, suspended in place and fully prepared to fire in . . . Weiss glanced at his watch . . . forty-nine minutes. Unless he called in to stop it, he supposed.

The professor backed the Chevy in by one of the instrument stands. He left the engine running. With the car pointed west he could reach one of the observation bunkers in ten minutes, or the trenches dug by the Marines who'd been the subject of last month's test.

Not that he was entirely sure he'd bother. He took one last look at the Geiger counter. The walker's path was more radioactive than before. Getting closer to the cause of that trail would in all probability be lethal, particularly the way the dust was kicking up, carrying the radiation into his lungs.

"Hello, there!" Weiss called up when he reached the foot of the tower. He didn't suppose the fellow would feel like talking after being shot at so much, but as it hadn't stopped him, perhaps he wouldn't mind. At least he had evidently reached his destination. "Mind if I come up?"

There was a moment when Weiss thought there would be no

answer. Then an answer came, in a harsh, guttural, and strangely accented voice.

"Come if you wish. You are aware my nature is antithetical to your own?"

"Yes," called up Weiss. He set his foot on the ladder and reached for a rung. "I am. I don't suppose you know how swiftly it will kill me?"

"Should we touch, you would die instanter," said the man. "But stay beyond arm's reach, and you may live to see another season."

"My name is Weiss," said the professor as he gained the platform. He took care to stay as far away from the walking man as possible, and kept the bulk of the bomb between them. "Professor Weiss. May I ask who you are?"

"A sinner," said the man, "who seeks to make up his last accounts."

He stood and pushed back his hood. Weiss stared at the dark red, large-scaled flesh and the blue, human-seeming eyes that were set so strangely in their reptilian sockets.

"I see. Ah, what planet . . . what distant star have you come from?"

"No star, no far planet," muttered the man. "Yet from the far side of this world, I have come."

"From the far side of this world," repeated Weiss. He kept looking at the man. Was he some sort of mutant? But it was not biologically possible to be so radioactive and continue to live.

"I have sought such a thing as this for many, many centuries," said the man. He indicated the bomb. "Yearning for it as I once yearned for love, or wine. Yet even now, I delay, when at a touch I might have release . . ."

"You know what this is?" asked Weiss. "An atom bomb. It is set to explode soon and it will kill—"

"Aye," interrupted the man. "It is a hope made real. I learned of it from a woman who came to my cave in Cappadocia, as so many have done, seeking the healing power of my inner fires. She died, but it was a slow death, and she told me many things, and taught me more of this tongue we speak. I had learned it once before, a long time past, but had forgotten it."

"Cappadocia?" asked Weiss. "In Turkey? You come from Turkey?"

He couldn't help but smile a little as he thought of the strangeness of this interview. Perhaps his mind was already affected, maybe this was all a morphine dream, the result of treatment begun to ease him through the horrors of death by plutonium poisoning.

"As it is now called," said the man. He licked the dust from his lips with a long, forked tongue, and sighed. "But I am no Turk. I was a good Christian, long ago, in the service of my emperor. Ah, how I long to shed this vile form, that I may join him in heaven!"

"Your . . . vile form," said Weiss. "You were not always—"

"Always thus? I was not. Once I was as well set-up a fellow as any might see . . . but so long ago. My own face is lost to me, gone so long I cannot see it, even in my mind's eye. . . ."

"How did you become . . . whatever you have become?" asked Weiss. He looked at his watch. Thirty-three minutes to detonation. Perhaps he had given up on life too early. It was not too late for him to have a genuine and great discovery to his credit, something truly remarkable, not just an accretion on top of the work of other, more gifted scientists. If he could study this altered man, learn the secret of radioactive life. . . . Others would have to continue the work, but if he could publish even the preliminary findings it would be a famous memorial of . . . or perhaps . . . perhaps he might even learn how he could live, learn some secret to purge the plutonium residue from his blood and bone. . . .

"How did I become what I am?" said the man. "I have told the story before, but perhaps none lived to repeat it."

"I think I would remember hearing about someone like you,"

said Weiss. "Maybe we would be more comfortable down on the ground? I mean if it's a long story—"

"The story is long, but I shall tell it short, and as the end lies here, it would not be meet to leave it."

"Sure," said Weiss. He looked at his watch again. Eleven twenty-nine. "Go on."

"I was an officer of the Empire, a high commander," said the man. "Of a good family, loyal to the Emperor, successful in war. This was in the reign of Ηράκλειος . . . you would say . . . Heraclius. I was a simple fellow, wishing only to do my duty, raise a family, have sons to rise to even greater glory . . . but it was not to be. It is strange, that this I am to tell you was so long ago, yet it is ever clear to me, when more recent times are but clouded mud, and I could not tell you what I did for a hundred years. . . ."

The minute hand on Weiss's watch moved to the six.

"It was summer, the end of a long, dry summer. I had gone to the mountains, to escape the heat, and hunt. The days were very long, and the evenings were of a gentleness that I never felt again . . . with the wind coming soft and cool from the snowy heights and the earth still warm from the sun. On such an evening, I saw a star fall, and it seemed to me to have fallen close, beyond the lake where my summer house stood on its oaken piles. I had my house slaves ready a boat, and they rowed me to the far shore, or almost to it, for there amidst the burning reeds was a great boat of shining silver. The slaves were frightened and backed their oars. Startled, I fell into the water. I called to them, but they were too afraid, and their fear made me angry, and braver than I should otherwise have been. I swam ashore, and seeing a hinged door open in the side of the silver ship, I went inside.

"It was cold inside that metal ship. Colder than the nights on the high plateau, when the ice storms blow sideways and no shelter is ever enough, and no fire can adequately warm you. But I was still angry, and I thought to see the glow of lamplight upon golden plate. Greed overcame me, and I struck deeper into the craft."

"What did you find?" asked Weiss anxiously. There were only twenty-eight minutes left now, and he would need five minutes at least to reach a fixed phone. Now that death was so imminent, he wanted to do more to postpone it, and this strange, cursed, voluble creature might be the means of doing so.

"Not gold. I found a creature. A great shining lizard-thing, trapped in the wreckage of its chamber. Longer than this tower, it was, and only one vast clawed arm free, but that was enough. It was quick, as quick as the small lizards that dart across the stones. Even as I drew back, it gripped me and took me in. Its grasp burned and my flesh boiled away at its touch, and the pain . . . the pain was mercifully cut short, as I lost my senses and fell into a swoon. It was while I was insensible that it tried to do its work—"

"Hold that thought!" cried Weiss, unable to listen to any more, his eyes fixed upon his watch and the inexorable circling of the minute hand. "I must . . . I must send a message from below. I'll be back."

He had his feet over the edge of the platform and was feeling for a rung when he felt a terrible, burning pain across his forearms and was dragged bodily back up. The walking man set him down in the corner and quieted his screams with a firm but final tap to the middle of his forehead.

"Tried to do its work," he continued, speaking, as he had done so often, to a corpse. "To make me into what it was, to serve its purpose. But I did not wish to be a dragon, and with the grace of God, it could not complete its foul purpose, and so I have remained at least half a man."

He bent down and kissed Weiss on both cheeks, his lips leaving a burning brand. "Half a man, who cannot touch a lover, and who cannot be slain, nor drown, nor die at all. Or so I thought, until at last Mrs. Harrison told me that my prayers were answered, and that there is a way to slay my dragon."

Weiss's watch said sixteen minutes to twelve, and the detonation was set for noon, as set by a bank of electric clocks and three separate control cables. But when the dragon embraced the bomb and tightened his grip, it was enough.

Nine miles away, as he stood mute while being scrubbed in the decontamination showers, Karadjian felt the floor shake for several seconds, and the flow of water from the showerhead slowed, stopped, then restarted again. It was a much bigger shock and a heavier ground wave than for a mere ten-kiloton test.

"Hey, Sarge," called out Anderson. "Reckon that guy went up then, with the bomb?"

"What guy?" asked Karadjian. "There never was no guy."

He was right. Five minutes later, still wet from the showers, they signed the forms that said so, while the mushroom cloud fell into itself in the middle distance.

INFESTATION

They were the usual motley collection of freelance vampire hunters. Two men, wearing combinations of jungle camouflage and leather. Two women, one almost indistinguishable from the men though with a little more style in her leather armor accessories, and the other looking like she was about to assault the south face of a serious mountain. Only her mouth was visible, a small oval of flesh not covered by balaclava, mirror shades, climbing helmet, and hood.

They had the usual weapons: four or five short wooden stakes in belt loops; snap-holstered handguns of various calibers, all doubtless chambered with Wood-N-Death® low-velocity timber-tipped rounds; big silver-edged bowie or other hunting knife, worn on the hip or strapped to a boot; and crystal vials of holy water hung like small grenades on pocket loops.

Protection, likewise, tick the usual boxes. Leather neck and wrist guards, leather and woven-wire reinforced chaps and shoulder pauldrons over the camo, leather gloves with metal knuckle plates, Army or climbing helmets.

And lots of crosses, oh yeah, particularly on the two men. Big silver crosses, little wooden crosses, medium-size turned-ivory crosses, hanging off of everything they could hang off.

In other words, all four of them were lumbering, bumbling mountains of stuff that meant that they would be easy meat for all but the newest and dumbest vampires.

They all looked at me as I walked up. I guess their first thought was to wonder what the hell I was doing there, in the advertised meeting place, outside a church at 4:30 p.m. on a winter's day while the last rays of the sun were supposedly making this consecrated ground a double no-go zone for vampires.

"You're in the wrong place, surfer boy," growled one of the men.

I was used to this reaction. I guess I don't look like a vampire hunter much anyway, and I particularly didn't look like one that afternoon. I'd been on the beach that morning, not knowing where I might head to later, so I was still wearing a yellow Quiksilver T-shirt and what might be loosely described as old and faded blue board shorts, but "ragged" might be more accurate. I hadn't had shoes on, but I'd picked up a pair of sandals on the way. Tan Birkenstocks, very comfortable. I always prefer sandals to shoes. Old habits, I guess.

I don't look my age, either. I always looked young, and nothing's changed, though "boy" was a bit rough coming from anyone under forty-five, and the guy who'd spoken was probably closer to thirty. People older than that usually leave the vampire hunting to the government, or paid professionals.

"I'm in the right place," I said, matter-of-fact, not getting into any aggression or anything. I lifted my 1968 vintage vinyl Pan Am airline bag. "Got my stuff here. This is the meeting place for the vampire hunt?"

"Yes," said the mountain-climbing woman.

"Are you crazy?" asked the man who'd spoken to me first. "This isn't some kind of doper excursion. We're going up against a nest of vampires!"

I nodded and gave him a kind smile.

"I know. At least ten of them, I would say. I swung past and had a look around on the way here. At least, I did if you're talking about that condemned factory up on the river heights."

"What! But it's cordoned off—and the vamps'll be dug in till nightfall."

"I counted the patches of disturbed earth," I explained. "The cordon was off. I guess they don't bring it up to full power till the sun goes down. So, who are you guys?"

"Ten!" exclaimed the second man, not answering my question. "You're sure?"

"At least ten," I replied. "But only one Ancient. The others are all pretty new, judging from the soil."

"You're making this up," said the first man. "There's maybe five, tops. They were seen together and tracked back. That's when the cordon was established this morning."

I shrugged and half unzipped my bag.

"I'm Jenny," said the mountain climber, belatedly answering my question. "The . . . the vampires got my sister, three years ago. When I heard about this infestation I claimed the Relative's Right."

"I've got a twelve-month permit," said the second man. "Plan to turn professional. Oh yeah, my name's Karl."

"I'm Susan," said the second woman. "This is our third vampire hunt. Mike's and mine, I mean."

"She's my wife," said the belligerent Mike. "We've both got twelve-month permits. You'd better be legal too, if you want to join us."

"I have a special license," I replied. The sun had disappeared behind the church tower, and the streetlights were flicking on. With the bag unzipped, I was ready for a surprise. Not that I thought one was about to happen. At least, not immediately. Unless I chose to spring one.

"You can call me J."

"Jay?" asked Susan.

"Close enough," I replied. "Does someone have a plan?"

"Yeah," said Mike. "We stick together. No hotdogging off or chasing down wounded vamps or anything like that. We go in as a team, and we come out as a team."

"Interesting," I said. "Is there . . . more to it?"

Mike paused to fix me with what he obviously thought was his steely gaze. I met it and after a few seconds he looked away. Maybe it's the combination of very pale blue eyes and dark skin, but not many people look at me directly for too long. It might just be the eyes. There've been quite a few cultures who think of very light blue eyes as the color of death. Perhaps that lingers, resonating in the subconscious even of modern folk.

"We go through the front door," he said. "We throw flares ahead of us. The vamps should all be digging out on the old factory floor, it's the only place where the earth is accessible. So we go down the fire stairs, throw a few more flares out the door, then go through and back up against the wall. We'll have a clear field of fire to take them down. They'll be groggy for a couple of hours yet, slow to move. But if one or two manage to close, we stake them."

"The young ones will be slow and dazed," I said. "But the Ancient will be active soon after sundown, even if it stays where it is—and it's not dug in on the factory floor. It's in a humungous clay pot outside an office on the fourth floor."

"We take it first, then," said Mike. "Not that I'm sure I believe you."

"It's up to you," I said. I had my own ideas about dealing with the Ancient, but they would wait. No point upsetting Mike too early. "There's one more thing."

"What?" asked Karl.

"There's a fresh-made vampire around, from last night. It will still be able to pass as human for a few more days. It won't be dug in, and it may not even know it's infected."

"So?" asked Mike. "We kill everything in the infested area. That's all legal."

"How do you know this stuff?" asked Jenny.

"You're a professional, aren't you," said Karl. "How long you been pro?"

"I'm not exactly a professional," I said. "But I've been hunting vampires for quite a while."

"Can't have been that long," said Mike. "Or you'd know better than to go after them in just a T-shirt. What've you got in that bag? Sawed-off shotgun?"

"Just a stake and a knife," I replied. "I'm a traditionalist. Shouldn't we be going?"

The sun was fully down, and I knew the Ancient, at least, would already be reaching up through the soil, its mildewed, mottled hands gripping the rim of the earthenware pot that had once held a palm or something equally impressive outside the factory manager's office.

"Truck's over there," said Mike, pointing to a flashy new silver pickup. "You can ride in the back, surfer boy."

"Fresh air's a wonderful thing."

As it turned out, Karl and Jenny wanted to sit in the back too. I sat on a toolbox that still had shrink-wrap around it, Jenny sat on a spare tire, and Karl stood looking over the cab, scanning the road, as if a vampire might suddenly jump out when we were stopped at the lights.

"Do you want a cross?" Jenny asked me after we'd gone a mile or so in silence. Unlike Mike and Karl she wasn't festooned with them, but she had a couple around her neck. She started to take a small wooden one off, lifting it by the chain.

I shook my head and raised my T-shirt up under my arms, to show the scars. Jenny recoiled in horror and gasped, and Karl looked around, hand going for his .41 Glock. I couldn't tell whether that was jumpiness or good training. He didn't draw and shoot, which I guess meant good training.

I let the T-shirt fall, but it was up long enough for both of them to see the hackwork tracery of scars that made up a kind of T shape on my chest and stomach. But it wasn't a T. It was a tau cross, one of the oldest Christian symbols and still the one that vampires feared the most, though none but the most ancient knew why they fled from it.

"Is that . . . a cross?" asked Karl.

I nodded.

"That's so hardcore," said Karl. "Why didn't you just have it tat-tooed?"

"It probably wouldn't work so well," I said. "And I didn't have it done. It was done to me."

I didn't mention that there was an equivalent tracery of scars on my back as well. These two tau crosses, front and back, never faded, though my other scars always disappeared only a few days after they healed.

"Who would—" Jenny started to ask, but she was interrupted by Mike banging on the rear window of the cab—with the butt of his pistol, reconfirming my original assessment that he was the biggest danger to all of us. Except for the Ancient vampire. I wasn't worried about the young ones. But I didn't know which Ancient it was, and that was cause for concern. If it had been encysted since the drop it would be in the first flush of its full strength. I hoped it had been around for a long time, lying low and steadily degrading, only recently resuming its mission against humanity.

"We're there," said Karl, unnecessarily.

The cordon fence was fully established now. Sixteen feet high and lethally electrified, with old-fashioned limelights burning every ten feet along the fence, the sound of the hissing oxygen and hydro-gen jets music to my ears. Vampires loathe limelight. Gaslight has a lesser effect, and electric light hardly bothers them at all. It's the intensity of the naked flame they fear.

The fire brigade was standing by because of the limelights, which though modernized were still occasionally prone to massive accidental combustion; and the local police department was there en masse to enforce the cordon. I saw the bright white bulk of the state Vampire Eradication Team's semitrailer parked off to one side. If we volunteers failed, they would go in, though given the derelict state of the building and the reasonable space between it and the nearest residential area it was more likely they'd just get the Air Force to do a fuel-air explosion dump.

The VET personnel would be out and about already, making sure no vampires managed to get past the cordon. There would be crossbow snipers on the upper floors of the surrounding buildings, ready to shoot fire-hardened oak quarrels into vampire heads. It wasn't advertised by the ammo manufacturers, but a big old vampire could take forty or fifty Wood-N-Death® or equivalent rounds to the head and chest before going down. A good inch-diameter yard-long quarrel or stake worked so much better.

There would be a VET quick response team somewhere close as well, outfitted in the latest metal-mesh armor, carrying the automatic weapons the volunteers were not allowed to use—with good reason, given the frequency with which volunteer vampire hunters killed one another even when only armed with handguns, stakes, and knives.

I waved at the window of the three-story warehouse where I'd caught a glimpse of a crossbow sniper, earning a puzzled glance from Karl and Jenny, then jumped down. A police sergeant was already walking over to us, his long, harsh, limelit shadow preceding him. Naturally, Mike intercepted him before he could choose who he wanted to talk to.

"We're the volunteer team."

"I can see that," said the sergeant. "Who's the kid?"

He pointed at me. I frowned. The kid stuff was getting monotonous. I don't look that young. Twenty at least, I would have thought.

"He says his name's Jay. He's got a 'special license.' That's what he says."

"Let's see it then," said the sergeant, with a smile that suggested he was looking forward to arresting me and delivering a three-hour lecture. Or perhaps a beating with a piece of rubber pipe. It isn't always easy to decipher smiles.

"I'll take it from here, sergeant," said an officer who came up from behind me, fast and smooth. He was in the new metal-mesh armor, like a wetsuit, with a webbing belt and harness over it, to hold stakes, knife, WP grenades (which actually were effective against the vamps, unlike the holy water ones), and handgun. He had an H&K MP5-PW slung over his shoulder. "You go and check the cordon."

"But lieutenant, don't you want me to take—"

"I said check the cordon."

The sergeant retreated, smile replaced by a scowl of frustration. The VET lieutenant ignored him.

"Licenses, please," he said. He didn't look at me, and unlike the others I didn't reach for the plasticated, hologrammed, data-chipped card that was the latest version of the volunteer vampire hunter license.

They held up their licenses, and the reader that was somewhere in the lieutenant's helmet picked up the data and his earpiece whispered whether they were valid or not. Since he was nodding, we all knew they were valid before he spoke.

"Okay, you're good to go whenever you want. Good luck."

"What about him?" asked Mike, gesturing at me with his thumb.

"Him too," said the lieutenant. He still didn't look at me. Some of the VET are funny like that. They seem to think I'm like an albatross or something. A sign of bad luck. I suppose it's because wherever the vampire infestations are really bad, then I have a tendency to show up as well. "He's already been checked in. We'll open the gate in five, if that suits you."

"Sure," said Mike. He lumbered over to face me. "There's something funny going on here, and I don't like it. So you just stick to the plan, okay?"

"Actually, your plan sucks," I said calmly. "So I've decided to change it. You four should go down to the factory floor and take out the vampires there. I'll go up against the Ancient."

"Alone?" asked Jenny. "Shouldn't we stick together like Mike says?"

"Nope," I replied. "It'll be out and unbending itself now. You'll all be too slow."

"Call this sl—" Mike started to say as he tried to poke me forcefully in the chest with his forefinger. But I was already standing behind him. I tapped him on the shoulder, and as he swung around, ran behind him again. We kept this up for a few turns before Karl stopped him.

"See what I mean? And an Ancient vampire is faster than me."

That was blarney. Or at least I hoped it was. I'd met Ancient vampires who were as quick as I was, but not actually faster. Sometimes I did wonder what would happen if one day I was a fraction slower and one finally got me for good and all. Some days, I kind of hoped that it would happen.

But not this day. I hadn't had to go up against any vampires or anything else for over a month. I'd been surfing for the last two weeks, hanging out on the beach, eating well, drinking a little wine, and even letting down my guard long enough to spend a couple of nights with a girl who surfed better than me and didn't mind having sex in total darkness with a guy who kept his T-shirt on and an old airline bag under the pillow.

I was still feeling good from this little holiday, though I knew it would only ever be that. A few weeks snatched out of . . .

"Okay," panted Mike. He wasn't as stupid as I'd feared but he was a lot less fit than he looked. "You do your thing. We'll take the vampires on the factory floor."

"Good," I replied. "Presuming I survive, I'll come down and help you."

"What do . . . what do we do if we . . . if we're losing?" asked

Jenny. She had her head well down, her chin almost tucked into her chest, and her body language screamed out that she was both scared and miserable. "I mean if there are more vampires, or if the Ancient one—"

"We fight or we die," said Karl. "No one is allowed back out through the cordon until after dawn."

"Oh, I didn't . . . I mean I read the brochure—"

"You don't have to go in," I said. "You can wait out here."

"I . . . I think I will," she said, without looking at the others. "I just can't . . . now I'm here, I just can't face it."

"Great!" muttered Mike. "One of us down already."

"She's too young," said Susan. I was surprised she'd speak up against Mike. I had her down as his personal doormat. "Don't give her a hard time, Mike."

"No time for anything," I said. "They're getting ready to power down the gate."

A cluster of regular police officers and VET agents were taking up positions around the gate in the cordon fence. We walked over, the others switching on helmet lights, drawing their handguns, and probably silently uttering last-minute prayers.

The sergeant who'd wanted to give me a hard time looked at Mike, who gave him the thumbs-up. A siren sounded a slow *whoop-whoop-whoop* as a segment of the cordon fence powered down, the indicators along the top rail fading from a warning red to a dull green.

"Go, go, go!" shouted Mike, and he jogged forward, with Susan and Karl at his heels. I followed a few meters behind, but not too far. That sergeant had the control box for the gate and I didn't trust him not to close it on my back and power it up at the same time. I really didn't want to know what 6,600 volts at 500 milliamps would do to my unusual physiology. Or show anyone else what *didn't* happen, more to the point.

On the other hand, I didn't want to get ahead of Mike and Co., either, because I already know what being shot in the back by accident felt like, with lead and wooden bullets, not to mention ceramic-cased tungsten-tipped penetrator rounds, and I didn't want to repeat the experience.

They rushed the front door, Mike kicking it in and bulling through. The wood was rotten and the top panel had already fallen off, so this was less of an achievement than it might have been.

Karl was quick with the flares, confirming his thorough training. Mike, on the other hand, just kept going, so the light was behind him as he opened the fire door to the left of the lobby.

Bad move. There was a vampire behind the door, and while it was no ancient, it wasn't newly hatched either. It wrapped its arms around Mike, holding on with the filaments that lined its forelegs, though to an uneducated observer it just looked like a fairly slight, tattered-rag-wearing human bear-hugging him with rather longer than usual arms.

Mike screamed as the vampire started chewing on his helmet, ripping through the Kevlar layers like a buzz saw through softwood, pausing only to spit out bits of the material. Old steel helmets are better than the modern variety, but we live in an age that values only the new.

Vamps like to get a good grip around their prey, particularly ones who carry weapons. There was nothing Mike could do and, as the vamp was already backing into the stairwell, only a second or two for someone else to do something.

The vampire fell to the ground, its forearm filaments coming loose with a sticky popping sound, though they probably hadn't penetrated Mike's heavy clothes. I pulled the splinter out of its head and put the stake of almost two-thousand-year-old timber back in the bag before the others got a proper look at the odd silver sheen that came from deep within the wood.

Karl dragged Mike back into the flare-light as Susan covered him. Both of them were pretty calm, I thought. At least they were still doing stuff, rather than freaking out.

"Oh man," said Karl. He'd sat Mike up, and then had to catch him again as he fell backward. Out in the light, I saw that I'd waited just that second too long, perhaps from some subconscious dislike of the man. The last few vampire bites had not been just of Mike's helmet.

"What . . . what do we do?" asked Susan. She turned to me, pointedly not looking at her dead husband.

"I'm sorry," I said. I really meant it, particularly since it was my slackness that had let the vamp finish him off. Mike was an idiot, but he didn't deserve to die, and I could have saved him. "But he's got to be dealt with the same way as the vampires now. Then you and Karl have to go down and clean out the rest. Otherwise they'll kill you too."

It usually helps to state the situation clearly. Stave off the shock with the need to do something life-saving. Adrenaline focuses the mind wonderfully.

Susan looked away for a couple of seconds. I thought she might vomit, but I'd underestimated her again. She turned back and, still holding her pistol in her right hand, reached into a thigh pocket and pulled out a Quick-Flame™.

"I should be the one to do it," she said. Karl stepped back as she thumbed the Quick-Flame™ and dropped it on the corpse. The little cube deliquesced into a jelly film that spread over the torso of what had once been a man. Then, as it splashed on the floor, it woofed alight, burning blue.

Susan watched the fire. I couldn't see much of her face, but from what I could see, I thought she'd be okay for about an hour before the shock knocked her off her feet. Provided she got on with the job as soon as possible.

"You'd better get going," I said. "If this one was already up here, the others might be out and about. Don't get ahead of your flares."

"Right," muttered Karl. He took another flare from a belt pouch. "Ready, Susan?"

"Yes."

Karl tossed the flare down the stairs. They both waited to see the glow of its light come back up, then Karl edged in, working the angle, his pistol ready. He fired almost immediately, two double taps, followed by the sound of a vamp falling back down the stairs.

"Put two more in," I called out, but Karl was already firing again.

"And stake it before you go past!" I added as they both disappeared down the stairs.

As soon as they were gone, I checked the smoldering remains of Mike. Quick-Flame™ cubes are all very well, but they don't always burn everything, and if there's a critical mass of organic material left then the vamp nanos can build a new one. A little, slow one, but little slow ones can grow up. I doubted there'd been enough exchange of blood to get full infestation, but it's better to be sure, so I took out the splinter again and waved it over the fragments that were left.

The sound of rapid gunshots began to echo up from below as I took off my T-shirt and tucked it in the back of my board shorts. The tau cross on my chest was already glowing softly with a silver light, the smart matter under the scars energizing as it detected vamp activity close by. I couldn't see the one on my back, but it would be doing the same thing. Together they were supposed to generate a field that repulsed the vampires and slowed them down if they got close, but it really only worked on the original versions. The latter-day generations of vampires were such bad copies that a lot of the original tech built to deter them simply missed the mark. Fortunately, being bad copies, the newer vampires were weaker, slower, less intelligent, and untrained.

I took the main stairs up to the fourth floor. The Ancient vampire would already know I was coming, so there was no point skulking up the elevator shaft or the outside drain. Like its broodmates, it had been bred to be a perfect soldier at various levels of conflict, from the nanonic frontline where it tried to replicate itself in its enemies to the gross physical contest of actually duking it out. Back in the old days it might have had some distance weapons as well, but if there was one thing we'd managed right in the original mission, it was taking out the vamp weapons caches and resupply nodes.

We did a lot of things right in the original mission. We succeeded rather too well, or at least so we thought at the time. If the victory hadn't been so much faster than anticipated, the boss would never have had those years to fall in love with humans and then work out his crazy scheme to become their living god.

Not so crazy perhaps, since it kind of worked, even after I tried to do my duty and stop him. In a halfhearted way, I suppose, because he was team leader and all that. But he was going totally against regulations. I reported it and I got the order, and the rest, as they say, is history. . . .

Using the splinter always reminds me of him, and the old days. There's probably enough smart matter in the wood, encasing his DNA and his last download, to bring him back complete, if and when I ever finish this assignment and can signal for pickup. Though a court would probably confirm HQ's original order and he'd be slowed into something close to a full stop anyway.

But my mission won't be over till the last vamp is burned to ash, and this infested Earth can be truly proclaimed clean.

Which is likely to be a long, long time, and I reminded myself that daydreaming about the old days is not going to help take out the Ancient vampire ahead of me, let alone the many more in the world beyond.

I took out the splinter and the silver knife and slung my Pan Am bag so it was comfortable, and got serious.

I heard the Ancient moving around as I stepped into what was once the outer office. The big pot was surrounded by soil and there were dirty footprints up the wall, but I didn't need to see them to know to look up. The vamps have a desire to dominate the high ground heavily programmed into them. They always go for the ceiling, up trees, up towers, up lampposts.

This one was spread-eagled on the ceiling, gripping with its foreleg and trailing leg filaments as well as the hooks on what humans thought were fingers and toes. It was pretty big as vamps go, perhaps nine feet long and weighing in at around two hundred pounds. The ultrathin waist gave away its insectoid heritage, almost as much as a real close look at its mouth would. Not that you would want a real close look at a vamp's mouth.

It squealed when I came in and it caught the tau emissions. The squeal was basically an ultrasonic alarm oscillating through several wavelengths. The cops outside would hear it as an unearthly scream, when in fact it was more along the lines of a distress call and emergency rally beacon. If any of its brood survived down below, they'd drop whatever they might be doing—or chewing—and rush on up.

The squeal was standard operating procedure, straight out of the manual. It followed up with more orthodox stuff, dropping straight onto me. I flipped on my back and struck with the splinter, but the vamp managed to flip itself in midair and bounce off the wall, coming to a stop in the far corner.

It was fast, faster than any vamp I'd seen for a long time. I'd scratched it with the splinter, but no more than that. There was a line of silver across the dark red chitin of its chest, where the transferred smart matter was leeching the vampire's internal electrical potential to build a bomb, but it would take at least five seconds to do that, which was way too long.

I leapt and struck again and we conducted a kind of crazy ballet across the four walls, the ceiling, and the floor of the room. Anyone watching would have gotten motion sickness or eyeball fatigue, trying to catch blurs of movement.

At 2.350 seconds in, it got a forearm around my left elbow and gave it a good hard pull, dislocating my arm at the shoulder. I knew then it really was ancient and had retained the programming needed to fight me. My joints have always been a weak point.

It hurt. A lot. And it kept on hurting through several microseconds as the vamp tried to actually pull my arm off and at the same time twist itself around to start chewing on my leg.

The tau field was discouraging the vamp, making it dump some of its internal nanoware, so that blood started geysering out of pinholes all over its body, but this was more of a nuisance for me than any major hindrance to it.

In midsomersault, somewhere near the ceiling, with the thing trying to wrap itself around me, I dropped the silver knife. It wasn't a real weapon, not like the splinter. I kept it for sentimental reasons as much as anything, though silver did have a deleterious effect on younger vamps. Since it was pure sentiment, I suppose I could have left it in coin form, but then I'd probably be forever dropping some in combat and having to waste time later picking them up. Besides, when silver was still the usual currency and they were still coins, I'd gotten drunk a few times and spent them, and it was way too big a hassle getting them back.

The vamp took the knife-dropping as more significant than it was, which was one of the reasons I'd let it go. In the old days, I would have held something serious in my left hand, like a deweaving wand, which the vampire probably thought the knife was—and it wanted to get it and use it on me. It partially let go of my arm as it tried to catch the weapon, and at that precise moment, second 2.355, I feinted with the splinter, slid it along the thing's attempted forearm block, and, reversing my elbow joint, stuck it right in the forehead.

With the smart matter already at work from its previous scratch, internal explosion occurred immediately. I had shut my eyes in preparation, so I was only blown against the wall and not temporarily blinded as well.

I assessed the damage as I wearily got back up. My left arm was fully dislocated, with the tendons ripped away, so I couldn't put it back. It was going to have to hang for a day or two, hurting like crazy till it self-healed. Besides that, I had severe bruising to my lower back and ribs, which would also deliver some serious pain for a day or so.

I hadn't been hurt by a vamp as seriously for a long, long time, so I spent a few minutes searching through the scraps of mostly disintegrated vampire to find a piece big enough to meaningfully scan. Once I got it back to the jumper, I'd be able to pick it apart on the atomic level to find the serial number on some of its defunct nanoware.

I put the scrap of what was probably skeleton in my flight bag, with the splinter and the silver knife, and wandered downstairs. I left it unzipped, because I hadn't heard any firing for a while, which meant either Susan and Karl had cleaned up, or the vamps had cleaned up Susan and Karl. But I put my T-shirt back on. No need to scare the locals. It was surprisingly clean, considering. My skin and hair shed vampire blood, so the rest of me looked quite respectable as well. Apart from the arm hanging down like an orangutan's, that is.

I'd calculated the odds at about five to two that Susan and Karl would win, so I was pleased to see them in the entrance lobby. They both jumped when I came down the stairs, and I was ready to move if they shot at me, but they managed to control themselves.

"Did you get them all?" I asked. I didn't move any closer.

"Nine," said Karl. "Like you said. Nine holes in the ground, nine burned vampires."

"You didn't get bitten?"

"Does it look like we did?" asked Susan with a shudder. She was clearly thinking about Mike.

"Vampires can infect with a small, tidy bite," I said. "Or even about half a cup of their saliva, via a kiss."

Susan did throw up then, which is what I wanted. She wouldn't have if she'd been bitten. I was also telling the truth. While they were designed to be soldiers, the vampires were also made to be guerrilla fighters, working among the human population, infecting as many as possible in small, subtle ways. They only went for the big chow-down in full combat.

"What about you?" asked Karl. "You okay?"

"You mean this?" I asked, threshing my arm about like a tentacle, wincing as it made the pain ten times worse. "Dislocated. But I didn't get bitten."

Neither had Karl, I was now sure. Even newly infected humans have something about them that gives their condition away, and I can always pick it.

"Which means we can go and sit by the fence and wait till morning," I said cheerily. "You've done well."

Karl nodded wearily and got his hand under Susan's elbow, lifting her up. She wiped her mouth and the two of them walked slowly to the door.

I let them go first, which was kind of mean, because the VET have been known to harbor trigger-happy snipers. But there was no sudden death from above, so we walked over to the fence and then the two of them flopped down on the ground and Karl began to laugh hysterically.

I left them to it and wandered over to the gate.

"You can let me out now," I called to the Sergeant. "My work here is almost done."

"No one comes out till after dawn," replied the guardian of the city.

"Except me," I agreed. "Check with Lieutenant Harman."

Which goes to show that I can read ID labels, even little ones on metal-mesh skinsuits.

The sergeant didn't need to check. Lieutenant Harman was already looming up behind him. They had a short but spirited conversation, the sergeant told Karl and Susan to stay where they were, which was still lying on the ground essentially in severe shock, and they powered down the gate for about thirty seconds and I came out.

Two medics came over to help me. Fortunately they were VET, not locals, so we didn't waste time arguing about me going to the hospital, getting lots of drugs injected, having scans, etc. They fixed me up with a collar and cuff sling so my arm wasn't dragging about the place, I said thank you, and they retired to their unmarked ambulance.

Then I wandered over to where Jenny was sitting on the far side of the silver truck, her back against the rear wheel. She'd taken off her helmet and balaclava, letting her bobbed brown hair spring back out into shape. She looked about eighteen, maybe even younger, maybe a little older. A pretty young woman, her face made no worse by evidence of tears, though she was very pale.

She jumped as I tapped a little rhythm on the side of the truck.

"Oh . . . I thought . . . aren't you meant to stay inside the . . . the cordon?"

I hunkered down next to her.

"Yeah, most of the time they enforce that, but it depends," I said. "How are you doing?"

"Me? I'm . . . I'm okay. So you got them?"

"We did," I confirmed. I didn't mention Mike. She didn't need to know that, not now.

"Good," she said. "I'm sorry . . . I thought I would be braver. Only when the time came . . ."

"I understand," I said.

"I don't see how you can," she said. "I mean, you went in, and you said you fight vampires all the time. You must be incredibly brave."

"No," I replied. "Bravery is about overcoming fear, not about not having it. There's plenty I'm afraid of. Just not vampires."

"We fear the unknown," she said. "You must know a lot about vampires."

I nodded and moved my flight bag around to get more comfortable. It was still unzipped, but the sides were pushed together at the top.

"How to fight them, I mean," she added. "Since no one really knows anything else. That's the worst thing. When my sister was in . . . infected and then later, when she was . . . was killed, I really wanted to know, and there was no one to tell me anything."

"What did you want to know?" I asked. I've always been prone to show off to pretty girls. If it isn't surfing, it's secret knowledge. Though sharing the secret knowledge only occurred in special cases, when I knew it would go no further.

"Everything we don't know," sighed Jenny. "What are they, really? Why have they suddenly appeared all over the place in the last ten years, when we all thought they were just . . . just made-up."

"They're killing machines," I explained. "Bioengineered self-replicating guerrilla soldiers, dropped here kind of by mistake a long time ago. They've been in hiding mostly, waiting for a signal or other stimuli to activate. Certain frequencies of radiowaves will do it, and the growth of cell phone use. . . ."

"So what, vampires get irritated by cell phones?"

A smile started to curl up one side of her mouth. I smiled too, and kept talking.

"You see, way back when, there were these good aliens and these bad aliens, and there was a gigantic space battle—"

Jenny started laughing.

"Do you want me to do a personality test before I can hear the rest of the story?"

"I think you'd pass," I said. I had tried to make her laugh, even though it was kind of true about the aliens and the space battle. Only there were just bad aliens and even worse aliens, and the vampires had been dropped on Earth by mistake. They had been meant for a world where the nights were very long.

Jenny kept laughing and looked down, just for an instant. I moved at my highest speed—and she died laughing, the splinter working instantly on both the human nervous system and the twenty-four-hour-old infestation of vampire nanoware.

We had lost the war, which was why I was there, cleaning up one of our mistakes. Why I would be on Earth for countless years to come.

I felt glad to have my straightforward purpose, my assigned task. It is too easy to become involved with humans, to want more for them, to interfere with their lives. I didn't want to make the boss's mistake. I'm not human and I don't want to become human or make them better people. I was just going to follow orders, keep cleaning out the infestation, and that was that.

The bite was low on Jenny's neck, almost at the shoulder. I showed it to the VET people and asked them to do the rest.

I didn't stay to watch. My arm hurt, and I could hear a girl laughing, somewhere deep within my head.

THE HEART OF THE CITY

Gerard MacNeacail, lieutenant in the Garde Écossaise of His Majesty King Henri IV of France, stamped his feet to warm them, his red-daubed, gilt-spurred boot heels smashing through a remnant sheet of ice that lay in the shadowed curve of the bastion, where he stood in an attempt to stay out of the way of the morning traffic that crowded the Pont Neuf.

MacNeacail was trying to be inconspicuous, an effort doomed to failure from the beginning. He was one of the tallest people in Paris, standing six foot four inches in his stockings, and his hair and beard were as bright as a burning hayrick, a legacy of his Scottish heritage, for all that he was of the fourth generation to serve a French king and had never even seen the Western Isles.

In addition to his remarkable height and the brightness of his hair and beard, MacNeacail had incautiously opened his cloak, revealing to any curious onlooker that he wore the saffron-yellow doublet of the Scottish Guard, its upper sleeves slashed to show the cream shirt beneath; he had a sword on his right side and *main gauche* on his left, indicating that he was left-handed; and there were two pistols thrust through his belt. To cap off this imposing appearance, several angel-blessed charms in the shape of gold bees hung from the brim of his broad felt hat.

"A monk," remarked his shorter, darker, more handsome, and better-proportioned companion, who was similarly attired but had not opened his cloak, as he felt that the winter sun had not sufficiently warmed the air and, though known for his bravery, was always concerned for his health. This was Armand de Vitray, a fellow lieutenant in the Scottish Guard, and a close companion. Like MacNeacail's dead father, his own parent had been one of the guardsmen who had saved the King from the madman Ravaillac fifteen years earlier, an event commemorated by the bronze equestrian statue that rose out of the river on its own foundation and abutted the bridge some forty feet away, opposite the entrance to the Place Dauphine.

"A monk astride a white horse, being led by a scarlet woman," continued De Vitray. There was a popular legend to the effect that if you stood on the Pont Neuf long enough, you would eventually see a monk, a white horse, and a prostitute—but not at the same time and certainly not traveling together, as appeared to be the case with this unlikely trio.

"*Abbé?*" MacNeacail asked the grey-clad ecclesiastical gentleman who was peering over the side to the waters of the Seine below, a small silver object that might be a pocket watch—a Nuremberg egg, perhaps—in his hand. "Is that significant?"

The *abbé*, who was an incessantly cheerful Irish Jesuit priest by the name of Cathal Gallagher, turned swiftly around, tucking the silver object into the silk gauntlet cuff of his right glove. He peered through the crowd upon the bridge, gaze darting over the ox cart laden with something noisome, between the three mules carrying sacks of dye, and then without pause over the heads of many pedestrians of every stripe, quality, and persuasion, before fixing on this unusual embodiment of the popular myth.

"Monk, white horse, whore," muttered Gallagher. "It must draw near . . . strange, I had thought there was a vibration upon the river . . . *Shelalhael,* are you here? *Shelalhael?*"

The three in the bastion heard no answer, but Gallagher suddenly pointed, and MacNeacail and De Vitray saw the equestrian statue stamp its bronze foreleg twice, and the bee charms in the Scotsman's hat gave a warning murmur. An angel was present, ready to work magic at the Irishman's behest.

"Warn your men," said Gallagher. "The monk, the woman, and the horse may be only a warning, an indication that it comes."

"What . . . ah . . . exactly is *it*?" asked De Vitray.

Gallagher shook his head and shrugged, indicating that he knew but would not tell, which in anyone else would have driven De Vitray to issue an immediate challenge, priest or not, but Gallagher's smile assuaged the insult. Besides, he was not only a priest, he was also the Duc de Sully's agent, and Sully, despite the incessant plots against him, continued to be the chief minister and primary confidant of the King. Besides all that, Gallagher owed De Vitray twenty-seven *écus* lost playing *lansquenet* in the guardroom the night before.

"Secrets," muttered De Vitray. "Always secrets. No one tells me anything. Do you know, MacNeacail?"

"I do not wish to know," said MacNeacail. He took off his hat and waved it three times above his head. Throughout the crowd, along both stretches of the bridge, hats waved back in response. The number of people on the bridge was so great that this coordinated movement appeared to attract little attention, but immediately afterward, the pace of movement to either bank noticeably increased, and several itinerant booksellers toward the middle of the main span began to hurriedly pack their wares. One particularly perspicacious fellow—most likely a survivor of the religious wars and so finely attuned to trouble—didn't even bother to pack up, but immediately swung his tall basket onto his back, tucked several loose volumes under his arm, and loped away at a pace considerably faster than a normal walk.

MacNeacail carefully repositioned his hat so that it would not fall over his face should fighting commence—as had once occurred, to his eternal embarrassment—and loosened his sword. De Vitray pushed back his cloak and immediately coughed, wincing as he did so, as if struck by a sudden pleurisy.

Gallagher looked up at the windows of the house opposite, on the southwest corner of the Place Dauphine. No one else heard *Shelalhael* speak, but the angel's voice was clear inside the Irishman's head, sharp as a needle to the brain.

The garret window, on the right-hand side. A match is applied to a gun.

"Stand before us!" shouted Gallagher, and he saw his companion angel manifest itself in the air above the bridge, just as a small cannon fired from an upper window. White smoke billowed out, and there was the sound of hail upon shingles as two handfuls of old nails and broken iron spattered ineffectually against the angel's folded wings; or as most of those on the bridge saw it, simply fell short and rained down without effect upon the eastern parapet, as if discharged with insufficient powder.

For a few seconds, all was still, as if everyone on the bridge was held in thrall till the last echo of the cannon's boom should fade. After those few seconds, the quiet was replaced by a hubbub of urgent noise and activity.

"Guards!" shouted MacNeacail, pointing up at the house with his sword. "Seize that cannon!"

"Keep De Lartigue and Despreaux," muttered De Vitray, as if to the air. He didn't look at MacNeacail, but kept his gaze upon the populace of the bridge, most of whom were now in sudden flight to either bank or onto the Île de la Cité.

"Ah, De Lartigue and Despreaux!" called MacNeacail. "Stay, if you will."

Two guardsmen struggled toward him, beating a path through the terrified crowd with their sword-hilts, while the remaining dozen charged across the bridge to throw themselves in a fevered assault upon the bronze-studded door of the house in question, which opened a moment before the full weight of the soldiers could be brought to bear upon it. The two foremost fell inside and were promptly trampled by their fellows.

Amid the shouting, the screams of the panicked, and the general riot, it was noticeable that apart from the guardsmen, there were two distinct groups of travelers upon the bridge who did not take to their heels. The first of these was the trio of the monk, the white horse, and the flaxen-wigged prostitute, who had continued their steady way along the bridge, going against the tide of fleeing pickpockets, dog-barbers, peddlers, toothpullers, and less immediately identifiable Parisians, which flowed south.

The second, some hundred paces behind this trio, was an ox-drawn conveyance that plodded on its way, its driver unfazed by the fact that he alone of all the various drivers on the bridge had not only chosen to stay with his cart, but also to keep driving it. His team of four oxen was also unusual, in that they maintained their pace with equanimity, unlike the various horses, donkeys, and palanquin bearers who had either joined the rout or, in the case of the animals not free to do so, were kicking, rearing, and shrieking in their traces.

"Is that the cart?" asked MacNeacail cautiously. "Its load is much as described."

He referred to the description given to them some hours before, in the dark before dawn, by the Duc de Sully in the anteroom adjoining the King's bedchamber. Though he had not expected it to be drawn by oxen, the box upon the cart was at least sixteen feet long and six feet high, and it was curiously narrow, so that it did resemble an overlarge coffin. Apart from the driver's seat, the cart was shrouded in rough sackcloth that had been daubed here and there with mud, which to some might look as if the contents were agricultural, but to MacNeacail smacked of an ineffectual attempt at subterfuge.

"Yes . . ." replied Gallagher distractedly. He had a terrible headache, the result of getting his angel to perform a significant feat of magic, and he could feel a faint trickle of blood from his nose running down the back of his throat. It was difficult to concentrate, and he could no longer feel a strong connection to *Shelalhael*. "I have to sit down."

He slumped to the pavement and reached into his doublet to draw out a silver-chased flask of *eau de vie.*

MacNeacail looked down at Gallagher and frowned. While it was true that practitioners of angelic magic were extremely useful to have around, as for example when being fired upon from ambush, they had a regrettable tendency to fall over after they had worked what to him seemed to be only minor miracles. But then he had not seen the angel's protective wings, only the fall of shot.

"De Vitray and Despreaux," said MacNeacail. "You stop the oxcart. De Lartigue, we shall speak with this monk and his . . . attendant."

MacNeacail strode out as he spoke, his sword still in hand, and struck a pose in the center of the bridge, curling his rather thin moustache as an afterthought. De Lartigue stood beside him, with a pistol held ready, the lock pulled back.

"Stop!" called out MacNeacail when the woman was some ten feet distant. But she did not stop, and though her blond wig was capacious and partly shielded her face, he noted that the one eye he could see was fixed on the far end of the bridge, and she seemed unaware that he stood in her way.

"Stop, in the name of the King!" commanded MacNeacail again, when the whore was almost upon him, but she walked on, and even when he pushed his hand against her shoulder, she still kept trying to walk forward, her slippered feet tracing the same steps over and over again.

"She sleeps," said the monk, and he threw back his hood.

Both MacNeacail and De Lartigue retreated a step. The monk's eyes were silver and shone with an unearthly light, the feared and awful sign that indicated he was more than a common practitioner of angelic magic, much more—that he had entered into the closest possible bond with an angelic being, an angelic being who was not an entity of the first or second hierarchies, but of at least the third.

MacNeacail bowed clumsily, since he was still holding the woman back with one hand. He had no doubt that this was the man they had been sent to meet, with orders to escort him and whatever he had brought into the city, wherever he wished to go. He was sure of this, even though no mention had been made that the fellow was a monk. However, MacNeacail was used to following directives from the King or his right-hand man, the Duc de Sully, that were intentionally roundabout and thus could be easily denied or laughed away as the mistake of a well-intentioned but youthful officer.

"But I am not always a monk," said the man. "I might have chosen to appear in a different guise."

He smiled thinly, at some private joke, then continued, "So no one could have told you to expect a monk."

MacNeacail felt a slight pain in his forehead, and his bee charms buzzed. He blinked rapidly, like an owl, or a prematurely awakened lackey, which was supposedly a method of preventing one's thoughts being read, while still continuing to see, which was preferable in the current case to the more foolproof method of screwing your eyes shut and looking the other way.

The pain lessened and the bees fell silent.

"Come, let us proceed," said the monk.

MacNeacail let his arm fall and stepped aside so that the woman could continue her somnambulic stroll. As she did so, her overlarge wig slipped a little to one side, and MacNeacail got a good look at her face.

"Irene Amytzantarants!" he exclaimed, gazing at her perfect, olive-skinned, oval face. She was one of the ladies-in-waiting to Helen Palaeologus, the niece of the Byzantine Emperor, who had married the Dauphin Louis three years previously. Though Louis still lived with his mother at the Luxembourg Palace, he and the Dauphine Helen were frequent visitors to the Louvre, and MacNeacail had been conducting inconclusive flirtations with several of the ladies-in-waiting, including Irene, who was herself a noblewoman of high distinction in the vast empire of the Greeks.

"A noblewoman, certainly, but also an agent of Constantine," said the monk. "She found me at Etampes last night and sought to divert me from my course."

MacNeacail frowned but didn't bother to blink, as there seemed little point in trying to resist. Now he had a nasty, vertical headache that was forcing its way from the back of his head out through his right eye.

"Where do you want—" MacNeacail started to ask, but he had to stop as the bees on his hat vibrated so much they began to bounce and clang against one another, reacting far more vigorously than they would to the simple act of mind-reading.

"Ventre gris!" swore the monk, and he twisted around on his horse to look behind him. "Protect the cart!"

As he did so, Irene stopped, cried out something in a language MacNeacail recognized as Greek but could not understand, looked down at her immodest scarlet dress in surprise, then clapped her hands to her wig, finding that also to be an unwelcome addition to her ensemble. She was about to throw it off when she stopped and instead pulled it down more firmly on top of her head, once more obscuring her features. Then she thrust herself against MacNeacail, insinuating herself into a one-armed embrace, though he managed to keep his sword-arm free.

"Monsieur MacNeacail," gasped Irene. "You must help me. I do not know how I came to be here, save by some foul magic."

MacNeacail was unable to immediately answer this appeal, as De Lartigue stepped past him and fired his pistol, the report of the shot immediately followed by shouts and the clash of steel. Over by the ox cart, De Vitray and Despreaux were beset by half a dozen small, masked bravos who, while no taller than children, had extraordinarily long arms and elegant tails that twitched and pounced behind them. More of these creatures, who wielded poniards and hatchets, were climbing over the side of the bridge, to advance upon the beleaguered guardsmen.

"Alas, I have my duty," said MacNeacail. Pushing her away, he pulled the wig firmly down over Irene's face, turned her about, and projected her in the direction of Father Gallagher, who had just managed to get to his feet.

"Secure her!" MacNeacail shouted over his shoulder as he ran toward the combat. The monk had caracoled his horse about at the same time, and was just ahead of him.

"To me!" roared De Vitray, swinging his sword like a scythe, as the bravos crowded him from all sides. Despreaux was already down, ashen-faced, with a poniard in his leg above the knee and his blood running to the gutter.

MacNeacail ran faster, extending his sword arm, and then—he felt a rush of wind, far greater than even the notably errant airs encountered on the bridge. His hat sailed off his head, the bee charms spread gossamer wings and took flight back toward him, and the tailed bravos shot into the sky, chattering and screaming as the breeze carried them higher and higher till they were lost in the winter clouds.

The monk pulled his hood forward once more. As he did so, MacNeacail shivered, for he saw the shadow of a vast wing move across the bridge, in unison with that motion.

"Thank you," said De Vitray, doffing his hat to the monk. "I daresay I would have managed, but—ah, Despreaux!"

Despreaux, pale as a ghost, lay upon the pavement, a slight, philosophical smile upon his face. He tried to raise his head as De Vitray bent down and ripped off his sleeve to fasten a bandage, but failed and fell back.

"Dead," remarked De Vitray. "He always did neglect his guard."

He turned his companion slightly, revealing the dagger thrust to the kidney that had finished him, though he would likely not have survived the leg wound in any case, unless one of the angels about had chosen to intervene, which they hardly ever did. Those angels who chose mortal companions were usually of the most combative sort, and were not known for their interest in the fragility of the flesh that clad immortal souls.

"It is such an annoyance to have to cross this particular bridge at the appointed hour, particularly when everyone knows it," said the monk.

"Everyone?" asked MacNeacail. He himself had no idea what the monk was talking about, though it had already cost Despreaux's life.

"Everyone concerned in the current matter," said the monk. "That is to say, His Majesty the King and those who serve him; the Dauphin Louis; the Dauphine Helen, or rather her uncle, the Emperor Constantine; the Spanish whose soldier-monkeys they were, brought from the Americas; the English; the Pope; and I suspect, the Dauphin's adviser, Cardinal Richelieu."

"*Cardinal* Richelieu?" asked MacNeacail. "He was only an Archbishop yesterday."

"He has his hat," said the monk. "It will be all the news of Paris by tomorrow. Come. We have to get the cart out of the sun. It must be kept cold."

MacNeacail looked up. There was little sun to speak of, and he did not like to think what might be in the coffin-shaped box on the cart that needed to be cold.

"If everyone does know it, monseigneur, why cross the bridge at this time?"

MacNeacail called him "monseigneur" because it seemed fitting but also from caution. Whoever this man was, he was not a mere monk. Apart from the powerful angel who kept him company, there was a look about him that seemed familiar. Something about the nose reminded MacNeacail very much of His Majesty the King, and at the back of his not very retentive mind he dimly remembered some story about a cousin who had taken holy orders.

"Ritual," replied the monk. "It is as the ancient ceremony dictates. Summon your men. We will need them to carry it inside."

MacNeacail wanted to ask about the "ancient ceremony" and investigate exactly what "it" and "inside" might mean, but he knew better. Instead, he looked up at the house in the Place Dauphine, and saw one of his men in the window.

"Cauvignac! What occurs?"

"We have been fighting apes, or perhaps monkeys, I know not what to call them!" called down Cauvignac. "They had a falconet, but lacked practice in reloading."

"Come down!" ordered MacNeacail. Already the braver citizens of the city were venturing back onto the bridge, emboldened perhaps by the distant drumming that announced that a force was marshalling in the Châtelet upstream on the right bank, and would soon—but not too soon, due to the innate caution of the city watch of the Prévôt des Marchands—march forth to investigate the disturbance.

He also belatedly noticed the flash of a scarlet dress as Irene Amytzantarants left the northern end of the bridge and disappeared down the steps to the quay. Gallagher, who he had supposed to be detaining her, instead appeared on the other side of the horse and bowed his head most subserviently to kiss a ring on the monk's hand, which confirmed MacNeacail's wisdom in using a polite address.

"I beg your pardon, monseigneur," said MacNeacail, striding around the horse's head. He bent down to Gallagher's ear and whispered, "Where is Ir . . . the woman? I told you to secure her!"

"I am a priest," Gallagher whispered back. "I cannot be holding on to harlots and whores."

MacNeacail chose not to respond to this, though knowing Gallagher as he did, he could offer several examples of occasions when the Jesuit had chosen to be less the priest and more the man, for example quite recently with a certain young and beautiful widow who favored the Irishman for her confessions. Besides, he knew it was probably more to do with politics than the public display of a suitably holy aversion to women. Irene, and more importantly her mistress the Dauphine, would now owe the priest a favor for letting her go.

"The woman is not important," said the monk. "You must bring the cart to a house on the northern end of the rue de Harlay, just short of the quay. There are carvings of orange trees around the door. Bring the box inside. I must go ahead and open the way. Quickly now!"

"At once!" cried MacNeacail. He ran back to the cart and leaped onto the driver's seat, but almost fell off again when the fellow emerged from beneath it and took up the reins.

"Through there!" commanded MacNeacail, pointing to the entrance to the Place Dauphine. The driver grunted and rolled his eyes insolently, but MacNeacail didn't notice, distracted by his guardsmen who were emerging from the house. He called out to them to fall in around the cart, while he stood next to the driver and struck a commanding pose. It was his habit to do so, acting upon the deathbed instruction of his father, who had told him to take the high ground at every opportunity and make himself obvious. That way, according to the older MacNeacail, he would be noticed. If noticed by enemies, they would be drawn into acting against him so that they could then be defeated; if noticed by friends, they would rally to him; and if noticed by superiors, they would see his actions, which might then lead to rewards and honor.

Gallagher and De Vitray picked up Despreaux's corpse. The priest muttered a prayer as they carried him into the house on the Place Dauphine that had housed the monkey-soldiers' cannon, and instructed the householder to keep the dead guardsman's body and possessions safe, upon pain of having his house ransacked and destroyed by the entire Scottish Guard. The man, a water merchant already terrified at the prospect of retribution for unwittingly allowing his attic to be infested with enemies of the state, bowed and groveled and promised the utmost care.

As the cart trundled through the Place Dauphine with a file of guardsmen on either side, MacNeacail looked back at the mud-washed sacking. One corner was torn, revealing a finely shaped and inlaid panel of chestnut and ebony, and this made whatever lay upon the cart's axles look even more like a coffin. A very large coffin, made for a giant.

"To the left," instructed MacNeacail as they approached the rue de Harlay. This time he did see the driver roll his eyes, and awarded him a judicious blow to the head for insolence.

"Thank 'ee, sir," croaked the driver. He ceased to roll his eyes and passed on his punishment by flicking his whip across the backs of the oxen, who paid it no more heed than they did the flies that clustered in columns along their ridged backs.

The house with the carvings of orange trees was the second-to-last one before the quay. The white horse was tied up outside it, and the door was open, but there was no sign of the monk. The oxcart stopped outside the door, the oxen lowering their heads in dumb obedience to their driver, who immediately jumped down and began to pull the sacking away to reveal the ornate, polished box.

MacNeacail swung himself casually off the cart and glanced inside the doorway. He was surprised to see not an entrance hall or room, but a garden. The house was a mere shell, without a roof or upper floors. The high, windowless stone walls enclosed a narrow but very long paved courtyard that had two lines of bare, ancient olive trees, one down either side. At the far end, the monk kneeled in front of an ancient standing stone that had a cross crudely carved into its granite surface.

"Make haste!" ordered the monk, without looking back.

"Curious," muttered De Vitray, who had to peer past MacNeacail's elbow, as he could not see over his shoulder. "A very secret garden. I wonder—"

"Best not to wonder," warned MacNeacail.

He turned about and negligently waved at the box, as if it were a handkerchief or something he had left behind on a chair.

"Cauvignac! Montausier! All you fellows. Be kind enough to bring that box over here."

The guardsmen looked at him in surprise. Carry a box as if they were lackeys, rather than noblemen serving in the Scottish Guard of His Majesty? Impossible!

MacNeacail knew this, and was drawing breath to attempt a rephrased and cajoling rendition of the same request, when Gallagher, smiling as ever, got in first.

"Gentlemen! This is not some mere box! It contains a holy relic of great importance to His Majesty the King and to France. In usual times it is borne on the shoulders only of princes of the blood, but in the present circumstances, noble birth shall suffice."

"Why didn't you say so!" exclaimed Cauvignac to MacNeacail.

MacNeacail sighed and looked suspiciously at Gallagher, but he couldn't tell whether the tale of the holy relic was the truth or some invention. At the same time he was trying to remember long-forgotten sermons and readings of scripture. Was there a saint who was a giant whose body had been preserved by some miracle? Or was that a children's story his nurse had once told him?

The task being properly explained, the dozen guardsmen made short work of lifting the box from the cart. Taking it on their shoulders, they carefully followed MacNeacail and Gallagher into the courtyard. De Vitray shivered as he crossed the threshold and drew his cloak tightly around his neck. It was much colder inside, though the roofless courtyard was no more shaded than the street.

Close to the standing stone, MacNeacail noticed that the worn grey pavers underfoot became a faded but still wonderful mosaic, partly obscured by dirt. He could not pause to inspect it, but from surreptitious glances down as he trod over it, he took in a narrative of some kind, the mosaic telling a story of the construction of a city, dealings between angels and men, a titanic battle, and all of it ending near the stone with a glorious sunburst, the disc of the sun immediately beneath the kneeling monk.

The monk crossed himself and stood to receive the guardsmen and their burden.

"Lift it up," he instructed. "Set the foot of it here, upon the sun."

The guardsmen did as they were told, lifting one end of the box so it stood upright, like a small, narrow house and less like a coffin.

"Strip the sacking away," said the monk.

With the sacking torn off, the box was revealed to be of very fine construction, rich chestnut panels bordered with ebony and a large fleur-de-lis in coromandel wood, ivory, and gold leaf set in the middle of the front panel.

It also had bronze hinges on three edges, and a huge latch upon the other.

"It is a cabinet!" exclaimed De Vitray.

"Indeed," said the monk. "De Vitray, is it not?"

"Yes, monseigneur," replied De Vitray, puffing out his chest at being recognized.

"Take your men and guard the doorway. Allow no one to enter without my word. MacNeacail, you will remain here with Father Gallagher."

De Vitray doffed his hat and bowed, but did not say anything, as he was no longer pleased. He snapped out a command and stalked off to the doorway, without a backward glance, the other guards following. Most of them did look back, as they wished to see what might be in the case.

"Welcome to the heart of the city, gentlemen," said the monk.

"This is the heart of Paris?" asked MacNeacail. He looked around again at the bare walls and the bare trees. "Surely not?"

"Since time immemorial," snapped the monk. "Do you take me for an idiot?"

"I beg your pardon," said MacNeacail. He bowed in some confusion and would have doffed his hat, but he'd forgotten to pick it up. The bee charms, which were now attached to his hair, rustled as his fingers brushed them.

"No matter," said the monk. "It has been a long journey, and I am tired. Please, gentlemen, open the cabinet."

MacNeacail and Gallagher undid the latch and eased the front of the cabinet open. A wave of chill flowed out, even colder than the winter air. This unnatural frost intensified as they pulled the sides of the cabinet fully open to reveal that what lay inside the box was not the body of a giant saint, as MacNeacail had suspected, but a throne. An immense throne carved out of a single block of ice, the back and arms covered in lines and lines of tiny incised letters in an alphabet that MacNeacail didn't even recognize, let alone was able to read.

"The throne of ice of the Parisii," whispered Gallagher as he stepped back. "I had never thought to see it."

MacNeacail nodded dumbly. He had never even heard of it, but he was impressed.

"Step back," warned the monk. "We must not touch the throne until after the ceremony."

MacNeacail stepped back quickly. Gallagher lingered for a moment, then came to stand by him. The monk pushed back his hood and the sleeves of his habit, and kneeled before the throne. He muttered a short prayer, then stood up and raised his arms. As he did so, dark shapes moved up the walls, the broad shadow of spreading wings. MacNeacail's bee charms huddled closer together in his hair, but did not buzz.

"*Bellinus*! Protector of the city! I, Charles de Guise, a prince of the blood and Archbishop, with my companion *Ophaniel*, bring you the throne of ice!"

MacNeacail backed away another step and almost fell over Father Gallagher. As he did so, the bee charms in his hair buzzed in alarm. Gallagher pushed him upright and looked around wildly, his expression distant. He fumbled in his glove for the silver object and flipped open its cover. This time MacNeacail saw it was a watch, but instead of hands, it had a silver cross mounted on the central dial. The cross spun wildly and then pointed at the blank wall to the south.

"*Shelalhael* . . ." whispered Gallagher. "What occurs? Show me . . . ah!"

He bent down on one knee. Blood gushed from his nose as he looked up at the monk and cried out, "There is a tunnel dug from the house opposite, they have placed a mine . . . another angel opposes—"

Gallagher gave a gargled, choking cough and fell forward to the ground.

The monk still faced the throne, his arms stretched up to the sky in supplication. But the shadow of the wings disappeared, and the southern wall suddenly rippled, as if all the bricks were momentarily water and something had dived through.

"*Bellinus*! We keep the compact!" called out the monk, in a parched, high voice. He slowly sank to his knees, and his arms quavered closer to his head, as if he were trying to hold up a great weight. Then he collapsed, and a trickle of blood ran from the corner of his mouth to the foot of the throne of ice.

MacNeacail was left alone in the courtyard. Both the monk and Gallagher were unconscious, and their angels thus no longer present, or at least no longer acting under the persuasion of their mortal companions. Gallagher had muttered something about a mine, but there was nothing he could do to stop that exploding, if the fuse was already lit on the other side of the wall.

It was very quiet. The bees were completely still, and he could not even hear the usual, muffled noises of the city beyond.

Man, said a voice inside his head.

MacNeacail turned around and then quickly looked down at the ground, blinking furiously. There was something on the throne of ice now, something that he could not gaze directly upon, though it was not bright, but simply too terrible to behold.

Man? said the thing upon the throne.

"Yes," mumbled MacNeacail. He edged sideways and prodded the monk with the toe of his boot, hoping desperately that he would return to his senses. Or that Gallagher would recover, that some priest used to dealing with angels could speak to—

But I am not an angel.

"Oh dear Father in heaven," whispered MacNeacail. It must be a demon. He reversed his sword and held it by the blade, the hilt in front of him to make a cross. "Save me."

Not like Shelalhael *or* Ophaniel, *who flutter about me here. Long ago, the Parisii called me a god. Later, in the book Enoch wrote, he named me Archangel.*

This revelation did not calm MacNeacail, but he did take up a more usual grip on his sword.

Are you to conclude the compact?

MacNeacail kicked the monk harder, no matter that he was a prince of the blood.

Are you to conclude the compact?

"Ah, yes," said MacNeacail.

But you do not know how.

"No . . . I do not."

It is simple enough. The throne of ice is my worldly temple. When I am called to inhabit my temple, my worshippers may ask my favor. It is usual to ask me to protect the city for whoever rules it, or wishes to do so. That is the compact I made long ago, MacNeacail.

"You know my name now?"

He sensed the archangel's amusement. It was like remembering an uncle's distinctive laugh from some festive occasion of his childhood, something forgotten that had risen to the surface, unbidden.

I have looked inside your head, Gerard MacNeacail. It has been a very long time since I looked inside a mortal's head. . . .

"MacNeacail . . ."

It was the monk, spitting blood-specked foam from his lips as he spoke.

"Tell *Bellinus* to protect the city in the name of His Majesty, King Louis! Quickly! The English prepare to fire their mine!"

"But Louis is not yet king!" protested MacNeacail. "I serve King Henri!"

"Fool!" hissed the monk. "Henri is sick and dying. You must—"

Whatever the monk was going to say was lost in a titanic blast of noise and fury. MacNeacail was knocked down by the explosion, and then as he struggled to get up, the earth gave way beneath his feet and he was drawn down into a newborn ravine that extended from the collapsing southern wall to just underneath the mosaic. Bricks rained down around him as he struggled to claw his way out of the dirt.

Just as he got his upper body free of the gripping soil, the throne of ice slowly toppled over and fell upon him. MacNeacail had only a moment to twist and roll so that he was in front of the seat, instead of being instantly crushed to death by the back or the lower half of the throne.

But that meant he was balled up in a hole in the ground, under a huge block of ice, and he shared that small, shifting space with the awful, unknowable thing that was *Bellinus.*

He did not look at it, and he shrank away from it the little distance that he could.

So the compact is no more, said *Bellinus*. *I shall return to* ★★★★★★★★★★★★.

The last word was not something MacNeacail could comprehend. Hearing it created a pressure inside his head, such a pressure that he thought his skull would explode and his eyes burst like punctured wineskins. But he knew he had a duty to perform. He must somehow make *Bellinus* remain, to protect the city, in the name of the King.

"Stay," he said, and reached out, as if he might hold the angel back.

As he touched it, MacNeacail's heart stopped. He felt it halt, felt the sudden absence of rhythm. A terrible pain filled his chest and he tried to scream, but only a pathetic, rattling croak came out.

An instant later, he died.

The pain and the bewilderment immediately stopped, and MacNeacail felt the sudden warmth of summer sun on his skin, welcome after the long winter. He stood up out of his body, left the hole, and walked up an unseen slope into the sky.

He looked down as he climbed, watching his friends engage the Englishmen who had emerged through the hole in the wall. The monk, or rather, Charles de Guise, lay with his head crushed under one corner of the throne, very evidently dead. Gallagher was alive, on his knees, digging furiously at the middle of the throne. Curiously, MacNeacail could now also see *Shelalhael*, hovering in the air above the priest.

The guardsmen had the Englishmen well in hand, MacNeacail noted with approval. The enemy had obviously mistimed the mine, since most were blackened and in rags, and kept falling over, their balance lost with deafness. It was surprising, given their national fascination with blowing things up, but perhaps De Guise's angel had intervened.

The dueling figures below got rapidly smaller as MacNeacail found himself several hundred feet above the courtyard and rising, giving him a hawk's-eye view of the city. There was still quite a commotion on the Pont Neuf. It appeared that the troops of the city watch had thought a common disturbance was in progress and in their attempts to quell the imagined uproar had actually started a riot. A barge had also run into one of the piers, though this was probably the method of delivery for the Spanish monkey-soldiers. Behind him, the great bourdon bell of Notre Dame was tolling, though whether this was for the riot or to mark the hour, he did not know.

Very well, said *Bellinus*, inside MacNeacail's head.

"What?" asked MacNeacail idly. He could not see *Bellinus*, but he could sense his presence. The archangel was next to him, one great wing brushing his shoulder. The nearness did not trouble him now, nor did anything else. He felt completely calm, more so than he had ever done before.

I will stay.

MacNeacail screamed as the pain came back and he plummeted earthward like a flung stone, far faster than he had risen. Inside an instant, he was back in his body, and pressed into the mud, with the rapidly melting throne of ice above him.

There is work to be done upon you, said *Bellinus*.

The pain in his chest went away and with a galvanic thump, MacNeacail's heart started to beat. He sighed in relief, then screamed again as his eyes were burned by a terrible fire, a fire that entered into his brain and threatened to entirely consume everything that defined his consciousness and identity.

It is complete.

With these words, the pain disappeared, leaving MacNeacail sobbing, choking, and threshing in a pool of mud. Water was flooding over his face, and the dread of drowning lent him strength as he tried to claw a tunnel out from under the ice. Then he felt a hand brush his, and he gripped it with panicked strength and so was drawn out of his entombment by Father Gallagher.

Leaving MacNeacail gasping facedown on the flagstones, Gallagher kneeled beside him and whispered urgently, "Did De Guise reaffirm the compact? In whose name?"

The Scotsman coughed or almost vomited up a mouthful of dirty water, then slowly turned his head. The priest gasped and bit the knuckle of his hand, rapidly crossed himself, then tore a broad strip from his sleeve and bound it tight around MacNeacail's eyes.

"What . . . what are you doing?" rasped MacNeacail. He reached up to strip the blindfold away, but stopped as he saw that it did not impede his vision. He could see straight through the cloth.

Hiding our eyes, said Bellinus. *Our silver eyes.*

"Silver . . . my eyes . . . but I am not a priest. . . ."

I have decided to accompany you, MacNeacail. We shall look after the city together.

"Is *Bellinus* with you?" whispered Gallagher. He was holding the silver egg. The cross was whirring around the dial like the vanes of a storm-swept windmill.

MacNeacail nodded slowly.

"Say nothing to anyone!" said Gallagher.

"I don't . . . I don't understand what has happened," said MacNeacail.

"The impossible," said Gallagher shortly. "An ancient entity— one some would call an archangel—has chosen to companion you, which has not occurred for a thousand years, and you are not even ordained! And the angel is *Bellinus*, the guardian of Paris! The city has lost its greatest defender! We must go to Cardinal Richelieu, he has great knowledge of angelic—"

"No," said MacNeacail. He looked at Gallagher and saw into his subtle mind, saw all the cunning schemes and stratagems that the priest was part of, and the multiple masters he served, as he prepared for the passing of Henri and the decline of Sully, and the consequent rise of Louis, the Dauphine Helen, and her Cardinal. "We must go to the King. Whatever has happened to me, I am still the King's man."

He slowly stood up and looked around. De Vitray was standing upon the rubble of the breached wall, supervising the guardsmen as they dispatched the mortally wounded Englishmen and tied up the survivors. The throne of ice had almost entirely melted, so that there was merely a muddy waterhole where it had been.

Only part of the mosaic had survived. A sliver of the sun, smeared with mud.

"For such a city," MacNeacail said. "It is very small, this heart."

It is not the heart that makes a city, said *Bellinus*. *It is the head.*

"Where is the head?" asked MacNeacail. He thought of the Louvre, where the King resided, though the power there was fading as Henri sank toward his death.

It is not a place, answered the archangel. *It is all the people. Come, let us walk amongst them. It is long since I looked at Paris through mortal eyes.*

MacNeacail nodded and clutched at Gallagher's shoulder. He felt the priest flinch, and *Shelalhael* also, as they felt some small part of the power of *Bellinus* in his touch.

"Lead me," he said, for he knew there was sense in Gallagher's warning to keep his eyes bound. "Let us look upon the city, as we go to see the King."

AMBROSE AND THE ANCIENT SPIRITS OF EAST AND WEST

Ambrose Farnington was not particularly well equipped to live an ordinary life. An adventurer in the Near East before the Great War, the war itself had seen him variously engaged in clandestine and very cold operations in the mountains between Turkey and Russia; commanding an infantry battalion in France and Belgium; and then, after almost a day buried in his headquarters dugout in the company of several dead and dismembered companions, as a very fragile convalescent in a nursing home called Grandway House in Lancashire.

Most recently, a year of fishing and walking near Fort William had assisted the recovery begun under the care of the neurasthenic specialists at Grandway, and by the early months of 1920 the former temporary Lieutenant-Colonel Farnington felt that he was almost ready to reemerge into the world. The only question was in what capacity. The year in the Scottish bothy with only his fishing gear, guns, and a borrowed dog for company had also largely exhausted his ready funds, which had been stricken by his remaining parent's ill-timed death, his father putting the capstone on a lifetime of setting a very bad example by leaving a great deal of debt fraudulently incurred in his only child's name.

Ambrose considered the question of his finances and employment as he sorted through the very thin pile of correspondence on the end of the kitchen table he was using as a writing desk. The bothy had been lent to him, with the dog, and though both belonged to Robert Cameron, a very close friend from his days at Peterhouse

College in Cambridge, his continued presence there prevented the employment of bothy and dog by a gamekeeper who would usually patrol the western borders of Robert's estate. Besides, Ambrose did not wish to remain a burden on one of the few of his friends who was still alive.

It was time to move on, but the question was on to what and where?

"I should make an appreciation of my situation and set out my qualities and achievements, Nellie," said Ambrose to the dog, who was lying down with her shaggy head on his left foot. Nellie raised one ear, but made no other movement, as Ambrose unscrewed his pen and set out to write on the back of a bill for a bamboo fishing rod supplied by T. H. Sowerbutt's of London.

"Item One," said Ambrose aloud. "At twenty-nine, not excessively aged, at least by time. Item Two, in possession of rude physical health and . . . let us say . . . in a stable mental condition, provided no underground exercise is contemplated. Item Three, a double-starred First in Latin and Greek, fluent in Urdu, Classical Persian, Arabic, Spanish, French, German; conversant with numerous other languages, etc. Item Four, have traveled and lived extensively in the Near East, particularly Turkey and Persia. Item Five, war service . . ."

Ambrose put down his pen and wondered what he should write. Even though he would burn his initial draft on completion, he was still reluctant to mention his work for D-Arc. Even the bare facts were secret, and as for the details, very few people would believe them. Those people who would believe were the ones he was most worried about. If certain practitioners of some ancient and occult studies discovered that he was Agent Çobanaldatan, the man who had so catastrophically halted that ceremony high on the slopes of Ziyaret Dağı, then . . .

"I suppose if I am not too specific, it can't matter," Ambrose said to Nellie. He picked up the pen again, and continued to speak aloud as he wrote.

"Where was I . . . war service . . . 1914 to 1915. Engaged by a department of the War Office in reconnaissance operations in the region of . . . no, best make it 'the East.' Returned in 1916, posted to KRRC, rose to brevet Lieutenant-Colonel by May 1918, commanded the 8th Battalion, wounded 21st September, 1918, convalescent leave through to 5th March, 1919 . . . no, that looks bad, far too long, will just make it 'after convalescent leave' resigned temporary commission . . . how do I explain this last year? Writing a paper on the Greek inscriptions near Erzerum or something, I suppose, I do have one I started in '09. . . . Let's move on. . . ."

He paused as Nellie raised both ears and tilted her head toward the door. When she gave a soft whine and stood up, Ambrose pushed his chair back and went to the window. Gently easing the rather grimy curtain aside, he looked out, up toward the rough track that wound down from the main road high on the ridge above.

A car was gingerly making its way down toward the bothy, proceeding slowly and relatively quietly in low gear, though not quietly enough to fool Nellie. It was a maroon sedan of recent European make, and it was not a car that he knew. To get here, the driver had either picked or more likely cut off the bronze Bramah padlocks on both the upper gate to the road and the one in the wall of the middle field.

Quickly, but with measured actions, Ambrose went to the gun cabinet, unlocked it with one of the keys that hung on his heavy silver watch-chain, and took out his service revolver. He quickly loaded it and put the weapon and another five cartridges in the voluminous right pocket of his coat, his father's sole useful legacy, an ugly purple-and-green tweed shooting jacket that was slightly too large.

He hesitated in front of the cabinet, then, after a glance at Nellie and at a very old pierced bronze lantern that hung from a ceiling beam, he reached back into the cabinet for a shotgun. He chose the lightest of the four weapons there, a double-barrel four-ten. Unlike the other guns and against all his usual principles, it was already loaded, with rather special shot. Ambrose broke it, whispered, *"Melek kılıç şimdi bana yardım"* close to the breech, and snapped it closed.

The incantation would wake the spirits that animated the ammunition, but only for a short time. If whoever came in the maroon car was an ordinary visitor, the magic would be wasted, and he only had half a box of the shells left. But he did not think it was an ordinary visitor, though he was by no means sure it was an enemy.

Certainly, Nellie was growling, the hair up all along her back, and that indicated trouble. But the bronze lamp that Ambrose had found in the strange little booth in the narrowest alley of the Damascus bazaar, while it had lit of its own accord, was not burning with black fire. The flame that flickered inside was green. Ambrose did not yet know the full vocabulary of the oracular lantern, but he knew that green was an equivocal color. It signified the advent of some occult power, but not necessarily an inimical force.

Readying the shotgun, Ambrose went to the door. Lifting the bar with his left hand, he nudged the door open with his foot, allowing himself a gap just wide enough to see and shoot through. The car was negotiating the last turn down from the middle field, splashing through the permanent mud puddle as it came through the open gate and the narrow way between the partly fallen stone walls that once upon a time had surrounded the bothy's kitchen garden.

Ambrose could only see a driver in the vehicle, but that didn't mean there wouldn't be others lying low. He raised the shotgun and thumbed back both hammers, suddenly aware of a pulsing in his eardrums that came from his own racing heart. Nellie, next to his leg, snarled, but, well trained as she was, did not bark or lunge forward.

The maroon sedan stopped a dozen yards away. Past the gate, and within the walls of the garden, which might or might not be significant. When he had first moved in Ambrose had planted silver sixpences in every seventh stone, and buried three horseshoes in the gateway. That would deter most of the lesser powers, particularly those already distressed at being so far west of the old Giza meridian. Which meant that his visitor was either mundane or not one of the *lesser* powers that stalked the earth. . . .

The car door creaked open, backward, and a tall man in a long camel-colored coat with the collar up and a dark trilby pulled down over his ears hunched himself out, his arms and legs moving very oddly—a telltale sign that told Ambrose all he needed to know. As the curious figure lurched forward, Ambrose fired the left barrel at the man's chest and a split second later, the right barrel at his knees.

Salt splattered across the target and burst into flame where it hit. Hat and coat fell to the ground, and two waist-high creatures of shifting darkness sprang forward, salt-fires burning on and in their mutable flesh.

Ambrose pulled the door shut with one swift motion and slammed down the bar. Retreating to the gun cabinet, he reloaded the shotgun, this time speaking the incantation in a loud and almost steady voice.

A hissing outside indicated that the demons had heard the incantation and did not like it. For his part, Ambrose was deeply concerned that his first two shots had not disincorporated his foes, that they had freely crossed his boundary markers, and that they had gotten to his home without any sign of having aroused the ire of any of the local entities that would take exception to such an Eastern presence.

He looked around the single room of the bothy. The windows, though shut, were not shuttered, and there was probably not enough sunshine for the glass to act as mirrors and distract the demons. If they were strong enough to cross a silver and cold iron border, they would be strong enough to enter the house uninvited, though not eager, which was probably the only reason they had not yet broken down the door or smashed in a window—

Nellie barked and pointed to the fireplace. Ambrose spun around and fired both barrels as the demons came roaring out of the chimney. But even riddled with ensorcelled salt, the demons came on, shadowy maws snapping and talons reaching. Ambrose threw the now useless shotgun at them and dived to one side, toward the golf bag perched by his bed, as Nellie snarled and bit at the demons' heels.

Demon teeth closed on his calf as his hands closed on his weapon of last resort. Between the irons and the woods, Ambrose's fingers closed on the bone-inlaid hilt of the yataghan that bore the maker's mark of Osman Bey. Tumbling the golf bag over, he drew the sword and with two swift strokes, neatly severed the faint red threads that stood in the place of backbones in the demons, the silvered blade cutting through the creatures' infernal salt-pocked flesh as if it were no more than smoke.

The demons popped out of existence, leaving only a pair of three-foot lengths of scarlet cord. Nellie sniffed at them cautiously, then went to nose at Ambrose's leg.

"Yes, it got me, damn it," cursed Ambrose. "My own fault, mind you. Should have had the sword to hand, never mind how ridiculous it might have looked."

Ambrose looked over at the oracular lantern, which had gone out.

"Possibly inimical, my sweet giddy aunt," he muttered as he pushed down the sock and rolled up the leg of his plus fours. The skin was not broken, but there was a crescent-shaped bruise on his calf. Next to the bruise, the closest half inch of vein was turning dark and beginning to obtrude from the skin, and a shadow was branching out into the lesser blood vessels all around.

Ambrose cursed again, then levered himself upright and hobbled over to the large, leather-strapped portmanteau at the end of his bed. Flinging it open, he rummaged about inside, eventually bringing out a long strip of linen that was covered in tiny Egyptian hieroglyphics drawn in some dark red ink. Ambrose wrapped this around his calf, tapped it thrice, and spoke the revered name of Sekhmet, at which the hieroglyphics faded from the bandage and entered into his flesh, there to fight a holding battle against the demonic incursion, though it was unlikely that they would entirely vanquish the enemy without additional sorcerous assistance. Egyptian magic was older and thus more faded from the world, and though Ambrose had immersed the bandage on his last visit to the Nile, that had been many years before, so the hermetic connection was no longer strong.

Ambrose had nothing else that might work to hand. Nor was there anyone he could easily turn to for assistance. In fact, he thought wretchedly, there were only two possible sources of the kind of help he needed within a thousand miles. One he had hoped to stay away from, and the other was very difficult to reach without extensive and unusual preparations that would simply take too long.

"First things first," muttered Ambrose. Using the yataghan as a crutch, but also to keep it close to hand, he limped to the table. Lighting a match against the back of his chair, he applied it to the bill for the fishing rod and watched his recent appreciation crumble into ash, dousing the blaze with the last half inch of cold tea from his mug when it threatened to spread to the other papers.

"Just like the war," he said wearily to Nelly. "Bloody thing was obsolete as soon as I wrote it. I suppose I shall have to—"

Nellie lifted her ears.

Ambrose whipped around to check the oracular lantern. The flame had relit and was even higher now, burning red and gold, signifying danger, but not immediate, and allies. Not friends, but allies.

"I'm not trusting you," Ambrose said to the lantern. Still leaning on the yataghan, he retrieved his shotgun and reloaded it, though this time he did not speak the words. Nellie stayed by his side, her ears up and intent, but she was not growling.

As the sound of a car being driven a shade too fast for the rough track grew louder, Ambrose cautiously opened the door and looked out.

He was not very much surprised to see that the second car was a green Crossley 20/25, the usual choice of the Secret Service Bureau and so also of its even lesser-known offshoot, D-Arc. He even recognized the two men in the front, and could guess at the other two in the backseat. Nevertheless, he kept the shotgun ready as the Crossley skidded to a halt behind the maroon sedan and the men got out. Three of them, two with revolvers by their sides and one with a curiously archaic bell-mouthed musketoon, stayed close to the car, watching the bothy, the maroon car, and the hillside. The fourth, a man Ambrose knew as Major Kennett, though that was almost certainly not his real name, advanced toward the bothy's front door. The quartet were dressed for the city, not the country, and Ambrose suppressed a smile as Kennett lost a shoe in the mud and had to pause to fish around for it with a stockinged foot.

"I see we're a little late," said Kennett as he pulled at the heel of his shoe. He was a handsome man, made far less so as soon as you saw the chill that always dwelled in his eyes. "Sorry about that."

"Late for what?" asked Ambrose.

"Your earlier guests," answered Kennett. He held out his hand. After a moment, Ambrose balanced the shotgun over the crook of his left arm and shook hands.

"You knew they were coming?" asked Ambrose.

Kennett shook his head. "We knew something was coming. Quite clever, really. We've been keeping tabs on a private vessel for days, a very large motor yacht owned by our old friend the Emir and captained by Vladimir Roop. It docked at Fort William, the car was lowered, and off it went. Nothing . . . unwelcome . . . touched the earth, you see, and it's a hard top, windows shut, keeping out all that

Scottish air and lovely mist and those who travel with it."

"Did you know I was here?"

"Oh, yes," said Kennett. He looked past Ambrose, into the simple, single room of the bothy. "Rather basic, old boy. Takes you back, I suppose?"

"Yes, it does," said Ambrose, without rancor. Kennett, like most D-Arc operatives, was from an old and very upper-class family. Ambrose was not. Everything he had achieved had come despite his more difficult start in life. He had taken a long series of difficult steps that had begun with a scholarship to Bristol Grammar at the age of seven, the first part of a challenging journey that had taken him far, far away from the ever-changing temporary accommodations shared with his father, at least when that worthy was not in prison for his various "no-risk lottery" and "gifting circle" frauds.

"Each to his own," remarked Kennett. "I take it you've dealt with the visitors?"

"Yes."

"We'd best take you away then," said Kennett. "Lady S wants to have a word, and I expect you'll need that leg looked at. Demon bite, is it?"

"Lady S can go—" Ambrose bit back his words with an effort.

"Quite likely," replied Kennett. "I wouldn't be at all surprised. But I don't see the relevance. Lady S wants to see you, therefore you will be seen by her. Unless, of course, you want to stay here and turn into something that will have every Gaelic-speaking entity of wood, air, and river rising up to assail?"

"No," replied Ambrose. He knew when it was pointless to rail against fate. "I don't want that. Do we have to go all the way to London? I don't think I can make—"

"No, not at all," said Kennett. "Lady S is on a progress through the far-flung parts of the D-Arc realm. She's in Edinburgh, taking stock of our new medical advisor."

"New medical advisor?" asked Ambrose. "What happened to Shivinder?"

Kennett turned his cold, cold eyes to meet Ambrose's gaze, and held it for a second, which was sufficient reply. Whatever had happened to Dr. Shivinder, Ambrose would likely never know, and if he did find out by some accident of information, he would be best to keep it to himself.

"The new chap is quite the prodigy," said Kennett. "Oxford, of course, like all the best people."

Ambrose sighed and limped a step forward toward the car. There were tiny wisps of smoke issuing from under the hieroglyphic bandage as the small angels of Sekhmet fought the demonic infestation. While it wouldn't actually catch alight, the pain was quite intense, which was another sign that the demons were winning.

"Spare me the jibes," he said. "Can we just go?"

"Yes, we should toodle along, I suppose," said Kennett. "Jones and Jones will stay to secure the place, and they can bring your gear along later and so forth. Do we need to shoot the dog?"

Ambrose bent down, gasping with the pain, and took Nellie by the collar. Turning her head, he looked deeply into her trusting brown eyes, and then ran his hand over her back and legs, carefully checking for bites.

"No, she's clear," he said. "She can go back to the big house. Nellie! Big house!"

He pointed to the garden gate as he spoke. Nellie cocked her head at him, to make sure he was serious, yawned to show her lolloping red tongue, and slowly began to pick her way through the mud.

She had only gone a few yards when Kennett shot her in the back of the head with his revolver. The heavy Webley .455 boomed twice. The dog was shoved into the puddle by the force of the impact, her legs continuing to twitch and jerk there, even though she must have been killed instantly. Blood slowly swirled into the muddy water, steam rising as it spread.

Ambrose fumbled with his shotgun, swinging it to cover Kennett. But it was broken open, and Kennett was watching him, the revolver still in his hand.

"There was demon taint in her mouth," said Kennett, very matter-of-fact. "She wouldn't have lasted a day."

Ambrose shut his eyes for a moment. Then he nodded dully. Kennett stepped in and took the shotgun, but did not try to remove the yataghan that Ambrose used to lever himself upright.

"You're all right?" asked Kennett. "Operational? Capable?"

"I suppose so," said Ambrose, his voice almost as detached as Kennett's. He looked down at Nellie's body. Dead, just like so many of his friends, but life continued and he must make the best of it. That was the litany he had learned at Grandway House. He owed it to the dead, the dead that now included Nellie, to live on as best he could.

"Did you do that to test me? Did Lady S tell you to shoot my dog?"

"No," replied Kennett calmly. "I had no orders. But there was demon taint."

Ambrose nodded again. Kennett could lie better than almost anyone he knew, so well that it was impossible to know whether he spoke the truth or not, unless there was some undeniable evidence to the contrary. And there could have been demon taint. Of course, with the dog's head shattered by hexed silver fulminate exploding rounds, there was no possible way to check that now.

Leaning on his yataghan, Ambrose trudged to the standard issue departmental car. He had hoped to avoid any further involvement with D-Arc, but he had always known that this was a vain hope. Even when he had left the section the first time in 1916, escaping to regular service on the Western Front, there had still been occasional reminders that D-Arc was watching him and might reel him in at any time. Like the odd staff officer with the mismatched eyes, one blue and one green, who never visited anyone else's battalion in the brigade, but often dropped in on Ambrose. Always on one of the old, old festival days, sporting a fresh-cut willow crop, a spray of holly, or bearing some odd bottle of mead or elderberry wine. Ambrose's adjutant and the battalion's second-in-command called him "the botanist" and thought he was just another red-tabbed idiot wandering about. But Ambrose knew better.

Once in the car, Ambrose retreated almost immediately into a yogic trance state, to slow the effects of the demon bite. Possibly even more helpfully, it stopped him thinking about Nellie and the long roll call of dead friends, and as it was not sleep, he did not dream. Instead he experienced himself traveling without movement over an endless illusory landscape made up of Buddhist sutras.

Ambrose came out of this trance to find that the car had stopped. He looked out the window and saw that the sun was setting. The gas lamps had just been lit, but it was still quite bright enough for him to work out that they had reached Edinburgh, and after a moment, he recognized the street. They were in South Charlotte Square, outside what at first glance appeared to be a hotel, till he saw a discreet brass plate by the front door that read "St. Agnes Nursing Home."

"New Scottish office, more discreet," grunted Kennett, correctly interpreting Ambrose's expression. D-Arc's previous Scottish office had been co-located with the SSB, tucked away in a temporary building on the outer perimeter of Redford Barracks, a position that provided physical security but made more arcane measures difficult to employ.

Kennett led Ambrose quickly inside, through the oak and silver outer doors, past the mirrored inner doors, and across the tessellated, eye-catching tiled floor of the atrium, all useful architectural defenses against malignant spirits. The demon had grown enough in

Ambrose's leg for him to feel its attention drawn by the mirrors, and his leg twitched and twisted of its own accord as he crossed the patterned maze of the floor.

Kennett signed them into the book at the front desk, at which point Ambrose was relieved of his yataghan and revolver in return for a claim ticket, before being helped upstairs.

"Lady S will see you first," said Kennett. "Afterward . . . I suppose the medico can sort out your leg."

Ambrose caught the implication of that phrasing very well. Any treatment would be dependent on Lady S and how Ambrose responded to whatever she wanted him to do: which was almost certainly about him returning to active duty with D-Arc again.

"In you go," said Kennett. He rapped on the double door, turned the knob to push it open a fraction, and released his supporting grip on Ambrose's elbow.

Ambrose limped in, wishing he was elsewhere. Kennett did not follow him, the door shutting hard on Ambrose's heels with a definitive click.

The room was dark, and smelled of orange zest and the sickly honey scent of myrrh, which was normal for any chamber that had Lady S in it. Ambrose peered into the darkness, but did not move forward. It was better to stay near the exit, since he knew that only a small part of this room was actually connected to the building and to Edinburgh itself. The rest of the room was . . . somewhere else.

He heard a rustling in the dark and swallowed nervously as the strange smell grew stronger. A candle flared, the light suddenly bright. Ambrose hooded his eyes and looked off to one side.

Lady S was there, some feet away from the candle, again as expected. He could see only her vague outline, swathed as she was in gauzy silks that moved about her in answer to some breeze that didn't reach the door.

"Dear Ambrose!" exclaimed the apparition, her voice that of

some kindly but aged female relative welcoming a close but morally strayed junior connection. "How kind of you to call upon me in my hour of need."

"Yes," agreed Ambrose. "I could not, of course, resist."

Lady S laughed a hearty laugh that belonged to a far more fully fleshed person, someone who might have triple chins to wobble as they guffawed. The laugh did not match the narrow, dimly perceived silhouette in her fluttering shrouds.

"Oh, you always could make me laugh," she said. "I don't laugh as much as I should, you know."

"Who does?" asked Ambrose, unable to keep the bitterness from his voice.

"Now, now, Ambrose," said Lady S. Something that might be a finger wagged in the air some distance in front of his face. "No petulance. I can't abide petulance. Tell me—your father, he of many names and aliases, may he rest in peace—his birth name was really Farnowitz and he *was* born in Germany?"

"You know he was," said Ambrose tightly. "It's in my file and always has been. My mother was English, I was born in Bristol, and what's more I have served my country more than—"

"Yes, yes dear," comforted Lady S. "We're not holding it against you. Quite the contrary. We need someone with a modicum of the art who also has German blood. Apart from the King, who naturally isn't available to us, the combination is rather scarce among our ranks."

"What do you need me to do, and what do I get out of it?"

"Oh, my dear young man, such impatience and, dare I say, rudeness, will not serve you well. But perhaps it is the demon that is gnawing its way up your leg? I will make some allowance for that."

"I beg your pardon, Lady S," muttered Ambrose. Even at the best of times it did not pay to offend Lady S, and this was far from the best of times.

"Oh, do call me Auntie Hester," cooed the apparition in the darkness. "You know I do like all my young men to call me Auntie Hester."

"Yes, Auntie Hester," said Ambrose reluctantly. He could not suppress a shiver, as he knew exactly what she was: a revenant who survived only thanks to powerful magic, numerous blood sacrifices, and a budget appropriation that was never examined in parliament. Lady Hester Stanhope had been dead for eighty years, but that had not ended her career in one of the predecessor organizations of D-Arc. She had gone from strength to strength in both bureaucratic and sorcerous terms since then. Though she was severely limited in terms of normal physical interaction with the world, she had many other advantages. Not least were her unrivalled political connections, which ran all the way back to the early nineteenth century, when she had managed the household of her uncle William Pitt the Younger, then Prime Minister of Britain.

"Very good. Now, it has come to our attention that someone exceedingly naughty in Solingen . . . the Rhineland, you know . . . is trying to raise a *Waldgeist*, and not just any sixpence-ha'penny forest spirit, but a great old one of the primeval wood. They've gotten hold of the ritual, and three days from now they're going to summon up the old tree-beastie and set it on our occupying forces—and we can't allow that, can we? Therefore, Ambrose my darling, you will dash over to Solingen, call up this Waldgeist first, and bind it to our service, then have it destroy the second summoner. Are you with me so far?"

"I know very little Teutonic magic," said Ambrose. "Surely there must be someone else better—"

"You'll have a grimoire, dear," said Lady S. "You *can* read Old High German?"

"Yes, but—"

"That's settled then!" exclaimed Lady S. "Our new doctor will cut that demon out for you, he's a darling boy and such a fine hand with the blade. Major Kennett will accompany you to Solingen, by the way. In case you need . . . assistance."

"What about the attack on me today?" asked Ambrose quickly. The windswept figure was retreating further into the dark, and the candle was guttering. "They were Anatolian demons! Why would the Emir be sending them against me now?"

"You will be protected," said Lady S. Her voice was distant now. "D-Arc takes care of its own."

"I know it does!" shouted Ambrose. "That's why I want to know who really sent those demons! Did you set this all in train—"

"Au revoir, my dear," said a very remote voice, no more than a whisper on the wind.

The door behind him snapped open, and an inexorable force propelled Ambrose back out through the doorway. Landing on his injured leg, he fell and sprawled lengthwise across the carpeted hall. Kennett looked down at him for a moment, sniffed, and helped him up.

"Doctor Lambshead is all ready for you," he said. "Gunderbeg is standing by to eat the demon when it's cut out, and we have all the recuperative apparatus prepared. Best we get a move on, I think."

Ambrose looked down at his leg. The bandage of Sekhmet was now just a few strands of rag, and it was being chewed on by a mouth that had grown in his calf muscle, a black-lipped, razor-fanged mouth that was trying to turn itself upward toward his knee.

"Yes," said Ambrose faintly. "If you don't mind."

At noon the next day, his leg salved, bandaged, and entirely demon-free, Ambrose and Kennett were on the boat train to Dover and thence to Calais. An uneventful channel crossing was complete by midnight and after changing trains only twice, they were in Solingen the following morning.

Ambrose spent a good part of their traveling time reading the grimoire that Kennett had handed to him in Edinburgh. The book had come wrapped in a piece of winding cloth cut from the burial shroud of the Scottish sorcerer Thomas Weir, a fabric made to stifle sorcery, indicating that the D-Arc librarian believed the grimoire had the potential to act of its own accord. Accordingly, Ambrose treated it with care, using reversed gloves to turn its pages and marking his place with a ribbon torn from a child's bonnet.

The grimoire was a typeset version of a much older text. It had been printed in the late sixteenth century, and according to the letter with it, was attributed to the German sorcerer and botanomancer Bertin Zierer, though as the flyleaf was missing and the original binding had been replaced several times, this was noted as being speculation rather than fact.

The section of the grimoire dealing with the Waldgeist of the Primeval Wood that had once stretched across much of modern Germany was, as per usual, couched in rather vague language, apart from the description of the actual ritual. It did not describe the form the Waldgeist usually took, or go into any details of its powers, beyond a warning that these would be employed against anyone who dared wake it who was "not of the blood of Wotan." The only clue to the nature of the Waldgeist came from an etching that showed a disc of ground covered in trees rising from a forest. Entitled, in rough translation, "Tree Spirits Rising," it did not help Ambrose very much, though it did make him wonder if the Waldgeist manifested as some sort of gestalt entity composed of a whole section of modern forest.

Apart from the grimoire, the duty librarian had also included a large-scale map of the area around Solingen and some typed pages of research and observation. The map indicated that the locus of the Waldgeist was in the middle of a small but very old wood some twenty kilometers south of Solingen. The notes cross-referenced the ritual cited in the grimoire with other known practices of Teutonic magic and affirmed that it looked to be complete and not designed to trap or harm the caster by some omission or intentional change.

Shortly before their arrival, both men assumed their appointed disguises, which had been placed by unseen hands in the next-door compartment. Ambrose became a full colonel from the staff sent to join the British forces of occupation on some mission that was not to be denied or inquired about by anyone. Kennett, on the other hand, simply put on a different and more conservative suit, topped with a grey homburg identical to that worn by the late King Edward, and thus assumed the appearance of a mysterious civilian from the upper echelons of Whitehall.

They were met at the Ohligs Wald station in Solingen by a young subaltern of the Black Watch, whose attempt at an introduction was immediately quashed by Kennett.

"You don't need to know our names and we don't want to know yours," he snapped. "Is the car waiting? And our escort?"

"Yes, sir," replied the young second lieutenant, a blush as red as the tabs on Ambrose's collar spreading across his cheeks. "As per the telegraph message."

"Lead on then," said Kennett. "The sooner we take care of this, the better."

The car, commandeered from the divisional general, was accompanied by four motorcycle outriders and three Peerless trucks carrying the nameless subaltern's infantry platoon and a machine gun section.

"We hardly need all this carry-on," protested Ambrose as he settled into the grandly upholstered backseat of the general's car and Kennett climbed in next to him. "Surely it would be better for me to get changed and just walk into the wood as a tourist or something?"

"I don't think so," replied Kennett. "The fellow who is hoping to . . . carry out this deed . . . is the leader of gang of militants called

Die Schwarze Fahne, and they have quite a membership of former soldiers and the like. We'll have the jocks establish a cordon around the wood, then you and I will go in."

"You're coming with me?" asked Ambrose. "The grim—"

He stopped himself, aware that the driver and the subaltern in the front seat were so obviously trying to not listen that they must be able to hear everything, even over the noise of the engines as the whole convoy got under way. "That is, the reference is specific about German heritage and the . . . subject's response if . . . ah . . . in contact with others."

"M' grandmother was Edith Adler, the opera singer," drawled Kennett out of the side of his mouth, so only Ambrose could hear. "So I have a drop or two of the blood. But I'll keep well back, just the same."

Ambrose nodded slightly and tried not to show how much he was discomfited by Kennett's disclosure. Even from such slight information he would now be able to positively identify the man. Which meant that Kennett was either taking him into some inner echelon of trust, or he didn't think Ambrose would be around long enough for it to matter.

It only took forty minutes to reach the fringes of the wood. Ambrose sat in the car for a few minutes while everyone else got out, and read the relevant pages of the grimoire for perhaps the twentieth or thirtieth time. The ritual was not complex, but he had to memorize it. It would not be possible to refer to the book in the middle of the process.

He felt quite calm as he slipped the grimoire inside his tunic and did up the buttons. They looked like the usual brass, but were in fact silver-gilt, part of the sorcerous protection that Ambrose hoped would help him if things went only slightly awry. Of course, when dealing with an entity like a primeval tree spirit, it was far more likely that if something did go wrong it would be on a scale so immense that no amount of sorcerous protection would make the slightest difference.

The lieutenant's platoon, under the direction more of a leather-lunged sergeant than the pink-faced officer, were forming up in three ranks on the verge. The trucks were parked across the road to block other vehicular traffic, and the Vickers machine gun was in the process of being emplaced on its tripod some way off, up a slight rise, to enfilade the road.

Ambrose got out and orientated the map to north by the sun, shifting it slightly to get the road in the right relationship, map to real topography. The map indicated the beginning of a footpath a dozen or so yards beyond the machine gun position, and sure enough, there was a stone cairn there and a rotting wooden signpost that once upon a time had had something written on it.

"We'll follow the footpath," said Ambrose, indicating the way. He folded the map and slipped it in with the grimoire. "It goes to the . . . the agreed rendezvous."

Kennett nodded and turned to the anxiously waiting lieutenant.

"Send one section to patrol the perimeter of the wood to the west and one section to the east. Keep one section here. Your men are not to enter the wood, no matter what you hear. Cries for help, orders that sound like they come from me or the colonel, all are to be ignored unless we are actually in front of you. If we do not come out within three hours—my watch says ten twenty-two, set yours now—return to Solingen, report to your CO, and tell him to imme-diately contact General Spencer Ewart at the War Office and relay the code phrase *defectus omnes mortui*."

"But that's . . . uh . . . fail . . . failing . . . failure . . . all dead," said the lieutenant, busy trying to scribble the phrase in his notebook and set his watch, all at the same time.

"Did I ask you to translate?" snapped Kennett. "Do you have the code phrase?"

"Yes, sir!" replied the lieutenant. He closed his notebook and managed to successfully set his watch, his platoon sergeant surreptitiously leaning in to make sure he'd gotten it right.

"Finally, fire two warning shots over the heads of anyone approaching. If they continue, shoot to kill. It doesn't matter who they are. Civilians, women, children, whoever. Here is a written order to that effect."

"Yes, sir," said the lieutenant. There was considerable doubt in his voice and his hand shook a little as he unfolded the letter, his eyes flickering across the typewritten lines before widening enormously as they came to the short signature—just a first name and a capital letter—at the bottom of the page.

"Yes, sir!" he repeated, much more vigorously.

"Presuming we return, I'll want that back," said Kennett. "Carry on."

The lieutenant saluted and whirled about, speaking quickly to his sergeant, who a moment later began to bellow orders. Ambrose ignored the sudden bustle of military activity and began to walk toward the footpath. His eyes were on the fringes of the wood, looking for signs of arcane disturbance. But there were none visible. This part of the wood was composed of beech trees, their trunks green and mossy, their foliage a darker green. The light changed under the trees, gaining a soft, green tinge, but this was the natural magic of leaves and sun, not anything sorcerous.

It was also cooler under the canopy of the forest. Ambrose led the way, with Kennett a dozen yards behind. They walked in silence, save for the occasional squelch of soft ground, or the snapping of a fallen twig where the footpath wound through higher, drier ground.

A half mile or so in, the beeches began to give way to oaks. They were much older, and grew closer together, the footpath leading into relative darkness. As they left the beech forest behind, Ambrose noticed that it was quieter among the oaks as well. All the bird-sound had vanished, and all he could hear were his own and Kennett's footsteps. Then, not much farther on, Kennett's footsteps stopped.

Ambrose looked back. Kennett was leaning against the broad trunk of one of the ancient oaks. He nodded and waved Ambrose on. Clearly this was as far as Kennett cared to go into the heart of the wood, and as he was far more in practice and so currently more attuned to the occult than Ambrose, this probably meant he had sensed the locus of the Waldgeist somewhere close ahead.

Indeed, no more than fifty yards ahead, there was a forest glade where the oaks parted around a clear expanse of grass. In the middle of this small clearing was an incredibly ancient, stunted tree, a king-oak that could well be thousands of years old. Blown over by some long-forgotten storm, it still lived, its branches spreading horizontally, its trunk twisted and gnarled, its bark as hard as iron.

Ambrose could feel the Waldgeist now, the sense of the sleeping spirit that had been born of thirty million trees, and would not fade until the last of those trees was gone. Humans had decimated the primeval forest, but the spirit still remained. It only slept, and in Ambrose's opinion it would be best left to do so. But he knew he had no real choice. If Lady S wanted the Waldgeist awoken, then he had to do so.

He knelt by the trunk of the king-oak, and paused, just for a moment, to gather his thoughts, mentally going through each step of the ritual. Satisifed that he had remembered it all, he laid out everything he needed on the forest floor.

First of all was the silver athame, his sacred knife, the one he had used in Turkey and thought he had lost when he was at the Front, only to find it had been stored away in the D-Arc armory against his later use. They had always presumed he would come back.

Second was an acorn from this same wood, though from long ago. It was so old it was almost petrified, and though he had been assured its origin had been checked by thaumaturgic assay as well as in the D-Arc records, it was the one element that he doubted. If it was from somewhere else, it might well help to raise the Waldgeist, but it would not be a friendly awakening.

The third thing was not in the ritual. Ambrose took his revolver from its holster and laid it down, to be ready at hand. If things went very badly wrong, he intended to shoot himself. It would be a far quicker and kinder way to die. Ancient spirits were not known for their sense of mercy.

That done, it was time to begin. Ambrose began to recite the words of the waking ritual. His voice was steady, and he spoke the words carefully as he sliced the end of his left thumb with the athame and let the bright blood drip onto the ancient acorn. As the blood dripped, the words became a chant, rhythmically repeated over and over again.

The acorn soaked up the blood like a sponge. When nine drops had fallen, Ambrose cut his right thumb and let another nine drops fall, without faltering in his chant. The guttural Old High German words sounded very loud in the stillness of the wood, but Ambrose knew it wasn't so much the words themselves that mattered. It was the thoughts behind them, the blood, and the aged seed.

He finished the chant at exactly the same time he pushed the acorn into the soil with both his bleeding thumbs, and sat back.

Nothing happened. Ambrose waited, sitting cross-legged next to the ancient oak, his hand on the butt of the revolver, ready to lift it up to his temple and fire.

A slight breeze swooped down and rustled the leaves on the low, spreading branches. It was cold, ice-laden, and out of time and place, in this splendid German summer.

"So it begins," whispered Ambrose. He could feel the Waldgeist stirring all around, the spirit waking in the wood. He looked up and saw the branches of the king-oak lifting, and then a moment later the trunk groaned and creaked as it began to straighten up. It was becoming the great tree of old, when it had stood sixty feet high or more, tall and straight and strong.

If it was a typical manifestation of a tree spirit, the tree itself would respond to Ambrose's summoning, either to whisper with the soft sussuration of leaves, or to pin him down with a heavy branch and send a thousand green shoots to penetrate his body, slowly growing through skin and flesh until they did fatal damage to some vital organ. Or, even worse in some ways, the Waldgeist might force itself into Ambrose's mind, remove everything of his personality, and create for itself a human puppet. That was likely one of Kennett's main reasons for accompanying him, to guard against this eventuality, with his revolver and its exploding silver bullets.

The wind blew stronger, and the tree grew taller. Ambrose made his fingers uncurl from the revolver, though he kept his hand close. It was important not to appear with weapons in hand, for that in itself might sway the Waldgeist to enmity.

Then the ground shivered and sank beneath Ambrose. It was an unwelcome sensation, delivering sudden uncertainty, and even worse, the sharp memory of being buried alive. Wildly, he looked around, and saw that just as in the etching in the grimoire, the king-oak and all the trees around the glade had risen from the surrounding forest, as if a disc had been cored out and lifted straight up.

Ambrose looked down and saw the earth crumbling beneath him. His fingers closed on the revolver and he managed to get it halfway to his head before he was suddenly pulled down, taken into the earth as a shark drags down a swimmer, without mercy or any possibility of resistance.

The ground closed over Ambrose's head, the revolver landing with a thud to mark the spot. Grass grew in an instant through the bare soil, eager tendrils of green wrapping around the blued metal of the gun, until in a moment it was covered in green and lost to sight.

Deep underground, Ambrose screamed and screamed and screamed, all inside his head, for his mouth was shut with soil. He relived the sudden concussion of the German shell, the blankness in his ears, the earth silently cascading into the dugout, the last glimpse of Peter's terrified face, the lantern snuffed out in an instant . . . and then the darkness, the pressure of the earth, everywhere about him save for a tiny air pocket between two fallen beams, where he had pressed his face.

Then there had been the terrible, never-ending time of being trapped, not knowing whether he would ever see daylight again, or breathe the clean air, untainted by earth and fumes and the slowly building stench of the corpses of his friends as they began to rot around him. Alone in the earth, held in an implacable grasp and wreathed in silence. Slowly dying, but not quickly enough for it to be an escape.

Now it was all happening again.

But it was not the same, some fragment of Ambrose's still-screaming mind observed. He was completely buried in the earth, this time, and so should already be well on the way to asphyxiation. But he felt no need to breathe.

Also, he could hear. He could hear his own heartbeat, beating a sharp tattoo of panic, but he could also hear the movement of the earth. But there was something else, as well, something that as his panic lessened, he realized was a voice, the voice of the Waldgeist.

What he heard was not words, at least not in any human language. It was the sound of the woods, of the wind, and the trees, and the birds, and the insects, somehow ordered and structured to become something that he could understand.

The Waldgeist of the primeval forest was whispering to him as it took him into its embrace. Its true heart was down in the tangled roots where he lay, not in the tree above. He could feel those roots now, twining around him, gripping him lightly, but ready to rend him apart should the spirit's feelings change.

It wanted to know why he had awoken it, and for what purpose.

Ambrose told it, not bothering to open his mouth. It took his explanation and went into his mind for more, its presence like a sudden shadow on a summer's day, cool and crisp as it slowly spread through his memories and mind. Ambrose's panic shrank before this shadowy touch, and he grew quiet, almost asleep himself, the Waldgeist growing more awake.

As the tree spirit wandered in his thoughts, Ambrose relived them too, slowly and sleepily. All the wonders and horrors of his life, from his earliest recollections to the events of the last few days. All were looked at by the tree spirit, and as they progressed, in no particular order, Ambrose felt that each memory, and everything he had done or not done, was being weighed up and catalogued, added to the Waldgeist's careful inventory of all the other living things in its forest domain.

Eventually, it finished looking. Ambrose was very tired by then, so tired that he could barely formulate the question that constituted his mission, visualizing each word in his mind as if he were writing it down on an order pad, the question carefully contained within the rectangular grid.

So	you	will	not	answer	this	other
summoner	in	the	days	to	come?	And
you	will	be	content	to	rest	until
I	call	you	from	your	sleep	again?

No answer came. Ambrose tried to ask the question again, but he was too tired. Fear and panic had exhausted him, but now he felt a different weariness. He was warm, and comfortable, and the tree roots that cradled him felt as comfortable as the ancient armchair by the fire in the bothy, the one with the sheepskins laid over its creased and faded leather upholstery.

Ambrose slept, and did not dream.

When he awoke, it was with a start. There was bright sunshine on his face, making him blink, and the blue sky above was bordered with green. He sat up and saw that he was at the foot of the king-oak, which was once again bent and bowed by the passage of time. There was no sign of his revolver or athame, but when he stood up and checked himself over, everything else seemed to be unchanged. The grimoire was still in his tunic, as was the map. There was some earth caught under his Sam Browne belt, and his uniform was somewhat mussed, but that was all.

Everything else looked normal. There was no risen disc of trees, and though he could feel the Waldgeist, it was very faint. It slept again, and was sleeping very deep. Whether he had convinced it or not to remain quiescent, it would take far more than the blood of two thumbs and the ritual he had used to wake it now.

Ambrose frowned, but it was a merry frown. He didn't really understand what had happened, but he knew his object had been achieved. He also felt surprisingly good, almost as happy in himself as he had been in the far-off, golden days before the War.

He clapped his hand against the king-oak in friendly farewell and set off along the path. Several paces along, he was surprised to find himself whistling. He frowned again, and stopped, standing still on the path. He couldn't remember when he had last felt like whistling.

There was a rustle up ahead. Ambrose's attention immediately returned to the present. He snuck off the path and crouched down behind a lesser but still substantial oak, regretting the loss of his revolver. Someone was coming very cautiously up the path, and it could be a German anarchist as easily as Kennett, and even if it was Kennett, Ambrose couldn't be sure of his intentions, and he was no longer so ready to just let Kennett kill him. There would be time enough to join his friends.

"Ambrose?"

It was Kennett. Ambrose peered around the trunk. Kennett was coming along the path, and he wasn't brandishing a weapon. But very strangely, he was no longer wearing the grey suit and homburg. He was in tweeds, with a deerstalker cap, and there was something about his face . . . a partially healed scar under his eye that hadn't been there . . .

"Ah," said Ambrose. He stepped out from behind the tree and raised his hand. "Hello, Kennett. How long have I been away?"

Kennett smiled, a smile that as always contained no warmth whatsoever, and was more an indication of sardonic superiority than any sense of humor.

"A year and a day," he said. "Just as the grimoire said."

"Not the copy you gave me," said Ambrose.

"Naturally," replied Kennett. "You might have refused to go. But from the whistling, the general spring of the step and so forth, I presume the cure has been efficacious?"

"I do feel . . . whole," admitted Ambrose. He paused for a moment, eyes downcast, thinking of his own reactions. "And I believe . . . I am no longer afraid to be underground."

"That's good," said Kennett. "Because we have a job to do, and I'm afraid a great deal of it is deep under the earth. High, but deep. I'm not fond of the Himalayas myself, but what can you do?"

"Was there actually a German adept who wanted to raise the spirit?" asked Ambrose as they began to walk together back along the path.

"Oh, yes," said Kennett. "It's doubtful if he would have succeeded, and the timing was not quite what we said, but Lady S thought we might as well try to get two birds with one stone. The new doctor brought it to her attention, that this old spirit had a two-fold nature, that as well as trampling the undeserving and so on, it also traditionally sometimes healed the sick and those of 'broken mind.'"

"Broken mind," repeated Ambrose. "Yes. I suppose that I wasn't really getting any better where I was. But those demons—"

"They *were* the Emir's," interrupted Kennett. "Forced our hand. Couldn't be helped."

"I see," said Ambrose, with a swift sideways glance at Kennett's face. He still couldn't tell if the man was lying.

They walked the rest of the way out of the wood in silence. At the road, there was a green Crossley 20/25 waiting, with Jones and Jones leaning on opposite sides of the bonnet, each carefully watching the surrounding countryside. They nodded to Ambrose as he walked up, and he thought that Jones the Larger might even have given him the merest shadow of a wink.

Ambrose's yataghan was on the floor behind the front seat and there was a large cardboard box tied with a red ribbon sitting in the middle of the backseat. Kennett indicated the box with an inclination of his head.

"For you," he said. "Present from Lady S."

Ambrose undid the ribbon and opened the box. There was a velvet medal case inside, which he did not open; a silver hip flask engraved with his name beneath a testimonial of thanks from an obscure manufacturer of scientific instruments in Nottingham; and a card with a picture of a mountaineer waving the Union Jack atop a snow-covered mountain.

Ambrose flipped open the card.

"'Welcome back,'" he read aloud. "'With love from Auntie Hester.'"

HOLLY AND IRON

S ix men-at-arms, all mounted," reported Jack. He paused to spit out some nutshells, a remnant of his transition from squirrel-shape to human form, before he added, "Three in front of the litter, three behind."

"And the litter bearers?" asked Merewyn. She didn't look at Jack as he put his clothes back on, her sharp blue eyes intent on the party that was making its way along the old Roman road that cut straight through the valley, only a hundred yards below their hiding place high on the densely wooded slope.

"Slaves," said Jack. "Our folk, from the look of them. They all wear braided holly charms on their ankles. So there is no ironmaster hiding among them."

"An ironmaster can stand holly for a short time, longer if it is not against their skin," corrected Merewyn. "Or they might make false holly from paper or painted wood. You're absolutely sure?"

Jack nodded. He was a big man, six feet tall and very broad in the shoulder. Even in his smallest squirrel-form he was almost two feet tall, and he could also shape himself as a large boar or bear. Even so, he was a head shorter and fifty pounds lighter than his younger brother, known as Doublejack, who stood silently by, awaiting Merewyn's instructions. Doublejack would probably take the shape of a cralle dog—a huge beast the size of a pony—if they were to attack the Norman in the litter and his guards.

Jack and Doublejack were the only shape-shifters in Merewyn's band. It was a very rare talent, found only among the Inglish. It was an ability not often used for the most part, as a shifter needed to eat a huge amount of fresh meat upon returning to their human form, something not easily obtained. Even now, Jack was eyeing the freshly dressed deer hanging by its hind leg from a nearby branch. Going down in size made him less hungry than going up, but he would still eat a haunch or two, leaving the rest for Doublejack to gorge on later.

"Six men-at-arms," mused Merewyn aloud. "A curious number. Why only six? Everyone knows we're in these woods. They look sun-dark, too, maybe pullani mercenaries . . . not household troops, which is also curious. And there is something strange about that litter. I cannot truly say I sense it, but I suspect some Norman magic is at work. Something of cold iron . . . yet I cannot be sure. . . . Robin?"

Robin shook her head impatiently, indicating she felt no Norman magic at work. She did not want to feel any, so she did not focus her full concentration on the litter.

"Do we attack or not?" asked Robin impatiently.

Like the men and her half sister Merewyn, Robin was dressed in a heavy woolen tunic over leather-booted hose, but apart from the clothes neither she nor Merewyn tried to disguise their femininity. Both had long hair, braided back and pinned with silver and amber, offering some protection against Norman magic workings and helpful for their own Inglish magic.

Silver and amber looked perfectly normal against Merewyn's blond hair. She was all Inglish, tall and muscular, a fair-faced warrior woman who could wrestle down a stag and stab it in the neck, or send a cloth-yard shaft from her longbow two hundred yards through a Norman man-at-arms, brigantine and all.

Robin, to her eternal embarrassment and shame, looked more Norman than Inglish herself. She was shorter and stockier than her sister, dark-haired and grey-eyed, and always very brown from their outdoor life. She took after her mother, her father's second wife. The one he had stolen from her Norman father, unwittingly setting in train not only his own death but also the loss of his kingdom to that self-same Norman, and the chain of events that led to his two daughters lurking in the fringe of trees above a valley, the elder leading a band of what could variously be described as bandits, rebels, or the last remnants of the army of the true King of Ingland.

"I am uneasy," said Merewyn. She looked up at the sky. The sun was still a full disc, but low and near the western hills. Two ravens circled overhead, black shapes against the darkening sky. "We will lose the light very soon, and we do not know who is in the litter."

"Only six guards," said Robin. "It can't be anyone important . . . or dangerous."

"It could be someone confident enough to need no larger escort," said Merewyn. "An ironmaster hiding his charms and devices until the last."

"Let's attack before it is dark," urged Robin. "We haven't had a chance like this for weeks."

Merewyn didn't answer. Robin frowned, then tugged at her sister's sleeve.

"This'll be the third Norman we've let go if you don't give the order! What's wrong with you?"

"There is nothing wrong, Robin," said Merewyn softly. "Knowing when not to attack is as important to a leader as being up front swinging a sword."

"That's not leading!" snapped Robin. "This is leading!"

She snatched the horn from Merewyn's shoulder and before her sister could stop her, blew a ringing peal that echoed across the valley. That done, she darted forward, drawing her sword as she ran.

The horn blast set the well-prepared ambush in motion. The heavy reverberation of axes on wood sounded ahead of the Normans' party. A few seconds later, a great tree came twisting down across the path, testament to the woodcutters' skill in keeping it balanced all afternoon on the thinnest spire of uncut trunk.

As the tree crashed, archers stepped out from their hiding places on the edge of the cleared area on the side of the path and began to shoot at the guards' horses. The guards responded by charging the archers, bellowing oaths and cursing. Unusually, the litter bearers didn't simply run away, toppling the litter, but set it down carefully before sprinting off between the trees.

Robin ran on the heels of a shaggy, slavering dog that stood higher than her shoulder. Merewyn and Jack came behind her, with a dozen of their band, all armed with swords, spears, or bill-hooks. They were the blocking force, to prevent an escape back along the path, as the fallen tree prevented any escape the other way.

But there was no attempt to flee. One of the guards was dead on the ground, killed instantly by an arrow that found a chink in his mail coif. Two more were trapped under dead or dying horses. The remaining three had realized the impossibility of riding down archers hiding in the forest fringe and had turned back.

"Surrender!" called Robin. She was out of breath from the mad charge down the slope and had to repeat the call. "Surrender!"

The three men-at-arms looked at the archers who were once again stepping out of the green shadows, at the huge cralle dog that chose that moment to howl, and at the fifteen armed bandits approaching.

"You will die if you try to charge through," said Merewyn loudly, correctly observing the intention announced by the tensing of the men's arms and the flick of their horse's heads. "We will give quarter."

Two of the men-at-arms looked at the third, who nodded and threw down his sword. His companions did likewise. Then they dismounted and stood by their horses' heads, casting dark looks at Robin and Merewyn and nervous glances at Doublejack, who was sniffing around the litter.

Merewyn made a signal and the archers moved closer, arrows still nocked and ready to loose. Six of her men raced forward and threw the men-at-arms to the ground, binding their hands as they also removed their daggers, boot-knives, and, in the case of the leader, a tiny knife scabbarded in the back of his gauntlet.

"Who is in the litter?" asked Robin. There had been no movement from it, not even the twitch of a curtain pulled aside. Doublejack was still sidling around it, his huge nose wrinkled much as a human forehead might frown in thought.

"An old Norman merchant," said one of the men-at-arms, the one the others had looked to. He had the faded, crescent scar of a slave tattoo on his cheek. "Going to the baths at Aquae Sulis."

"Not until he's paid his toll, he's not," said Robin. She strode over to the litter, hacked off the knots that held the curtain to the frame, pulled the rich but travel-stained velvet drapes aside, and trampled them under her heels.

There was a man inside the litter, sitting upright, wrapped in a thick cloak of blue felt, the hood pulled up and forward, so his face was shadowed. He had a chess-table set before him, of dark mahogany and ivory. There was a game in progress, though no one sat opposite him, slate-grey pieces in movement against softer, smaller ones of cherry-wood.

"You are our prisoner," said Robin. She extended her sword arm, the point hovering a few inches from the man's hooded face. "And we will want a suitable ransom. What is your name?"

Instead of answering, the man lifted one of the slate-grey knights from the chessboard. Robin had only a moment to register that all the grey pieces were knights when she suddenly felt her sword twist violently out of her hand and hurtle up and behind her, almost impaling Doublejack.

Robin immediately snatched her necklace-garrote of holly beads from her belt, but before she could do anything with it, the Norman flung down the grey knight. As it hit the ground, there was a clap of thunder, strange and terrible in the still air. Heat washed over Robin, as if she'd stepped into a forge, and there was no longer a chess piece between her and the palanquin, but an eight-foot-tall warrior, made entirely of iron, bearing a sword of blue-edged star-steel and a kite shield green with verdigris.

The iron warrior pushed his green shield at Robin, a blow that would have knocked her to the ground if she had not flung herself backward. Losing her garrote in the fall, she rolled and wriggled away as the iron warrior stomped toward her, its feet leaving deep impressions in the soft forest soil.

Robin heard Merewyn shouting, "Flee!" but her sister did not follow her own orders. Instead, she rushed forward to help Robin up. The ground was damp and the leaf mulch slippery, and they slid apart as Robin got to her feet, with Merewyn behind her.

In that instant, the iron warrior was upon them. Merewyn tried to pivot on guard as it slammed its iron shield toward her, but it was too quick. The iron rim of its shield caught her full in the neck. There was a sickening crack, all too like a snapping branch, and Merewyn was hurled to the ground. She lay there, her head at an impossible angle.

Robin could do nothing but run. There were thunderclaps all around as the ironmaster threw out his chess-pieces, iron warriors rising up where the knights fell. Robin ducked, weaved, and zigzagged to the treeline, with iron warriors smashing their way through saplings, shrubs, and bushes toward her.

She paused when she reached the trees, twisting back to take a look. The nearest iron warrior was a dozen paces away, allowing Robin a few seconds' grace to take in the scene before she had to run again.

A full dozen iron warriors stalked the clearing, and there were two more standing in front of the palanquin, their shields raised to protect the ironmaster from archery. Not that there was anyone shooting at him. Merewyn's band had vanished like a summer shower. The only signs that they had ever been there were the men-at-arms working away at their bonds—and Merewyn's body, a dozen paces from the palanquin.

Robin waited another second she couldn't afford, hoping that she would see Merewyn move, that her sister would suddenly get up and sprint away. But she didn't move. Deep inside, beneath the barrier of hope, Robin knew that Merewyn wouldn't get up, now or ever. She'd been hit too hard.

The iron warrior struck at the tree in front of Robin, its sword shearing through the wrist-thick branches she was sheltering behind, a spray of woodchips chasing Robin as she fled deeper into the forest.

Not long after dawn the next morning, with the inexplicably insistent and enduring iron warriors left behind only a few hours before (and at least one of them struggling in one of the forest's more extensive bogs) Robin wearily climbed up onto the broad, ground-sweeping branch of an ancient oak and used it as a bridge over the narrow ravine known to locals as Hammerbite.

She looked for the two sentinels on the upper branches, but no one was there. There didn't seem to be anyone in the camp either, when she rounded the trunk and looked out through the lesser trees at the row of leather tents, carefully pitched under the overhang of a huge ledge of shale, an outcrop from the grey hill whose bare crown poked out of the forest a hundred yards above the camp.

Robin whistled dispiritedly, not really expecting an answer, and so was not surprised when there wasn't one. She trudged over to the fire pit and looked down into it. The fire was emplaced about three feet down to disguise the smoke, and it was fed only good, dry wood, so it would burn clean. It was always kept alight, for there was never any knowing when fire might be needed.

But it was not burning now and was clearly many hours dead.

Robin picked up the bent iron rod that doubled as poker and pot-hanger and stirred the ashes, but not one bright coal emerged.

She kept poking it long after this was clear, for want of anything better to do. It seemed symbolic to be stirring dead ashes, the ruins of a once-bright fire. Merewyn was dead, and it was all Robin's fault. She had gotten her own sister killed. The fact that none of the band had returned to the camp indicated that they thought so too, perhaps coupled with the distrust of her Norman heritage that had always simmered beneath the surface, kept in check only by Merewyn's authority.

She stabbed the poker hard into the ashes, wishing that it were the heart of the Norman ironmaster. Flames suddenly erupted from the dead ashes and Robin jumped back. Not in fear of the flames, but of what she had just done, without thinking.

"That's a right Norman trick. Iron magic," said Jack, making Robin jump again, this time almost into the fire.

"I . . . I didn't . . ."

Jack shook his head and crouched down to pick up a gnarled knot of ancient beech, which he threw down onto the fire.

"You needn't fear, lass," he said. "I always knew you had the iron magic from your mother. There's no one here to see but me and Doublejack, and he's across the Hammerbite, eating up a gobbet of something I didn't care to look at."

"Did you see . . ." asked Robin quietly. "Is Merewyn . . ."

Jack took the poker and made sparks fly. He didn't look at Robin.

"The Princess is dead," he said finally. "I took the squirrel-shape and went back to be sure, though the Ferramenta chased me anyway. Her neck was broken. They took the body."

"I killed her," whispered Robin. She picked up handfuls of dry dirt and smeared them across her face, then she stood up and screamed, her words flying back at her, reflected by the overhanging shale. "I killed my sister!"

She reached for the hot coals of the fire and would have taken two handfuls but Jack caught her in a bear hug and lifted her away, with her still kicking and screaming and quite out of her head with shock and grief and exhaustion. He carried her to the tent that was their makeshift surgery and hospice, patting her on the head and crooning the nonsense words he'd used long ago to calm young dogs when he was the King of Ingland's master of hounds.

When her threshing stopped and the screaming had subsided into a dull, inward keening, he laid her down and, taking up a small leather bottle, poured a cordial of dwale down her throat. Within a few minutes, the potent combination of hemlock, Italian mandragora, poppy juice, henbane, and wine calmed her and only a little later sent her into a dreamless sleep.

When she awoke, Robin felt strangely calm and distant, as if a veil of many months lay between her and Merewyn's death. But she knew that the dusk she could see outside was the partner of the Ferramenta-haunted dawn. Even dwale-sleep could not hold someone for more than nine or ten hours.

The taste of the herbal brew was still in her mouth and her breath stank as if she had vomited, though she was clean enough. Her hands had been washed, and the scratches smeared with yarrow paste. Robin stared at the scratches and for a few seconds couldn't remember how she had gotten them. She sat for a minute or two, thinking, then she slowly unfastened her dark Norman hair and hacked it short with her dagger, so short that her scalp bled and had to be staunched with cloth.

Jack and Doublejack were sitting by the fire, occasionally passing a wineskin between them, with an even more occasional word or two. They looked around as Robin emerged from her tent, started at her changed appearance, then got up and bowed as she approached. Deep, courtly bows, out of place for outlaws in a wild woodland den.

"Don't," said Robin. "Not to me."

"You are the Princess Royal now," said Jack. "Heir of Ingland."

"Ruler of all I survey," muttered Robin, gesturing at the empty camp. She held out her hand for the wineskin and poured a long draught down her throat before handing it back.

"You are King Harold's daughter," said Jack. Doublejack nodded in emphasis, almost spilling the wine. "You are the rightful Queen of Ingland."

Robin laughed bitterly.

"Queen of nothing," she said. "We should have found another way, not this bandit life, skulking in the trees, while Duke William's rule grows ever stronger."

"We have been biding our time," said Jack. The words came easily to his lips, the familiar speech he had made to doubters before. "The Duke is old and has no sons. The Normans will fight each other when he dies, and we shall have our chance. The true Inglish will flock to your banner—"

"No," said Robin. "They won't. They might have come to serve Merewyn. They won't serve me. Besides, Duke William looked well enough yesterday eve. He might live for years, even beget himself new sons."

"It was the Duke?" asked Jack. "I wondered—"

"It must have been," said Robin. "Fourteen Ferramenta, walking for hours, never wavering in their purpose. Duke William is the only living ironmaster who wields such power. It was him. My grandfather was my sister's bane. Though I also must bear the fault—"

"Nay," interrupted Jack quickly, as he saw the grief begin to twist Robin's face. "None can escape their doom. The Princess was fated to fall as she did."

Robin did not answer for a full minute, her gaze locked on the fire. When she at last lifted her chin, her eyes were red, but there were no tears. A plan . . . or at this stage just a notion . . . was already swimming up from the dark depths of her mind.

"Who stands to inherit from the Duke should he die now?" she asked. Merewyn had always kept up with the many machinations, plots, counterplots, and deaths among the Norman nobility, but Robin chose not to know, as part of her repudiation of that side of her heritage.

"I think three of the eight grand-nephews still live, his sister's son's sons," replied Jack. "And the son of his brother's leman, the Bastard of Aurillac, has something of a claim to Normandy alone."

He hesitated, then added, "None of your cousins has as good a claim to the Duke's lands as you do, highness."

"I am not a Norman heir!" protested Robin. "My claim flows from my father, the true and Inglish King! Besides, the Duke has already tried to slay me, as his iron servants slew Merewyn!"

Jack tilted his head just a fraction, indicating his doubt that the Ferramenta had actually tried to kill Robin. But she did not see it, her eyes on the fire and her mind on other things.

"If I die, Jack, who stands next in the true line?"

Jack looked at her, trying to fathom what she was thinking. He had known her since she was born, but even as a little girl it had been hard to gauge her thoughts or predict her actions. She was always headstrong, a fault usually tempered by intelligence. She never did the same stupid, impetuous thing twice. Though sometimes once was all it took for lifelong regrets.

"None stand clear," replied Jack slowly. "The kin of your father's brother's wife in Jutland. King Sven would claim by that right, I think. But he would gather no following among our people here—"

"Is there no other Inglish heir?"

"There are distant cousins of your family, but none with the name or blood to stir the hearts of the people. Even fewer could wield the holly magic or the rowan, as you do."

The fact that Robin could also wield the iron magic was left unsaid between them. The magics of holly and rowan were Inglish, born of the land, bred true in the royal line. Iron magic was not native to the island kingdom; it was an alien power, like the Norman invaders themselves. It was also magic much more suited to war and conquest.

"What do you intend, highness?" asked Jack.

Robin did not answer.

"I know . . . I suppose . . . you will wish to see the rites conducted for Princess Merewyn. But we cannot bring a priest here, or linger ourselves. The Ferramenta may not cross the Hammerbite, but men-at-arms could, and this place is known . . . and the local folk may not hold out against questioning."

"Not now they know Merewyn is dead," said Robin bitterly. "Tell me, does that fat priest still haunt the cave near the whitestone glade?"

Jack looked at Doublejack.

"Aye, he does," said the huge man.

"Which god does he serve?"

Doublejack shrugged. "He keeps to himself. I would guess the Allfather."

"Not the best—" said Jack.

"Can he sing a death?" interrupted Robin.

"He sang for Wat the miller's son," said Doublejack. "Not at the cave, though."

"Her death should be sung at the High Chapel in Winchester," said Robin bitterly. "But we cannot go there, or to any temple or church that I can think of. So we will go to the fat priest, no matter which god he worships."

Jack and Doublejack bowed, though it was clear Jack would have argued more, if Robin had allowed it.

"We should take what we can from here, highness," said Jack. "We will not be able to come back."

"I will gather what is needed from our . . . my tent," said Robin.

She walked the little way over to the small leather tent she had shared for so many years with Merewyn. There was little enough to pack inside. She took Merewyn's bow, which was better than her own, but left everything else. Of her own stuff, she took a quiver, among its dozen arrows one ivory-tipped, black-fletched shaft, made for killing Norman ironmasters; a small purse of silver pennies; and more hunting clothes.

Then she reached under her straw-stuffed bed and retrieved a leather case. It contained two books. One, bound in bright blue calfskin, was a primer for the Inglish magics of holly, rowan, and oak. The other, bound in dull bronze and black leather, was her mother's grimoire, an ironmaster's compendium of spells and lore.

Robin took everything outside to pack and sort. She could feel grief and raw emotion rising up in her again, overcoming the numbing dregs of dwale that still coursed through her blood. But she forced the complex mix of guilt, rage, and sorrow back down and concentrated on balancing her case, bow, quiver, and sack of clothes. It took her only a very few minutes, for quick departures had been part of her life for six years. Even so, Jack and Doublejack were already ahead of her, the hawker's baskets on their backs full of everything of worth that needed to be carried away.

It was a long walk, via the most hidden paths in the deep forest. The night was light enough for travel, with the moon waxing and near full, and the stars bright save for a single long wisp of cloud on the horizon. Robin gave little thought to where she put her feet or to the green world around her. She simply followed Jack, with Doublejack behind, her mind mostly stuck on a narrow path of its own, a constant repetition of those fateful seconds when the Ferramenta stepped forward and swung its shield at Merewyn.

To try and break out of this pattern, Robin began to focus on a plan that was slowly gathering momentum in her mind. An act that if successful, might make some small amends to Merewyn's shade, to her father, and to the people of Ingland.

It was near midnight when they reached the cave. Though they were quiet and came so late, the priest was waiting for them on the high ledge outside the cavemouth.

Merewyn's band knew him as the fat priest, for he had carried much excess flesh when he'd first arrived in the forest. But that was two years past, and he was now gaunt, great folds of skin around his cheeks and neck the only signs of his previous corpulence. It was unlikely anyone from his past, before he came to the cave, would recognize him. Particularly since, in addition to being a much-reduced man, he had also chosen to cut out his left eye in honor of his god.

The priest went down on one knee as Robin climbed up the stone steps to the cave entrance, Jack pushing past him to make sure no one lurked inside.

"I welcome you, highness, in the Allfather's name," the priest intoned quietly.

"I am honored," replied Robin. It was best to be civil to priests and particularly to those who served the Allfather. "I suppose since you know who I am you also know what I wish of you."

"To sing Princess Merewyn beyond this world," replied the priest. "A raven came to me with the dawn, with the news of her death, and what would be required of me. But come, set down your burdens. I have prepared ale and oatcakes within."

"We do not worship the Allfather," said Robin. "And do not wish to be beholden to him. We will set our packs down here, sit on these steps, and sup on our bread and water, while you sing."

"As you wish," said the priest. He got to his feet creakily and went into the cave, emerging a few minutes later with a harp that had only four strings, a cup of ale, an oatcake, and a silver-bound ox horn. He set all but the harp upon the ground. Taking the instrument under his arm, the priest looked to the starry sky and began to slowly pick out a tune. It began simply, but grew more complex, and Robin felt sure she could hear the strings that weren't there.

Then the priest began to sing as well. His voice was hoarse, but strong, and after the first few words, it echoed strangely, almost as if someone far distant had joined in the singing.

Robin shivered as the song grew louder and stranger, with the unseen voice beginning to drown out the priest. Then suddenly Robin heard Merewyn, clear through the layers of song, in between the harp notes.

"Robin! Seek new beginnings!"

Robin sprang to her feet and rushed toward the priest, but even as she gripped him, screaming, "Merewyn! Merewyn!" her sister's voice was gone, as were the others. There was only the priest, silent now himself, plucking one last note.

"She is gone," said the priest. He stepped back out of Robin's grasp. She did not try to restrain him. "You had best begone yourself, highness, before your men wake."

Robin looked behind her. Jack and Doublejack were sprawled against the steps, chests slowly rising and falling in the rhythm of deep sleep.

"Duke William is at Winchester," said the priest. His single eye reflected the moonlight with a red glint, as if there were also fire in the sky. "You wish to kill him, do you not? Have your revenge?"

"Yes," said Robin warily. She was not entirely sure who she was talking to now, whether it be the priest or the one he served. She could feel the sudden attention of the oaks in the forest. They would not bend themselves to listen to a mortal. But it was not safe to seek the Allfather's favor. He was a god who loved battle and dissent and delighted in sudden treachery.

"Your servants would try to prevent you going to Winchester," said the priest. "But they will sleep here till the dawn, and by then you will be at the gates of Winchester, with your black arrow."

"I do not want your aid, whoever or whatever you are," snapped Robin. "Wake my men!"

"I only wish to be of service," wheedled the priest. "Duke William is a powerful adversary. How will you strike at him, without more powerful allies?"

"I asked only for what any kin may ask of any priest, to sing my sister's death," said Robin. "I will take nothing else and owe no debt. Wake my men!"

"Very well," said the priest. "I will wake them."

He snatched up the ox horn and blew it mightily, its peal echoing out across the forest. It was answered not just by Jack's and Doublejack's sudden, surprised oaths, but by many voices on the forest path below, accompanied by the jangle of arms, armor, and harness.

Robin looked down and saw a column of men-at-arms stretching back along on the path, their helmets glinting in the moonlight. They were leading their horses and there were at least two score of them, perhaps more.

When Robin turned back, the priest was gone, as were horn, cup, and oatcake. Shouts from below showed that she had been seen. Within a few seconds there would be Norman men-at-arms charging up the steps.

"Into the cave, highness!" exclaimed Jack. He pushed Robin out of the moonlight, into the dark entrance. "You must escape!"

Robin knew there was a wide, natural chimney at the rear of the cave, but she couldn't see it and she didn't even try to find it. Instead she turned back toward Jack and Doublejack. Two silhouettes, etched in moonlight, standing in the cave entrance with drawn swords. From beyond them came the crash of soldiers charging up the steps and sudden war cries that echoed and danced around the cave.

"Go!" shouted Jack. He didn't turn around. A moment later, he and Doublejack were beset by three men-at-arms, all that could attack the cavemouth at one time. But many more waited their turn on the steps or the forest floor below.

Robin tried to think of some magic she could do, something that might hold the soldiers off long enough for Jack and Doublejack to disengage. But no Inglish spell came to mind, not one that would work in a cold stone cave. And she had none of the apparatus or the prepared objects that would let her work any serious Norman magic.

But she had her sword. She ran forward and, crouching between her two housecarls, stabbed out at the knee of one of the attacking men-at-arms. Her thrust struck home, sliding under the skirts of the man's mail byrnie. He stumbled back, teetered on the edge of the cave's natural porch, was helped along by a swordthrust from Jack, and fell over the edge.

One of the other men-at-arms was already dead on the ground. The third backed toward the steps. A commanding voice from the forest floor below bellowed out, "Bring up the archers!"

"Take the princess and flee!" ordered Jack to his brother. Doublejack shook his head. It started as a human headshake but ended up as a dog's. His shredded clothes and basket fell to the ground, and a huge cralle dog crouched ready to spring. With a deep bass howl that Robin felt from her feet up through her breastbone, the huge beast leaped forward, straight at the terrified men-at-arms, who tried to jump back, beginning a mass fall down the steps.

Jack watched for two long seconds, then whirled around, gripping Robin's arm with considerable force.

"To the chimney!"

Robin tried to wriggle out of his grasp as they ran into the cave. She couldn't see a thing, but Jack obviously could, for they didn't run into anything.

"We have to go back! Doublejack—"

"They'll shoot us down. Don't waste his gift!"

Robin stopped struggling. Jack dragged her along another half dozen steps, then abruptly picked her up. Tilting her head back, Robin could see a faint circle of lighter darkness above her.

"There are iron staples," said Jack. "I hope."

"There are," said Robin. She knew where they were, without having to see them. Iron called to her, she could feel its resonance deep in her bones. She reached out blindly, her fingers closed around the first staple, and she started to climb.

The chimney was about fifty feet high. Robin emerged on the side of a steep slope, between stunted trees that clung to the rock with gnarled, exposed roots. Jack climbed out behind her.

Both of them looked down the slope. The cavemouth was hidden from them, but they could see at least forty Norman men-at-arms standing ready on the path below it, including half a dozen archers who stood in a semicircle, laughing and joking. From their triumphant demeanor and the snatches of talk that drifted up the hill it was clear Doublejack's furious attack had ended under a hail of arrows.

"Doublejack—"

"He's dead," said Jack. "Come on. Some brave fool will try the chimney, sooner or later, and the wiser will come up the easy side of the hill."

Using the exposed roots as handholds, Jack started to make his way diagonally across and up the slope. Robin followed more slowly. Jack no longer had his basket to weigh him down, but Robin had managed to keep her leather bag and quiver, though Merewyn's bow lay on the cave steps below.

It was a hard scramble to the top of the hill, followed by a frantic, dipping, ducking run between, under, and around the trees and bushes that followed the ridgeline, as the Normans had already raced up the easier side of the hill. Fortunately they were much slower and clumsier in the forest than Jack and Robin and could not simply bull their way through the undergrowth like the Ferramenta.

At last, when the noise of their pursuers faded and there was only the expected sound of the night forest, Jack stopped before a vast, lightning-struck remnant of a royal oak. It was split in several places, revealing a hollow chamber within, but none of the holes were large enough to allow even a child passage.

"Highness, can you make us a way?"

Robin touched the oak, her palm flat on the ancient trunk. If the tree had been alive, she would have felt its green spark at once. But this oak was long dead. Only its shade remained, contained within the collective memory of the forest.

Robin stopped breathing and stood as still as she could. She felt the forest mind slowly drift into her head, like a fog gliding across the moor. She felt what it was to be a sapling reaching for the sun, to have leaves trembling under heavy raindrops, branches reaching out and dividing many times, a trunk thickening its girth for year after year, century after century.

She became the oak, took its place in the memory of the forest. Green shoots sprang out around her palm. Old, dry bark quickened under her skin. One of the holes in the trunk groaned and split farther, a tiny twig growing out from one side. The split expanded, and the twig became a branch, tiny shoots forming on its edges, leaves unrolling from the green buds a few moments later.

"Enough," said Jack.

Robin heard him from far away. But she did not want to let go, did not want to leave the forest. She was the oak, and all her human pain and guilt and fear were somewhere else, far away and alien.

More branches grew around the split, questing outward.

"Enough!" said Jack again, more strongly.

Robin shuddered and withdrew her hand, tearing the skin where the bark had grown around the fleshy mound between thumb and wrist.

She sucked at the graze as she ducked through the split and into the warm, dry, and remarkably roomy chamber that occupied perhaps a quarter of the royal oak's broken stump. The interior was lined with thick moss, which Robin gratefully lay down on, letting the exhaustion she'd held back flow through her limbs.

After a few minutes, Jack, who was propped up near the split, said, "We'll be safe enough here till the dawn. After that, it might be best to make for the convent at Avington. You could claim sanctuary there."

"No," said Robin. "I'll not run from the Allfather to Christ Godsson."

"What shall you do then, highness?" asked Jack. His voice was weary, so weary that he stumbled on his words. Robin looked at him, and for the first time in her young life, saw that Jack was old. Forty at least, perhaps even older. She hadn't noticed that he was grey with fatigue, for Robin had been thinking only of herself.

"I'm sorry, Jack," she said quietly. "For everything. If I hadn't been so impatient to attack, none of this . . . Merewyn . . . Doublejack . . ."

"If not then, it would have been soon anyway," said Jack. All his usual confidence was gone, his tone strange to Robin. "Princess Merewyn knew it. We had more than two thousand men in the months after Senlac Hill. How many stood with us two days ago? Four and thirty! I fear to say it, highness, but I think the time has come for you to treat with your grandfather."

"What?" snapped Robin.

Jack closed his eyes for several seconds before forcing them open again with obvious effort.

"Let us speak of this in daylight, highness," he whispered. "I am weary, so weary . . . perhaps it is weariness and despair which speaks. Let us talk on the morrow. . . ."

His voice trailed off, his head slumped to one side, and his breathing slowly changed, clear indication that he had fallen into an exhausted sleep.

Robin stayed awake, anger frothing about inside her, but she could not maintain her rage. Jack had served her father and her sister faithfully for far longer than Robin had lived. He was mistaken, of course. It might seem as if the Inglish were defeated, but Robin had no intention of falling on her knees before her grandfather and begging forgiveness. She had other plans.

Other plans that meant forcing herself to wake before the dawn and creep from the hollow oak, leaving Jack still asleep. She looked down at him for a few moments, wondering if she was doing the right thing, and found herself reaching out to wake him. But she stopped, her hand wavering a few inches from his shoulder. Jack would not allow her to do what she intended.

Even so, she felt she could not leave him without a word or sign to show that she had gone of her own free will, and not been taken by enemies. So she took the silver-set amber hairpin that no longer had a place to go on her shorn head, and stuck it in the ground by Jack.

By the time the sun was well up and warming the air, Robin was hidden amid long grass, watching the Roman road that ran down from Newbury to Winchester. A lone rider had passed by just after the dawn, but Robin was looking for a large group of travelers, or better yet, a train of merchants, that she could join and mingle with. To better do so, she had thrown away her quiver, keeping only the ivory-tipped arrow, which was uncomfortably tied to her waist under her tunic. She had cut it short, throwing away the flight end, for Robin did not intend to shoot this arrow.

A small group of broad-hatted, staff-wielding pilgrims followed the lone rider an hour after the dawn had yielded to the bright sunshine of a summer day. Robin ignored them too. She would stand out like a dark toadstool in a basket of mushrooms amid the pilgrims.

The next group was much more promising. It looked like the whole population of a village, going to the fair at Winchester to sell their produce. More than thirty men and women, with half a dozen handcarts and three ox-hauled wagons.

Robin stepped out of the trees, pulling her tunic down and hose up, as if she was returning to the road after modestly finding a more private toilet than the roadside ditch.

Thirty pairs of suspicious eyes watched her approach. But when they saw that she had neither sword nor bow, and was not the precursor of a throng of armed bandits, some called out a greeting, the words unclear but the intention friendly.

They were from two villages, Robin found as she walked and talked among them. She had thought they might be wary of her, with her Norman looks, but if they were, they didn't show it. Toward midmorning, a grandmother even invited Robin to ride with her on an ox-wagon, making one of her granddaughters step down. Robin accepted gratefully, for she was very weary.

They did not talk at first. But after a mile of silence, save for the rumble of the wheels, the creak of the cart, and the occasional snuffling bellow from the oxen, the woman asked a question. Her dialect was thick, but Robin understood her well enough.

"Where are you from, boy? Who is your master?"

"Winchester," said Robin, glad that, as she hoped, she had been taken for a boy. "I am a freeman. My name is . . . Wulf."

The woman nodded three times, as if impressing the information into her head.

"I am Aelva," she said. "Widow. My sons are also freemen, holding a hide of land from Henry Molyneux."

"Is he a good lord?" asked Robin.

"Aye, better than the last."

"The Normans have many bad lords," said Robin. She saw the woman's gaze slide across her shorn hair and added, "My father was Inglish. My mother Norman."

"The last lord before Sir Henry was Inglish. We danced when

the tidings came of his end at Senlac Hill."

Robin glared at her and stood, ready to jump off the cart. But the woman caught her elbow.

"I meant no harm, lad. Inglish or Norman lords, it matters not to me, but I'll say no more."

Robin slowly sat back down. They did not talk again, but after a while settled into a companionable silence, the moment of tension between them left on the road behind.

Instead of talking, Robin watched the countryside, enjoying the fresh air and the sunshine. It was years since she'd been out of the forest in daylight. The land looked more prosperous than she remembered. There were more sheep on the hillsides, and more farm buildings, and the road was well mended.

The villagers stopped to rest the oxen and themselves when the sun was high. Robin thanked Aelva and wished them all well, and continued on her way. She felt much more rested in body, but her mind was besieged by new thoughts, brought on by the peaceful road, the contentment of the villagers, and the wealth of the country around her. She tried to tell herself that it was fattened as a lamb was fattened for the slaughter, but this did not rest with what she could see, or with the demeanor of the people.

A mile farther on, she caught her first look at the city of Winchester, the ancient royal capital of Ingland. Once it had been her home, but she had not seen it for more than three years. She had expected it to look exactly the same, for it had not changed in the first twelve years of her life. But it was different, very different, and Robin stopped on the road and stared.

The old wooden palisade was gone, replaced by a much higher one of white-faced stone that incorporated the three old stone watchtowers and had four new towers as well. At first she thought nothing remained of the old royal palace, a large hall that had used to perch atop a low hill, then she realized it had been incorporated into the fabric of a new castle, a fortification that would completely dominate the city were it not balanced by the abbey, whose belltower was as tall, if not so martial. The abbey had also been extended and rebuilt since Robin had seen it last. Harold had not favored the followers of Christ Godsson, but William was said to hold their priests in high esteem.

Entering the city through a new gate of freshly worked stone with masons still finishing the facade, Robin found herself in a crowd and for a few moments was struck with a sudden, nameless fear. She wasn't used to the noise, to the bustle, to the accidental touches as people moved all around her. But she kept pushing forward, making for the market square, where there would be more room. Surely, she told herself, that would not have changed overmuch.

Yet, when she came to it, she found the square also completely different to her expectations, as it was neither an empty field, as it used to be seven days out of fourteen, nor awash with buyers and sellers, goods, and smaller livestock as it would be on the seven fair days.

Instead, the whole field was roped off with muddy red cord fixed to iron pickets driven into the ground. Small groups of men-at-arms lingered at each corner of the field, and right in the middle there was a huge roughly hewn lump of sandstone lying on its side like a toppled sarsen stone. It had a sword stuck right in the middle of it. Even sixty feet away Robin could feel the iron magic involved. The sword had been plunged into the stone by some great magic.

But there was also something of Inglish magic there. Robin couldn't make it out, but there was something on the stone next to the sword. Some sticks, or a bird's nest, or something like that, only it emanated a strong sense of holly magic, and rowan, too. It gave her a strange, slightly nauseating sensation to feel the two magics so close together.

"Strange, ain't it?" whispered a voice near her elbow. "Kiss my hand with silver and I'll tell you the tale."

Robin looked down and stepped back. A crippled man, both of his legs lost at the knee, was grinning up at her and holding out his hand. He would have been tall and strong once, Robin could see, a handsome Inglish man. Now he was a beggar, though she guessed he must be a successful one, for he had decent-enough clothes and good padding on his stumps.

"Did you lose your legs at Senlac?" she asked. If he were one of her father's men, she thought to give him a coin.

"Nay," the man said, and smiled. "It was an accident, building the castle. The King's reeve paid me leg-money, but that's long gone. Go on, give me a scratch of silver and I'll tell you about the sword."

"No," said Robin. She turned away and headed back toward the busy, closed-in streets. The cripple shouted after her, but in good nature. Something about it being a story worth hearing but only if told well.

The crowd swallowed Robin up and buffeted her. It took a while for her to get her bearings again and to try and find the human currents that would carry her in the direction she chose, rather than force her back or push her into the more dubious side streets.

Her destination was always visible to Robin, no matter how the streets turned or the people thronged about her. The castle was a constant landmark, its towers looming above the rooftops.

Finally, she reached the gate and stood alone, between the commercial hurly-burly of the city and the guards who glanced at her with casual disinterest. The gatehouse was new, of the same white-faced stone as the city wall. But the twin leaves of the gate were the old ones, the palace gates of ancient oak, etched with the names of all the kings and ruling queens of Ingland back to Alfred.

Robin found her father's name there. Duke William had not removed it, as she thought he might. But his own name was there, too, clear-cut and bright on the old wood, above Harold's and the Edwards, Edgars, Edmunds, and others fading into illegibility below.

Robin coughed to clear her throat and the guards looked at her again. She stared back, suddenly aware that this was a moment just like when she had snatched Merewyn's horn. If she stepped forward and spoke, her plan would be put irrevocably in motion. Her fate would be decided by its success or failure, and the fate of Duke William, and the fate of the whole kingdom of Ingland, and perhaps the world.

If she stepped forward and spoke.

One of the guards let his hand drop to the hilt of his sword. Three of them were watching her now, wondering why she did not finish her gawping and turn away, as so many did.

Robin stepped forward. At the same time, she reached out to the iron in the guards' swords, helmets, and mail, feeling the weight of it, the currents of attraction and repulsion that moved in the metal. She made a ritual gesture with her hand, closing her fist and shaking it, and as her hand moved, everything of iron on or about the guards let out a keening wail, a crescendoing shriek that was loud enough to make the youngest guard screw his face up and move a little out of position.

It was the iron cry, the announcement of the arrival of a Norman noble ironmaster. Everyone in the castle would have heard it. But even the ironmasters would not recognize this particular cry, because Robin had never used it. From the Duke down, they would be wondering who could have summoned such a loud, pure call.

The guards reacted instinctively, bracing to attention. Robin might look like a vagrant boy, but there was no denying the iron cry. She walked toward them, stopped under the gate, and spoke.

"I am Princess Robin. I wish to be escorted to my grandfather, Duke . . . King William."

More guards ran out to stand at attention, lining both sides of the gate passage. A knight, busy buckling on his sword, followed them, marching up to Robin. He bent his knee briefly and smiled, a cheery, honest smile that had no hint of the Norman duplicity Robin always suspected.

"Greetings, your highness. I am Geoffrey of Manduc. The King has been expecting you, and awaits you in the Great Hall. This way."

"Expecting . . . me?" asked Robin, confusion and fear suddenly gripping her throat, so the words came out hoarse and broken.

"Indeed, all the King's heirs are here," said Geoffrey happily as he bounced along one step behind, still fumbling with his sword belt. He reminded Robin of a hunting dog she'd had, long ago when her father had been alive. Or rather, it was a dog supposed to be a hunter, but despite its enthusiasm, it kept tripping over its own paws and running around in cheerful, ever-decreasing spirals. "When the King returned from the forest yestereve he told the court that you had chosen to end your self-imposed exile. You are very welcome, highness."

"That's not . . ." said Robin. She was already trying to work out what the Duke was up to, and how it might affect what she planned. "Never mind. You said all the King's heirs are here?"

"Yes, they have all been summoned here, though none know why," burbled Geoffrey. "The King has not spoken, though many believe it has something to do with his sword, which he set in a stone down in the market field last settling day."

"A beggar said he could tell me the story of the sword," said Robin, though she felt like someone else was speaking. Most of her attention was on the passage through the gatehouse, and then on the clear space of the outer bailey beyond. She noted the guards' positions and looked for a postern gate or any other way out of the castle.

"I'm sure he did!" laughed Geoffrey. "Stories being the stock of beggars. But surely Highness, you have better stories of your own. Surely, to live as a priestess of the easterner's Moon Goddess must have given you many stories—"

"What?" asked Robin. "I haven't been a priestess for any god, let alone the Easterner's Moon mistress. I've been . . ."

Geoffrey leaned in, intent on her words, and Robin realized that he was probably not the fool he appeared. He was some sort of functionary, but at a royal court, and already he was trying to gain some advantage, some secret knowledge of the King's granddaughter.

"Is it not known where I have been these last four years?" she asked quietly as they rounded the base of the motte hill, heading toward the Great Hall rather than climbing the steps to the Keep.

"No, highness," said Geoffrey. "But there have been many tales."

"What of . . . what of my sister, the Princess Merewyn? What do these tales tell of her?"

Geoffrey looked surprised.

"The Princess Merewyn? She died of a fever only three days after Senlac Hill, did she not?"

Robin shook her head, unable to speak. It was becoming clear to her that her life of the last four years had been largely irrelevant to the Normans, to the people, to . . . everyone in the world outside the forest. They had just been another band of robbers, hiding in the greenwood as robbers so often did. Not even a big enough nuisance for proper tales to be told about them.

The huge doors of the Great Hall were open. As they approached, Robin could hear voices raised in uproar, immediately followed by the harsh clang of Ferramenta beating their swords on their shields.

"I suspect the King has explained the matter of his sword," said Geoffrey. He lengthened his stride and began to hurry. Despite the booming bell-noise of the Ferramenta, the shouts and impassioned voices inside had not subsided.

It was much louder inside the Hall. A vast, high-roofed building, it was a sea of shouting men and a smaller number of equally loud women. Down the far end, a line of twenty Ferramenta held the crowd back from a dais with a simple wooden throne on it. Only four of them were striking their shields, the insistent clangor slowly quieting the crowd. Behind the Ferramenta were a score of archers who wore the black surcoat of Duke William's guard.

The Duke himself stood in front of the throne, calmly waiting for quiet. If he saw Robin, he did not show it. As Geoffrey led her through the crowd toward the throne, Robin realized that nearly everyone around her was a follower of one or the other of William's heirs. The Hall was packed with Norman nobility and the most important knights and ladies of William's realm, most of them either angry, shocked, or excited, the end result being a lot of noise.

Robin didn't speak to any one of them, but every few yards, Geoffrey would grab an elbow and exchange a few words and there would be a bit of space for Robin to squeeze through.

They were only halfway through the crowd when Robin suddenly felt a cold, biting pain behind her right eye. It only lasted a moment, but it also made a strange and sudden anger well up inside her. Anger that was directed at Duke William. He had slain her father, and her sister, and usurped the crown that was rightfully hers. He had to die!

Robin stopped. She had certainly felt anger toward the Duke. She planned to kill him, it was true, but that had been a cold decision, not born of anger. This sudden fury felt strangely out of place, as if it had come from somewhere else. She looked around, and saw only Normans looking to the throne.

Then she looked up and saw a raven staring down at her from the rafters. Its beady black eye was fixed upon her, but its gaze was not that of a bird. She felt it almost like a wind, something invisible but powerful and cold.

Robin shook her head and looked at the floor, mud and rushes overlaying the white flagstones. The fury was still there, but she knew it was not hers. It was the Allfather, trying to force her to play her hand too early.

"Are you well, highness?" whispered Geoffrey. Robin jerked

her head up, suddenly aware that the Ferramenta had stopped their clanging, the people their shouting, and the Hall was growing quiet. She took a slow breath, forcing out the anger that would not help her.

"Yes," she answered. "But before we go on, tell me what has caused this commotion?"

"The King has announced that his heir will be——"

Geoffrey stopped as the King suddenly spoke, his voice strong and penetrating, echoing above Robin's head.

"I have spoken. It is as it is. Who will be the first of my blood to try my test?"

Silence greeted the King's words for several seconds. Then a short but very broad-shouldered man with the back of his head shaved to the crown pushed to the front and walked between the Ferramenta. The iron knights let him pass, and the black-clad archers merely watched as he strode to the foot of the dais. He did not bow, but did incline his head a fraction.

"Aurillac," whispered Geoffrey to Robin.

"I protest, Uncle!" snorted the Bastard of Aurillac. "There should be no test! I claim to be your heir by right of blood. There is no need for this foolery with swords——"

"There are others with an equal or better right of blood," said William. "More is needed from one who would be heir to the King of Ingland and Normandy both. I have proclaimed the manner of my choosing. If you do not dare attempt it——"

Aurillac snorted like a bull.

"I am a greater ironmaster than any here save you, Uncle. I will go now and take your sword from the stone!"

He did not wait for permission but bent his head a little once more, then turned and strode toward the doors. His lesser barons and knights, perhaps a quarter of all those present in the Hall, turned to follow him. Shouting and scuffling broke out again, intensified as the Ferramenta suddenly tromped into a wedge formation and began to march for the doors, with the King and his archers within the wedge.

Geoffrey gingerly pinched Robin's sleeve, being careful not to touch her, and tried to draw her back.

"Best we withdraw and follow the King," he said. "This crowd is too great to draw near to him."

Robin nodded and followed his twisting, winding progress between people to the side of the Hall. She could feel the ivory-tipped arrow at her side and her hand ached to draw it out and plunge it into William's chest. But she could not get close enough now. Later, she would have her chance.

She would be slain soon after, Robin knew, but at least she would die knowing that she had avenged her sister's and father's deaths, and that William's heirs would plunge Ingland and Normandy into war. Though from the look of things, the Bastard of Aurillac might well win that struggle quickly, for his entourage was by far the largest and most warlike. He would also be here, in the capital. . . .

A shadow of doubt slowly slid into Robin's mind. If she slew William, then she might be giving Ingland to Aurillac, who by all accounts would be a far worse master than the Duke. And did she really want Ingland to be stricken by yet another war? These thoughts felt disloyal and were slipperier and harder to grapple with than the pure anger she felt toward William. But they were also persistent, and they stuck with Robin as she followed the crowd out of the castle and down through the town to the market field.

The commotion from the castle, with the sudden parade of the King, the Ferramenta, and more than four hundred Norman nota-bles caused an even greater sensation in the town. It seemed to Robin that absolutely everyone within the city walls was streaming toward the market field, townsfolk and country visitors mingling with the outer edges of the procession from the castle.

With Geoffrey's deft help, whispered words to barons and knights ahead of her, and directions via her sleeve, Robin found herself only just behind the wedge of Ferramenta when they reached the field. There, the iron knights and the bowmen, reinforced by the men-at-arms already at the field, formed a cordon thirty yards out from the sword in the stone, holding back the crowd, which to Robin now seemed to number in the thousands.

Within the cordon, William stood alone with Aurillac. Geoffrey tugged at Robin's sleeve and gently maneuvered her to a position at the very front, so she could see clearly between two Ferramenta. She shivered as she stood up close to them, blinking as she felt the hot spirits contained within the metal bodies reach out to touch her mind. She was both repulsed and attracted to that mental touch. She had not felt it for many years, not since her lessons with her mother. She had been too busy fleeing from them two days before.

Aurillac was shouting something at William. Robin forced her attention away from the iron knights in order to listen to the Bastard.

"—the commoners away! I shall not be tricked, Uncle, in front of the mob!"

William said something Robin couldn't hear and gestured at the sword. Aurillac snarled and strode over to it. He climbed up on the stone and planted his feet on either side of the sword, grasping it with both hands. His muscles tensed, and at the same time, Robin felt a surge of iron magic emanating from him. He was trying to manipulate both the metal of the sword and the more unwielding stone, which William had melded together.

"You must also wear the crown!" called out William. He indicated what Robin had thought was a bird's nest, an irregular ring of sticks and berries, before she'd sensed its magic.

"What?" shouted Aurillac, his nose and cheekbones bright with fury and exertion. "You push me too far! I'll not wear some fool's cast-off casque—"

"It is King Alfred's crown," William said, and though he did not shout, his voice penetrated through the crowd and Aurillac's anger, quietening both. "Lost these two centuries, now found again. Wear the crown of holly, Aurillac, and draw the sword of iron, and you shall succeed me as King of Ingland and Normandy."

"Is this yet another insult?" asked Aurillac. "I am pure Norman, no matter that my parents were not wed. I cannot wear a crown of holly!"

"That is nonsense, born of tales and fancy," said William. He walked over to the stone and reverently picked up the ancient crown. He held it aloft for a few moments, then gently placed it on his head. There was a collective gasp from the crowd, but William neither sweated blood, nor fainted, nor showed any of the other signs Norman ironmasters were supposed to when touched by good Inglish holly.

Aurillac stared at William, then a slow smile crept across his face. It was obvious to Robin that he thought the crown some kind of trick, a thing of paper berries and painted sticks. But she could feel its power too, like a cool and separate pool, riven by currents of hot iron magic that flowed between the Ferramenta, William, Aurillac, and . . . herself.

"Give me the crown!" Aurillac demanded. He stretched out his hand, but William stepped back and held the crown aloft.

"Let the crown of King Alfred choose my successor!" he intoned. Aurillac grunted and climbed down from the stone. He bent his head slightly to allow William to place the crown on his head, then he stood up.

The smile faded from his flushed face as thorns suddenly grew from the holly, long thorns that scraped and scratched like claws toward his eyes. Blood suddenly gushed from his nose and his breath came in harsh, wheezing gasps. He fell to his knees, with his hands pressed over his eyes to protect them from the thorns. William stepped forward and lifted the crown from his head, the thorns retreating.

Robin stared. She had felt the holly magic surge, its calm

replaced by a sudden chill blast, like a freezing wind off the sea. But she had also sensed that the crown had not reacted to Aurillac's Norman blood, but to some other sense of wrongness. She vaguely remembered her mother saying too much was made of the Norman antipathy to holly and oak, but it was widely believed—and that belief had its own power. There were rare people—even rarer than shape-changers—who did not believe in magic at all, and they were extremely resistant to all spells, and sometimes could even prevent magic being done at all. Savants speculated that this was a type of magic in itself.

Two of Aurillac's knights helped him up. The Bastard wiped his bloody face, stared at William, then turned on his heel and strode to join his followers. There he held a quick conversation and his men began to turn around and start pushing the common folk, to create a path away from the field.

"Aurillac!" William called out. "I have not given you leave to go. There are others of my blood here. If one succeeds, all must swear allegiance to my chosen heir."

Four Ferramenta moved as William spoke, the iron knights lumbering closer to where Aurillac paused, fury expressed in his clenched fists and caution in his twisting torso, as he turned back to face the sword in the stone.

William looked at another knot of knights and men-at-arms, behind three young men who all stood scowling at the stone. Unlike Aurillac, they were not in mail, and their bright garb was in stark contrast to most of the other men.

"Well, nephews?"

"We will wait till you're dead, Great-uncle," said the one with the bright blue tunic and the silver-tipped cap. He looked over at Aurillac and added, "Then split everything between us equally."

William laughed.

"Honest as ever, Jean. But I do not intend to die for some time.

I think I will find my heir today—and you will swear allegiance."

"Who?" asked Jean. "Aurillac could not draw your sword, and my brothers and I know better than to attempt it. There is no one else."

William smiled again and turned to face the crowd. He didn't speak, but stood waiting. A hush fell upon the crowd, the silence spreading till the only sound Robin could hear was the thumping of her heart, the blood vessels in her neck hammering like a drum.

"The iron call outside the castle," Jean said suddenly, his voice strange and reedy in the silence of the crowd. "Who was that?"

A raven cawed its lonely cry and flew over the field. A one-eyed man pushed to the front of the crowd, right behind Robin and Geoffrey.

She reached inside her tunic to grasp the broken end of her ivory-tipped arrow, but still hesitated. She would never have such an opportunity again to kill William, but still—

The one-eyed man touched Geoffrey on the small of the back with his little finger, a touch that would not have crushed a fly. The Norman courtier fell forward and would have hit Robin, but she had already started forward, bursting into the clearing, where she appeared like a sprung child's toy from between the two Ferramenta.

There was a collective gasp from the crowd as Robin slowly walked toward William. To them it looked like a poor Norman boy, a peasant, was approaching the King of Ingland and Normandy—with head held high.

"Princess Robin," said William.

"Grandfather."

A shriek came from the crowd as she spoke, and nervous laughter, followed by many voices calling for quiet. Aurillac started forward, and the Ferramenta moved fast, blocking his way. William made a sign and his black-clad archers moved closer, their eyes on the Bastard and his entourage.

"What is to be, then?" asked William softly, so no one else could hear. "What do you hold there? A wooden stake? Will you hear me first?"

Robin nodded, though instantly she felt that this was a mistake. Her courage and fury, pulled taut as a bowstring, could not be held so long. She gripped the arrow more tightly and told herself that a minute more would not matter. William would merely die a little later.

"Kill me and you will die," said the King. "Ingland will be riven by war. Everything your father held dear will be lost—"

"You slew my father!" Robin whispered hoarsely, while all the crowd leaned forward, desperate to hear what was being said.

"He died in battle, with a sword in his hand, as did your sister. I regret their deaths, particularly Merewyn's. My death will not return them to the living, Robin. Your death will serve no purpose. Wear the crown and take my sword, and within a year or two at most, you will be Queen of Ingland and Normandy!"

William spoke fiercely and reached out to grip Robin's shoulders. She shuddered under his touch and half drew the arrow. He was so close, it would be so easy to punch the arrow up through his old ribs and into his heart. All the charms and protections every ironmaster wrapped themselves in would be as nothing to the sharp ivory point.

Robin raised her elbow and began to draw the arrow out through the fold in the front of her tunic.

"You are my granddaughter," whispered William. He closed his eyes and leaned forward, as if seeking an embrace. "Do what you will."

"Seek new beginnings," whispered Merewyn. Though her voice was nearly drowned by the sudden cawing of ravens overhead, it sounded to Robin like her sister was just behind her.

But she wasn't. There was only her old grandfather, his eyes still closed, his hands on her shoulders. There was the crowd beyond, a great mass of excited expectation, aware that they were witnesses to a great and strange event. The three grand-nephews, staring at her as if she were some strange creature. Aurillac, his stare that of an enemy, held in check only by temporary weakness.

Robin remembered grabbing the horn from Merewyn. Remembered charging down the slope. Remembered the sound of Merewyn being struck by the iron knight.

Knowing when not to attack . . . seeking new beginnings . . . Merewyn's voice echoed in her head, as it would probably echo for as long as Robin lived.

Slowly, she pushed the arrow back under her tunic, through her belt, and pulled her hand free.

"I will never forgive you," she whispered. "But I will take your sword."

Then she spoke loud enough for the crowd to hear.

"Give me the crown."

A cheer rippled through the mass of onlookers, though Robin wasn't sure whether they were cheering her on or hoping to see a repeat of what had happened to Aurillac.

William held the crown high, and Robin felt the magic within it. It was like a seed, a container of potent force waiting for the right conditions to burgeon forth.

Robin bent her head and felt the rough touch of the holly leaves scrape through her hair. She tensed, waiting for the sharper stab of thorns, or for a sudden, shocking attack of nausea. But the crown sat comfortably on her near-shaven head, and her stomach was no more stricken with anxiety than it had been before.

"The sword!" someone shouted from the crowd, a cry that was taken up in seconds, to become a chant, several thousand voices all calling at once.

"The sword! The sword!"

Robin reached up to steady the crown and was startled to find her fingers touching flowers and green shoots rather than dried sticks and wizened berries. She was even more startled to find that the stubble on her scalp was no longer harsh and fuzzy. Her hair was growing back impossibly fast, and was already as long as the first two knuckles on her little finger.

"The sword," said William. Robin couldn't hear him, the chanting was so loud, but she knew what he was saying. She dropped her hands from her newfound hair and the flowering crown, flexed her fingers, and stepped up onto the stone.

The sword radiated iron magic like a miniature sun. Robin felt the heat wash across her face and breathed hot air through her mouth. But she knew this was not real heat, and it would not burn her unless she feared it would.

Without hesitation, she gripped the hilt of the sword with both hands, accepting the heat and the magic, letting them flow through her body, taking in the strength of the iron to add to her own.

She felt no conflict from the crown, but rather an acceptance that this, too, was part of her. Her heritage was of both the green forest and the hot stone that lay deep beneath the earth, and they did not clash within her.

The chant grew louder and more frenzied as Robin bent her knees and focused both her strength and her will upon the sword in the stone. She could feel how William had meshed blade and rock, but it was no easy matter to undo what he had done. But slowly she compelled sword and stone to separate, and with a screech like some tormented beast of legend, the weapon came free, an inch at a time.

Sweat poured from Robin's face and pain coursed through her lower back and forearms, but with one last outpouring of strength and determination, the stone gave up its prize. Robin whipped the sword around and held it aloft, too breathless to shout or even speak.

Not that even her shouts would be heard above the noise of the crowd.

William held up his hands for silence, the Ferramenta booming and clanging to punctuate his demand. As the crowd stilled, William turned to the stone and started to walk the few paces over to Robin.

At that moment, Aurillac and his men suddenly charged, the Bastard himself leaping up on the stone, sweeping his great sword out of its scabbard as he jumped.

Robin ducked under his first blow, Aurillac's swordpoint skittering off the stone in a spray of sparks. She parried the next, but the blow was so strong William's sword was smashed out of her hand, and her fingers were suddenly numbed and useless.

Three arrows bounced off the Bastard, repelled by his charms, as he struck again. Robin jumped backward off the stone, landed well, and backed away, the crowd receding like the tide.

A sweeping glance showed Robin that William, his bowmen, and the Ferramenta were wreaking bloody havoc among Aurillac's men and this stupid battle would not last more than a few minutes.

But that was all the Bastard would need to kill her.

He jumped from the stone and charged toward her as Robin tried to pull out the black arrow with her left hand. She tensed, ready to try and dodge, the arrow still stuck in her clothes. But as Aurillac raised his sword, he was suddenly struck from behind by a huge lump of snarling brown fur that was either a dog or a small bear, that had jumped from the fringes of the crowd straight on his back.

At the same time, more than a dozen unarmed men—townsfolk or simple peasants—charged in front of Robin. One fell beneath Aurillac's sword, but the others fell on him as the bear brought the Bastard bellowing down. More men and women surged from the crowd to form a human shield-ring around Robin.

All were shouting the same thing.

"Ingland! Ingland! Ingland!"

Then Robin was being lifted up, onto the shoulders of the taller men of those about her. Aurillac lay dead nearby, or good as dead, as eight or nine people hacked at him with small knives, hatchets, and even their hands. The bear that had felled him sat up on its haunches, the crowd giving it space as it licked its paw and muzzle clean of blood.

Robin looked at the bear and it met her gaze with a human understanding.

"I thank you, Jack," said Robin softly.

The bear got up and stood on his hind legs. Then he slowly sank to one knee and bowed his head. All around him, the people followed suit. It was like the wind pressing down a field of corn, as heads suddenly lowered and men, women, and children all sank to one knee. The peasants and townsfolk were first, but then the Norman men-at-arms followed suit, and then the knights and lords and ladies, into the bloodied mud where Aurillac's followers lay dead or wounded.

Only William still stood. Even the men who carried Robin had sunk to their knees, so she was seated on their shoulders. Her hair had grown long and now framed her face, and the holly flowers of her crown had grown and spread too, to make a mantle that fell down her back like a rich, royal cloak.

William walked to her. Halfway, he held out his hand, and his sword flew into it. He reversed it to hold the blade. Then he proffered the hilt to Robin, and she took it in her left hand, and held it high.

So the Princess Robin came into the inheritance she had never sought; amid blood, but not of her choosing; welcomed by a grandfather she had always feared and hated; hailed by the Normans she looked like and the Inglish who she felt were her true people.

Overhead, two ravens cawed once in disgust and flew northeast, biting and snapping at each other as they flew. As they fled, a one-eyed man coughed and died where he lay on the ground between two of Aurillac's dead men, the arrow that had chance-hit him buried deep in his chest.

a wink and a nod

lighthearted tales

THE CURIOUS CASE OF
THE MOONDAWN DAFFODILS MURDER

As Experienced by Sir Magnus Holmes
and Almost-Doctor Susan Shrike

H olmes is here, Inspector," announced the Sergeant, peering around the door of Inspector Lestrade's office, which
was currently occupied by the newly promoted Inspector
McIntyre, as Lestrade was on his holiday. "In a manner of speaking,
that is."

McIntyre, aware of the susceptibility of the newly promoted to
pranks from those less fortunate, chose to play a straight bat.

"What do you mean, in a manner of speaking?" he asked calmly,
placing the file he had been reading slowly down upon Lestrade's
desk. "Is he, or is he not, present in the antechamber?"

"Well, he is present," said the Sergeant, whose name was Cumber
and whose intellect was not particularly finely honed. "Only it isn't
Mr. *Sherlock* Holmes, as was invited."

McIntyre set both his hands flat on the table, as they trembled
with visible tension.

"You don't mean to say that Mr. Mycroft Holmes has come to
see me!"

McIntyre was well aware of Mr. Mycroft Holmes's importance
within the government, and the range and power of his influence.
He also knew that the elder Holmes never left his club, and he could
not even begin to consider just how much more serious the case
before him must be if Mycroft Holmes himself had come to consult

upon it. Why, it was more than the mountain going to Mahomet, it was unprecedented, it was—

The Sergeant broke into McIntyre's slightly panicked thoughts.

"No, it isn't Mr. Mycroft Holmes. It's a Sir Magnus Holmes."

"Sir Magnus Holmes . . ." muttered the Inspector. "I don't believe I've even heard of the fellow."

"He has a woman with him," said the Sergeant darkly. "One of them modern women."

"What!?" exploded McIntyre. "If this is all some sort of joke, Cumber, it's gone too far."

"Not a joke," said Cumber. He paused for a moment to reflect, then added, "Least, not that I know of. Shall I send them in?"

"No!" roared McIntyre. He thumped his fist on the desk, making the file jump and his half-empty teacup rattle on its saucer, the tea inside almost slopping over the edge.

"Very good, sir," replied Sergeant Cumber. He started to close the door, but just before it snapped shut, he added, "'E did say Mr. Sherlock sent him over, sir."

The door shut before McIntyre could answer. He sat there with his mouth open for an instant, then, with an explosion that this time did send his tea slopping over the saucer and onto the desk, he erupted from behind the chair and stalked to the door. A big man, who had fought heavyweight for his uniformed division before joining Scotland Yard, he flung the door open with a weighty fist and was all set to bellow again when he saw that he was being stared at by a lady and a gentleman, and by Cumber, who clearly had not quite gathered the intellectual power to tell them to go away in a nice fashion suitable to their obvious gentility.

McIntyre saw a relatively young man, perhaps twenty-eight or thirty, with a not very memorable face, short pale hair, and something on his upper lip and chin that could charitably be viewed as a Van Dyke beard. He was only of medium height, had a slight build,

and was wearing a very well-cut grey morning suit, made somewhat eccentric by a curiously shaped and very heavy gold watchchain
visible on his waistcoat, which was surmounted by a pearly white
stiff-necked shirt with a dark red ascot tie, again made odd by the
large and peculiar tiepin that was thrust through it, which had the
appearance of being made of a bundle of small golden sticks and so
looked rather raffish.

The woman next to him was a very different matter. She was of
a similar age, but where he was very much of average appearance,
she was striking. Dark-haired, blue-eyed, her charms were subdued
under her not very flattering black-and-white dress that was somewhat reminiscent of a uniform, though it was drawn in tightly at the
waist and had an elegant ruffled neck of obviously very expensive
lace. She also carried a small leather Gladstone bag, which was not at
all a normal item of apparel for a lady of quality. McIntyre automatically noted she wasn't wearing a wedding ring.

"Inspector McIntyre!" called out the man. "We were just trying
to impress on the good sergeant here that we had come to call upon
you, at the express request of my cousin Sherlock."

"Mr. Sherlock Holmes?" asked McIntyre warily. "He is your
cousin?"

"Second cousin, actually," said the man. "Something to do with
our grandfathers, I can't quite recall, but my father grew up with
Sherlock, and when my grandfather gambled away the old place and
my father had to turn to trade, Sherlock was one of the few who
stood by him, or so father always said, though I don't—"

"And you are?" asked McIntyre, cutting short what otherwise
seemed likely to be a long discourse of Holmes family history.

"Oh, I'm Sir Magnus Holmes," said the man happily. "Just plain
Magnus Holmes till father dropped off the perch last year. He was
made a baronet in '87, services to the Worshipful Company of Tallow
Chandlers . . . lucky for me, if they'd left it any later I'd have missed

out inheriting. Makes it easier to get a decent table, don't you know, and theater tickets—"

"Indeed," said McIntyre. He looked at the door to the corridor, which had a glass window and thus might show the shadows of any observers, as he was beginning to wonder whether Mr. Sherlock Holmes himself was playing a trick upon him. Seeing nothing untoward, he glanced at the lady, who had maintained her station a pace or two away from Sir Magnus and was looking with detached interest at both the Inspector and the Baronet.

"And Miss . . ."

"Allow me to introduce Almost-Doctor Susan Shrike," declared Sir Magnus. "My . . . um . . . keeper."

McIntyre's brow lowered, a frown compressing his rather bull-like features, now accentuated by the narrowing of his mighty nostrils.

"I don't appreciate having a May-game made of me—" he began.

"I beg your pardon, Inspector," interrupted Susan Shrike. Her voice was cool and commanding and both soothed and dominated all the menfolk in the room. "Magnus sometimes gets carried away. My name is Miss Susan Shrike, and I *am* almost a doctor, in that I am in the final year of my medical studies at the London School of Medicine for Women. I also am upon occasion employed to care for certain patients who are allowed excursions from Bethlem Royal Hosp—"

It was the Inspector's turn to interrupt. He raised a finger to point at Magnus.

"You mean . . . you mean to say he's a lunatic from Bedlam!"

"Well, I am getting better," said Magnus reasonably. "I wouldn't be allowed out, otherwise, even with Almost-Doctor Susan."

"Sir Magnus is not at all dangerous," said Susan. "He has been at the hospital for a few months recovering himself after an unfortunate accident. He is now well enough to begin to resume everyday activities. My presence is merely a precaution insisted upon by his aunt."

Magnus grimaced.

"Lady Meredith Foxton," he said in a stage whisper. "Ghastly woman. Specializes in making people miserable."

"Now then, Inspector," said Susan. "As I must have Sir Magnus back at the hospital before nightfall, perhaps you would be kind enough to tell us exactly what your problem is and we shall see if Sir Magnus can assist you."

"Sir Magnus, assist me?" asked McIntyre. He was having difficulty comprehending what was going on and was wondering if perhaps he wasn't better suited to a more lowly rank after all. If only Lestrade hadn't gone on holiday!

"I like to help," said Sir Magnus brightly. "Sherlock said you had a case that was right up my alley and that . . . let me see . . ."

He strode to the fireplace and leaned one elbow on the mantelpiece, then turned his head back to look at the Inspector. Somehow his face had assumed an entirely different aspect, and he now looked far more hawklike and acute, with a hint of suppressed arrogance.

"Magnus, my boy," he drawled, in a voice that McIntyre recognized as a very good imitation of Sherlock's. "When you have eliminated the impossible, whatever remains, however improbable, must be the truth—and the very highly improbable is I suspect exactly what Mr. McIntyre is facing. As this is very much more your area of expertise, I suggest that you answer the Inspector's clarion call and leave me to my practice."

Magnus dropped his elbow, and the likeness with it.

"Revolver practice, that was, not violin," he added in his own voice. "Shooting initials in the wall. And they say I'm mad."

"What is your area of expertise, Sir Magnus?" asked McIntyre. He felt that this was perhaps a foolish question, but the truth of the matter was that he needed help, and if Sherlock Holmes really had said those words, which, after seeing that impression, he was inclined to believe, then perhaps this unlikely lunatic might be of some assistance.

"I am a s . . . s . . . s . . ." Magnus started to say, stopping suddenly as Susan looked at him intently. "That is, I have made a study of the unusual, the arcane, and the occult. Also I make things. I am an inventor, and have a supple and surprising mind. Sherlock said that too, by the way. Mycroft says that I am a throwback to another era and should be burned at the stake, but he doesn't mean it, not after that business with the . . . the . . . things that I'm not supposed to mention. Let's go into your office, shall we, Inspector?"

McIntyre surprised himself again by allowing Magnus to slide past him, and he held the door open for Susan Shrike, letting it swing shut behind him on Cumber's inquisitive face.

"Go and get my guests some tea," ordered McIntyre through the door.

"Yes, sir," came the muffled response.

"I trust he won't have to wait for the tea," said Sir Magnus.

"No, I shouldn't think so," replied McIntyre, rather baffled by this new conversational sally. He returned behind his desk, and indicated the chairs on the other side. "Please, do sit down."

"If he had to wait in a line then he would be a queue Cumber," said Magnus.

"What?" asked McIntyre, who had opened the file again and allowed his thoughts to wander. "What?"

"Hush," said Susan Shrike. "Why don't we let the Inspector tell us about the matter in question."

"Queue," muttered Sir Magnus. "If he grew his hair long at the back, he could—"

"Magnus," said Susan Shrike, quite softly.

Magnus nodded.

"Yes, yes, awfully sorry. Please do explicate the matter, Inspector."

McIntyre picked up the top paper from the file, gripping it as if he might hurl it to the ground and throw himself upon it in a wrestling check.

"These are the salient points," he said. Clearing his throat, he began to read.

"On the morning of the ninth instant, that is to say, yesterday, at twenty-one minutes past five o'clock in the morning, P.C. Whitstable was proceeding upon his usual beat and had reached the corner of Clarges Street and Piccadilly, when he heard a shout on the other side of the road, at the point where a path exits from The Green Park. Dawn was approaching, the gas lamps were still lit, and there was no fog. He clearly saw a man in a long coat and unusual wide-brimmed hat run out of the park and start to cross the road. But on seeing P.C. Whitstable approaching, this man turned to the left and increased his speed. P.C. Whitstable, blowing his whistle, set off in pursuit, and was joined by Park Keeper Moulincourt—"

"Moulincourt?" asked Sir Magnus. "I knew a fellow called Moulincourt. He wasn't a park keeper though—"

McIntyre shook his paper and resumed reading.

"—Moulincourt, who had in fact raised the alarm by shouting. Though Moulincourt, who had already pursued the coat-wearing man for some distance, fell back, P.C. Whitstable, a keen footballer, soon caught the fellow. However—"

"There's always a however," said Sir Magnus. "Had to be. I was expecting it to come in before this. However."

"However!" blasted McIntyre, shaking his paper in barely suppressed fury. "When Whitstable gripped the fellow's arm, the coat and hat came off, and there was no one inside, only a great shower of daffodils that fell onto the road."

Sir Magnus tilted his head until it was completely sideways, and peered at McIntyre.

"Daffodils," he repeated. "Stolen from the park?"

"Yes," said McIntyre, through gritted teeth. "Stolen from the park, and a park keeper murdered in the process."

"Not Moulincourt, obviously," added Sir Magnus, whose head was slowly righting itself again. "Were they the first daffodils of the spring?"

"I don't know!" protested McIntyre. "No one's ever tried to steal flowers from the park before. There are daffodils all over the place. Why bother with those ones? And anyway, how did the bloke escape—"

"First flowers of spring from a royal park, cut with a silver blade between dawn and moonset," said Sir Magnus. "Your park keeper had his throat cut?"

"Yes, how on earth . . ."

A look of suspicion crossed the Inspector's face. Perhaps Sherlock Holmes was not playing a game with him, but sending him a suspect.

"Where were you yesterday morning between five and six o'clock?"

"Locked up," replied Sir Magnus. He looked across at Susan Shrike and gave her a cheery smile.

"Yes, that's true, Inspector," said Susan. "Sir Magnus is locked inside his rooms at the hospital from dusk to dawn. It is part of his treatment."

"Then how did you know about the throat cutting?" asked McIntyre. "None of this has been in the papers. Did Sherlock tell you? He has his ways of finding out."

"No, Sherlock didn't tell me," complained Sir Magnus. "Why does everyone always think Sherlock does my thinking for me? No, I deduced it, from my knowledge of folklore and ritual."

"What are you talking about?" demanded the Inspector.

"It's quite simple, really," drawled Sir Magnus. He slid his chair away and leaned backward for a moment, precipitating a mad grab at the edge of the desk as he almost tipped over. "There is a . . .

belief . . . among certain quarters, that flowers from a royal park, if cut with a silver knife at a particular time, will enormously enhance their natural poison. Lycorine, as Sherlock would tell you. Nasty stuff in general, but a moondawn daffodil's poison is far, far more dangerous."

"That can't be true," protested McIntyre. "How could it make any difference?"

Sir Magnus shrugged.

"Whether it does or not, clearly someone believes they need moondawn daffodils to make a terrible poison. I wonder what they intend to use it for?"

"And what about the empty coat?" asked McIntyre. "The running man who was . . . was just daffodils?"

"Oh, that's easy," said Magnus. "The Adept would have cut the keeper's throat, and when the blood spilled on the earth he quickly fashioned a kind of simple golem from the resulting mud, using cut daffodils for the arms and legs, he threw his own coat and hat over it and sent it away to create a diversion."

"Magnus," warned Susan Shrike. "Remember?"

"Or, far more likely," Magnus continued without pause, "in the relative darkness—he was between two gaslights, I expect, in a balletic movement as the constable took his arm, the murderer spun about, at the same time turning himself out of the coat and throwing the daffodils at the policeman's face, blinding him for the few seconds required to drop to the ground and then crawl away along the shadow of the park railings."

"I prefer the second explanation," said McIntyre. He stared at Magnus for a few seconds, then stood up, casting an air of finality over the proceedings.

"Thank you very much for your time and thought, Sir Magnus," he said, shaking hands over the desk. "You have given me something to think on, to be sure. A pleasure to meet you, likewise, Miss

Shrike. Sergeant Cumber will show you out. Please pay my respects to Mr. Sherlock Holmes when next you see him."

"But the Adept . . . the murderer . . . you'll need my help to find him and bring him to justice," protested Sir Magnus.

"We'll get our man," said McIntyre. "Thank you again, but this is pure police business now. Good day."

"Sherlock said that apart from Lestrade and . . . and Gudgeon or someone . . . you were—"

"Sir Magnus! We really must be going," said Susan forcefully. "Thank you, Inspector."

Outside the Inspector's office, Sir Magnus turned to Susan.

"We didn't even get our tea," he grumbled.

"I expect there was a queue, after all," said Susan. She took Magnus by the arm and led him out into the corridor, hustling him along past the startled Sergeant Cumber and his silver tea tray.

"You know we can't let you out if you will insist on telling people the truth," she admonished him as they climbed into their hackney cab, which was not, despite its very ordinary appearance, one for hire by the general public.

"I can't help it," said Sir Magnus. "Krongeitz really knew what he was doing with a curse."

"It is fading, though," remarked Susan. "You'll be right as rain in a few months."

"If the *other* fades as well," said Magnus.

"My, you are cheerful today. Magister Dadd says it will go in time, with the treatment, and he should know."

"He also said it will get worse before it gets better," said Sir Magnus. He leaned over and took Susan's hand. "Promise me that you'll act at once if it seems to be . . . spreading into the daylight hours, of its own accord."

Susan gently withdrew her hand and rested it on her Gladstone bag.

"You know I will do whatever is necessary, Magnus," she said.

"But I am sure it won't be necessary. Now tell me, do you have any thoughts about who might be behind this moondawn daffodil business?"

"An Adept who can make a golem from blood, mud, and flowers on the fly? And who wants moondawn daffodils to reap their poison? I'm not sure we should try to find whoever it is."

"Magnus. We can't leave it to the police. Tell me about this moondawn poison business. Does it really make the flowers that much more dangerous?"

Magnus chuckled grimly.

"I didn't even tell the Inspector the best part. If you transform the poison properly, you don't even have to deliver it physically to the target. You can use the poison on something sympathetically attuned to a similar object the victim will use. A comb is quite popular, because it merely needs to touch."

"I see," mused Susan. "And is this process of transformation difficult to manage? Does it require any particular apparatus?"

"Yes, it does," said Magnus. "And I see what you're thinking. Interestingly, and I never realized it before, it also ties in with the popularity of a comb being the typical sympathetic object of moondawn daffodil poisoning."

"Why?"

"Because the ritual partly involves the daffodils being cut up with a silver blade and placed in a retort with a scented oil. A silver razor, or scissors, would work a treat—"

"And Macassar oil for the retort," added Susan. "What else?"

"It needs to take place underground, with the usual harmonization requirement," mused Magnus. "Old Mithraeum, something like that. An Anglo-Saxon crypt would work, maybe a Norman one at a pinch."

"How long does the ritual take? How much time do we have?"

"I'm not entirely sure, never having undertaken the dastardly deed myself. But I seem to recall the daffs have to fester for several days in the oil, with lots of highly repetitive incantation . . ."

"So we need to look for an underground barbershop on the site of an old temple or church."

"Yes . . . it will also be close to Green Park, as the daffodils have to be in oil before the sun is fully up. Even so, it could take a while to find out somewhere that matches all that. Damned tedious as well."

"Unless you ask your cousin."

"Sherlock? He hates this kind of . . . oh . . . Mycroft. I suppose I could think about that."

"It might even be in his bailiwick, as it were," said Susan. "After all, who would our Adept be wanting to poison in this way? Someone difficult to reach by other means."

"Yes," said Magnus. "The Queen is the obvious target. Or perhaps the Prime Minister. Mycroft might even be polite."

He tapped the ceiling twice, and the small hatch beneath the driver's seat slid back.

"Carstairs! The Diogenes Club, thank you."

Following his visit, Sir Magnus returned to the hackney in a bad mood and handed Susan a note on which an address was written in Mycroft's distinctive copperplate.

"It really is the most boorish place," complained the Baronet. "All I said was 'Good morning, Mycroft.' I whispered, but you would have thought I was Marie Lloyd in full flight from the way they carried on. Mycroft wouldn't even talk to me, I had to write everything down for him."

"You know their rules," said Susan. "I believe you talk just to annoy him. Anyway, you got an address."

"Gregory Cornet's in Curzon Street is the only barbershop that fits all the criteria," said Sir Magnus. "Its lower cellar was a temple to Bast, once upon a time."

"The Egyptian goddess?"

"Yes, the fiscal procurator for several successive Roman governors was Egyptian and had a thing for the old cat. . . . I get my hair cut at Cornet's by old Radziwill. I do hope he's not involved. A good barber is hard to find."

"Really?" asked Susan, pointedly staring at the not very successful Van Dyke which was a fairly recent addition to Magnus's upper lip and chin.

"Yes. It makes the whole thing so much more difficult. Maybe we should hand this over to Dadd."

"Because of your barber?"

"No. Yes. I don't know. I suppose I've lost confidence after the whole Krongeitz business."

"I think we should go to Cornet's and you should get your beard shaved off," said Susan. "I will wait and observe, making caustic comments, in the role of your fiancée."

"I wish you would be my fiancée."

"You know we're not going to talk about that until you're completely recovered," said Susan. "As I was saying, this will allow us to get a feel for the place, and we may well sense any unusual vibrations that would confirm the location."

"So we walk into what is probably an enemy lair and I sit down and ask to have a razor put to my throat," said Magnus. "Besides, what do we do if it *is* the place?"

"I doubt the barbershop, or your Radziwill, is actually involved," said Susan. "Think about it. They've been there too long, and it's too public. I expect we'll find they've a new odd-jobs man, who lurks in the cellar, or something like that."

"Maybe," replied Magnus. "But it could be they're all in it, a secret society of barber-illuminati."

"Yes, it could," admitted Susan. "In which case, I will quickly give you the blue pill."

Magnus looked at her very seriously.

"I think that's why I don't want to go. I really would prefer it didn't come to that. Are you sure we shouldn't hand this over to Dadd?"

"No," replied Susan. "But here we are. Do we go in?"

"You wish me to shave the beard?" asked Radziwill. "It has barely had a chance to begin."

"Cut off in its youth," sighed Sir Magnus. He rolled his eyes to where Susan was sitting primly on a chair, apparently reading a copy of *The Englishwoman's Domestic Magazine*. "But it has to go."

"Interesting place you have here, Mr. *Razorwell*," said Susan, over the top of the magazine. "I've never seen anywhere like this."

"Ladies do not usually come inside," said Radziwill. He began to strop his razor, which both Magnus and Susan noted was silver-handled, and possibly the blade was silver too. "It is a gentleman's establishment."

"Where does that charming little stair go?" asked Susan. She pointed past the row of curtained booths to the end of the room, where a brass-railed stair curled down beside a wall of massive, ancient stones.

"The cellar, ma'am, where we store our scents and oils," said Radziwill.

"Oh, I should like to see that!" exclaimed Susan. She got up and started to walk toward the stair. But she had hardly taken a step when the curtains of every booth on either side slid back, to reveal twelve other barbers, each holding a silver razor. Radziwill made the thirteenth, and there were no customers in sight.

"Damn," exclaimed Magnus, delivering a savage kick to Radziwill's groin at the same time he leaped out of the chair. The barber grimaced and swung back with the razor, which Magnus countered by swirling around the sheet that had been over his shoulders a moment before.

Susan sat back down and opened her bag with a click. Reaching quickly inside, she pulled out a large blue pill.

"Magnus!"

Magnus turned his head and opened his mouth. Susan threw the blue pill unerringly down his gullet and immediately reached into the bag to withdraw a necklace of shimmering blue stones, which she dropped over her head.

"I really wish you weren't involved in this, Radziwill," said Magnus, parrying another swipe. "You're an excellent barber. . . . Argh!"

Radziwill looked at his razor in puzzlement. He had swung, but as far as he could tell had cut only the sheet, which Magnus had been employing as something between a baffle and *main gauche.*

Magnus screamed again and raised his arm. Only it wasn't an arm anymore, but a loathsome tentacle, lined with huge suckers that were ringed with glistening fangs.

One of the barbers, presumably the Adept, apparently knew what Magnus was becoming. He shouted something and ran for the door, only to be shot in the back by Susan, who was standing on the chair with her back pressed to the wall, the glowing necklace on her breast and a lady's purse revolver in her hand, the barrel now smoking.

Magnus's screams quickly became no longer human, there were many tentacles, and within a minute at the most, there were no more living barber-illuminati. The thing that Magnus had become slid across the floor of the shop, squelching through blood and torn flesh toward the front door and the street.

Susan put her revolver away, took a twisted paper packet from her bag, and stepped off the chair. The thing paid her no attention. One long tentacle began to caress the door, feeling for how it might be opened.

Susan lifted off the necklace with her left hand. Instantly the monster swung about. Two tentacles shot toward her, sucker-rings protruding, all the teeth out. She calmly ducked aside and threw the contents of the paper across the tentacles, creating a cloud of blue dust that very slowly twisted and danced about on its slow way to the floor.

It took a few minutes for Magnus to become human again. Susan spent the time preparing a slow match to the store of hair oil in the cellar, being careful not to disturb the daffodil brew that was bubbling on the Aga in one corner.

When she came back up, Magnus had managed to get most of the blood and matter off himself, and was wearing a clean robe with a towel wrapped around his head. He had not managed to completely clean the vomit from the corners of his mouth, and his eyes were wild.

"He . . . the Adept . . . put a s-s-silence charm and interrupt-me-not on the d-d-door," he said, teeth chattering. "It will break when you pull it open. N-n-nice of them, don't you think?"

"Very handy," agreed Susan. She took him by the arm and pulled the door open, putting two fingers in her mouth to whistle for Carstairs. The cab was just down the street and it came smartly up, so that Susan and Magnus could jump inside and be away at least thirty seconds before smoke began to billow from the underparts of the barbershop.

"What was I this time?" asked Magnus as they sped away.

"I don't know," replied Susan. "Something with tentacles."

Magnus was silent for a while. He looked out the window at the city and all the people and the life beyond. Susan watched him. Finally, he turned to her and spoke.

"Sometimes I think you're too ready to use the blue pill."

"I'm sorry," said Susan. "I really didn't expect to that time. I never thought they'd all be in it, or that they would suspect us and be ready. I mean how could they . . . oh, I see."

"Yes," agreed Magnus. "Mycroft also, is too ready to use the blue pill. Especially against enemies of the state."

Susan nodded, and reached out to pull him down, so that his head was on her lap. Magnus resisted for a moment, then relented. Susan took off the towel and lightly scratched his head through his hair.

"Mann said I'll get better," whispered Magnus. "No blue pill then, and my nights will be my own."

"Yes," said Susan. "You will get better."

She did not look at her bag, and its box of Krongeitz pills, the blue . . . and the yellow. Magnus did not know about the yellow pills.

Susan hoped he never would.

AN UNWELCOME GUEST

There's a girl in the south tower," reported Jaundice, the Witch's marmalade cat. "The same one as almost got in last year."

"Well, go and bite her or something," said the Witch. She was busy stirring a huge bronze cauldron. She had twelve coworkers coming for lunch and was mixing up a batch of jelly, which had to be poured into an architectural mold and put in the ice cave before eleven.

"Can't," purred Jaundice. "She's in the top chamber."

"What? How did she get up there? I spelled the lower doors shut!"

"She's grown her hair," said Jaundice as if this explained everything, and started licking her paws. The Witch stopped stirring the jelly, ignoring the sudden series of pops as several frogs jumped free.

"How does that relate to her getting into the top chamber of the south tower, pray tell?" asked the Witch sternly. Jaundice, like all witch's cats, prided herself on her independence and liked to tease her mistress. The Witch didn't usually mind, but she was feeling flustered. The last thing she needed was a girl trespassing on the premises. Particularly a repeat offender.

"She's grown her hair *very long*," said the cat.

She paused to lick her paws some more, till the Witch lifted her ladle and started dripping jelly mixture toward her familiar.

"And braided it into a rope . . . with a grappling hook woven into the end," continued Jaundice, leaping to the Witch's favorite chair, ensuring her safety from dripping jelly.

"She climbed up the south tower using her own hair as a rope?" asked the Witch. "How very enterprising. I suppose I'll have to take care of the matter myself then?"

"It shouldn't be my job, anyway," said Jaundice. "Mice, rats, goblins, and intruders no taller than four feet, that's my province. Not great tall galumphing maidens with ten ells of yellow hair woven into a hawser. She's a sight too handy with that hook, as well. You want to be careful."

"I *am* a witch," said the Witch. She carefully put the ladle aside and began to undo her "A Cook's Kitchen Is Her Castle" apron.

Jaundice muttered something inaudible and her whiskers twitched.

"What was that?" asked the Witch sharply.

"Nothing," said Jaundice. "Just remember I told you about the grappling hook."

The Witch nodded thoughtfully and instead of taking up the traditional pointy hat she'd gotten out for the luncheon, she put on her bicycle helmet instead, and for good measure, added the leather apron she wore when silversmithing. Last but not least, she went to the broom closet and after briefly considering several of her favorites, took out Minalka, a sturdy Eastern European besom with a rough-stained ash handle and a thick sweep of bundled birch sticks.

"You can call up everyone and tell them lunch is off," said the Witch as she greased the broomstick with flying ointment.

"But I want to see what you do to Rapunzel," complained Jaundice.

"Rapunzel," said the Witch. She shook her head, the rat bones woven into her three pigtails clattering on her shoulders. "I knew she had a stupid name. But stupid name or not, you know I can't do anything to her, since she's already inside. Not without upsetting the Accord. I'll just ask her nicely to leave, that's all. You get on with those calls, Jenny."

"Don't call me Jenny!" spat the cat, her back arching in agitation. "My name is Jaundice! I am the evil servant of a wicked witch!"

"You aren't even yellow," pointed out the Witch. "You're orange. And I saw you put that mouseling back in its nest yesterday. Call that evil?"

"I was full," said Jenny, but her heart wasn't in it. She let her back smooth out and jumped over to the telephone, batting off the receiver with a practiced paw.

"And I've never been wicked," said the Witch firmly. "Least, not by my measure. Just independent-minded."

"Wickedness depends on where you're standing, doesn't it?" said Jenny. She thrust out a single claw and started pushing phone buttons. "Want me to call Rapunzel's parents after I've done the coven?"

"Yes!" exclaimed the Witch. Having been born fully adult by a process of magical fission from an older witch, she had no parents and tended to forget such things existed.

"Won't do any good, but I'll call," said Jenny. She winked at the Witch, one emerald eye briefly shuttering, then turned her head to the phone as someone answered. "Hello? Oh, Fangdeath, is that you—"

"Fangdeath?" interrupted the Witch. None of her coworkers were called Fangdeath.

Jenny held a paw over the receiver and quickly whispered, "That's what Bluebell calls himself. You know, Decima's familiar."

The Witch nodded and sighed again, hitching up her tartan skirt and the leather apron as she straddled her broom. Sometimes she wondered if the familiars regretted entering the Accord, the agreement that had brought peace, order, and security for both ordinary folk and those who either practiced magic, had magic, or were magic in themselves.

Not that the Accord was perfect. There were a few little loopholes and both sides had been known to exploit them now and again.

This girl Rapunzel had managed to find just such a loophole, and as the Witch flew out her kitchen door and rocketed up toward the south tower, she wondered just what she might be able to do to get rid of her unwelcome guest.

Rapunzel was eating ice cream straight out of the silver cornucopia and watching television when the Witch flew in through the tower window and screeched to a hard-brush landing that scrunched up the carpet and made the coffee table slide into the wall.

The girl put her spoon down and slowly turned her head to look at the Witch. She had to turn her head slowly because her hair weighed a ton, even with most of it coiled up next to her on the sofa.

"Hello," Rapunzel said brightly. Apart from her ridiculously impossible hair, she looked just like any of the other thirteen-year-old girls that the Witch often saw playing soccer on the oval across the road from her Witchery. She was even wearing her sports uniform, complete with cleated soccer boots. They had probably come in useful for wall climbing.

"You know you're not supposed to be here," said the Witch. "This is private property and you're trespassing. You have to leave at once."

"Why don't you call the police, then?" asked the girl snarkily, her face twisting into a disrespectful moue. "You old bat."

The broom shivered in the witch's hand, Minalka eager to leap forward and smack the insolent brat who had tilted her head to one side and was smirking in a very self-satisfied way.

"You know I can't call your police," hissed the Witch. This was one of the problems of the Accord. If Rapunzel had been detected trying to get into the tower, it would be a matter for the police. But she was already inside, and under the Accord, the ordinary folks' police could not enter the Witchery.

Usually this wouldn't be a problem, as the Witch could deal with intruders any way she liked. But there was another loophole, and Rapunzel knew it and had taken advantage of it. She had not just moved in to any part of the Witchery. She was in the Witch's guest room, and she had eaten her bread and drunk her wine. Or in Rapunzel's case, eaten the Witch's ice cream and drunk her lemonade.

From the moment she had done so, she was no longer an intruder, but a guest. An unwelcome one, but that made no difference. The Witch could not use magic against her without inviting the retribution of numerous magical entities that defended the guest right with both vigor and cunning.

One of them was watching now, the Witch noticed, from next to the television. A brownie in the shape of a porcelain Labrador. It winked and stuck out its tongue as it saw her looking.

"I think I'll stay for quite a while," announced Rapunzel. She collapsed back into the sofa and picked up the cornucopia and her spoon. "I like it here."

"Why don't you move in permanently?" asked the Witch in her nicest tone.

Rapunzel waggled the spoon at her.

"You think I'm stupid? The second I agree to that I turn into a housemate and the second after that, probably a toad, right? I'm a guest, right?"

The Witch snarled and looked at the brownie, calculating the odds. It bared its teeth and flicked an ear at the big armchair. The cushion there tilted up to reveal a host of dust-fey, fully caparisoned for battle, many of them mounted on shiny black cockroaches.

The Witch closed her eyes and willed herself to be calm, at the same time tightening her grip on Minalka. The broom had gone beyond wanting to smack Rapunzel. Now it wanted to beat her up.

"Bye-bye, old bat!" mumbled Rapunzel, her mouth full of ice cream. "Don't forget to bring a different cornucopia up tomorrow morning. And some clean towels and an extra blanket. And get some more channels for your television, this one's pathetic."

The Witch closed her eyes down to narrow slits, to hold back the magical glare that she knew was pent up behind her lids. The brownie and the dust-fey moved and muttered, but the Witch knew they would not attack unless she gave Rapunzel a full Force 10 eyeball assault—which she dearly wanted to do, but knew she could not.

It took some effort to tear Minalka away and aim her at the window, but the Witch managed it. Firmly astride the angry broomstick, she tried to think of some cutting farewell remark, but nothing came, and Rapunzel had changed the channel to a music video station and turned up the volume, a blaring song driven by overcranked bass beginning to shake the room.

The Witch flew out the window. Out in the open, she opened her eyes and let her rage paint the sky above the neighboring sports field with a temporary but very colorful aurora.

Two hours later, the bass from the tower was still pumping and the Witch was still seething. All her nine brooms jiggled and hummed around her as she sat in her favorite chair, and Jenny was curled up on her lap, trying to calm the Witch with a gentle purr.

There had been a brief moment of calm and possibly even hope an hour before, when Rapunzel's parents had shown up, but it hadn't lasted. The girl's father said he washed his hands of his daughter, that she never listened to him and hadn't for years, and anyway he had to go and milk the sheep or there'd be no specialty cheeses in the shop the next week to keep house and home together. Rapunzel's mother had sobbed and cried and raved about the Witch stealing her little girl away until her husband had shouted at her to face reality and accept that they'd raised a monster and then both of them had stormed out, leaving the Witch no better off.

"There must be some way of forcing her out without upsetting the guest right," muttered the Witch. "A lure of some kind, perhaps."

"Not her," said Jenny. "She knows too much."

"Knows too much," repeated the Witch. "She does, doesn't she? Far more than any soccer-playing farm girl ought to. . . ."

"She reminds me of someone," said Jenny.

"Her hair is too long, too strong," added the Witch. "It's unnatural."

Cat and witch sat thinking and the nine brooms gently swept around them in a mystic pattern that was possibly conducive to deep thought.

"She's one of the Bad Old Ones come back," said Jenny finally.

The Witch wrinkled her nose. "Possibly. Even if she is, she's still a guest."

"We could ask for help," suggested Jenny tentatively. "I mean, if she is one of the Bad Old Ones reborn . . . we could ask Decima and Nones and perhaps that smith by the crossroad. . . ."

"No," said the Witch. "That would show weakness. I am not weak."

"It would show common sense," said Jenny.

"Shush," said the Witch. "I'm thinking. I can't force a guest to leave, can I? Not unless I want all those under-folk and eaves-dwellers on my back."

"No," said the cat.

"What about if I force a guest to stay?" asked the Witch, and her lips curled back a fraction, not quite enough to show teeth or be called a smile.

"But we don't want her to stay! How would making her a prisoner . . ." said Jenny, her ears pricking up in sudden attention. Then she did smile, showing her sharp little teeth. "Oh, yes. I see."

□ □ □

Rapunzel was asleep in the Witch's second-best feather bed, when the brownie licked her face. She sat up at once and tried to slap the porcelain dog, but it ducked under the blow.

"What do you want?" she asked. "Is that old hag up to something?"

"Yes and no," said the brownie. "I just wanted to tell you that you're not under our protection anymore."

"What?" shrieked Rapunzel. "Why not?"

"The Witch has declared you a prisoner," said the Brownie. "So we're clearing off. Bye!"

The brownie vanished and from under the bed there was a sudden flourish of trumpets.

Rapunzel flounced out of bed and ran into the living room, hair uncoiling behind her like an astronaut's tether. Everything was as it was. She touched the cornucopia and ordered a milkshake and it was there, fresh and cold. The television came blaringly on at the touch of the remote.

"Stupid old fashion disaster," said Rapunzel. "I don't want to leave anyway! There's things I can do here."

She sat on the sofa and wound in her hair, thinking evil thoughts, while animated monsters fought with each other on the television. But after a few minutes, she began to hear something annoying outside. She tried to ignore it, but it just didn't stop and she thought she could hear her name. Finally she cracked, flicking the television off and flinging open the window.

There was a man at the base of the tower. Or, a boy, rather. He was dressed in a red and yellow uniform and was carrying a large flat cardboard box.

"Delivery! Rapunzel! Pizza delivery for Rapunzel!"

Rapunzel scowled. The cornucopia didn't do pizza, and she was hungry. She stuck her head out the window.

"Who ordered me a pizza?" she asked. She could smell pep-peroni and anchovies and it was extremely tempting.

The boy looked up. He was slightly odd-looking, Rapunzel thought. His ears were a bit long and his hair was white, rather than blond.

"We got the prison contract," he said. His voice was high too, and Rapunzel lowered her estimate of his age. "We do the city jail, the police cells, and now here. How do I get up there?"

"You don't!" snapped Rapunzel. She lugged her hair over to the window and started lowering the braided tresses. She'd taken the grappling hook off before she went to bed. "Just tie this rope around the box and I'll pull it up."

"The pizza'll get mushed up though."

"Do as you're told!"

"Whatever," said the boy, and shrugged. Even his shrugging looked a bit strange as if his shoulders were oddly proportioned. "Say, you know, my brothers and I, we do rescues as well as pizza delivery."

"Just tie up the box and clear off," said Rapunzel. Her hair-rope was almost at full stretch, dangling just above the boy's head. He reached up and pulled it down. As he grabbed the hair, two other, almost identical boys jumped out from where they'd been hiding behind the hedge of thorn bushes and also took hold of the braid.

Rapunzel just had time to brace herself in the window frame before the three boys gave her hair rope a hefty jerk, and she was bent in two, her scalp burning with the sudden strain on her head.

"What are you doing, you idiots!" she shrieked.

"Rescuing you," shouted the three boys, and they hauled on her hair again.

Rapunzel shrieked again and something inside her, something old and cold and strange that should never have come back to the world, bubbled up from where it was hiding and used her voice to speak a spell. The carefully pruned thorn bushes shivered in answer and their branches suddenly grew long and the thorns much sharper, and they lashed out at the three boys, scratching horribly, tendrils seeking their pale red eyes.

"Do something!" said Jenny to the Witch. They were both on Ellidra, fastest of the brooms, hovering just behind the corner of the kitchen garden wall.

"I can't," said the Witch. "Not until she's rescued."

"But it's not even her," protested the cat. "It's one—"

"Blind!" screamed one of the boys. He let go the hair and clutched at his face. "I'm blind."

"Pull," whispered the Witch. "Pull! She's almost out!"

The two remaining boys pulled on the hair as hard as they could, even as the thorns scratched at their eyes. Rapunzel clung to the windowsill with one hand and one foot, as whatever was inside her screeched spells and imprecations, most of which were diverted by the charms and defenses of the Witchery gardens.

Then the remaining two boys let go, both with their hands pressed to where their eyes had been. As Rapunzel's hair whipped away from them, one of her stray curses undid the magic that the Witch had used upon them, and instead of three blind pizza delivery boys, three mice scampered in circles, squeaking and crashing into one another.

Rapunzel laughed and began to climb back through the window.

"We'll never get her out," said Jenny despondently.

At that moment, the brownie appeared and gave Rapunzel a good kick in the back. Completely unprepared, she lost her balance and fell from the window, her nails scoring the bricks as she frantically tried to get a hold.

As she fell, the Witch and Jenny flew over her on Ellidra, faster than any swift or swallow, almost too fast to see. A sparkling powder fell from the Witch's hand, and Rapunzel found herself landing on a great soft coil of hair, and she bounced high before landing on her back in the soft earth of a flower bed.

A second later, the Witch and Jenny landed. The cat leaped from the broom to sink her claws into Rapunzel's chest and the dark shadow there that was trying to sink back below the girl's skin and into her heart. The Witch, brandishing a set of silver scissors she'd made herself long before the Accord had brought peace to the witching world, cut the braid from Rapunzel, very close to the back of her head.

The braid twisted and writhed like a snake and even began to rear up, and the shadow on Rapunzel's chest reached out to it. But Jenny's claws held tight and the Witch's scissors flashed, snipping the braid into shorter and shorter lengths. Finally, the hair moved no longer, and Jenny tore the shadow from the girl and flung it on the ground, where it withered in the sun.

Witch and cat stepped back and both took a breath. Rapunzel sat up and scratched the back of her head.

"Go home," said the Witch.

Rapunzel stood on shaking legs and began to cry. Then she started to run, the thorn bushes arching to make a gate for her exit.

"She'll make the sheep-milking at that speed," said Jenny. "Now where are those mice?"

The Witch held out her cupped hands. Jenny sniffed at them, then retreated back several paces. The Witch breathed upon what she held and whispered a word. Then she bent down, opened her hands and three fully-sighted mice dashed away to a hole in the tower wall, with Jenny not quite close enough behind them.

"Glass of milk?" said a voice near the Witch's foot.

The Witch looked down at the brownie and nodded.

"I'll pour you one," she said. "Then I think I might go into town."

"Town?" asked Jenny, returning mouse-less from the hunt. "What for?"

"I need a haircut," said the Witch, and she shook her head, scowling as her pigtails clashed together.

A SIDEKICK OF MARS

I guess you, like what seems to be most of the world these days, have read about John Carter, and his adventures and whatnot on the red planet we call Mars and the locals there call Barsoom. But I bet you've never read nothing about one Lamentation of Wordly Sin Jones, who was right there by J.C.'s side for more than a sixth of the time by my calculation but don't get a mention at all in any of the write-ups. Not even under the name by which Carter knew me, which wasn't the full moniker my god-fearin' parents dished up but the shorter, easier to get your mouth around Lam Jones.

See? I bet you're castin' your mind back through all those books and not remembering any Lam Jones, which is a downright insult, being as I was there, as I said, some eighteen percent of the time, only to get left out when Carter got back to Earth and decided to tell his tales to that nephew of his.

Not that Carter told it all, oh no, he was right reticent on a couple of matters. He could be downright *closemouthed* when it suited him, and probably still is, since for all I know he's living yet, me not having seen him for some considerable time due to him being back on Barsoom and me being back here on this green Earth. Where I hopes I will stay, though for how long that will be is anyone's guess, there not being anyone alive who knows what in God's name that buffalo hide scroll I took off the body of that Indian did to me, aside from wrestling me right out of my flesh and flinging me off to the fourth planet and back again like a damn hot chestnut juggled between two hands.

Let me tell you how I first met up with Captain John Carter. . . .

But I s'pose I'm getting ahead of myself. As I was saying, Lam Jones is what I been known by since I was going on fourteen, except for a period in the Union Army when I was called Private Jones and then Corporal Jones and finally Quartermaster-Sergeant Jones, but as soon as the war was done with I got back to being plain old Lam Jones again.

Me fighting for the North probably was the first thing that put Carter off me, him being a rebel and all. Or maybe like a lot of hot-blooded, rip-roaring cavalry types he just hated quartermasters. There must have been a dozen or more occasions when I had to face down some shouting colonel or major who wanted something that I either just didn't have in the stores, or couldn't give them without a paper signed by the appropriate officer, not just any jumped-up brigadier-general. Why, sometimes what they wanted had to be approved by General Meigs himself, and it was a marvel to me that those officers couldn't understand a simple procedure and put their request through the proper channels in an approved fashion.

Now I'm getting behind. Suffice to say that at the end of the War, there I was, plain old Lam Jones again, left by the tide of battle (though not the sharp end of it) in a three-saloon town, with a meager bounty from a grateful government, that being I got to keep my Spencer carbine, a rusty old saber I'd never used, and $202 in back pay, most of it paper money which passed at a discount in favor of gold.

Gold! Like a lot of folks around then, I was mad for the yellow metal, and I'd set my sights on getting a whole lot more of it than the three Miss Liberty coins I had in my poke. That's why I went west as soon as I could, and sure enough I struck it lucky right away in Arizona, when I met a fellow called Nine-Tenths Noah, an old-time miner, who reckoned he knew a prime spot for a strike, only he needed a partner and a stake on account of him being a vagrant drunk.

To cut a long story down to size, we did well in our gold-diggings. Despite Nine-Tenths Noah being a soak of the first degree, being pretty much permanently pickled (as the nine-tenths referred), he knew his business and he provided the brains of the operation, while I provided the stake and then the digging power. I guess I ain't mentioned that short as I am from foot to crown, I am nearly as wide as tall, and all of it muscle. Some folks even tried calling me the Block, on account of my physique, back in the regiment, until I showed 'em I was against it.

That might well be another reason Carter misliked mentioning me in his stories. Sure, he was taller and had the looks and all, but I was stronger. He could jump farther, having the better balance, but when it came to grip and lift, I left him in the red dust. We had a thoat-lifting contest once (I 'spect you know a thoat is a Martian horse-thing) when we were both sozzled on the stuff that passes for whiskey on Mars. I lifted my thoat clear above my head, and he only got his to shoulder height. It kicked him when he threw it down, too. He was kind of upset about the whole thing the next day, and blamed me for it, though it had been his idea all along. He wasn't a drinker, in a usual way, so maybe his wife, that Dejah Thoris, gave him a scold when he staggered back to the palace.

Anyways, that was much later. Back on Earth, old Noah's nose had led us right, and I was digging out a lot of gold. All through the winter of 1866 we kept at it, and it was only when spring had started to come over and the snow melt begun that we realized that we were down to the final nasty-looking hunk of salt beef, there was but one sack of flour left, and Noah was having to dive headfirst into his puncheon of snakebite whiskey to dip his cup. We'd left it kind of late to resupply, which might surprise you what with me being a former quartermaster and all. It was the gold that did it. As long as more of it kept coming out of the mine, neither of us could bear to stop.

The nearest town was four days away, walking. I don't hold much with riding, being as I said, more square than rectangular in shape. I had to shorten stirrups so high as to provoke ridicule, and there weren't many horses that liked my weight none, either. So leading three mules, I left Noah behind to guard the mine, on account of him being incapable of walking any considerable distance. There was even a chance he might sober up while I was gone. He couldn't ever ration his drinking and there was only six gallons left.

Only I never did make it back in the nine days I'd reckoned, which was four to walk out, a day's business, and four days back. In fact, I hardly got a mile from the mine.

It was Indians that done this, leastways one particular Indian. We hadn't seen any Indians at all over the winter, though we knew we were on Apache land. The mine was in a narrow mountain canyon, with few trees or foliage, and no hunting to speak of, so I suppose it wasn't worth a visit. I didn't know much about the Apache myself, or Indians in general, having been raised in Pennsylvania and never being in the West before. Noah had taught me a few signs to get along, but I hoped I'd never get close enough to need 'em, nor my Sharps carbine or the Colt Army .44 I had stuck in my pants neither.

I wasn't thinking about Indians, or much else neither, 'cept the slap-up meal I was going to have in town, when I just about tripped over the legs of a fellow, lying straight across the narrow path that was the only way out of the eastern end of the canyon. I jumped back into my lead mule, who protested at this kind of unexpected treatment. It let out a bray that echoed down the canyon walls and that didn't help me none as I was scrabbling to get my Colt out, it having slipped down a piece and the hammer getting stuck under my waistband.

With the gun in my hand I steadied a little, maybe also because the fellow wasn't moving at all. His bare legs were across the trail, but the top half of him were stuck in a little cave mouth I'd never noticed before, in the almost sheer canyon side. I called out to him, but he never moved. So I bent down and dragged him out, and had to jump back again as a huge snake come out with him, sounding its damn rattle as it lunged at me. I fired at once, and blasted it in half, the gunshot and the snake rattlin' and writhing about making my lead mule decide to push past me and take off, with the others at its heels.

I was knocked back by the mules, and had a bad dance with the front half of that rattler, who still wasn't done till I stomped on its head, put my full weight on it, and screwed my heel around a few times.

After I'd calmed down a piece, I turned the Indian over. He was naked, save for a breechclout, and his head was pretty swole, with six or mebbe seven snake-bites across his face and down his neck. I was a mite surprised that an Apache had stuck his head into that little cave, but I s'pose anyone can get caught out by a rattler if it's sitting quiet.

The dead man had a roll of some kind of parchment, probably scraped buffalo hide, clutched in his hand. I muttered an apology to him, in case of ghosts, and made the sign that I thought meant *It's a pity things is the way they are but what can you do*, and pulled the scroll out of his closed fingers, which took some doing, because he sure had a right death grip on it. Then I wandered on a few yards to get away from that hole and maybe more rattlers, and sat down on a boulder and put my back against the canyon wall. I knew the mules would be along all right, when they regained their senses, and I figured I'd take a look at that parchment while I waited.

I started to unroll it, and saw the beginnings of a picture. To this day I can't say what it was a picture of, or what the colors were, or nothing like that. As soon as my eyes set on it, I felt mighty strange. I got cold and stiff all over, like I was becoming part of the rock I leaned against, and then I got awfully tired. I tried to look away from that cursed drawing, but my eyes wouldn't move, and I couldn't stop my eyelids drifting south.

When I woke up, I was standing 'bout ten yards farther along the path. I glanced back to where I'd been sitting and had the terrible shock of seeing myself a-sitting there, still as a statue!

I rushed over, and reached out to my own shoulder, thinking perhaps I could shake myself awake. But my hand was like a ghost's, and for the first time in my life I couldn't get a hold of anything.

Then I figured I must have gone and died without knowing it. Maybe another rattler had got me, quick and quiet, while I was setting down. Or my heart had give out, like what happened to Sergeant Ducas that day in the mess hall, raising his spoon one second and dead the next.

Only I didn't feel dead and for sure I wasn't in heaven, or hell, neither, as my parents always said I would end up. I felt fine, save for a kind of itchy yearning at the back of my neck that made me want to crick it back and look up. Which eventually I did, seeing there was no reason not to.

I looked up along the narrow walls of the canyon, up to the sky above, which was a lot darker than I expected, with the stars already coming out. It was already night, so I guess I'd slept the day away.

One star caught my eye. A red star that grew brighter and brighter still. With nary a thought from me, my arms reached up toward that star, as if I might somehow drag it down, or be lifted up toward it.

I remember thinking very clearly, *This ain't right*, then everything went red, as if I was passing through a fire, a huge fire that filled up the world, but a cold fire, 'cause I never felt it burn.

The next thing I knows I was facedown in a tidy parcel of dust. I pushed myself up, noticing that once again I could feel the earth. I felt greatly relieved that I had been restored to my flesh, and now all would be well, that the strangeness would be over and done with.

Only I was mistaken about that. The first thing I saw when I stood up was the strangest figure of . . . a man, I guess . . . only he was some fifteen feet high, with two pairs of arms atop a pair of mighty legs, and an overall color reminiscent of a green tree frog,

which is not exactly green but a kind of yellow greenness. He had a
harness of leather and metal on his upper body and in each of his topmost hands he bore a long straight blade of some whitish metal. To
top off this nightmarish aspect, his great head was riven by a mouth
that bore enormous tusks, and his eyes were an evil red.

Naturally I reached for my weapons, only to discover that not
only did I have neither Colt nor knife, I was barebuck naked into
the bargain! The green warrior, correctly judging that motion of
mine, raised both blades and swung them down. Seeking to dodge,
I lunged forward, and was surprised to find myself projected into the
midriff of the creature as if shot from a cannon! Despite his great
size, my impact knocked him down and he did not immediately rise.
I gripped his huge hand and twisted, planning simply to disarm him
and take one of the blades to defend myself. But under my grip bones
cracked and flesh tore, so I fair messed up that hand before I got hold
of his sword.

The green man tried to rise and lift his other three blades. But
before he could do so, I raised up the sword I had taken and plunged
it deep into his chest. Again, my new strength surprised me, the
blade driving through flesh and bone and into the ground beneath,
so far that I could not easily withdraw it, particularly not when balanced upon a green giant undergoing the pangs and tremors of death.

But with a great exertion I did pull the blade free and jumped,
only to find myself hurtling high through the air once more, to land
not next to the man as I'd thought, but dozens of yards away!

Given a moment's respite from fighting the big green fellow, I
looked around and saw that while I was indeed in a canyon of sorts, it
was not the canyon of my mine. It was shallower, and wider, and the
rock wasn't bare, but covered in some sort of moss or maybe lichen.
The sun wasn't right neither, being smaller and punier than it should
have been.

But I only glanced at the strange, distant sun, because beyond the green man I had killed, only a few hundred yards along the canyon or valley, there was a whole damn regiment of those green four-armed men, only they was sittin' atop those thoat things I mentioned, what were like horses but with eight legs.

Unlike John Carter, the first thought in my head when spotting a right army of huge green warriors is not to wander over and beat up on the general and maybe the staff as well, just to make sure of the matter. The thought that was jumping to attention in my brainbox was how I was going to get the hell out of there. Only no answer occurred as the green men lowered their spears and their eight-legged mounts began to charge toward me.

There was nowhere to hide, and nowhere to run, and the enemy was coming on at a rush. My head almost turned completely around on my neck as I tried to find some way out, but there was no way out. Within a minute or two, I would be ridden down, speared, and trampled to death.

Then I saw that between me and the green man I had killed, there was a perfectly round pattern in the dusty ground, like the hatch to a cellar, too regular to be natural. I jumped toward it and even though I'd held back on my full strength, I overshot my mark. Then, trying to run back, I kept bouncing up into the air, as if the very force of gravity that bound me to the earth had lessened—as it had, I would later confirm.

But I managed to get back to that circular depression and, using the green man's sword, swept the red dust aside. There *was* a cellar hatch there, a round door of metal. But there was no handle, ring, or lever with which to open it. Reversing my blade, I banged on the strange door with the hilt, but there was no response, save the distant clang resulting from my blows.

Things was about as desprit as they get then, for the green cavalry was almost upon me. I turned to face them, a thousand thoughts of all the things left undone in my life racing through my mind, but chief among them was regrettin' all that gold I'd never get to spend.

Then, as the thunder of the charging thoats filled the canyon, and the green giants and their spear-points were only yards away, I was suddenly lifted into the air from behind and yanked up into the sky like a fish jerked out of the water by a long-handled gaff.

Which ain't poetical talk, but a true saying, save that I'm no fish, and it was a boat of the sky that had lifted me aboard, the hook employed being very skillfully thrust through the back of my make-shift kilt, so that I had only a quarter-inch-deep cut across one buttock to show for it and no more blood lost than a canteen might hold.

Later on I learned that John Carter himself had swung the hook, which was all to the good. Any normal fellow would probably have taken my head off. When it came to wielding a sword, gun, or even a hook, Carter really was the best. I often wondered how he might fare against Bill Hickok, who was a wonder with a pistol. I met Hickok much later in what you might call my career, not on Mars, you understand. But even against Hickok, I reckon Carter might have had the edge.

So there I was, splayed and bleeding on the floor of this fly-ing machine which was accelerating mightily toward the rim of the canyon, while an ordinary-looking fellow with a regular Earth-size number of arms and legs fired a long-barreled rifle of unfamiliar design over the stern and someone I at first took to be an Indian on account of him having the red skin that Indians was supposed to have (but didn't in actual fact) was directing the craft from a half cockpit forr'ard.

Sharp explosions sounded behind us in rapid succession, send-ing up clouds of dust where they struck the ground, obscuring our rapid retreat. The Earthman fired a few more rounds, then lowered his strange rifle and turned about. He jabbered something at the red man, who laughed, before he turned his attention to me, removing the hook from my belt without paying much attention to the blood that was flowing readily down my leg. Then he jabbered some more, at me this time, in a language I could not even begin to recognize.

"I fear I do not—" I started to reply.

This obviously surprised him greatly. Carter—for of course it was he—was never one to show much emotion in his face, but in this case both his eyebrows lifted for an instant, and a spark flashed across his steel-grey eyes.

"You speak English?" he interrupted. "Or have you learned it this moment from my mind?"

"I cain't read minds," I replied. "I've always spoken English, and a little Dutch and German, on account of being raised in Berks County, Pennsylvania."

"You're an Earthman!" exclaimed Carter. "I took you for some kind of White Dwarf Martian, emerged from the subterranean fastness back there."

"I ain't a dwarf, Martian or otherwise," I replied stiffly. "And I don't let no man call me one, neither. The name is Lam Jones, Arizonee miner, late quartermaster in the headquarters of General Sheridan."

"A Union man," said Carter, his manner immediately less friendly. "Allow me to introduce myself, Mr. Jones. I am Captain John Carter of Virginia, and a Prince of Helium, here on Barsoom."

"Pleased to meet you, Captain . . . that is to say . . . Prince," I said weakly. I didn't want to look, but I could feel the blood trickling down my leg, and it felt like there was a lot of it. "The War being over and all. Uh, where might Barsoom be, your honor?"

"It is the fourth planet of this solar system," said Carter. "You would call it Mars."

"Mars?" I asked. "I'm on *Mars*?"

"Yes," said Carter. There was still a mighty chill in his voice. "You are only the second Earthman to come here, as far as it is known."

I kind of got the message then that he liked it better when there was only the *one* Earthman on Mars.

"Mars," I repeated, looked down, saw my own blood spreading across the deck, and fainted.

When I awoke, I found myself on a kind of padded shelf of silk, with my ass bandaged up and a fur robe loosely tied around me, the kind of fur robe that would have cost more than a hundred dollars from one of the finest stores in Philadelphia, like I was going to buy with my gold. The whole store, I mean, not the fur robe.

Apart from my buttock wound, I felt refreshed, so with only a little difficulty in the sitting-up department, I swung myself off that shelf and took stock of my surroundings. I could see from the tall arched window opposite that I was in some kind of tower room, a room straight out of the color plates in the book of Araby that Captain O'Hoolihan of the New York Zouaves had lent me once, in return for three more hogs over his company's allowance. It was all silk curtains and suchlike, that room, and more cushions than a madam's fancy-house.

No sooner had I got down than a woman rose up out of those cushions, a mighty fine-looking woman, with that real red skin like the fellow who'd been driving the flying boat. She bent her head and then looked straight at me, her eyes seeming to bore into my head, and I felt something twitch and give inside my brain, right behind my eyes.

Suddenly I knew her name: Kala. It was just there, as if I'd a-knowed it all along. Prancing along behind, straight into my head, came some other words, and before I really caught on what was happening I was answering back to her, without either of us uttering a word.

That's how I got started with that Martian mindtalkin' business, though I never got as good as Carter. I could talk with folks, but I couldn't read their minds. He could, right enough, except for mine. I used to think up some pretty insulting thoughts sometimes, about Johnny Reb and all, but he never caught on.

I was stuck in that tower for nigh on a week before Carter showed up to see how I was going. I guess he'd been off slaughtering some of the Warhoon greens or similar activities of which he was right fond.

Straight away he wanted to know how I'd got to Barsoom, though he never told me nothing about his own journey. I read it years later, like everyone else, and wondered why he'd kept it secret. He wanted to know if I was an immortal too, or couldn't remember my childhood. I reckon he was pleased to find out I was no one special in that regard.

'Course, I'd met quite a few folk along the way who couldn't remember their childhoods, like old Noah for one, but I never suggested to Carter that it might be whiskey that done in his memory. I knew right early he wasn't a man to trifle with. He killed too easily, and had it all sorted within himself. Just like my ma and pa. They would have whipped me to death over the smallest thing and said it was all for the best, just the way God intended.

Only Carter had his honor instead of God, and that honor only had room for Virginian gentlemen and Martian princesses. Everyone else was pretty much window-dressing, providing a pretty frame for him and his lady to stand in the sunlight.

I asked him as soon as I might how I could get back to Earth and my gold (only I never mentioned that, and I never knew he was a miner too, neither), as polite as anything, well larded with "Sirs" and "Highnesses" and "Your Grace" and all. But either he didn't know—which he didn't, as it turned out—or he wouldn't tell me. Besides, since he didn't want to go back himself, he found it sort of peculiar that I wanted to. By this stage he'd sort of adopted me, not exactly as the First Earthman to the Second Earthman, but more like he might pick up a pet. I reckon I ranked somewhat lower than his foul dog-thing Woola.

He also put me to work. Though expressing the opinion that a Union quartermaster was only worth the merest part of a good Virginian quartermaster, or, at a pinch, an Alabaman, he still considered that a cut above the Martian variety. I was given a Martian assistant and, with Kala to help translate, was assigned the task of putting in order the stores and armories of Helium, the city which Carter's old-man-in-law was the mayor or the governor or whatever Jeddak signified.

I didn't mind the work, for to tell the truth, those Martians already had things pretty well sorted. It was just Carter wanted things done the way he was used to, and him being such a hero to all of them Heliumites, they was happy to oblige.

I didn't mind the living either, once I worked out that Kala wasn't just provided to teach me the lingo but was happy to warm me up on that silk shelf as well. She wasn't a princess, but a princess wouldn't have suited me anyhow. If it wasn't for my gold waiting for me I s'pose I could have got used to the quiet life as a quartermaster in Helium.

So the weeks went past, and then months. I might be there still if John Carter hadn't got it into his head that a fellow Earthman like himself must be pining for the excitements he got into every day, speeding about in flyers, shooting up green folks from miles away with a radium rifle, engaging in desperate hand-to-hand combat with a critter eight times his size, and all them larks.

"I've been thinking about that subterranean lair you found where we picked you up, Lam," he says to me one day, suddenly turning up as I was quietly counting bandoliers in a nice little corner armory where hardly no one ever visited. "You said you noticed a round trapdoor or some such, I think?"

"Yes, sir," I replied enthusiastically, before I let my face fall.

"Only I'd never find it now, all that red dust and moss looks the same to me."

"Not to me," says Carter. "I have a complete recollection of the area. We'll pick up Kantos Kan and go and take a look. I've been wondering what's under there, and there's nothing much else on at the moment."

Kantos Kan, I should have said, was the fellow who'd been driving the air boat when I was rescued. He was Carter's best friend and as mad a cavalry type as he was. Kind of an equivalent to General Custer, inasmuch as he'd do something crazy as heck just because he could, everyone would follow, and he'd come out the other side smiling even if most of the followers didn't. Only that don't always work, as Custer found out on the Greasy Grass. Kan had better luck than Custer all round, but I reckon he probably got ten times as many Heliumite soldiers killed in his time than Custer managed with the Seventh Cavalry.

"You and Kantos have fun then, sir," I said, turning back to my bandoliers. Intentionally misunderstanding him, you see. Only Carter could play that game one better, for he really *didn't* understand why anyone would not want to go out on some crazy expedition with him.

"You have to come!" he laughed, clapping me on the back hard enough to kill a Thark. "Satisfy your curiosity, man!"

I muttered something about not having any damned curiosity, but not too loud. Like I said, I never wanted to push Carter too far.

We left that night in a three-man flyer, Kantos Kan naturally leapin' at the opportunity to stick his nose in somewhere dangerous. He laughed at me as I found it difficult to sit on what passed for a seat in them Martian flyers, but it wasn't because of the buttock wound. That had healed up right nicely. I just was a little awkward what with my three radium pistols, sword, knife, water bottle, and haversack, all of it worn over a fur robe 'cause I felt the cold. Carter and Kan, as per usual, were wearing outfits that would have got them arrested just about anywhere civilized, just a few leather straps, a pouch over the unmentionables, and some bits of metal stuck on here and there that Carter told me in his case meant much the same as Grant's three stars.

The valley where they'd found me was quite some distance away. I forget how far in Martian haads or karads, but it was nine hundred miles, give or take, about six hours' flight. Shame we ain't got those flyers here on Earth, 'cause they beat the railroad hollow for speed, and you don't get covered in soot, neither.

We arrived soon after the Martian dawn, and sure enough, Carter knew almost exactly where to go. Kantos Kan dropped the flyer down where Carter pointed, and then the three of us took no more than ten minutes looking about before we found that circular hatch.

As before, there weren't no way of opening the thing, but this didn't put Carter off. He knelt down by it, and just *thought* at it for a while, while I fidgeted about nearby and Kantos Kan went back and leaned on his flyer.

Even knowin' what I did about Carter being able to read Martian minds and all, I was still taken aback more than a bit when that trapdoor started to turn about, making a noise like a railroad engine straining for grip on a greasy rail. Then the whole dang thing rose up out of the ground, turning as it came, till there was a cylinder some ten foot high and six feet in diameter sticking up out of the dust.

Carter rapped on the side of it with his knuckle, and a door slid open. There was a Martian standing there, dressed up in the kind of driving outfit folks wear here nowadays, with the long leather coat and the goggles and all. I guess I was staring like a fool, while Carter had stepped a little to the side—he always was in the right place—so when the Martian suddenly raised up this bellows thing and blew a cloud of green gas it went straight at me, and afore I knew it, I'd sucked it into my chest.

I don't know what was in that gas, but as soon as I breathed it down, I was stuck fast where I was, unable to move a muscle. I watched Carter lean in and stick the goggle-wearing Martian with his sword, then haul him out by his coat and throw him a good dozen yards away to die in the dust. Then he came back to me, and I saw his mouth moving, but I couldn't hear any words, and my eyes were already closing, being as I was unexpectedly come over weary.

I think he was saying summat along the lines of "Why did you stand there, idiot?" which fair sums up our usual dialogue, then and later. I reckon he thought I was willfully stupid, which was why he was always having to push me out of the way, or rescue me and all. Not that he ever complained when it was Dejah Thoris who needed rescuin', which happened a damn sight more to her than anyone might expect. I guess I was never much of a hero, but at least I weren't kidnapping-prone like Miss Dejah Thoris.

She never liked me, neither. Maybe because of the time I was checking over Carter's accounts and couldn't make them balance, though I never said a thing about it being kind of peculiar that her new jeweled doo-dah cost the same as the missing money.

That was much later, anyhow. After I sucked that gas and was knocked out or put to sleep, the next time I opened my eyes I was no longer on Mars! I was back in my own body, sitting in the canyon mouth, with my back against the wall. There was a kind of lean-to built over my head, and dry-stone walls up to near my waist, and sitting alongside of me in a rocking chair was my partner, Nine-Tenths Noah.

"You awake, then?" he said, pausing in his rockin' to take a gulp of what had to be water, on account of I couldn't smell it.

"Reckon I am," I said wonderingly. "How long has it been?"

"Five months and a week," replied Noah.

I slowly stood up, marveling that all my muscles and faculties worked as they should. I flexed my fingers, and right then noticed that I was no longer holding the Indian painting or whatever it was.

Noah saw me looking at my empty hand.

"Real bad medicine," he said. "I threw it back in that there cave it come from, where it should have stayed."

I looked at him properly, taking in his unusually bright eyes and pink skin. Forcible laying off the whiskey had done him good service, it seemed, but I was kind of puzzled how come he was still alive.

"What you been eatin' while I was out of my head, Noah?"

"Mules," he replied. "You up to walkin'?"

"Yep," I replied. I felt fine, and mighty relieved to be back where I belonged. For good, or so I thought at the time, little knowing that I'd be back on Mars within the year, once again running along behind John Carter, and wishing I wasn't.

"We gotta go spend some gold," said Noah. "Where you been, anyhow? I seed you was spirit-walking."

"Mars," I said. "It ain't all it's cracked up to be."

"Mars," mused Noah, an odd, far-away expression passing across his face. "They got any gold up there?"

Anyhows, that's how I first met up with the all high-and-mighty John Carter of Mars, even if he don't care to recollect it himself, what with him being Warlord and Jeddak of Jeddaks and all that stuff. Or maybe he was still cantankerous about the South losing the War and all. He always did get all maudlin when he was back on Earth, whining about missing Dejah Thoris, and reminiscin' something horrid about what went wrong at Chancellorsville and suchlike.

I tried to tell my old general, Phil Sheridan, that the folks in Washington ought to keep an eye on Mars, because there was a Johnny Reb up there itching to start over if he could figure a ways of getting his army alongside of Earth. But then I disappeared back to Barsoom myself, and by the time I returned, Phil was dead.

I guess if J.C. does decide to attack the United States, I'll probably be there with him, dang it. I don't know how it's worked out like this, but I just can't get rid of the fellow, at least not permanent-like.

Or maybe it's that he can't get rid of *me*?

UNDER OTHER SKIES

SCIENCE FICTION

YOU WON'T FEEL A THING

I t started with a toothache.

The Arkle had it, in one of the great hollow fangs at the front of his mouth, which would have been simple canines before the Overlords changed him, in the process of turning him into a Ferret. Not that the Arkle was entirely a Ferret. He'd escaped from the Dorms when he was eleven, so he still looked mostly human. A very thin, elongated human, with his face and jaw pushed out so that it wasn't quite a snout but you could tell it would have been one if he hadn't gotten away.

The Arkle also had a taste for blood. Not the full-on bloodlust the Ferrets had, because he could control it. But when the Family killed a chicken to roast, he would cut its throat over a bowl and drink the blood down like a kind of predinner cocktail. Sometimes he put parsley in the cup, as a garnish. Or, as he said, for those extra vitamins. The Arkle didn't eat a lot of greens.

He was one of the younger members of the Family. He'd come out of the city four years before, more dead than alive, his body covered with sores and his gums receding from malnutrition. He'd lasted almost six months on his own after escaping from the Dorms, which was no mean feat, but he wouldn't have lasted much longer if he hadn't been lucky enough to have been found by Gwyn, on one of the latter's last foraging expeditions into the city fringe.

Gwyn was the first to notice the Arkle behaving strangely. They were working together, moving one of the portable henhouses to its new location, when the Arkle stopped pushing and pressed his fingers into his jaw, using the middle knuckle so he didn't slice himself with his talons.

"What are you doing?" asked Gwyn, annoyed. As always he was providing most of the muscle, and though the Arkle's participation was mainly for show, the henhouse wheels *were* stuck in the mud, and even a slight amount of assistance would make it easier for Gwyn to free them.

"Toothache," muttered the Arkle. He stretched out his jaw and ground it from side to side. "Annoying me."

"Doc had better look at it right away," said Gwyn. He'd had a toothache himself a few years back, and there was still a hole at the back of his mouth where Doc had pulled out a big molar. But that was better than what could happen if it was left to rot. Gwyn had seen that too, in other survivors. And Ferret teeth were certain to be trickier than more nearly human ones.

"It's not too bad," muttered the Arkle. He winced as he closed his mouth, though, and tears started in his eyes.

Gwyn set down the chicken-house and lumbered around, towering over the Arkle. Gwyn was the big brother of the Family, and the second oldest. He'd been thirteen when the Change swept through, removing everyone over the age of fourteen. Like most of the surviving children, he'd then been caught up by the suited figures driving their centipede trains, and been taken to the Dormitories. Big for his age and well muscled, he'd gone straight into the Myrmidon track, fed alien steroids and exercised to the limits of torture, but like the Arkle he'd managed to escape before the final conversion in the Meat Factory.

Even so, he was seven feet tall, measured four feet across the shoulders, and had arms roughly the same diameter as the massive logs he split for the winter fire, wielding a blockbuster that most of the others couldn't even lift.

"Go and see Doc now," ordered Gwyn. Like the few other

almost-Myrmidons who had gotten away from the Dorms, his voice was high and reedy, a by-product of the chemical infusions that had built his muscle while also effectively making him a eunuch.

But high voice or not, the Arkle knew that when Gwyn spoke, he meant what he said.

"All right, all right, I'm . . . ow . . . going," he said. "You sure you can move this by yourself?"

"I guess I'll manage somehow," replied Gwyn.

The Arkle nodded sheepishly and trudged back through the sparse forest where the five henhouses were arranged. At the edge of the trees, he climbed over the old, rusted fence with the sinuous grace of a true Ferret, pausing to tip a finger at Ken-Lad, who was on sentry halfway up the ancient tree that served as the western lookout post. Ken-Lad made a ruder gesture back, before resuming his steady, regulated gaze staring up at each quadrant of the sky.

The Farm lay in a deep valley, more than a hundred kilometers from the city. The creatures had never come to fight their battles there, and even the Wingers never flew overhead. But very occasionally, one of the Overlords' flying machines did, and that was why the sentries watched. The Family could not afford to have a curious Overlord sweep down and see free humans, for the creatures would surely come then, correcting whatever oversight had kept the valley secret for the eight years since the Change.

The Farm had been a giant dope plantation before the Change, and the camouflage nets were still in place over a good thirty acres of land. The Family had poked a few holes in the nets, here and there, to let in a little more light for the much smaller portion they had under cultivation. That provided vegetables, and the chickens provided meat and eggs, and there was hunting for wild game as well. There had been a lot of tinned and dried food earlier on, but it was mostly saved for special occasions now, since it was too risky to venture toward the city and the riches that still awaited there.

Doc Carol had found the Farm almost five years before. She'd never told the others whether she knew it was there, or had simply stumbled upon it and then worked out that it was safe from the creatures.

She never told anyone how she knew so much about medicine and healing either. Gwyn probably knew, and some of the older ones, but they never talked about anything the Doc said or did. All the others knew was that she had been a day short of her fifteenth birthday when the Change came, a day short of being old enough to go wherever it was that most of humanity went. If they went anywhere, as opposed to simply ceasing to exist.

The Arkle spat as he remembered the caterpillar train that he had willingly climbed aboard. He'd been seven years old at the time, and his mother had vanished in front of his eyes, and he'd been desperately afraid. The train had looked a bit like the one at the fairground, and it was already loaded with children. He even knew some of them from school.

So he'd gotten on, and it had taken him to one of the first established Dorms. A tracking and ID device had been injected beneath the skin of his wrist, and he'd been subjected to a series of tests at the hands of those silver-visored, faceless, suited humanoids. The tests had said "Ferret" and from then on, everything he did or that was done to him was designed to make him both less and more than human.

The Arkle looked at the strange purple welt on his wrist as he loped through the high grass that surrounded the main house. They cut the grass occasionally, using scythes, just to reduce the risk of fire, but never enough that it would look new-mown.

The tracking device in his wrist had been removed by Tira, a girl in the Dorm, though the Arkle didn't know exactly how she'd done it. She simply touched her finger to the lump that showed where the tracker lay under the skin, and there had been a moment of pain so terrible that the Arkle had blacked out. When he'd come to, there was no lump. Just the purple welt.

Of course he knew that Tira had used a Change Talent of some kind. He had one too, only it wasn't as useful. Or at least it was only useful for one thing. The Arkle grinned as he thought of that, then grimaced and almost sobbed as the pain in his tooth came back, darting from his mouth up into his head, savaging him right behind the eyes.

The pain in his tooth was even worse than that remembered pain in his wrist.

Tira had taken her device out, too, and they had run together. Only she never made it over the perimeter wire. Tira was the one who had first called him "the Arkle." He didn't know why, but he'd kept the name, just to remember her, his truest friend from the Dorms.

Greenie was on the verandah of the house, carefully potting up seedlings of some plant or other that the Arkle didn't recognize. She looked at him with her head on one side, and he could tell she was wondering why he had come in early. But even then, most of her mind was probably on the plants. Greenie had a Change Talent too, and though like all Change Talents hers was very weak down in the valley, she still had a special empathy for vegetable life. Greenie could always tell when a plant needed water, or more shade, or sun, or was being strangled by its neighbors.

"Got to see Doc," said the Arkle. He tried to smile, but it hurt too much, so he waved instead and hurried on inside.

The Arkle could see Doc Carol through the small square window that was set high in the inner door to her lab, even though the thick glass was smeared all around with sealant. Doc was clearly cooking up something fairly toxic, since she was wearing a gas mask and an ex-Army NBC suit.

The Arkle hesitated, then knocked on the window. He didn't

want to disturb Doc, but his tooth was getting worse, a lot worse. The pain had been around for a few weeks, but had come and gone, and hadn't ever gotten too bad. But for the past few days it had escalated, ebbing occasionally but never going away, and when it hit full force he could hardly think or see and he just wanted to smash his face into something hard and just destroy the bastard tooth. Only he didn't, because he knew it wouldn't work.

Doc looked over, her eyes just visible through the round lenses of the gas mask. Doc had weird eyes. They were kind of violet, and bigger than normal. The Arkle had heard that up out of the valley they shone in the dark, and Doc had to wear sunglasses all the time. He'd never seen it, but he believed it.

"That you, the Arkle?"

Her voice was muffled through the mask and the heavy door, but clear enough.

"Yeah. Can I come in?"

Doc was almost the only person in the Family who called the Arkle by his chosen name. Most of the others called him Arkle, or Ark, or Arkie, which he hated.

"Wait a minute," called out Doc. "This stuff won't do you any good. I'll be out in a minute. Go into my office."

The Arkle retreated through the outer door. Doc's office was the biggest room in the old house. She slept there, as well as worked. Her bed was behind the desk. The Arkle looked at it and wondered what it would be like to share it with her. He'd slept with nearly all of the women and at least half of the men on the Farm, because his Change Talent was for seduction and even the pale version of it that worked down in the valley was enough to help out his natural charm, and since everyone had pretty much grown up in the Dorms, there was no such thing as a normal human body anymore. So his snouty face and fangs and slimmest of waists was not a bar to relationships.

Doc was the one closest to old human, and even then, she had those eyes. But the Arkle had never dared try his Talent on her, had never even had a few minutes alone with her to see if it might be worthwhile adding that into the natural equation of liking and desire.

He couldn't even daydream about sex with Doc, not with the pain in his tooth. He lay down in the patient's chair, the old banana lounge that sat in front of the desk, and shut his eyes, hoping that this would somehow lessen the pain.

It didn't, and the sudden waft of a harsh chemical smell alerted him to Doc's presence. She was leaning over him, the gas mask off, her short brown hair pressed down in an unnatural way, showing the marks of the straps. Her violet eyes were fixed on his jaw.

"Your jaw is swollen," remarked Doc. She went behind the desk, put down her mask, and stripped off the suit. It gave off more chemical smells as she opened the window and hung it on the hook outside, ready to be hosed down later.

She was only wearing a pair of toweling shorts and a singlet underneath. The Arkle's eyes watered as he looked at her ruefully. The tearing up wasn't from the remnant chemical smell, but from the pain. A pain so intense he couldn't even appreciate his first real look at Doc without the white lab coat she nearly always wore inside— and there it was, slipping over her shoulders and getting done up at the front, far too swiftly for his liking.

"Is it a tooth pain?" asked Doc.

"Yeah," whispered the Arkle. He raised one hand and gestured toward the left-hand fang. "It's got . . . pretty . . . bad. Just today."

"That never got this bad in a day. You should have seen me when it first started," said Doc. She dragged a box over next to the banana lounge and sat on it. "Open wide."

The Arkle opened wide, in a series of small movements, because he couldn't do it all in one go, it hurt too much. Doc leaned over him, looking close, but not touching. Some distant memory made the Arkle shut his eyes. For a moment, he was six again, and in the dentist's chair, and his mother was holding his hand. . . .

"Keep your hands still," ordered Doc. "Stay there. Just lie quiet."

The Arkle heard the box slide back and Doc move. He opened his eyes and saw her go over to the door to the cellar. It had two big padlocks on it, and only Doc and Gwyn had the keys. The Family's hard-won pharmacopoeia was stored in the cellar. All the drugs that had been found in scavenging expeditions in the small towns nearby, and in the outer suburbs of the city, plus the things that Doc had been able to make.

The Arkle shut his eyes again. It didn't really help with the pain, but it did seem to make it easier to bear it. He didn't want to sob in front of Doc. He hadn't cried since Tira was killed, and he'd sworn he'd never cry again. It was hard not to now. This pain just went on and on, and it wasn't only in the tooth. It was all up the side of his face, and reaching deep inside his nose and into his brain.

"Ah, it's getting worse, it's getting worse," muttered the Arkle. He couldn't help himself. The pain was starting to make him panic, fear growing inside him. He'd been afraid before, plenty of times, felt certain he was going to die. But this was worse than that because the pain was worse than dying. He'd rather die than have this incredible pain keep going—

There was a sensation in his arm, not a pain exactly, more like a pressure inside the skin. Something flowed through his arm and shoulder, and with it came a blessed darkness that pushed the pain away and carried it off somewhere far away, along with his conscious self.

Doc put the syringe back in the sterile dish and placed it on the table. Then she put a blood pressure cuff on the Arkle's arm, pumped it up, and released it, noting the result. A check of his pulse followed, and a look at his eyes, gently raising each eyelid in turn.

Finally, she opened his mouth, being careful to place her hands so that some involuntary reflex wouldn't put a fang through her fingers. Even more gently, she touched the top left tooth. Despite the sedation, the Arkle flinched. Doc curled back the young man's lip and looked at the gum around the base of the tooth. She looked for quite a while, then let the lip slide back and stood up.

"Pal! You there?"

Pal came in a minute later. He was another of the oldsters, though unlike Doc he'd spent time in the Dorms. He had been destined to become a Winger, and was hunchbacked a little, and there were stubs on his shoulders where his wings had either failed to grow or been surgically removed.

"You called?"

Pal was the chief cook of the Family, and liked to pretend he was a particular butler, in some reference to the old time that only Doc and Gwyn understood. He always wore the same black coat, which had long tails that hung down at the back.

"Go get Gwyn, will you? He's moving the chicken-houses."

Pal looked down at the Arkle.

"Problem?"

Doc sighed.

"Big problem. Why don't they ever tell me when they first hurt themselves, Pal? A week ago this could have been sorted out with antibiotics. I mean, I've got enough broad spectrum stuff downstairs to treat a thousand patients, but it's got to be done early! Now . . ."

"Now what?"

"I'm going to have to cut out the tooth, and he's practically all Ferret in the jaw. Those teeth have roots four inches long, and nerve clusters around the blood-sucking channels . . . which I only know about in theory, since I never—"

She stopped talking suddenly.

"Since you never dissected a Ferret?" asked Pal.

"No," replied Doc. "Never a Ferret. At least a dozen Myrmidons, and quite a few Wingers . . ."

"Which was just as well for me," said Pal. "All things considered. I suppose you want Gwyn to carry the boy up to the ridge?"

Doc looked at the floor.

"Yeah, I guess I was thinking that. It's the only way I can do it."

"Risky," said Pal. "For everyone. I thought we agreed no more trips out of the valley?"

"What am I supposed to do?" asked Doc. "Arkle will die if I don't take out the tooth, and he'll die if I do it wrong. I have to be able to see inside!"

"You could try halfway up," said Pal. "Some of the Talents seem to work okay there. Gwyn's does."

"And mine doesn't," snapped Doc. "It kicks in at the ridgeline, never lower down. So can you go and get Gwyn now, please? I can't keep Arkle under forever. There's a big enough risk with what I've given him already."

"All right, all right, I'm going," said Pal. "I suppose you want to go alone, just you and Gwyn?"

"Yes," said Doc. "Better to lose two than any more."

"On that logic, better to lose just *one* in the first place," said Pal, inclining his head toward Arkle. "That's what Shade would do."

"I'm not Shade," said Doc. "That's why I left Shade. You sorry you left, Pal?"

"Nope," replied Pal somberly. "I was just checking to see if you were. You had a mighty fine surgery back there, and those spider-robots of his to be nurses and all. Yanking out a Ferret tooth there would be as easy as taking a piss."

"Maybe," said Doc. "But I reckon the Overlords have probably tracked down Shade by now, and whoever was dumb enough to stick with him, and the computers he lives in and the whole submarine and everything in it has probably been rusting away at the bottom of the bay for years."

"Could be," said Pal. "But I wouldn't be surprised if Shade is still going, even still looking for us. Another reason to be careful. Shade always did have his true believers, and he sends them far and wide. They could easily be more dangerous than the creatures."

"Just go get Gwyn," said Doc wearily. "While I get my kit together."

The Arkle came back to the world in total incomprehension. There was a terrible pain in his face, everything was on a strange angle, and he could see the sun in a very odd position. He groaned, and the angle shifted and the sun righted itself and moved away, to be replaced by Gwyn's broad face, up unreasonably close. It took the Arkle a few moments more to work out that it was so close because Gwyn was carrying him like a baby, across his chest.

"What's happening?" he croaked. It was hard to talk, because his mouth felt puffy and strange. His lips were swollen and too close together, his jaw wouldn't open properly, and there was this pain there, jabbing at him with every step Gwyn took.

"Stop for a moment," Doc said to Gwyn.

The Arkle blinked and tried to shift his head. Why was the Doc there? He vaguely remembered going to see her about something.

"Keep still, please, the Arkle," said Doc.

He obeyed, and something stung him in the arm.

"What is . . ."

The Arkle's words trailed off and he subsided back down in Gwyn's arms.

"He's not staying under as well as I thought he would," said Doc. "And I can't give him much more. We'd better hurry."

"Easy for you to say," said Gwyn. "You only got that case."

"You carried me a lot farther a lot faster once," said Doc. She could see the top of the ridge up ahead, the real top, not the false one that had famously fooled so many walkers in the old times, when there had been a popular trail that went along the ridge, weaving up and down on either side.

"Long time ago," said Gwyn. "You were lighter then."

Doc hit him on the arm, very lightly.

Gwyn laughed, a kind of giggling chuckle that sounded weird coming out of his barrel chest. Then he suddenly stopped, and his head snapped to the right, and he immediately crouched down, balancing the Arkle with his left arm as he drew his sword with his right. It was short, but broad-bladed, and streaked with gold. Gold was good at disrupting creature circuitry, the augmentation stuff they put in at the Meat Factory, completing the transformation from child to monster.

Doc had ducked down too. Gwyn's Change Talent was an extra sense. He could feel other life-forms, and track them, though he couldn't tell them apart. Doc drew her sword, too. Like Gwyn's, it was gold-plated, another relic of their service with Shade, the enigmatic computer personality who led what he liked to call the Resistance against the Overlords and their creatures.

"Where?" whispered Doc.

Gwyn pointed with his sword, across to a point below the ridge where the trees opened out and the undergrowth was not so thick.

Doc slid her sword back in its scabbard and reached inside her coat to take out a pistol instead. Since it was below the ridgeline, it was unlikely to be a creature.

Creatures were hard to kill with gunfire—the gold-plated swords worked better. But for a human, a gun worked fine.

And as Pal had said, Shade always did have plenty of true believers, escapees from the Dorms who did whatever Shade told them to do without question . . . even if that might include tracking down and killing humans who Shade would undoubtedly have labeled traitors.

Particularly Doc, who Shade had labored over for so many years, tailoring educational programs and simulations to train her as a doctor. But not to help save human life. Shade had only wanted her trained up to help him with his research into the creatures, to dissect captured prisoners, to try to discover exactly how they worked, and how they were augmented by the strange energy that could be detected in the city after the Change. . . .

A low branch quivered and whipped back, and something loped down the slope. It came toward them for a moment, till it caught their scent and suddenly changed direction, even before Doc recognized it and decided not to shoot.

"A dog," whispered Gwyn. "Better make sure it's gone."

Dogs and cats were rare, because the creatures killed them, as they killed anything that was not part of the complicated battles the Overlords played in the city, endless battles that soaked up the continuous production of the Meat Factory, and the dorms that fed it with their human raw material.

They waited for a few minutes, but the dog did not circle back.

"It's gone," said Gwyn. "Beyond my range, anyway. Let's go."

At the top of the ridge there was an old picnic station, an open structure with a galvanized iron roof and a single long pine table underneath. Gwyn set the Arkle down on the table, while Doc laid out her instruments and drugs.

"Tie him down," she said, handing over a package of bandages. "I can't put him down deep enough so he won't react."

Gwyn took the bandages. When he was done with the tying down, he looked over at Doc.

"Your eyes are bright," he said. "You seeing?"

"Yes," said Doc. She blinked and bent down low over the Arkle's open mouth. Her violet eyes grew brighter still, and she stared down, looking through the tooth, through the bone, seeing it all. Her eyes moved, following the blood from the roots up along the altered circulatory channels. She saw the infection flowing with the blood, swirling across the boy's face, flooding into his brain, to join the pool of bacteria where it already dwelled and prospered.

Doc straightened up and looked across at Gwyn. Her eyes were shining still, but it was not with the light of her Change Talent.

"Too late," she said. "Just *too* late. It must have been hurting for weeks, and he never said a thing, he never asked for help."

"They don't know how, the young ones," said Gwyn, who was all of twenty-one. "They just don't know how to ask."

The Arkle groaned, and one taloned hand fluttered under its restraint.

"Mom?" he whispered. "Mom?"

Doc picked up a hypodermic and plunged it deep, followed quickly by another. Then she took the Arkle's hand and held it tight, despite the talons that scored her flesh.

"It's all right, love," whispered Doc. "It's all right."

"You won't feel a thing. You won't feel a thing. You won't feel a . . ."

AUTHOR'S NOTE

This story is set in the same world as my 1997 novel *Shade's Children*, though it takes place about ten years before the events of that book.

PEACE IN OUR TIME

The old man who had once been the Grand Technomancer, Most Mighty Mechanician, and Highest of the High Artificier Adepts was cutting his roses when he heard the unmistakable *ticktock-tocktock* of a clockwerk velocipede coming down the road. He started in surprise and then turned toward the noise, for the first time in years suddenly reminded that he was not wearing the four-foot-high toque of state, nor the cloak of perforated bronze control cards that had once hung from his shoulders, both of which had made almost anything but the smallest movement impossible.

He didn't miss these impressive clothes, but the old man concluded that since what he heard was definitely a clockwerk velocipede, however unlikely it seemed, and that a velocipede must have a rider, he should perhaps put something on to receive his visitor. While he was not embarrassed himself, the juxtaposition of a naked man and the sharp pruning shears he held might prove to be a visual distraction, and thus a hindrance to easy communication.

Accordingly, he walked into his humble cottage, and after a moment's consideration, took the white cloth off his kitchen table and draped it around himself, folding it so the pomegranate stain from his breakfast was tucked away under one arm.

When he went back out, the former Grand Technomancer left the shears by the front door. He expected to be back cutting the roses quite soon, after he got rid of his unexpected visitor.

The surprise guest was parking her velocipede by the gate to the lower paddock. The Grand Technomancer winced and frowned as the vehicle emitted a piercing shriek that drowned out its underlying clockwerk ticktocking. She had evidently engaged the parking retardation muffler to the mainspring before unlocking the gears. A common mistake made by those unfamiliar with the mechanism, and yet another most unwelcome noise to his quiet valley.

After correcting her error, the girl—or more properly a young woman, the old man supposed—climbed down from the control howdah above the single fat drive wheel of the velocipede. She was not wearing any identifiable robes of guild or lodge, and in fact her one-piece garment was made of some kind of scaly blue hide, both the cut and fabric strange to his eyes.

Perhaps even more curiously, the old man's extraordinarily acute hearing could not detect any faint clicking from sandgrain clockwerk, the last and most impressive advance of his colleagues, which had allowed modern technology to actually be implanted in the body, to enhance various aspects of physique and movement. Nor did she have one of the once-popular steam skeletons, as he could see neither the telltale puffs of steam from a radium boiler at the back of her head nor the bolt heads of augmented joints poking through at elbow, neck, and knee.

This complete absence of clockwerk enhancement in the young woman surprised the old man, though in truth he was surprised to have any visitor at all.

"Hello!" called out the young woman as she approached the door.

The old man wet his lips in preparation for speech, and with considerable effort, managed to utter a soft greeting in return. As he did so, he was struck by the thought that he had not spoken aloud for more than ten years.

The woman came up to the door, intent on him, watching for any sign of sudden movement. The man was familiar with that gaze. He had been surrounded by bodyguards for many years, and though their eyes had been looking outward, he saw the same kind of focus in this woman.

It was strange to see that focus in so young a woman, he thought. She couldn't be more than sixteen or seventeen, but there was a calm and somewhat chilling competence in her eyes. Again, he was puzzled by her odd blue garment and lack of insignia. Her short-cropped hair, shaved at the sides, was not a style he could recall ever being fashionable. There were also three short lines tattooed on each side of her neck, the suggestion of ceremonial gills, perhaps, and this did spark some faint remembrance, but he couldn't pin the memory down. A submarine harvesting guild, perhaps—

"You are Ahfred Progressor III, formerly Grand Technomancer, Most Mighty Mechanician, and Highest of the High Artificier Adepts?" asked the woman, quite conversationally. She had stopped a few feet away. Her hands were open by her sides, but there was something about that stance that suggested that this was a temporary state, and that those same hands usually held weapons and shortly would again.

The old man couldn't see any obvious knives or anything similar, but that didn't mean anything. The woman's blue coverall had curious lumps along the forearms and thighs, which could be weapon pockets, though he could see no fasteners. And once again, he could not hear the sound of moving metal, not even the faintest slither of a blade in a sheath.

"Yes," he said scratchily and very slowly. "Ahfred . . . yes, that is my name. I was Grand Technomancer. Retired, of course."

There was little point in denying his identity. Though he had lost weight, his face was still much the same as it had been when it had adorned the obverse side of millions of coins, hundreds of thousands of machine-painted official portraits, and at least scores of statues, some of them bronze automata that also replicated his voice.

"Good," said the woman. "Do you live here alone?"

"Yes," replied Ahfred. He had begun to get alarmed. "Who . . . who are you?"

"We'll get to that," said the young woman easily. "Let's go inside. You first."

Ahfred nodded shakily and went inside. He thought of the shears as he passed the door. Not much of a weapon, but they were sharp and pointed. . . . He half turned, thinking to pick them up, but the woman had already done so.

"For the roses?" she asked.

Ahfred nodded again. He had been trying to forget things for so long that it was hard to remember anything useful that might help him now.

"Sit down," she instructed. "Not in that chair. That one."

Ahfred changed direction. Some old memories were coming back. Harmless recollections that did not threaten his peace of mind. He remembered that it didn't matter what armchair he took, they all had the same controls and equipment. The house had been well prepared against assassins and other troubles long ago, but he had not restarted or checked any of the mechanisms after . . . well, when he had moved in. Ahfred did not choose to recall what had happened, and preferred in his own head to consider this place his retirement home, to which he had removed as if in normal circumstances.

Even presuming that the advanced mechanisms no longer functioned, he now had some of the basic weapons to hand, the knives in the sides, the static dart throwers in the arms. The woman need merely stand in the right place. . . .

She didn't. She stayed in the doorway, and now she did have a weapon in her hand. Or so Ahfred presumed, though again it was not anything he was familiar with. It looked like a ceramic egg, and was quite a startling shade of blue. But there was a hole in the end and it was pointed at him.

"You are to remain completely still, your mouth excepted," said the young woman. "If you move, you will be restrained, at the expense of some quite extraordinary pain. Do you understand?"

"Yes," said Ahfred. There had always been the risk of assassination when he was in office, but he had not thought about it since his retirement. If this woman was an assassin, he was very much puzzled by her origins and motivation. After all, he no longer had any power or influence. He was just a simple gardener, living a simple life in an exceedingly remote and private valley.

"You have confirmed that you are Ahfred Progressor III, the last head of state of the Technocratic Arch-Government," said the woman. "I believe among your many other titles you were also Keyholder and Elevated Arbiter of the Ultimate Arsenal?"

"Yes," said Ahfred. What did she mean by "last head of state," he wondered. He wet his lips again and added, "Who are you that asks?"

"My name is Ruane," said the woman.

"That does not signify anything to me," said Ahfred, who heard the name as "Rain."

He could feel one of the control studs under his fingers, and if his memory served him correctly it was for one of the very basic escape sequences. Unlike most of the weapons, it was not clockwork-powered, so was more likely to have remained operational. Even the chance of it working lent him confidence.

"Indeed, I must ask by what right or authority you invade my home and force my acquiescence to this interrogation. It is most—"

In the middle of his speech, Ahfred reached for a concealed knife on one side of the chair, and the escape stud on the right-hand arm.

Something shot out of the egg and splatted on Ahfred's forehead, very like the unwelcome deposit of a bird. He had an instant to crinkle his brow in surprise and puzzlement, before an intense wave of agony ran through the bones of his skull and jaw and—most torturously for him—through his sensitive, sensitive ears.

Ahfred screamed. His body tensed in terrible pain. He could not grip the knife, but his fingers mashed the control stud on the chair. It rocked backward suddenly, but the panel that was supposed to open behind him slid only halfway before getting stuck. Ahfred was thrown against it, rather than projected down the escape slide. He bounced off, rolled across the floor, and came to rest near the door.

As the pain ebbed, he looked up at Ruane, who had kept her place by the door.

"That was the least of the stings I could have given you," said Ruane. "It is only a temporary effect, without any lasting consequence. I have done so to establish that I will ask the questions, and that you will answer, without further attempts to derail the proceedings. You may sit in the other chair."

Ahfred slowly got to his feet, his hands on his ears, and walked to the other chair. He sat down carefully and lowered his hands, wincing at the faint ringing sound of the escape panel's four springs, which were still trying to expand to their full length.

"I will continue," said Ruane. "Tell me, apart from you, who had access to the Ultimate Arsenal?"

"There were three keys," said Ahfred. "Two of the three were needed to access the arsenal. I held one. Mosiah Balance V, Mistress of the Controls, had the second. The third was under the control of Kebediah Oscillation X, Distributor of Harm."

"What was in the arsenal?"

Ahfred shifted a little before he remembered and made himself be still.

"There were many things—"

Ruane pointed the weapon.

"All the weapons of the ages," gabbled Ahfred. "Every invention of multiple destruction, clockwerk and otherwise, that had hitherto been devised."

"Had any of these weapons ever been used?"

"Yes. Many of the older ones were deployed in the War of Accretion. Others had been tested, though not actually used, there being no conflict to use them in."

"The War of Accretion was in fact the last such action before the formation of the Arch-Government, twenty-seven years ago," said Ruane. "After that, there were no separate political entities to go to war with."

"Yes."

"Was the absence of military conflict something you missed? I believe you served in the desert—in the Mechodromedary Cavalry—during the war, rising from Ensign to Colonel."

"I did not miss it," replied Ahfred, suppressing a shudder as the memory, so long forgotten, returned. The mechodromedaries had joints that clicked, and the ammunition for their shoulder-mounted multiguns came in bronze links that clattered as they fired, for all that their magnetic propulsion was silent. Then there had been explosions, and screaming, and endless shouts. He had been forced to always wear deep earplugs and a sound-deadening spongiform helmet.

"Did Distributor Kebediah miss military conflict? She, too, served in the Accretion War, did she not?"

"Kebediah was a war hero," said Ahfred. "In the Steam Assault Infantry. But I do not believe she missed the war. No."

"Mistress Mosiah, then, was the one who wished to begin some sort of war?"

Ahfred shook his head, stopped suddenly, and gaped fearfully at his interrogator.

"You are permitted to shake your head in negation or nod in the affirmative," said Ruane. "I take it you do not believe Mistress Mosiah was the instigator of the new war?"

"Mosiah was not warlike," said Ahfred. A hint of a smile appeared at the corner of his mouth, quickly banished. "Quite the reverse. But I don't understand. May I . . . may I be permitted to ask a question?"

"Ask."

"To what war do you refer?"

"The war that approximately ten years ago culminated in the deployment of a weapon that killed nearly everyone on Earth and has destroyed all but fragments of the Technocratic civilization. Did it start with some kind of revolt from within?"

Ahfred hesitated a moment too long. Ruane pointed the egg weapon, but did not fire. The threat was enough.

"I don't think there was a revolt," said Ahfred. Small beads of sweat were forming in the corners of his eyes and starting to trickle down beside his nose. "It's difficult to remember . . . I am old, you know . . . quite old. . . . I don't recall a war, no—"

"But a weapon of multiple destruction *was* used?"

Ahfred stared at her. The sweat was in his eyes now, and he twitched and blinked to try to clear it.

"A weapon was used?" repeated Ruane. She raised the egg.

"Yes," said Ahfred. "I suppose . . . yes. . . ."

"What was that weapon?"

"Academician Stertour, its inventor, had a most complicated name for it . . . but we called it the Stopper," said Ahfred, very slowly. He was being forced to approach both a memory and a part of his mind that he did not want to recall or even acknowledge might still exist.

"What was the nature and purpose of the Stopper?" asked Ruane.

Ahfred's lower lip trembled, and his hands began to shake.

"The Stopper . . . the Stopper . . . was a development of Stertour's sandgrain technology," he said. He could no longer look Ruane in the eyes but instead stared at the floor.

"Continue."

"Stertour came to realize that clockwerk sandgrain artifices could be made to be inimical to other artifices, that it would only be a matter of time before someone . . . an anarchist or radical . . . designed and constructed sandgrain warriors that would act against beneficial clockwerk, particularly the clockwerk in augmented humanity. . . ."

Ahfred stopped. Instead of the pale floorboards, he saw writhing bodies, contorted in agony, and smoke billowing from burning cities.

"Go on."

"I cannot," whispered Ahfred. He felt his carefully constructed persona falling apart around himself, all the noises of the greater world coming back to thrust against his ears, as they sought to surge against his brain. His protective circle of silence, the quiet of the roses, all were gone.

"You must," ordered Ruane. "Tell me about the Stopper."

Ahfred looked up at her.

"I don't want . . . I don't want to remember," he whispered.

"Tell me," ordered Ruane. She raised the egg, and Ahfred remembered the pain in his ears.

"The Stopper was a sandgrain artifice that would hunt and destroy other sandgrain artifices," he said. He did not talk to Ruane, but rather to his own shaking hands. "But it was not wound tightly, and would only tick on for minutes, so it could be deployed locally against inimical sandgrain artifices without danger of it . . . spreading."

"But clearly the Stopper did spread, across the world," said Ruane. "How did that happen?"

Ahfred sniffed. A clear fluid ran from one nostril and over his lip.

"There were delivery mechanisms," he whispered. "Older weapons. Clockwerk aerial torpedoes, carded to fly over all significant cities and towns, depositing the Stopper like a fall of dust."

"But why were these torpedoes launched?" asked Ruane. "That is—"

"What?" sniffled Ahfred.

"One of the things that has puzzled us," said Ruane quietly. "Continue."

"What was the question?" asked Ahfred. He couldn't remember what they had been talking about, and there was work to be done in the garden. "My roses, and there is weeding—"

"Why were the aerial torpedoes launched, and who ordered this action?" asked Ruane.

"What?" whispered Ahfred.

Ruane looked at the old man, at his vacant eyes and drooping mouth, and changed her question.

"Two keys were used to open the Ultimate Arsenal," said Ruane. "Whose keys?"

"Oh, I took Mosiah's key while she slept," said Ahfred. "And I had a capture cylinder of her voice, to play to the lock. It was much easier than I had thought."

"What did you do then?" asked Ruane, as easily as asking for a glass of water from a friend.

Ahfred wiped his nose. He had forgotten the stricture to be still.

"It took all night, but I did it," he said proudly. "I took the sample of the Stopper to the fabrication engine and redesigned it myself. I'm sure Stertour would have been amazed. Rewound, each artifice would last for months, not hours, and I gave it better cilia, so that it might travel so much more easily!"

Ahfred smiled at the thought of his technical triumph, utterly divorcing this pleasure from any other, more troubling, memories.

"From there, the engine made the necessary ammunition to arm the torpedoes. One thousand and sixteen silver ellipsoids, containing millions of lovely sandgrain artifices, all of them sliding along the magnetic tubes, into the torpedoes, so quietly. . . . Then it took but a moment to turn the keys . . . one . . . two . . . three . . . and off they went into the sky—"

"Three keys?" asked Ruane.

"Yes, yes," said Ahfred testily. "Two keys to open the arsenal, three keys to use the weapons, as it has always been."

"So Distributor Kebediah was present?"

Ahfred looked out the doorway, past Ruane. There were many tasks in the garden, all of them requiring long hours of quiet, contemplative work. It would be best if he finished with this visitor quickly, so he could get back to work.

"Not at first," he said. "I had arranged for her to come. A state secret, I said, we must meet in the arsenal, and she came as we had arranged. Old comrades, old friends, she suspected nothing. I had a capture cylinder of her voice, too. I was completely prepared. I just needed her key."

"How did you get it?"

"The Stopper!" cackled Ahfred. He clapped his hands on his knees twice in great satisfaction. "Steam skeleton, sandgrain enhancement, she had it all. I had put the Stopper on her chair. . . ."

Ahfred's face fell and he folded his hands in his lap.

"It was horribly loud," he whispered. "The sound of the artifices fighting inside her, like animals, clawing and chewing, and her screaming, the boiler when the safety valve blew . . . it was unbearable, save that I had my helmet. . . ."

He looked around and added, "Where is my helmet? It is loud here, now, all this talking, and your breath, it is like a bellows, all a-huffing and a-puffing. . . ."

Ruane's face had set, hard and cold. When she spoke, her words came out with slow deliberation.

"How was it you were not affected by the Stopper?"

"Me?" asked Ahfred. "Everyone knows I have no clockwerk enhancement. Oh, no, I couldn't stand it, all that ticking inside me, that constant *tick . . . tick . . . tick. . . .* It was bad enough around me, oh, yes, much too awful to have it inside."

"Why did you fire the torpedoes?" asked Ruane.

"Tell me who you are and I'll tell you," said Ahfred. "Then you may leave my presence, madam, and I shall return to my work . . . and my quiet."

"I am an investigator of what you termed the Rival Nation," said Ruane.

"But there is no Rival Nation," said Ahfred. "I remember that. We destroyed you all in the War of Accretion!"

"All here on Earth," said Ruane. The lines on her neck, that Ahfred had thought tattoos, opened to reveal a delicate layering of blue flukes that shivered in contact with the air before the slits closed again. "You killed my grandparents, my great-uncles and great-aunts, and all my terrestrial kin. But not our future. Not my parents, not those of us in the far beyond, in the living ships. Long we prepared, myself since birth, readying ourselves to come back, to fight, to regain our ancestral lands and seas, to pit the creations of our minds against your clockwork. But we found not an enemy, but a puzzle, the ruins of a once great, if misguided, civilization. And in seeking the answer to that puzzle, we have at last found you. *I* have found you."

"Bah!" said Ahfred. His voice grew softer as he went on. "I have no time for puzzles. I shall call my guards, assassin, and you will be . . . you will be . . ."

"Why did you fire the torpedoes?" asked Ruane. "Why did you use the Stopper? Why did you destroy your world?"

"The Stopper," said Ahfred. He shook his head, small sideways shakes, hardly moving his neck. "I had to do it. Nothing else would work, and it just kept getting worse and worse, every day—"

"What got worse?"

Ahfred stopped shaking his head and stood bolt upright, eyes staring, his back rigid, hands clapped to his ears. Froth spewed from between his clenched teeth and cascaded from his chin in pink bubbles, stained with blood from his bitten tongue.

"The noise!" he screamed. "The noise! A world of clockwerk, everybody and everything ticking, ticking, ticking, ticking—"

Suddenly the old man's eyes rolled back. His hands fell, but he remained upright for a moment, as if suspended by hidden wires, then fell forward and stretched out headlong on the floor. A gush of bright blood came from his ears, before slowing to a trickle.

It was quiet after the Grand Technomancer fell. Ruane could hear her own breathing, and the swift pumping of her hearts.

It was a welcome sound, but not enough, not now. She went outside and took a message swift from her pocket, licking the bird to wake it, before she sent it aloft. It would bring her companions soon.

In the meantime, she began to whistle an old, old song.

MASTER HADDAD'S HOLIDAY

The world was a bleak one. It was unable to support human life and didn't do very well with homegrown life-forms either. It had not been tek-shaped to improve its temperature, which was too hot, nor its atmosphere, which was thin and somewhat poisonous.

Thrukhaz Three did have a starport of sorts, built for a Prince who, on the basis of a single holographic image, had thought that the huge, carapaced beetles that were at the top of the local food chain might offer good hunting. When it turned out that they were easily frightened, basically herbivorous, and left luminous trails that made them ludicrously easy to track, the hunting was canceled. The infrastructure built for the hunting parties remained.

As Thrukhaz had once been claimed by a Prince, it technically remained within the Empire—but in practice it was part of the Fringe. Blessed with numerous wormholes to and from long-established Imperial worlds, shadowy traders and smugglers found that it was a useful place to meet, in order to buy, sell, and get away in quick time if it proved necessary.

Haddad, an assassin of the Empire, came to Thrukhaz Three, but his primary purpose was not to buy and sell. Though Haddad was aged only twenty-one in old-Earth years, he was already a senior apprentice, and was soon to be made a Master of Assassins.

That is, if he survived this final mission for his current Prince, which was doubtful. The Prince's probability calculator, Uncle Yukhul, had worked out that the chances of the overall plan succeeding were quite good, about 0.42. Haddad's chance of remaining alive was a much more disturbing 0.04.

But even the priests of the Temple of the Aspect of the Cold Calculator could not include all possible variables, particularly for missions outside the Empire. And no assassin expected to live a long time. They were expendable, particularly apprentice assassins. Perfect to use up in long-shot missions, like the one Haddad was engaged in right now.

It *was* unusual for an apprentice to be sent alone out of Imperial space, disguised as a Fringe-dwelling dealer in antique weapons. The transparent panels in Haddad's head were hidden, under Bitek simu-flesh that had spread and merged into his own skin. A living wig had been implanted into his scalp, giving him a dark red mane that stretched halfway down his back. A programmed Bitek scathe had burrowed red trails across his cheeks, creating in five minutes the effects of years of ritual scarification.

This was the fashion of a clan of independent traders, the Pralganians, who turned up from time to time in odd corners of the galaxy. There were no real Pralganians in the sector at the moment, or at least there should not be, according to Haddad's information.

To reinforce his disguise, Haddad wore a Pralganian trader's flax-gold shipsuit, with paler yellow boots and a belt of woven wires that supported twin sting-guns: handguns that fired low-velocity Bitek projectiles, suitable for use on a ship or in zero gravity. One gun had a red grip and was for crystalline darts charged with a lethal nerve poison. The other had a blue grip and was loaded with a mere knockout/paralysis combo. Or so the traders liked people to believe. It made their enemies watch the red-handled gun too closely.

A Bitek portable safe followed Haddad. Portable safes, with their ultratough armored hide, strong reptilian legs, and cacophonous hooting alarm snout, were very popular for transporting valuables in the Fringe, though some customers didn't like the idea of goods being stored inside the utility stomach of a living creature, even though it was designed for the purpose, and was both dry and disconnected from the alimentary system of the beast.

"Hup," said Haddad. He checked his breath mask and weapons and went out through the ion curtain that separated the breathable air of the starport arrival "hall" from the miasmic mist of the planet. The safe waddled after him, its sentience limited to obeying simple commands, knowing who its master was, and shrieking if anyone tried to cut it open or prize its massive, interlocking jaws apart.

Haddad had memorized a map of the Thrukhaz Three startown, but it was based on the interrogation of a trader who had been there several months previously. He noted the differences as he walked between buildings toward the caravansary that was his chosen destination. He had selected it from the data available in the Empire, and confirmed the choice with some judicious questioning of the other travelers who had descended with him from the tramp starship that ran a semiregular route between Thrukhaz and Sazekh Seven, the nearest Imperial system.

The caravansary was much as Haddad expected. He took a small room at the back, a bolted-on unit that had a ceiling hatch as well as a door, and reserved a rectangular patch of ground in the courtyard, where he would set up his booth. Leaving the traveling safe surrounded by a number of tiny telltales, Haddad wandered the startown, buying a few odds and ends for his booth and examining the wares of those who would be his competitors, selling antique or interesting weapons. None had anything of particular interest. He made a point of introducing himself, and invited the other dealers to come and see his wares.

Returning to the caravansary, Haddad found that, as he had expected, his room had been searched and surveillance established, and the traveling safe had been inspected, though not actually opened. Unless it had been opened with Psitek by either a Master of Assassins or a Prince, and he thought it was too early for either one to be here.

Haddad took out one of the items he'd bought, an obsolete Mektek Jhezhan spytracker, and set it going on his table. It unfolded its jointed legs and search tendrils and started looking for spy-specks.

After the spytracker had wandered for a few minutes without success, Haddad smiled, as if he were content he was not under observation. He already knew from a Psitek scan that it would take the spytracker a few hours to find and destroy the spy-specks, which were of a newer and superior make.

"Open."

The safe yawned wide, revealing the shelved space within. Haddad reached inside and gently ran his fingers over the items on each shelf. No one could see it, under false flesh and hair, but his temples were roiling with the blue fluid that indicated Psitek activity.

As far as he could tell, nothing had been interfered with, and nothing new had been introduced. For the benefit of those watching and listening via the almost invisible spy-specks up in the corners of the ceiling, he took out the most important item.

This was a small reddish box of real wood, not Bitek extrusion, at least five centuries old. Haddad flicked the bronze catch and opened it. Lined with velvet, it held a simple steel dagger, the bright blade rippled with tiny wave marks, the hilt and guard a darker, more ominous metal.

The weapon was at least three thousand years old, and came from ancient Earth. To a discerning collector, it was worth more than the entire Thrukhaz startown. In fact, it was so valuable, only one of the richest plutocrats in the Fringe could afford it—or a Prince of the Empire.

Not that Princes typically bought things. They just took them, unless they were already claimed by another Prince or a temple, or made inviolate by an order of the Imperial Mind.

But here, essentially outside the Empire, a Prince might find it easier to buy. Though there would probably be an attempt or attempts to steal it first. Not that such attempts would solely be the action of Princes. Many people would want that ancient dagger.

Haddad closed the box and returned it to the safe, taking out several other packages, which he laid out on his table.

"Shut and lock."

Interlocking teeth ground to closure. The safe hunkered down on its haunches.

Haddad sorted through the lesser wares he had taken from the safe, while he waited for the spytracker to finish. He had nothing else that was anywhere near as valuable as the dagger, but compared to what he had seen from the other weapon sellers, his basic stock was good. All old Imperial tek, proven in countless battles across the galaxy.

Like the blast projector he was examining, a lighter and shorter version of the basic mekbi trooper weapon.

Haddad heard faint footsteps in the corridor, and his Psitek senses picked up hostile intentions. Earlier than he had expected, but the indications were very clear. He lifted the blast projector and sighted at the door. It was locked, but whoever was outside had another key.

As the door slid open, the blindingly bright energy pulse from Haddad's weapon essentially vaporized the two thugs who were about to charge in, and badly wounded their boss, who was several paces behind.

Haddad moved, faster than a human should be able to move. Leaping over the remains of the two attackers, he ripped off a Bitek medaid patch that had been disguised as a button on his shipsuit and slapped it on the scorched face of the boss who had been lurking behind. The patch rippled, manipulating blood chemistry, injecting drugs, arresting shock, and arranging mental compliance—at least for the minute or two the man had left.

"Who sent you?" demanded Haddad.

"Contract," whispered the dying man. "Lerrue the Shubian."

"Kill and steal?"

"Yes . . . the safe . . ."

The man died. The medaid patch shriveled and fell off.

The next person in the corridor was the manager of the caravansary, suspiciously close and quick. She approached cautiously, her hands up and open.

"An attempted robbery," said Haddad. He didn't mention the fact that the intruders had a key, doubtless obtained from the woman. "I will require a different room. Number 125 will be suitable."

"It's rented . . ." the manager started to say. Then she looked at the energy projector in Haddad's hand, the smoking doorframe, and the dead thugs. "I mean . . . it will be ready in thirty minutes."

"Is there a legal process to be followed?" Haddad asked, who already knew the answer. "Authorities to be alerted?"

"No," said the manager. "We sort things out ourselves here. As you have done."

"Where would I find Lerrue the Shubian?"

Haddad already knew the answer to that as well, but, as always, he wanted separate confirmation.

The manager's mouth twitched.

"Lerrue?" she croaked. "The small green dome outside the starport arrival hall. But . . ."

"But what?" asked Haddad.

"Lerrue is a *Shubian*," said the manager.

The Shubians were known to the Imperial Mind. Haddad knew what data the Empire already possessed. Indeed, Lerrue the Shubian had a part to play in the plan, though he didn't know it yet.

"What does that signify?"

"Shubians set prices, put buyers and sellers together, for a commission. They don't do stuff themselves. Least, Lerrue doesn't."

"You mean that Lerrue did not send these people, but merely arranged their services to be supplied to whoever wanted me killed and robbed?"

"Yeah," said the manager. "And Lerrue, she's kind of important here, sort of like the unofficial . . . uh . . . governor, or whatever. She sorts things out, like I said, fixes the prices."

"Interesting," said Haddad. He had not known Lerrue's gender, though for Shubians this was not important, as they changed from time to time. "Let me know when my new room is ready."

The next morning was as greenish and congealed as any other day on Thrukhaz. Haddad finished securing his new room with a few choice devices, then left it via the hole he had cut into the adjacent storage closet. The portable safe stayed behind, hunkered down under a blanket.

Lerrue the Shubian was easy to find. There was a queue of breath-masked people waiting outside the exterior airlock door of the green dome. Obviously Lerrue didn't trust an ion curtain to keep the good atmosphere in and the bad atmosphere out. There were a couple of guards stationed outside who were performing a similar function to the airlock, only with visitors.

Haddad paid them to let him in. They took his sting-guns, and the J-knife from his boot, but only did a cursory scan for other weapons, making his misdirectional shuffle of items around his body purely a drill.

Lerrue was a nine-foot-tall humanoid with a shiny hide, big eyes, and several flapped holes in the side of her bald head that looked like ears but weren't. She was wearing a hundred-years out-of-fashion Imperial evening dress, which only reached as far as her thighs, or whatever Shubians called the part of their legs above their second kneecap.

"You arranged for three men to kill me and steal my traveling safe last night," said Haddad.

"I introduced a buyer of death and robbery to a seller of the same," said Lerrue. She had two voices that spoke together, one emanating from her mouth and one out of the orifices in the side of her head. The one from the mouth was that of a young human choirboy, pure, clear, and musical. The other voice was reedy and sounded almost mechanical.

"I do not wish to have to kill more murderers and robbers," Haddad stated. This was true. Though he had been trained from birth to kill, he did not want to waste his skills on nondesignated targets. He existed as a weapon of the Emperor, and of his Prince. He thought of himself as an entirely different being from the ordinary killers of the galaxy.

"Do you want others to undertake the killing for you?" asked Lerrue, in that strange double voice.

"I do not want anyone to even attempt to rob or murder me," said Haddad. "Including whoever paid for the first attempt."

"Understood," said Lerrue. "For how long should this state continue?"

"Twelve weeks, local," replied Haddad. He didn't need anything like that much time.

Lerrue named a sum in one of the credit systems commonly used in this part of the Fringe. Haddad nodded, pulled a ring from his hand, and handed it over. The ring was of no value in itself, but had a sum of money encoded in it that could be drawn on a bank only two wormhole transits away.

Lerrue scanned the ring and handed back a pile of plastic chips, likewise encoded with credit, in much smaller amounts. Haddad tried not to take them, but Lerrue pressed them on him.

"I am Shubian," she said. "Exact money always. No exceptions."

"Fine," replied Haddad. He pretended to hesitate. The Shubian was part of his original plan. She could accelerate the process. "There is another item of business you may be able to help me with."

"Specify this business."

"I am a dealer in unusual and antique weapons," said Haddad. "While I have my regular stock, on this occasion I also have obtained a very rare and extremely desirable item, a dress dagger from the first solar fleet of the second pre-Imperial epoch. What would you charge to find a buyer for this item?"

"Five percent of sale price," said Lerrue. "Standard commission. What is the price?"

Haddad told her the price.

Lerrue whistled through the holes in the side of her head.

"No buyers here," she said. "You want me to spread the word?"

"Yes," said Haddad.

"Maybe get attention you don't want," warned Lerrue. "Prince maybe. They like old-time Earth stuff."

"Maybe," said Haddad.

"Send battalion of mekbi drop troopers, you not see any profit," remarked Lerrue. "Me neither. We both be dead."

Haddad hesitated, again for show.

"I just came from Sazekh Seven," he said. Sazekh Seven was the closest Imperial world. "Apparently two Princes, both collectors, compete to be the new planetary governor. I think that means neither one will let the other use force to take what I have."

This part was true, or mostly true. There would be no naval task force, no mekbi troopers. But if all went as expected, Haddad would not be the last Imperial Assassin to come to Thrukhaz.

"I heard this," confirmed Lerrue. "It will be as you ask. I spread the word."

"Good," said Haddad. He bowed slightly, keeping his eyes on the Shubian and the bodyguard in the shadowed corner of the room, who he knew was there even though he couldn't see her due to some kind of portable distortion field. But he had noted the absence of presence in a particular pattern, heard her breathing and done a surface Psitek scan of her mind. A human bodyguard, like the other visible employees of Lerrue. It was quite likely the fixer was the only Shubian in the entire sector, or even the quadrant.

Haddad enjoyed the rest of the week. Though it was not something he had done before, he took to selling his goods like a Sad-Eye took to an undefended brain. Soon, he had sold all the stock he had brought with him, so he started buying as well, both from people who came to his booth in the busy courtyard of the caravansary and from booths or stores he encountered during his apparently random wanderings through the startown.

The wanderings were not random. Haddad was watching for the opposing Prince's Master of Assassins, or her apprentices, or for any sign they were using local people despite Lerrue's aegis of protection.

It took five days before the first one showed up. An apprentice, fairly junior, Haddad thought, and not sufficiently versed in narrow-cast Psitek interrogation. He felt her peering into the minds of other traders in the courtyard, seeking information about an antique dagger of immense worth. He was surprised that it was not an inquiry about a Pralganian trader. He had made it easy enough for them.

When his turn came, he felt the intrusion into the compartment of his mind that he had created for his Pralganian identity, and the slight shock, carefully controlled, inside the questioner's own mind when she "saw" the dagger, the box, the safe, and his room details all hidden there.

As she withdrew her mental probe, Haddad followed it back into her own mind. Just like a tiny rivulet of water joining the rush of a greater stream, he moved past the Psitek defenses that were meant to stop just such a move, defenses that were not adequately supervised by the apprentice's conscious mind.

Haddad saw what he needed to and made a few small adjustments that caused the apprentice to turn and hurry away, knowing only that she had found what her Master had sent her to find. The whereabouts of the dagger.

At least Haddad was fairly sure that was all she knew. There was always the chance that he had been suckered in turn, fed a prepared apprentice with a mind compartmentalized like his own for just such an occasion. But he didn't think so. It took quite some time to mentally prepare in this way, and everything about the plan was designed so that the opponents were reacting, rather than acting.

So he believed that the apprentice was with a team of only six. But most important, one of those six was Visknim, Master of Assassins to Prince Xerkhan. Which meant the Prince was also almost certainly nearby somewhere, perhaps in orbit, with the remaining eight of Visknim's apprentices. But significantly, no Master.

The wasp had been drawn to the honeypot.

They came that night, as Haddad had read in the apprentice's mind. An orthodox approach, when the toxic fog was thickest and most still. Two had infiltrated earlier, taking rooms, and these two stunned the door and roof guards. Two then climbed the back wall of the caravansary. Another used a zero-G harness to land on the roof.

Haddad tracked the five of them from their Psitek chatter, sparse as it was. But he couldn't locate Visknim, the Master. Haddad had his own spy-specks in place all over the caravansary, but they showed only the apprentices, moving toward Room 125. Five assassins, not six, and everything depended on the Master also being part of the assault.

The apprentices were converging. Haddad had to decide, to wait or move.

He moved, cloaked with every artifice of his Psitek, a vision distorter superior to the one used by Lerrue's bodyguard, and by sheer surprise. Dropping from the ceiling outside room 126, he killed the first two apprentices with his red-handled sting-gun as they opened the door to his room, confident till the very last millisecond that their own Psitek powers showed only a sleeping man in the room.

It was not a sleeping Pralganian trader they had detected, but a Bitek auxiliary brain in a box inside the safe, asleep forever, grown solely for the purpose of deception.

Dragging the bodies inside, Haddad shut the door and exited again through the hole in the wall to the storage closet, and from there into the corridor again.

The other apprentices, and Visknim—wherever she was—would have caught the last, dying Psitek screams and final vision of the two, with the open door. They would think their enemy was inside, and would be more careful.

At least they should have become more careful. The apprentice who had landed on the roof rushed down the ramp, thinking himself clear of the zone of action, still trusting to Psitek senses that showed no one lurking ahead. Haddad, waiting by the side of the ion curtain, simply stabbed him with an energy stick as he ran past. Straight into his head. He died so quickly there wasn't even a Psitek squeal. Just a sudden absence.

Three down. Two to go. And Master Visknim.

Haddad took the zero-G harness, checked its power status, and put it on. Then he went to the roof and launched himself off, floating silently down until he was halfway to the ground, level with the second floor.

The two remaining apprentices were shielding themselves properly now, their Psitek locked down. Haddad could not see them with his mind, but they had failed to take proper measures against all his spy-specks. He had strewn several varieties liberally across the ceilings and walls of the hotel, and most had survived the sloppy countermeasures employed by the intruders.

Consequently, he knew they were crouched on the other side of the wall, probably in a narrow-band mental debate about what they were supposed to do now three of their colleagues were dead.

Haddad cut their conversation short by tilting his hands back at the wrist to fire the single-shot energy lances that were mounted under his forearms. Two incredibly thin jets of energy, as hot as a sun, bored through the wall and very neatly through the heads of the apprentices, helmets and all.

Even the decrepit Bitek hazard alarm on the ceiling nearby had to take note of this event, sniffing smoke and sensing ridiculously high temperatures. It shrieked, and its batch-mates, those still alive after a century of inattention, took up the chorus. Very few of the inhabitants knew the detectors were screaming "Fire" in their original manufacturer's language, but the tone was clear. The caravansary began to stir. People started to shout. Doors and even some windows began to open.

Haddad dropped to the ground, ditched the zero-G harness, and reentered the building. He still couldn't feel any mental hint of Master Visknim, and though there was plenty of activity being shown by the spy-specks, all the movement was by people getting out of the caravansary.

Except for one person. She was going against the traffic, going deeper inside. The manager of the caranvasary, heading toward room 125.

Or was it the manager? Haddad noted that those of his spy-specks that communicated via Psitek were not functioning at all, and only one in six of the Mektek ones were beaming their images back to the screen inside his right eye. Those images showed a woman of the same height, build, general looks, and typical clothing of the manager, but the resolution was low.

The woman stopped and tapped on the door of 125. Again, the audio was too degraded for Haddad to identify the voice as definitely that of the manager. She tapped again, then used a key.

Haddad began to creep along the corridor, toward room 125. He stopped using his Psitek completely, depending on sight and hearing.

If Master Visknim had assumed the identity of the woman, as seemed most likely, then everything would succeed or fail in the next few minutes.

None of the alarms or defenses he had placed within his room announced their activation as he drew closer, which only confirmed that the person who had entered the room was not the manager, but a Master of Assassins.

A Master who would have additional augmentation that Haddad did not, making her as fast as a Prince, perhaps even faster, though not as highly durable. An apprentice, even a senior one like Haddad, could not match a Master in straight head-to-head combat.

Haddad sidled closer to the room. Visknim would know he was somewhere around, if she had not already located him. But her objective would be to take the dagger, not to kill a single apprentice.

She was probably already leaving the caravansary with the weapon, Haddad thought. Visknim could have mentally commanded the mobile safe to open in a matter of seconds, then perhaps a minute to disable some of the interior traps, another minute to leave via the hole in the wall, probably pausing to throw some kind of timed explosive back. . . .

Haddad whirled around and sprinted away from the ill-fated room 125, turning the corner not quite fast enough to completely escape the sudden, ferocious blast of a micromatter conversion bomb. Thrown forward, he skated along the floor till he came to rest in a pile of debris near the front door.

His red hair was smoldering, his back pricked all over with shrapnel damage, the blood already beginning to ooze. Haddad got to his feet, coming up with the red-handled sting-gun in his hand.

He got off one dart before a narrow beam of dark energy drilled through his hand, entering near his index finger and exiting underneath his little finger. Haddad threw himself aside, spinning around to get a view of his target, who had to be above him, as his left sleeve vomited fake-out targets, small holo-projectors that filled the air with moving images of himself.

Not that they would distract even an apprentice. It was just something to do, and even as Haddad twisted and turned, trying to get to the door, trying to get his blue-handled sting-gun in his left hand, he knew that the probability he wouldn't survive the mission had surely hit 100 percent.

If only that meant that the main mission had succeeded as well!

Another beam of energy glanced across Haddad's face, and half the world went dark as his right eye was blinded. He fired back in the general direction he thought the attack must have come from, full automatic, crystalline darts spraying up at the ceiling where Visknim would be scuttling like a spider, already gone from her last firing position.

Then the sting-gun was empty, and Haddad felt something at his neck, on the right side where he could no longer see. It was very sharp, and cold, and he knew it at once. The antique dagger, perfectly positioned, impossible for him to defend against in the microsecond before Visknim pushed it home.

But she didn't. Instead, he felt her voice inside his head.

:Are you relayed here?:

"No," croaked Haddad. It was an operational decision that he would not use mindspeech on Thrukhaz. He was alone, without relaying priests anywhere in range, and he had no contact with the Imperial Mind.

:Then know that Prince Xerkhan <identifier> was assassinated ninety-four seconds ago:

The knife left his neck. Visknim sighed audibly and clapped Haddad lightly on the shoulder.

Her Prince was dead. When reborn, he would demand a new Master of Assassins. Haddad was an apprentice who had succeeded in his graduating mission. He too, would be serving a new Prince.

For the time being, they were no longer antagonists. Just fellow priests of the Emperor in Hier Aspect of the Shadowed Blade.

"I knew it had to be a diversion," said Visknim as they left the caravansary by the back door, pausing before the ion curtain to fit their breath masks. "But His Highness insisted he had to have the dagger, come what may, and that I must go and get it. I suppose it is authentic?"

"Copy," said Haddad. "Made a thousand years ago, though. Valuable in itself."

"Should it go back to your Prince, I wonder? Your former Prince, I mean," mused Visknim.

Haddad caught the mental whisper as she queried the Imperial Mind, and also received the reply, as relayed by the priests in the now-deceased Prince Xerkhan's ship in high orbit above.

:Dagger to be disposed of at discretion of Haddad <identifier> promoted Master of Assassins new assignment Prince Lowkwol <identifier> Diplomatic Service Ambassador Three ship out former <Icerine Dagger> now <Mysterious Vanten> orbit Thrukhaz Three tranship Sazekh Seven any ship for Groghok sector receive new eye new augmentation then any ship for Prolkamh Two:

The Imperial Mind kept reeling off orders and information, which Haddad stored for later perusal.

"Congratulations, Master," said Visknim.

Haddad bowed. He felt no different. Perhaps when he received the additional augmentation, or became responsible for his new Prince . . .

Visknim handed the dagger to Haddad.

"What are you going to do with it? It's not of much practical use."

Haddad took the dagger and looked at it with his single eye.

"I think I'll keep it. Not as a weapon."

"What then?" asked Visknim. Casually she raised her hand, an egg-shaped weapon suddenly visible. A figure in the shadows by Lerrue's dome hastily raised her hands and stepped back. "The shuttle's over there. No need to go through arrivals, we'll just burn a hole in the fence."

"A reminder," said Haddad.

"Of what?"

"An enjoyable week," said Haddad. "What did the ancients call it? A time removed from normal cares?"

Visknim looked at Haddad curiously.

"A holiday," she said finally, and he could tell she had queried the Imperial Mind. "You know, I think you are going to be a very *odd* Master of Assassins."

Haddad inclined his head, perhaps in agreement, and followed her toward the landing field and the shuttle that would take him back to the ship above, and thence to the Empire.

His holiday was over. Soon, his real work would begin.

RETURN TO THE OLD KINGDOM

The long-awaited prequel from
New York Times bestselling author GARTH NIX

HARPER
An Imprint of HarperCollinsPublishers

www.epicreads.com

ALSO FROM *NEW YORK TIMES*
BESTSELLING AUTHOR
GARTH NIX

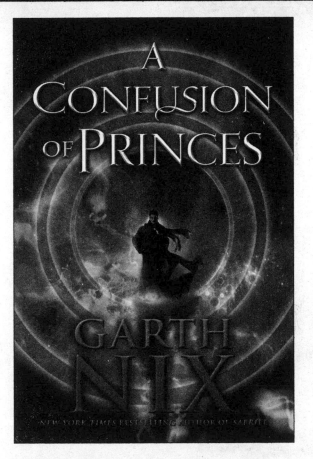

SUPERHUMAN. IMMORTAL.
PRINCE IN A GALACTIC EMPIRE.
THERE *HAS* TO BE A CATCH....

HARPER
An Imprint of HarperCollinsPublishers

WWW.EPICREADS.COM